credible *Ham and High*

ANN GRANGER

AN UNFINISHED MURDER

HEADLINE

First published in Great Britain in 2018 by
HEADLINE PUBLISHING GROUP

First published in paperback in 2018 by
HEADLINE PUBLISHING GROUP

1

Cataloguing in Publication Data is available from the British Library

ISBN 978 1 4722 5266 1

Typeset in Adobe Garamond by Palimpsest Book Production Limited, Falkirk, Stirlingshire

Printed and bound in Great Britain by CPI Group (UK) Ltd, Croydon, CR0 4YY

MIX
Paper from
responsible sources
FSC
www.fsc.org   FSC® C104740

Headline's policy is to use papers that are natural, renewable and recyclable
products and made from wood grown in well-managed forests and other
controlled sources. The logging and manufacturing processes are expected
to conform to the environmental regulations of the country of origin.

HEADLINE PUBLISHING GROUP
An Hachette UK Company
Carmelite House
50 Victoria Embankment
London EC4Y 0DZ

www.headline.co.uk
www.hachette.co.uk

A few years ago I wrote a series of fifteen crime novels featuring Alan Markby and Meredith Mitchell. I have since been asked many times for a 'new' Mitchell and Markby. But it is not so easy to pick up characters after a lapse of years. Are they still the same age? Or do they now qualify for a bus pass apiece? How has the world around them changed?

Well, yes, they have aged and Alan Markby is retired. But when an old case is unexpectedly reopened, he finds himself called upon by Superintendent Ian Carter and Inspector Jess Campbell to lend a hand.

So, this book is not only for friends of Campbell and Carter but also for all those fans of Mitchell and Markby. They're back!

Prologue

The bend in the lane was looming and Josh was getting ready. He knew that once they turned it, and were out of sight of the house, Dilys would hit him. She was a year younger than he was, only eight, and smaller, though chunkily built. But she moved like lightning. So, although Josh knew it was coming and was ready to dodge, he also knew that she'd still catch him a few painful kicks and punches before he got out of the way. He wasn't allowed to hit her back, because Auntie Nina said boys shouldn't hit girls. Well, perhaps so, but Josh knew they did, because the various boyfriends who passed through his mother's life frequently blacked his mother's eye, or worse.

While they'd lived with their mother (Josh still thought of it as 'when they lived at home'), the cops had been at the door every other day or night, or so it seemed. If it wasn't the fights that brought the uniforms, then it was tearing the place apart looking for drugs. Once, they burst in looking for a shotgun belonging to the current boyfriend. It was discovered under Dilys's bed and their mother had gone crazy when she realised that was where the boyfriend has stashed it. It took three of the uniforms to hold her back when she rushed at him, brandishing a pair of scissors. After this episode, the Social interfered and they'd ended up living with Auntie Nina.

Josh wasn't Dilys's only target. She had attacked other children in the new school they attended. This caused a lot of trouble. Dilys now knew she mustn't do that, but she still had the anger in her, so she took it out on Josh. The child psychiatrist Dilys had been sent to see explained it as Dilys and Josh having grown up in a violent home. It was a form of self-defence, the doctor said. She, Dilys, was making it clear to anyone who might be inclined to hit her that it wouldn't pay. She'd hit back. So, she hit out first.

Again, Josh reasoned, that might be so. But it didn't explain why *he* was included every time they got the lecture about not attacking other kids, because *he* hadn't done anything. That was the bitter injustice of it all. Josh didn't *want* to hit anyone. He hated the violence. He loved his sister. He'd loved his mother – still loved her, wherever she was – and not being able to protect her in the past had filled him with guilt.

Living with Auntie Nina was all right, if you accepted Auntie Nina's rules, which were many. At least, no one had fights or got drunk and vomited all over the place, and the police didn't come. That, said Auntie Nina, meant he and Dilys were Very Fortunate. They had the chance of a Normal Life. He could have argued about that, too, because he knew, from the parents who turned up at the school gates, that in a normal life children lived with their mothers, and not with the Auntie Ninas of this world. Most of the other children also had fathers. Josh didn't know who his father was; he had never asked, because he dreaded being told it was one of the tattooed boyfriends. Also, he suspected perhaps his mother didn't know. But he kept this and other opinions to himself, because if he'd learned anything, it was to keep quiet.

But he did speak now. 'Listen, Dilys! Don't start punching me, right?'

'I want to,' said Dilys simply.

'But I don't want you to!'

'It makes me feel better,' returned Dilys, after a moment's consideration of his argument.

'It doesn't make me feel better. I've got a big bruise on my arm from where you clouted me yesterday. Don't you like me?'

At this question Dilys began to cry quietly, tears rolling down her face. So, he put his arm around her consolingly, because he understood. It had always been too much for Dilys and she couldn't cope. She hadn't coped with the shouting of the terrifying men and the blood running down their mother's face. She hadn't coped with their mother slumped on the sofa in a drugged stupor, unable to respond to anything they said. She couldn't cope now with Auntie Nina's rules or the home-cooked meals Auntie Nina said were good for them. They had to eat everything, even though they'd never seen a Brussels sprout or a parsnip before. They had managed all their short lives, until they came here, on takeaways and microwaved pizza.

Dilys snuffled into his T-shirt for a moment or two until the tears stopped. Then she kicked his shin.

'Walk over there!' ordered Josh, as he hobbled a few feet away to one side.

'Where are we going?' asked Dilys quite calmly.

It was like that. The anger had been released from where it had been bottled up inside her, and now she was fine . . . until the next time.

'Auntie Nina says we have to go for a walk,' said Josh. 'But it's already nearly five o'clock and we have to be back by six, so we can't go far. Where would you like to go?'

'To the spinney,' said Dilys.

The spinney was a patch of woodland behind the row of council houses. Auntie Nina lived in the first house. But, although she could see the spinney from her kitchen window, she couldn't see into it, because it lay at the bottom of a downward slope. Thus, if they went there, they'd be out of range of her interference.

'All right,' Josh agreed.

Dilys smiled and began to sing a carol, 'Good King Wenceslas', which they'd learned at school months before, at Christmas. She liked the story it told and didn't worry that it wasn't the right time of year for it.

All the local children went to the spinney, not just Josh and Dilys. The kids clambered up into the low branches or made camps in the bushes and picked blackberries when they were in season. They seldom let Josh or Dilys into their camps, so Josh and his sister made their own camps in a different spot. But Josh was a first-rate climber, so if someone's hat was thrown up into the branches, or a ball, and lodged there, Josh would be called in to shin up and retrieve it. That would mean a temporary truce during which they were let into the other camps. The moment was fragile and soon broken because, inevitably, Dilys flew into one of her rages.

Josh and Dilys clambered over the stone wall around a field, walked across it to the far side, then scrambled down into a ditch where Dilys got stung by nettles, resulting in a rash of white spots that burned like anything. That meant ten minutes hunting for dock leaves to rub on the reddened flesh to soothe it. It put Dilys back into a bad temper. When they finally made it into the spinney, it was deserted. Josh was pleased they had it to themselves and didn't need to negotiate a play area with other kids. Dilys found a fallen branch and began to thrash the bushes with it and strike it against the trees. It was only a matter of time before she swung it at him, Josh reckoned. So, he walked ahead of her and turned off the path into the tangle of undergrowth, because it would take all Dilys's attention to negotiate a route – and that would absorb her energies, with any luck. He could hear her behind him, slashing wildly with the branch to clear her way.

He had been wrong in thinking they were alone in the spinney, because they weren't. Ahead of him, through the vegetation, he could see a patch of white and another of blue. He guessed someone had thrown rubbish away there. But when he got a little nearer, he could see there was someone lying on the ground, apparently sleeping. The person was half smothered with leaves and twigs, in some places more thickly than in others. It was as if someone had tried to cover up the sleeper but hadn't finished the job. The lower part of a leg in blue jeans and a foot in a white trainer hadn't been covered at all. Josh hesitated and then moved nearer. At the opposite end to the white trainer, a pale face peered through the leaves, tilted up as if to see who approached. The face belonged to a woman. Josh thought her quite a young woman – perhaps because she had long fair hair, like his mother's. Her head was turned to one side and he could see her forehead, nose and one eye. A hand poking up through the mulch pointed its pink-painted fingernails at him.

'Is she drunk?' asked Dilys, who had arrived alongside him, and was staring down at the woman critically. 'Perhaps she fell over last night on her way home from the pub.'

5

'No,' said Josh.

The eye was open and filmy. It stared at them without regis-
tering anything. This woman couldn't see them. She wouldn't see
anyone, now or ever again, because Josh knew she was dead. He
felt sick, but it was the sickness of despair not of revulsion.

Perhaps their mother was dead by now, like this, and no one
had told him or Dilys. It was something that worried him
constantly but he was afraid to ask Auntie Nina, because she might
have replied that, yes, his mother was dead. For as long as he
stayed in ignorance, there was a chance she might still be alive
and he'd see her again. But looking down at this woman, he began
to dread that this was how it had all ended for his mother.

'What, then, just asleep?' asked Dilys.

'Yes!' lied Josh. 'Come on, she might wake up and be cross.'

Dilys still had her branch and she waved it above her head. 'I
could hit her with this. That would wake her up.'

'No!' Josh grabbed her arm and pulled her back. 'Listen, we've
got to go back now, understand? You mustn't say anything about
this girl being asleep here. It will make trouble. We'll be blamed
for something. We always are.'

'I won't tell,' said Dilys sturdily.

Josh knew she wouldn't. Dilys didn't use words much. She
preferred action. Besides, she also knew the value of keeping quiet.

'Come on, then.' Josh released her arm and set off back the
way they'd come.

After a moment or two, he realised he couldn't hear Dilys. So,
he stopped and looked back. His sister was still standing by the
body. Seeing he was looking at her, she gave him a defiant stare.

'Come on!' urged Josh. 'Before she wakes up.'

Dilys set off towards him, and they made it back to the main path. The rest of the way home passed in silence until they'd climbed back over the stone wall into the lane. It was then, as Dilys scrambled down, that he saw she had something gripped in her grimy fist. It glittered.

'What's that?' he demanded and tried to grab her hand.

But Dilys was too quick, as usual. He just grabbed air.

'What is it?' he snapped at her and, for once, he must have sounded really angry, because Dilys reluctantly opened her fist and he saw it was a chain with little silvery objects attached to it. It was a charm bracelet. Their mother had owned one, until one of the boyfriends had stolen it and sold it to buy a fix.

'You took that off the girl in the spinney!' he gasped, appalled.

Dilys looked mutinous and obstinate, as only she could. 'It doesn't matter,' she said. 'It's not stealing, because she wasn't asleep. *I* think she'd *died*. She was cold and felt funny, like a dead fish.'

'*You touched her?*'

Josh's voice came out as a squawk.

'Only to take off the bracelet. It's nice.' Dilys held it up and stretched the chain out in a line from which the tiny objects dangled.

Josh could see now that the silvery objects weren't charms; they were letters of the alphabet. In a line now, as Dilys held the chain taut, he saw they spelled out the name R-E-B-E-C-C-A.

'Throw it away, now, at once!' he ordered.

'No!' said Dilys belligerently.

'Auntie Nina will see it.'

'No, she won't. I'll hide it. I'm good at hiding things from her. She's stupid. She's never found anything I've hidden.'

Josh had a nightmare vision of a stash of small stolen articles hoarded by his sister somewhere. 'If it's found we will get into a lot of trouble!' he said and then, inspired, added, 'And they'll tell that kids' head doctor they send you to!'

This made an impression on Dilys, who muttered and fidgeted but eventually threw the bracelet into a nearby clump of tall, pink wild flowers; 'ragged robin' Aunt Nina called those plants.

'Remember,' he warned his sister, when they reached the house. 'You don't say anything to anyone about this!'

Dilys nodded and gave his arm a punch by way of having the last word.

As agreed, they didn't speak of it. Not until many, many years later.

For the next twenty years, Josh had nightmares about that pale glazed eye staring up through the leaves; but he couldn't and wouldn't talk about it. Then, one day, he broke his silence.

He spoke to Mr Markby, and that was only because he had learned that Mr Markby had once been a policeman – a detective, and a top-ranking one.

So, Josh hoped, perhaps he wouldn't be shocked.

PART ONE

Chapter 1

'I'm retired,' said Alan Markby.

He said it casually, although he was curious as to what might have prompted the question.

'But you were a proper detective? Auntie Nina said you were.'

Josh Browning was a grown man but he still lived with the elderly lady who had once been foster parent to him and to his sister when they were children. Mrs Pengelly her name was, by rights, although Josh always referred to her as Auntie Nina. The sister had left the area, but Mrs Pengelly and Josh shared a home in the slowly crumbling row of social housing that had been erected in prefabricated sections in the second third of the previous century. It was named after a farmer from whom the land had been purchased to build them. At the time they were constructed the houses had been intended to be temporary. Elsewhere in the country such 'estates' had long since been demolished and replaced by more modern homes. Goodness only knew why no one had demolished Brocket's Row. But it had become the sort of project put at the back of every queue and eventually forgotten.

The houses had originally backed on to open country and woods. That had mostly disappeared under a trading estate and warehousing, originally described optimistically as a 'business park'. But Brocket's Row still stood. As far as Markby knew, Josh had

11

no other family, except for the sister he'd once mentioned in passing. Only the one time and then clammed up.

Josh didn't make conversation. He seldom spoke at all unless it was absolutely necessary. This led some people to think he was mentally backward but Markby knew this wasn't so. Josh was sharp enough and observant. He remembered what he saw, even the tiniest detail. Sometimes, shyly, he would remind Markby of some detail about the garden. There had been a rat hole under the fence a year ago but he, Josh, had filled it in. The rat hadn't come back, because Josh had poured strong disinfectant around the area and no animal liked that. This year, a jackdaw had taken to hanging around the garden waiting for scraps. It was always the same one, slightly lame, and Josh had not seen its mate. There were others in the church tower, next door, but the one that visited the garden roosted ther\e. It was a loner, 'like me', Josh had added with a rare smile.

He was an odd-job man by occupation and could turn his hand to most things. Alan Markby and his wife, Meredith, lived in a Victorian building, a former vicarage, and things always needed doing around the place. So, over the years, Josh had become a familiar visitor, painting, hammering, climbing up on the roof to replace dislodged slates after winter storms and, increasingly, doing the hard work around the large garden. That was where he was working alongside Markby today, digging over the vegetable plot and getting it ready for courgettes. Those were Meredith's idea.

But Markby had no idea what had led Josh suddenly to ask, 'You were a copper once, is that right?'

They were sitting in the shed, drinking coffee in a mid-morning break. Josh was tall and strongly built, and took up a lot of space.

He had a mop of red hair and features that looked as if they'd been chiselled by a sculptor who was still learning the craft. He had stretched out his legs and was contemplating, apparently, the soil-caked boots he wore. His question had come out of nowhere, just spoken without any preamble.

'Why?' asked Markby, because there had to be a reason. Josh didn't do purposeless chat.

'You were an important copper here in Bamford, Auntie Nina reckons.'

'I was a superintendent, and it was quite a while ago now. Does it matter?'

Markby kept his voice casual but he was watching Josh's averted face closely. Markby knew about witnesses. Long years of investigating serious crimes had taught him that they came in all sorts of guises. There were the liars and the fantasists, the inaccurate, the embroiderers, and occasionally the observant. There were always the ones who knew something but didn't want to trouble the police with it, because it mightn't be important, or it was something embarrassing to speak of. You couldn't make them talk but, when they were ready, they'd talk of their own accord, although it might take a long time for them to get round to it. Sometimes their information wasn't important and sometimes, annoyingly, it was. He wouldn't know which classification Josh's information fell into but he was absolutely certain Josh knew something – a secret – and he was trying to share that knowledge. The trouble was, Josh didn't know how to go about it and, having started the conversation, he now seemed to have exhausted his ideas and had plunged back into his normal silence.

'Funny how things happen . . .' said Markby into his coffee

mug. It was a shot in the dark and mentally he had his fingers crossed.

Josh brightened. 'That's it!' he agreed. 'You never know how they'll turn out.'

'So, how have they turned out?' Markby ventured to ask.

Josh drew up his legs so that his boots were planted firmly on the floor and twisted in his chair to look directly at Markby. 'I don't want you to get the wrong idea about our Dilys,' he said.

Dilys? Hang on; wasn't that Josh's mysterious sister?

'In what way?' asked Markby, adding, 'I've never met your sister, if that's Dilys.'

'Well, you won't now, or not for a while,' said Josh. 'She's in prison.'

'What did she do?' asked Markby. He couldn't remember the name of Dilys Browning in the local paper.

'She always did hit people,' said Josh earnestly. 'She didn't mean anything by it. She used to hit me. She hit kids in the playground at the school they sent us to, when we came to live here.'

'To live with Mrs Pengelly, your Auntie Nina?' Markby prompted.

Josh nodded, clearly encouraged. 'She does it because she's unhappy, see? When we were kids they sent her to see some fancy doctor – psychiatrist – but it didn't help. In the end, Dilys hit the doctor. She got passed around doctors a lot after that but it didn't do any good.'

'And does she still hit people? Is that why she's in prison now?'

'That's it!' Josh smiled unexpectedly. It was a smile of pure relief. 'I knew you'd understand. But that's all she's ever done, hit people. She's not a thief!'

14

'Has someone accused her of being a thief?'

'No!' said Josh indignantly. 'I haven't got to that bit yet.'

'Oh? Sorry! Go on.'

'They've banned her from a lot of clubs and pubs and places like that,' said Josh sadly. 'She's been up before the magistrates lots of times, up there in London, where she's been living. But this last time it was really bad. She glassed a guy in a pub and nearly cut his throat. There was blood everywhere, all over Dilys, too. They had to take him to hospital and get the gash sewn up. It was an accident; she didn't want to hurt him. She doesn't realise she hurts other people because of the hurt inside herself. It's all she's thinking, that *she's* hurting!' Josh gazed at him, willing him to understand. 'I can't explain. Only, she didn't mean it. She just struck out but she had a glass in her hand . . .'

Markby sighed at this only too familiar explanation. *I happened to be holding a bottle . . . I happened to be holding a breadknife . . .*

'And?'

'And they told her she'd be sure to get a custodial sentence this time, so she came to see me. She brought a cardboard box with her personal stuff in it, for me to keep it safe for her while she was in prison. She couldn't leave it where she'd been living. It'd have been pinched.'

'Quite,' said Markby, nodding.

'Well, after she'd left, Auntie Nina looked into the box and saw it was mostly clothes and a couple of DVDs, nothing much. But Auntie Nina said she didn't want an old box lying around and, anyway, the clothes would probably go mouldy if they were left like that. She told me to take everything out. She'd wash the clothes and put them away tidy – and any other bits and pieces

I should put somewhere in my room, in a drawer. So that's when I found it, at the bottom of the box.'

'Found?' Markby prompted. It was like drawing teeth. But they were getting to the important bit, he knew that. It was vital not to hurry Josh now.

'The bracelet. We found it – well, Dilys found it, sort of found it, when we were kids. She was only eight. Robbing dead bodies, that's a crime, isn't it?'

Josh stared at him, waiting for an answer. But the disconcerting leap from finding a bracelet to dead bodies had momentarily floored Markby.

'Dead bodies . . .' he managed to croak. What on earth was coming next? Who had robbed a dead body? 'It might depend on the circumstances,' he said carefully. 'Archaeologists find items in burials that end up in a museum.'

'I found – and Dilys came along just a few minutes later – a dead woman in the spinney, down the hill from the house. She had leaves and bits of branches over her but she wasn't covered over completely.'

'When was this?' yelped Markby, automatically reaching for his mobile phone and then dropping his hand, because he didn't want to interrupt Josh.

'Years ago, when we were kids. Dilys and me, well, other families didn't like us, because we'd come from a bad home; and Dilys kept hitting their kids, and we weren't local. We got the blame for all sorts of things, mostly things we hadn't done. So, I reckoned we'd get the blame for this, somehow. Not that we'd killed her, but that we shouldn't have gone poking about in the woods. I don't know . . .' Josh paused and shook his mop of red curls.

'They'd have found something to blame us for. So, I told Dilys she wasn't to speak of it ever. I'm only telling you now, because of the charm bracelet.'

Don't say anything! Markby warned himself silently. *Just wait. He's getting to it.*

'We left the body where it was and started off home. We were nearly there when I saw Dilys had something shiny hidden in her fist. It was a charm bracelet – a sort of charm bracelet, only it didn't have charms on it, just letters of the alphabet. She'd managed to slip it off the dead woman's wrist without me seeing. Dilys has always been very quick. I was really angry, I can tell you! Dilys wanted to keep it and said it wasn't stealing because the woman was dead. But I made her throw it away. She did. I watched her. She chucked it into some flowers growing on a bank. But I didn't know she'd snuck back later and found it and kept it hidden away all these years.'

Josh sighed. 'It's my fault. I should have realised she'd go back for it. I should have gone back before she could, and thrown it somewhere else where she couldn't find it. So there it is – was – at the bottom of the box she'd given me to keep safe. The thing is, I've kept thinking about that dead woman all these years. I thought perhaps she had family and they were looking for her. Perhaps she had kids, like us – like we were, then . . .'

Josh had slumped dejectedly. 'So, when Auntie Nina said you'd been an important copper once, I thought, well, you'd be the person to tell.' Josh looked up. 'It's time now to tell someone, isn't it?'

'Yes,' said Markby gently. 'You've done the right thing, Josh. Have you still got it, the bracelet?'

In response, Josh pushed his hand into his jeans pocket and

drew out a silvery piece of jewellery. He held it up, stretched out, so that Markby could read the letters: R-E-B-E-C-C-A.

'How old were you, Josh, when you found this? Dilys was eight, you say?' Markby knew his voice was shaking.

Josh nodded. 'I was nine, just coming up to ten.'

Markby made a quick mental calculation. 'Oh, my dear God . . .' he whispered. 'Rebecca Hellington! You and Dilys found Rebecca Hellington. Josh,' he said carefully, 'leave this with me and I'll see if I can sort it out. Someone may ask you to tell the story again, so they can write it down or record it on tape. It will be nothing to worry about, because that's normal procedure. Just tell it as you told me. And don't worry that you or Dilys will be charged with any crime. You were both under ten at the time, the age of criminal responsibility. It would have been better to have reported what you found – just telling your Auntie Nina would have done it. Then she could have contacted the police. But you can't be charged under the law with anything.'

'Oh, that's all right, then,' said Josh, relief sounding in his voice.

'You didn't tell Auntie—tell Mrs Pengelly, did you?'

Josh looked at him, his blue eyes wide with shock. 'We'd never have heard the last of it! Of course we never said . . .' He paused. 'Anyway', he added, 'the next time I went to the spinney, the body had gone.'

'When was that? When did you go back?'

Josh frowned. 'Not the next day, because it rained really hard. It would have been the day after that. And she wasn't there any more, like I said.'

'All right.' Markby stood and gathered up the empty coffee mugs. 'I'll take these back to the house.'

Josh unfolded himself from the canvas chair in which he'd been wedged and stood up, too. He had to bend his head, because the roof was too low to accommodate him. Markby himself was still a tall man. He hadn't lost much to age. But Josh must be about six foot three, he thought.

'I'll finish digging over that patch,' said Josh and set off towards the vegetable garden.

Markby walked thoughtfully back to his house and into the kitchen. It was empty. He put the mugs on the table and went in search of Meredith.

Chapter 2

Markby found his wife in the study, staring intently at her computer. Her tawny hair, still thick, with only a sprinkling of grey strands, fell forward around her face. Her fingers rested on the keyboard in a position that suggested she'd stopped typing suddenly, mid-sentence.

'Not going well?' he asked mildly.

'Going OK, but something isn't right . . .' She leaned back, stretched her arms above her head and turned to smile at him. 'So, what's new?' she asked.

Since retiring from her job with the Diplomatic Service, Meredith had taken to writing books – more specifically, detective stories. When she started on the first of them, he had protested, 'I'm all for you writing, but well, crime fiction . . . people will think they're real-life crimes I've told you about.'

'No, they won't,' she had returned, 'because I'm setting all my stories in the nineteen-twenties. Anyway, when people read them, they won't know I'm married to an ex-copper.'

'They'll soon find out,' he'd replied gloomily.

'So what? Anyway, the detective in my book is a piano tuner by trade.'

'You're serious about this? Why?' he'd asked incredulously.

'I've thought it through, you know!' She'd sounded nettled. 'In the nineteen-twenties having a piano was the fashionable thing. Like having a telly now. Pianos need tuning regularly. So, my piano tuner visits all kinds of homes to fix the piano. It's a time-consuming job, so he's there for an hour or so, just sitting quietly in the parlour and pinging the piano strings, while the household carries on around him and probably forgets he's there. He can overhear things, notice things, be there when odd things happen.'

'Right . . .' Markby had conceded the argument.

So, now he didn't know whether the question she posed was rhetorical – meaning that she'd hit a snag in a plotline – or she'd read his face, as she did all too well. That puzzle was quickly resolved.

She asked quietly, 'What's wrong?'

'Nothing . . . that is to say, I've learned about something that happened a long time ago. It's an old unsolved mystery and has to do with an investigation I carried out locally on behalf of the Gloucestershire force, years back. With conspicuous lack of success, I may add.'

'Don't tell me you and Josh have dug up a vital clue in the potato patch!'

Markby shook a warning finger at her. 'No joking! You're a lot nearer the mark than you imagine. The thing is, I've just had a curious conversation with Josh.'

Meredith raised her eyebrows. 'Having anything like a conversation with Josh is curious in itself, isn't it? I only manage to get single sentences out of him. It's generally a question about whatever work he's doing around the place and, once I've answered, he usually just nods and takes himself off again.'

'Well, this time we were having our coffee break in the shed, when he suddenly asked me if it was right I'd been a senior police officer, before I retired. He said his Auntie Nina – Mrs Pengelly – had told him I was.'

'She's his foster mother, or she was,' Meredith said, 'not a proper aunt. What made her suddenly tell him that you'd been with the police? I'm surprised he didn't already know.'

'I don't know why she told him; that's something I'll have to look into. I'm not really surprised he didn't already know, because he doesn't talk to people, does he? Look, let me tell you what he told me.'

She listened quietly while he repeated Josh's tale. 'Wow!' she said softly, when he stopped speaking. 'Who was Rebecca Hellington?'

'She's been a missing person these past twenty years. There's never – till now – been any evidence that she's dead. Her family – her father, at least – believed she must be, because she didn't get in touch with them. She normally phoned home at least once a week. She was a student at a West Country teacher training college, but her family lived in Bamford. They ran a travel agency in the town. Being reported missing doesn't necessarily mean the person is dead. People vanish from their usual haunts deliberately and don't contact anyone. They have all sorts of reasons. Her mother insisted for a long time there was some explanation and Rebecca would turn up. But I have to confess that the police were inclined to agree with her father at the time. The thing was, we had no *evidence* either way, whether she was dead or alive.' He fell silent.

'You looked for her here?' Meredith prompted when the silence lasted.

Markby started. 'Yes, in cooperation with the Gloucestershire force, as I told you. They were investigating her disappearance at their end. They liaised with us, because she had told two people at her hall of residence, plus her boyfriend, that she was thinking of going home for the weekend. If that was the case, she never turned up. The parents were in a terrible state.'

'I can understand that,' Meredith said quietly, 'particularly if they were expecting her. So, she had definitely informed her parents, and not just a couple of college friends, that she was coming for the weekend?'

'She'd mentioned it as a possibility but hadn't confirmed it. They'd been waiting to hear from her, to let them know what time her bus would arrive here. She was in the habit of travelling by National Express coaches, because it was so much cheaper than using the train.'

'Even cheaper, if riskier, would be to hitch-hike?' suggested Meredith.

'Her father assured me she wouldn't have done that. I remember he said she was too sensible. Also, he'd told her that if she was really broke and couldn't afford the bus ticket, he'd send her the money or a ticket. He'd made her promise she'd do that, because they didn't want her to hitch.' Markby's normally calm features formed a ferocious scowl. 'I don't even know if the spinney is still there! I should have asked Josh. I can remember when it was mostly open country behind those old council houses. I'm astonished those homes are still there – that Mrs Pengelly is still living in one of them. The land was developed over the years. Come to think of it, it was one of Dudley Newman's projects, could have been his last. You remember Newman? His vision of the future was to cover the surrounding countryside with bricks.'

'The builder? I remember him, though I never had much to do with him. But a body was found on one of the sites he was building houses on, I certainly remember that! It turned out to be quite a hairy episode for me! Don't tell me it's happened again. I might begin to worry about Newman!'

'Yes, I remember that one, too, but the later development behind Brocket's Row didn't involve houses. Newman got delusions of grandeur and put a sort of business park there. As far as I recall, nothing suspicious was found during the work on it – or it was never reported, if it was! The business park didn't do well and now, I believe, it's mostly storage units.'

'So, the spinney may have been concreted over to fulfil Newman's aim in life?'

'It may have been. I'll have to check that out before I go to Trevor Barker with my story.'

'You're reporting this to the police here at Bamford, then?'

'I have to report it as my citizen's duty. And I'm reporting it to Inspector Barker, because he'd be upset if I went over his head.' Markby sighed. 'My hope is, that particular patch of the spinney escaped Dudley Newman's attentions. Then there is a chance we can still find Rebecca. However, it seems likely her killer returned soon after the children found her, and moved her elsewhere. He'd heard the kids earlier, perhaps, and any intruders temporarily frightened him off. Or it might have made him decide the spinney was too popular a spot, so he moved the body somewhere else. All we know is that, after Josh and Dilys found her, no one else did. It would have been reported to us at the time. Josh did return to the spot two days later, but the body had disappeared.'

Meredith was ready with an objection. 'If she hadn't been

buried, just covered with leaves and twigs, surely someone else *must* have stumbled over her, as the children did.'

'Which suggests the body wasn't lying on the ground like that for long. As I said, either the killer went back and made a better job of burying her in the spinney later that same day, soon after the children saw her. Or he moved the body altogether and buried it somewhere else – and we have no clue where.' He transferred his gaze to the window and the view of the church beyond. 'So, Rebecca, where are you now?'

'This is going to make trouble for Josh,' Meredith said soberly. 'Will he cope? He likes to be left in peace to get on with a specific job. He won't like a lot of strangers arriving on the doorstep wanting him to talk.'

'I've warned Josh the police will want to interview him.' Markby sighed. 'But I do wonder how Inspector Barker will cope! He's not going to be happy when I tell him he may have to dig up a sizeable area of land to look for a body that might not even be there.'

'When I got up this morning,' said Inspector Trevor Barker, 'the only immediate worry I had was that I was losing even more hair.'

He swept a hand self-consciously over what was a distinctly thinning thatch. He wasn't old, for crying out loud, and he thought it unfair to be going bald. His mother told him it made him look distinguished. She reminded him that his father had also lost his hair early. But no man wanted to be told he looked like his father when said father was in his seventies and the son was only forty-four.

'I knew that once I got into work, I'd get the usual problems landing on my desk,' he added gloomily. 'What I didn't expect, Alan, was that you'd walk in here and tell me that your gardener found a body twenty years ago and didn't report it.'

And also walk in here looking like bloody Peter Pan. Why had Markby not lost any hair? Barker fumed inwardly. What's more, Markby had been blessed with that kind of fair hair that never quite seems even to be going grey. 'Ash blond' it was named in those preparations women buy to colour their hair. He knew, because his wife used such a beauty aid. He might even, had he been an uncharitable man, have thought that Markby dyed his hair. But he knew it wasn't so. Markby was lucky, that's all. He, Trevor Barker, had drawn the short straw. There was his visitor, who must be in his late sixties, looking the same age as Barker.

'Distinguished,' his wife had once described Markby to him, after a chance meeting with the retired superintendent and his wife in a local restaurant. 'And those blue eyes quite give me the shivers!'

Barker had sourly told his wife to, 'Chuck it in!'

'Josh was only nine years old at the time,' Markby reminded him. 'And he was in foster care. He didn't have a real mother he could run home to with the story. I've explained all this.'

'Oh, yes, you've explained it all very well!' Barker retorted, returning his attention to the matter in hand. 'I don't know the spot myself. Is the spinney, as you call it, still there?'

'I drove round that way and made a recce before I came in here this afternoon,' Markby told him. 'Most of it is still there but it's in a dismal state. It seems to be where the citizens of Bamford dump their unwanted old fridges and TVs. Not to mention sacks of garden waste and other rubbish. From Josh's description of it, as it was when he was a child, it was quite a pretty spot. Now you'd call it pretty horrible.'

Barker acknowledged the weak joke with a grimace. 'And you completely believe your gardener's tale?'

'Absolutely. Besides, he had the bracelet – that one.' Markby pointed to the surface of Barker's desk.

Barker stared gloomily down at the silver chain, now neatly encased in a little evidence bag. 'Well, I'll have to pass this higher up. I can't authorise an expensive fishing expedition like digging up the area without further authority. They won't be happy, I can tell you. Everything is costed now, down to the last penny. There is a Cold Case Unit in the county, but they're fighting for the finances to look into more promising cases than this one. Besides, they just don't have the personnel. So, just don't get your hopes up too high! We're talking about a bracelet found by kids twenty years ago on a patch of ground that has since been largely built over. The gardener says his sister took it off a corpse. But his sister might just have found it on the ground, lost months earlier. I can't remember in detail everything I did when I was nine. Can you?'

'I understand your doubts,' Markby said mildly. 'But it would be nice to be able to close the case.'

Barker leaned back and beat a tattoo on the desk with his finger-tips. 'Of course, it was *your* case, wasn't it? You'd want it sorted.'

'It was only my case at this end of things, and our involvement here was strictly limited to finding out if the girl had come home. The police in Gloucestershire handled the other end, the actual disappearance. They interviewed the students who knew Rebecca, and also her boyfriend.'

Barker's face set in a suspicious scowl. 'They checked the boy-friend out more carefully than just a chat, I suppose? Lovers' quarrel, perhaps, or maybe she wanted out of the relationship. The lad was jealous, you know the sort of thing.'

'I believe that he was questioned more than once, at the time. But there was nothing to suggest he knew anything about her disappearance. He was described to me as being very worried.'

'Sure he was worried!' snapped Barker. 'It might have been a guilty conscience!'

'Or just that he was a young man who'd never been in trouble and whose girlfriend had vanished, and he didn't know what to do or say. But I didn't interview him. That was the local CID's job, as I told you. I dealt with the parents here.'

'Are they still alive?' Barker asked. 'We'd need them to confirm this is her bracelet.' He touched the little plastic bag with the silver chain.

'Without checking, I couldn't say. I imagine they'd be elderly now, like me!' A fleeting smile crossed Markby's face. 'Yes, they could still be around.' Diffidently he added, 'There is one thing I might mention – just a coincidence, you understand.'

'Please do!' invited Barker sourly, and looking apprehensive.

'Well, at the time, when I was liaising with Gloucestershire, there was a young detective sergeant assigned to the case there, bright chap, graduate intake . . .'

'Oh . . .' said Barker simply.

'He's now a superintendent. His name is Ian Carter. He later moved around, as one does, but now he's back in Gloucestershire.'

'This is leading to something,' Barker said suspiciously.

'Only that, before I retired here, I had a newly promoted

inspector on my team called Jess Campbell. She was very young. She's now with the Gloucestershire force, working with Carter. A coincidence, as I said.'

There was a silence during which Barker looked thoughtfully up at the ceiling. When he lowered his gaze again he said, 'Fair enough. I'll pass this higher up. They'll want to speak to you, if nothing else.'

Markby chose to overlook the lack of encouragement, and rose to his feet. 'Thank you for listening to all this,' he said politely.

Barker, not to be outdone in courtesy, held out his hand. 'My pleasure, as I might say in other circumstances! Only it isn't good news you've brought me. For you, perhaps it is.'

'For me?' asked his visitor, gripping the proffered hand.

Barker smiled for the first time since greeting Markby on arrival. 'Not often an investigating officer gets a second bite at the apple long after he's retired.' Barker's smile widened. 'That is what you're after, Alan, isn't it? A second crack at an unsolved case?'

'I'm retired,' Markby said, for the second time that day.

'Well? What did Trevor Barker say?' asked Meredith impatiently. 'Are they going to dig in the spinney?'

Markby shrugged off his jacket and hung it up in the cavernous hallway of the old Victorian house. It was darker and gloomier than usual, because the light was fading. He had not done much in the garden, he thought. Once Josh had told his extraordinary tale, Markby had spent the rest of the working day driving round the area once covered by the spinney, and talking afterwards to Barker. Before coming indoors, he'd checked that Josh had finished the digging; he was slightly surprised to find that his gardener, after neatly cleaning the tools and putting them away in the shed, had gone home.

'Josh hasn't waited to find out how I got on,' he said to his wife. 'I suppose, now he's laid the burden of his secret at my feet, he's decided he doesn't have to worry about it any more. It's my pigeon.' He gave a rueful grin.

'And how did you get on?'

'Trevor's passing it up the food chain,' he said. 'Consulting his superiors. To be fair, he can do nothing else. To reopen the case would be a complicated and expensive business; so, unless there is really good reason to believe a body or some remains will be found, there may be reluctance to go ahead. In the end, it can't be Trevor's decision alone.'

'He doesn't believe Josh?'

'He knows I believe him; and I expect him to speak to Josh in person. Plus, we have the evidence of the bracelet. But it might not be enough. No one else stumbled over the body, only Josh and Dilys. Then it vanished, pretty soon afterwards – or someone else would have found it, as you said. The killer might even have been there when the two children came upon it. He heard them coming and hid, then emerged when they ran away.' Markby looked discontented. 'Barker and anyone else he consults will drag their feet.'

They had progressed to the sitting room where, in deference to a chilly evening, the bars of an electric fire glowed in the hearth. In wintertime, a real log fire burned there, but the weather was warming up, during the day, at least. Alan subsided on to the sofa with a sigh of relief.

'The cost of the operation will be a big factor!' said Meredith sapiently. She had followed Alan and was perched on the arm of the sofa. 'Someone will decide it can't be squeezed into the budget.'

'It's an important factor in any decision to be made about following this up. That, and assigning the manpower. Then there's all the paperwork – even if it's computerised, these days. Someone has to do it. It would mean finding out who now owns the land. And who owned it at the time, and whether it was put to any use other than just a scrap of woodland. Who had access? Who went there regularly? All that could be tricky. Although there is a possibility the Council now owns it, if the spinney formed part of the original plot of land bought from the farm for the houses to be built. But if it doesn't, then possibly the developers of the business park own it. That would be Dudley Newman's company, which itself is history. But they didn't incorporate all of it in the development, so perhaps it was outside their purchase. The farm is long gone, of course, so if the farmer retained ownership, it will be quite a job tracking down his heirs.'

'You're making it sound very difficult,' said his wife.

'It is difficult! Police work is difficult! Anyway, all you and I – and Josh – can do now is wait.'

Waiting did not sit well with his wife. 'We could go and take a look around that spinney, or what's left of it. It's been in public use for over twenty years, whoever owns it!'

'I did that on my way to see Trevor Barker. It's always been all too accessible! It's become an unofficial rubbish tip over the years and now it's a real eyesore. There is less of it than when Josh and Dilys made their grim discovery. I understand part of it is now under the parking area attached to the business park.'

'It's not difficult to dig up a parking lot!' said Meredith eagerly.

'They did it in Leicester and found King Richard the Third. People said that was a waste of time before they found the skeleton!'

'Hold your horses, Watson! This isn't our decision, remember!' He grinned at her. 'Much as you would like it to be! I've done my bit and told Barker. Now it's with him.'

There was a pause in the conversation but not an empty one. The atmosphere fairly vibrated with the unspoken. Markby picked up the daily paper, made an unconvincing stab at reading the headlines, and dropped it again.

'There's something else,' said Meredith. 'Is it something Trevor said?'

'He thinks I want an investigation to go ahead for my own satisfaction. I was, after all, in charge of enquiries at this end. It's unfinished business for me.'

'And would you like to finish it?'

Alan didn't answer at once. Then he said, 'I should like Rebecca's body to be found. At the time of her disappearance enquiries were concentrated in the West Country, where she was living and where she was last seen. We didn't find her *here* and, frankly, we didn't expect to. Perhaps we – I – should have looked harder. It is possible one or both of her parents are still alive. It would give them closure. Not knowing for sure what happened to a loved one is very hard to cope with. It's very sad having a body to bury. But not having a body means no one ever knows, and there is always a lingering hope. Usually a forlorn one. But I can do nothing now, even if a decision is reached to excavate the spinney. Besides, even if remains were found, it would mean establishing they are Rebecca's. DNA tests cost money and take time. The bracelet alone isn't enough.'

'And if Rebecca is found there?'

'Then the first thing Barker will do is tell me to keep out of it! It will be his case – or a matter for the Cold Case Unit. I'm retired, remember?' He heaved another sigh. 'Why do I keep saying that today?'

'Because you're like an old warhorse. When you hear the bugle call, you want to gallop ahead!'

'Thanks for the comparison!'

Meredith went to the bay window, leaned her hands on the sill and stared out at the view of the path to the front gate and the street beyond. The lamp posts had sprung into bright life. There must be something on in the church next door, because that was lit up, too, and people were walking past the house heading for it.

'Nothing says you can't make a few enquiries – look around – before Barker warns you off. After all, it was to you Josh told his story. You ought to check it out!'

Her husband jumped up from the sofa, dislodging the discarded newspaper. It slid to the floor, scattering its sheets across the carpet.

'You are absolutely right!'

Meredith spun round. 'You agree?'

'A hundred per cent. I should have checked it out more fully, before I went to Barker. I have confidence in Josh, but it's a lot to expect Barker to have the same belief in his story. When he interviews Josh, as he will, he may decide Josh isn't all that bright. He'd be wrong, but people do think it! Barker may decide it's all a wild goose chase and decide not to take it any further. I ought to have dug out some background detail to support it. It would be insurance for me, too. After all, the worst-case scenario is that Barker does take action, that all the permissions come through, the spinney is thoroughly excavated at great cost, and nothing's found!'

Markby was now walking up and down the room, gesturing with one hand and pushing back the fringe of hair that had fallen over his forehead with the other.

'You remember Jess Campbell? She joined my team when I made superintendent. She had just made inspector and it was her first posting in the rank.'

'Yes, of course I do. She bought my little house. Where does she come into it?' Meredith was beginning to be alarmed. She hadn't seen Alan so agitated about anything for a long time.

Quickly he told her about Ian Carter, who'd been in on the original enquiry and was now ranking superintendent. 'Jess is working in the West Country with him now . . .' He paused. 'I would have expected Jess to have been promoted upwards again by now. But the higher you climb the harder it gets. There are fewer officers in the higher ranks than in the lower ones, it's as simple as that.'

'Perhaps,' Meredith suggested, 'she doesn't want to be tied to a desk? She was one of those people who like to do things themselves, as I remember her.'

'It ran in the family,' her husband said. 'Her brother worked for some medical charity and always seemed to be in war zones. What I'm thinking,' he went on, 'is that I should phone Ian tomorrow. It's only courtesy, after all. Ian will remember the original investigation all too well. He'd not long been in CID and was keen to make his mark. The failure to clear it up has probably been gnawing at him all these years. I'd like to hear what he remembers. And perhaps I should pay a visit to Brocket's Row.'

'Do you mean talk to Auntie Nina, by any chance?'

'Absolutely talk to Auntie—I mean, talk to Mrs Pengelly. Although Barker might think that smacks of me doing my own investigation.'

'So, let me go and chat to her,' Meredith said calmly. 'Any call I pay on Mrs Pengelly is purely social and, um, in the way of a natural concern. Josh has become a familiar sight here. He's a friend. When officers come knocking on her door wanting to talk to him about the body in the spinney, the poor old lady will be very upset. We should forewarn her, if Josh hasn't done so already.'

'Fair enough,' said Markby, after considering the matter 'from all angles' in his wife's habitual phrase. 'Barker can't stop you. He hasn't told you to leave it with him. If he says anything to you, tell him it's your early training looking after distressed Brits in far-off places. While you're there, get Mrs P to reminisce about Josh and Dilys when they were kids. That shouldn't be difficult. It will probably be more difficult to stop her wandering down memory lane! See if she remembers the children coming home one day looking worried or particularly upset. Find out who else lived in the row of houses at the same time and if any of the residents still live there. Someone else might have seen something. Although, whether anyone will remember after twenty years is another matter!'

After a moment, during which Meredith stared at him thoughtfully, she asked, 'Alan, are you bored?'

Startled, he replied too quickly, 'No! No, of course not. How could I be bored?'

'Pretty easily, I imagine. I have been wondering about it, as a matter of fact, for some time.'

She had quite taken the wind out of his sails, she thought, watching as the startled expression on his face turned into one of puzzlement and then something approaching panic.

He leaned forward to ask earnestly, 'Do you mean, really mean, that I'm boring?'

'Of course I don't!' Now it was Meredith's turn to be startled. 'I just mean that back in the days when you were a copper, life was full of surprises. They weren't all nice ones, usually quite the opposite! Cases were shocking, distressing, frustrating perhaps – and downright infuriating, at times – but never dull. I know you dreamed about retirement. You and I would be together and live in a house we could both love, and you'd have time to garden and I wouldn't have to start every working day running down a station platform with a briefcase in one hand and a polystyrene cup of coffee in the other. Then, when we did get married and both of us retired, we had this house to knock into shape. There will always be something to be done; it's that sort of house. But the big tasks have been tackled and now the garden is planned out, and you've got Josh to come over and help out with that. I've got my writing . . . I have wondered, from time to time, if you were just a little bit bored.'

He smiled. 'How could life be boring when I'm married to you?'

'I accept the compliment – I suppose it was a compliment? But watching you now, and listening to you after you'd spoken to Trevor Barker, I realise that what you do want – really want – is a proper problem to sink your teeth into, like this mystery of Rebecca . . . what was her surname?'

'Hellington. Rebecca Elizabeth Hellington. Fair hair, blue eyes, five foot five in old measurements, and full of life. Everyone who knew her agreed about the last thing. She always had something planned, her father told me.'

'But she didn't plan to end up buried in the spinney behind Brocket's Row,' Meredith said.

'No,' Alan agreed soberly. 'But this is more than just a mental challenge.'

'I realise that.'

After a moment, Alan got to his feet, crossed to his wife and put an arm around her shoulders. 'I am not bored. I have never had the chance to be bored since the moment I met you. For that I thank you, really, very much indeed! But, if I'm honest, I have to admit Trevor Barker hit the nail on the head. I do want another crack at solving the mystery of what happened to Rebecca. I want it even more than I ever did, now that I know she died here, a mile away, behind Brocket's Row. Or her dead body was brought there, *and I didn't find it!* I let her down, Merry, and I let that family down.'

'I know you did everything you possibly could have done at the time,' she declared.

'But this morning, out of the blue and twenty years later, Josh handed me a silver bracelet. He told me how he and his sister found Rebecca, something I wasn't able to do. I can't just hand it over to Trevor and let it go at that.'

Chapter 3

Ian Carter put down the phone and sat for a moment with his hand still resting on the receiver. Then he stood up and walked to the window. It wasn't a great view, mostly showing the car park, an expanse of tarmac with half a dozen trees planted haphazardly here and there by way of a nod to landscaping. Nor was it a great day weather-wise. The sky was overcast, muddy in hue. A stiff breeze had sprung up since lunchtime. Probably the rain would sweep in tonight. Twenty years, he thought. The saying was that 'time flies when you're having fun'. In his experience, it flew by, anyway. If you were lucky, some of it was enjoyable, some of it routine and boring; and sometimes everything seemed to go wrong, as when his marriage fell apart.

Yet, from the career point of view, he'd done all right. He'd reached the rank of superintendent and doubted that he'd go any higher. Frankly, he had no ambition to rise further. But he could still remember how elated he'd been, twenty years before, when he'd just made detective sergeant. At the time of this advancement – hailed by his late parents, as only to be expected – Carter himself saw CID as a panorama of opportunity, opening out before his mental view.

Even then, things hadn't started too well and he'd been quickly disillusioned. One of the first cases he'd found himself working on had been the disappearance of a student at a local teacher training college, Rebecca Hellington. The team had collectively put in long hours on that one case alone, and got nowhere. He had interviewed Rebecca's boyfriend at length, uneasily aware that he, Carter, had not been that much older than Peter Malone, the young man being questioned. The theory advanced by Carter's boss at the time was that Malone would talk more freely to a younger officer. Carter, for his part, would understand Malone's thought processes – so went Inspector Parry's reasoning.

Carter's own opinion (as a junior, he'd been unable to express it, of course) had been that Parry's theory stood on shaky legs. If he'd thought it when Parry came up with the idea, he was sure of it after the first of several meetings with Malone.

So many cases over the years. So much water had flowed under the bridge. Why does one particular case stand out? Because it's gruesome? Because of its strangeness? No, thought Carter now. Because it's unsolved. You never forget those: the long hours, the frustration, the ultimate inevitable moment when you have to admit to yourself, and to others, that you've failed.

Also, over the years, some faces blur in recollection; but Carter could still picture Malone in extraordinary detail. Having been informed that Malone wasn't an aspiring teacher, like the missing girl, but was working towards qualifications in business studies, Carter had expected to meet an outgoing, self-confident future captain of industry, or a city banker.

He'd run him to earth in his lodgings where, in a room decorated with a carefully constructed tower of empty beer cans, he found a slim but sinewy, bespectacled youth with a mop of black hair. Malone's features had been finely drawn and his skin had been unusually pale. Rather to his own embarrassment, Carter had found himself reminded of Renaissance frescoes seen on a trip to Italy. Delicate-featured angels painted on the plaster blew trumpets with such energy they'd appeared about to leave the wall, and soar up into the church roof. But here sat one of those angelic heralds in a scruffy sweater and jeans, chewing on the end of a biro and scowling at him. He'd pushed his spectacles on top of his head, where they nestled in his black curls. Definitely an artist, not a banker, thought Carter, and then he'd wondered what had attracted Malone to the world of finance.

When Carter had arrived and introduced himself, Malone had clearly been nervous, which had been understandable. But he hadn't looked or sounded guilty. Nor, initially, had he sounded unduly worried about where his girlfriend might be. He'd been 'tetchy', if anything. He'd certainly stuck to his story. Rebecca had told him she might be going to Bamford to visit her parents that weekend. It was her father's birthday. No, he'd never been to Bamford himself but Rebecca had told him that was where her family lived. So, when he didn't see her around, he assumed that was where she'd gone. Malone seemed to feel that Rebecca was being inconsiderate in causing any problem.

'I've got enough on my plate!' he'd said crossly, taking the biro out of his mouth and jabbing it in all directions to indicate the untidy heaps of paper and books in his room.

'So have I!' Carter had snapped back. 'So, don't waste my time! Just answer my questions. How did the two of you meet up?'

'At a party!' Malone had snarled.

'Where?'

'Somewhere,' Malone had said, vaguely.

'I'm not here because I've got nothing else to do! So, let's do it the easy way. I ask and you answer.'

Carter had wondered, when he spoke so sharply, if he'd gone too far. But, surprisingly, Malone had removed his spectacles from his dark curls, squinted at his interrogator, and then smiled briefly.

'You can ask whatever you like, mate,' he'd replied. 'But I don't think for a minute I've got any of the answers.' Malone paused, frowning.

'OK, it happened like this,' he'd said briskly. 'I'm not the sporting type but I do belong to a local tennis club. Usually I play doubles. I know several other players, but generally only to play tennis. Otherwise we don't usually socialise. But one day, I got a call from a chap called Nick. I'd partnered him a few times, otherwise I didn't know him well. I was a bit surprised when he invited me to a party at his parents' house. It was out in the country somewhere. His people were away on holiday and he was throwing open the doors of the family home and inviting us all in. We drew lots among the tennis gang for the designated driver and Nick's mate, Henry, got the job. The rest of us piled into his car and he drove us there.'

'Any damage done to the house? What did Nick's parents find when they got back?' Carter wouldn't have been surprised if the unlucky homeowners had found the place trashed.

'They'd moved most of the furniture out into the garden ahead of our arrival,' Malone had said, defensively. 'Not my problem, anyway.'

'They?' Carter had pressed.

'Nick – the chap throwing the bash – and some of his friends. Anyhow, the downstairs rooms were practically empty of any furniture . . .' Malone had hesitated. 'Upstairs was probably

41

furnished, but I didn't go upstairs. Others did.' Malone had grinned briefly, looking less like a herald angel, for the moment, and more like a fallen one.

'But not you – and Rebecca.' Carter's scepticism had sounded in his voice.

'No! I hadn't met her before that evening! She didn't like it, the party. She'd come along with others, as I'd done, and quickly decided it wasn't her scene. She's a student at teacher training college and hadn't gone out much in the evenings since the beginning of term, so she'd thought the party would be nice. But it terrified her. Her people are very – um – respectable. There were so many partygoers and so much noise, everyone letting their hair down. That would be the polite way of describing it!' Malone had given a brief grin. 'I found her in the conservatory, hiding behind some big potted palm thing. She wanted to leave but she had no independent transport. She was on the verge of tears. I couldn't borrow someone's car keys and drive her back, because I'd been drinking. But I felt really sorry for the kid, so I said I'd organise something for her. She was pathetically grateful.'

'That was chivalrous of you,' Carter had commented. 'What, exactly, did you organise?'

'It wasn't easy,' Malone had grumbled. 'I looked for Henry, but he'd disappeared somewhere. No one else wanted to leave, only Rebecca. But she'd got into a bit of a state, like I said. So, I went to find Nick, as he was the host, and told him Rebecca felt ill. I couldn't tell him she was having a rotten time at his party, could I? Nick asked, "Who's Rebecca? Can't she go home with whoever brought her?" But I didn't know who'd brought her. So Nick went off to see if he could find someone, and he came back with a tall blonde girl he introduced as a cousin. She lived locally. She said she'd take Rebecca over to her family's place and Rebecca could doss down there until morning – use this girl's room. Then, in the morning, Rebecca could make her way home somehow by bus. She – Nick's cousin – said her parents were cool about that sort of thing. They were out for the evening, anyway, and if Rebecca used her bedroom, no one would know.'

'And this plan worked?' Carter had not so very long ago been a student himself, and he wasn't unfamiliar with ad hoc arrangements.

Remembering the conversation now, twenty years later, he realised how much older and wiser he'd grown. His daughter, Millie, was about to become a teenager – she'd be thirteen next month. He worried about her now. How much more was he going to worry in three or four years' time? Was that what 'wiser with age' really meant? You just worried over things that would never have troubled you when young?

Back then, Malone had been sanguine about the whole thing, and had said the plan worked out fine. Nick's cousin – 'Don't ask me her name, I haven't a clue!' – took Rebecca away and returned alone, saying it was OK; she'd left Rebecca in her bedroom. Malone himself had gone home by car, in the early hours of the morning – driven by Henry, who had just about managed to stay sober. But the next day, he went over to Rebecca's hall of residence and asked after her.

'Just checking, you know. She was there. She'd got back that morning on the bus. It had all gone to plan. I don't think the other girl's parents ever knew she was kipping in their house – or if they heard anything, they thought it was their own daughter.'

'And since then you've started seeing one another?'

'Yes, off and on. It isn't that serious.' Malone had shrugged.

The first Malone knew about Rebecca's disappearance being treated officially as suspicious was the moment Carter had turned up to quiz him. He had become aware that people, other than himself, couldn't find her, because it was going round 'on the grapevine'. But there could be any number of reasons for that, he'd pointed out. 'I don't know anything!' he'd concluded. 'If I did, I'd tell you. But I don't, OK?'

If Carter had been curious at Malone's manner, he'd put it down to the callousness of youth.

But there was no sign of Rebecca over the following days. So, Carter went back to talk to Malone again – and again. Eventually, Malone had become resigned, up to a point, to seeing Carter appear in front of him. The young man's original nervousness had gone and he veered now between visible exasperation and a sort of world-weariness.

'Do you know if Rebecca has ever gone missing before?' Carter remembered asking. He had been getting desperate himself by then.

'No, not missing exactly,' Malone had replied, testily. 'Look, quite often she says she'll do something and then changes her mind. It's like that party I rescued her from. She'd wanted to go and then decided she didn't like it. Or she'll be sidetracked by something she's found more interesting or urgent, or has just forgotten about. Ask anyone.'

He could account for his own movements, even though a lot of the time he'd been in his room with his head down, poring over his books. He'd been due to deliver a piece of written work to his tutor. He still hadn't finished it and Carter was taking up valuable time. Malone had grown steadily more resentful the more

Carter spoke to him. When Carter kept returning to question him again, his resentment became barely concealed anger.

'Why me?' he had demanded querulously on yet another, later visit. 'Why do you keep coming back and asking me?'

'Because you are close to her,' Carter had replied. And because he didn't have any other leads, he might have added, if he'd been honest. They'd still been working on the assumption that Rebecca was alive. Inspector Parry, a man of long years' experience, was saying he thought she was dead, but he had yet to put it in any report.

'OK, she's my girlfriend!' howled Malone. 'That doesn't make me her bloody minder! We don't go round everywhere holding hands! It's a relaxed sort of relationship. I've told you, I don't always know where she is. You're supposed to be looking for her. Why don't you go and do it?'

'That's why I'm here,' Carter had pointed out, doing his best to keep his temper. 'I am just wondering why *you* aren't out looking for her. Aren't you worried about her safety? You worried enough to organise her escape from that party when you'd only just met. This has now been almost two weeks. It isn't a question of a missed lecture or a broken date. No one's seen her. Her bed hasn't been slept in. There is no sign she's been in her room, and her post hasn't been collected from the pigeonhole. The police are asking for her. Surely you realise it's serious? You can't still be that relaxed, to use your word, about it!'

Malone had already been flushed with anger, but now he turned a deep red. 'Of course I'm worried now, with time going by and all that! You keep turning up! No one has any idea where she is. But what can I do? I've asked around her hall of residence. I've been to a couple of pubs we used to visit and asked there. Do you know what one barman said to me? He said all "student types" looked the same to him.' Malone had scowled ferociously. 'I nearly punched him.' He'd caught Carter's eye. 'But I didn't.'

As days passed Carter realised that, even though Malone had not been unduly worried at the outset, the young man was deeply worried now. Moreover, he was getting very twitchy. Whether this was on Rebecca's account – or on his own, because now the police had become involved and they might consider him a suspect in some as yet unspecified crime – Carter didn't know.

'You have no suggestions as to where else she might have gone if she changed her mind about going home?' he'd asked in one of their very last conversations, alarmed to catch a note of desperation in his own voice.

'How should I know?' Malone had leaned forward and spoken slowly, emphasising his words. 'We met at that party I told you about. We've gone around together a bit after that. We aren't a fixed item. We have friends in common here, sure. But I don't know how many friends she had before she came here, or has back home in Bamford. Half the town there probably knows her. She probably has dozens of friends. Why don't you track them down and ask them?'

'Someone at the Bamford end of police enquiries is doing that,' Carter had assured him.

That 'someone' had been Inspector Alan Markby. He'd reported exhaustive enquiries, all leading nowhere. Mr and Mrs Hellington were frantic with worry. It was quite out of character for Rebecca to take off like that. Yes, she'd mentioned coming home for her father's birthday. They'd waited for her to let them know the arrival time of the National Express bus. She never did.

She never contacted them again.

Markby had expressed his regrets at the failure of his team to turn up anything further. But from the career point of view, thought Carter now, it hadn't done Markby any harm, because six months afterwards Markby had gained promotion. He must have been successful in other cases. Indeed, over the years, Carter had learned this was so, because Markby had risen to superintendent and become something of a legend. In a weird sort of way, for Carter, this had been a small consolation. If the great Markby couldn't track the girl down, it wasn't such a disaster that he, Carter, couldn't.

But it was a failure, and somewhere along the line Carter began to feel he, personally, had screwed up. The disappearance of any young girl with her future ahead of her must be a tragedy. It was agreed, unofficially, that the missing girl was most likely dead; the body had been disposed of either out in the countryside or in the river. There were possibilities enough, and the budget couldn't be stretched out endlessly. The active search ground to a halt. Other matters, obvious crimes, took precedence: a murder, a bank robbery, a hideous case of child cruelty. In all of these instances there was physical evidence. But Rebecca had vanished as if in a puff of smoke – or like a genie in a fairy tale, dematerialising back into the lamp.

Eventually, the decision had been taken to put her disappearance on the back burner, in the absence of any new evidence – such as a sighting of her alive, or the discovery of remains – and she became a 'cold case'. But he, Carter, had never forgotten this failure in his early career as a detective.

This morning, to his astonishment, he had received a phone call and discovered that Alan Markby hadn't forgotten it, either.

Footsteps sounded now in the corridor outside his office.

Through the small window in the door he saw the head of Sergeant Morton passing by. He got up and hurried to the door, pulling it open just as Morton was about to disappear round a corner in the corridor.

'Phil?'

Morton backtracked and asked, looking wary, 'Sir?'

'You don't happen to know where Inspector Campbell is just at this moment, do you?'

'I believe she's gone down to lunch, in the canteen,' Morton told him. 'Should I fetch her up here?'

'Oh, no, no,' Carter said hurriedly. 'Don't disturb her. I'll see her later.'

Morton continued on his way, looking relieved that he hadn't been given any kind of new job.

A glance at his wristwatch confirmed that it was just after midday and, after a moment's deliberation, Carter decided to head down to the canteen and see if Jess was indeed there. An informal approach, that was the thing, he told himself. You couldn't get much more informal than the canteen.

He found Jess starting on an early lunch of macaroni cheese. She was staring down at it with a slight frown. Carter, rather self-consciously, had acquired a cup of coffee at the counter, together with a baked potato filled with not very much tuna and a lot of sweetcorn. The canteen assistant had served him with a puzzled look. He didn't know if that was because of his unexpected appearance in her workplace or because she knew something about the baked potato that he didn't. He wished now he'd gone for the macaroni. The large room echoed with the clatter of cutlery and subdued chatter; the air was damp and warm, and smelled of baked beans.

'Do you mind if I join you?' he asked.

'Of course not!' Jess replied, looking up and appearing startled, as he approached at her table. Then, and only then, he realised that she hadn't been staring down at the food but at what looked like a letter, rather a scrappy, scrawled one, lying on the plate beside the macaroni.

'Sorry, I'm disturbing you!' he exclaimed, embarrassed.

'No, not at all. It's just that we don't often see you in here.' As she spoke, she crumpled the letter up and pushed it into her pocket.

'Well, I thought I ought to show willing occasionally.' Ian ruefully indicated his baked potato.

She laughed. 'Why did you pick that, if you don't like the look of it?'

'Panic,' he said. 'I didn't like the look of any of it. Although, that cheesy thing looks nice.' He picked up a fork and prodded the potato. 'It's an excuse, I'll come clean. I wanted to have a word about a phone call I've just had. Oh, nothing to do with a current investigation!' he added hurriedly. 'It was more in the nature of a private call, although it relates to an old case. You, ah, remember Alan Markby?'

Surprised, Jess abandoned the macaroni cheese and stared at him. 'Of course! He was the superintendent directing a murder investigation I was attached to at Bamford, before I came here.'

'Mm, my acquaintance with him was well before that – and mostly conducted over the telephone. I did meet him a couple of times; he was a tall, thin, fair-haired chap. He was pleasant, cordial even, but he wasn't any help.' He sipped his coffee. 'I was with the

CID here and had just made sergeant. Markby was older than me. He was an inspector then. He'd reached superintendent by the time you knew him, you say?' Carter took a mouthful of the potato and filling, and it wasn't as bad as he'd feared. A bit dry, however.

'Yes, he had. This case you worked with him on, it was a murder case?'

'Missing person. Although, when we couldn't find any trace of her, we began to suspect we were looking for a body.' Quickly, Carter sketched in the background to Rebecca's disappearance. 'We found no trace at this end and Markby found none at the Bamford end. It's been an unsolved mystery ever since.' Hurriedly he added, 'I don't mean Markby didn't try and trace her. I'm sure he did all he could.'

Jess was frowning. 'He must be retired by now, Alan Markby.'

'He is retired. But he's been on the phone to me this morning.'

'The body's turned up!' Jess exclaimed. In her surprise she'd spoken more loudly than she'd intended, and heads turned. More quietly, she hissed, 'Something important must have happened. Is it a body?'

'Not a physical body. But evidence of a body, possibly. It's a bit more complicated than that. You know, I would have thought Markby would have forgotten all about it by now.' Carter abandoned the potato. 'Look, if you're free this evening, come and have a pub meal with me somewhere? Then I can tell you all about it. At the moment, it's not official business, nothing to do with us. But I have a sneaking feeling Markby is on the trail and, sooner or later, I'm going to be involved in some way. Hardly anyone else still professionally active now will remember the case. But I do!'

'Alan Markby was a keen gardener!' Jess remembered suddenly. 'He had a girlfriend in the Diplomatic Service.'

'Well, since the time you knew him, he's married the girlfriend, she's taken to writing detective stories, and he's acquired a gardener to help him with his hobby. That's what's led to the phone call.' Carter abandoned his lunch and stood up. 'Think of a pub you'd like to eat at tonight.'

Jess, left to contemplate the mangled shell of the potato on Carter's plate, thought resentfully, *So, what's it got to do with me!* Unless Ian just wanted to pick through her memories of Markby, ahead of any fresh involvement with him. 'Yes!' she muttered. 'That's it! Still, it will be nice to have a decent pub meal tonight, instead of something microwaved at home!'

The macaroni cheese, during her talk with Ian, had gone cold and rubbery. She pushed it away to join his abandoned potato, and hunted in her pocket for the now very creased sheet of paper.

Her twin brother, Simon, was a doctor working with a medical charity active in areas of conflict, resulting in camps of desperate refugees, ravaged by hunger and disease. Communications from him were sporadic, since he was usually out of the range of any mobile phone signal. Emails tended to arrive at odd intervals, and to consist of a couple lines saying he was OK and hoping she was, too. Letters were almost completely unknown, because postal services were early casualties of general mayhem. Besides, who had time nowadays to write letters? Simon certainly didn't. To receive one was nothing short of amazing. The letter read:

Sorry that this is such a scrawl. I have just heard that a courier is flying out and we've been told if we have letters we should hand them to him pronto, so I only have a few minutes. I am OK. Hope you are. I've scribbled a few lines

to Mum under separate cover. Do you remember Mike Foley?
He trained with me in London and he's been out here
working with us. He's been sick and is being sent back home
to recover. He'll be staying with an old uncle in Bath, the
only family he has left. Understand the old fellow is difficult,
deaf and set in his ways. So I hope you won't mind, but I've
given Mike your address and suggested he get in touch with
you when he gets to Bath. You will not be that far away.
Thought you might like a personal update of what I'm doing.
If you think it's all right, you could take him to see Mum
and he could chat to her, too. Only, don't take him if you
think it would upset her.

    Take care,
    Love,
    Simon

What did he mean, 'don't take him if you think it would upset
her'? Jess tapped the crumpled sheet thoughtfully. Their mother
would be delighted to have first-hand news of Simon. Her brother
knew that. So, the warning referred to something else.

Jess searched her memory for Mike Foley, and it supplied a
misty image of a tall, thin, muscular young man in running shorts
and vest. Track athlete, a middle-distance runner, as far as Jess
could recall. 'He's been sick and is being sent back home to
recover.' Recover from what?

No point in worrying about that now. When, and if, Foley
showed up, there would be time to sort that one out.

Chapter 4

Josh had not turned up at the Old Vicarage to work in the garden the following day. He'd phoned early to say he'd gone to deal with a blocked drain. Meredith took the call and thought Josh cut the link quickly once he'd delivered his message. He probably wasn't giving her a chance to ask him questions about the bracelet. But he didn't ask what Alan had done about it, either. That did surprise her.

Alan, when she reported this, gave as his opinion that Josh's memory of the body in the woods had been a burden for twenty years. Now he'd been able to put it down, he'd done just that. He'd handed it over to a suitable person and had walked away.

'I hope,' said Alan worriedly, 'that he'll come back to the garden again and not abandon us completely now.'

'If he's clearing out someone's drain,' said Meredith, 'it's a good moment for me to go and visit Mrs Pengelly. How old do you think she is?'

Alan considered. 'Possibly not extremely old. She was young enough, twenty years ago, to act as foster parent to a couple of disturbed kids. Perhaps more or less my age? And I don't consider myself to be old!'

Before tackling Trevor Barker the previous day, Alan had taken a few minutes to check out the spinney where Josh and Dilys had

53

stumbled on the body. So, Meredith decided to do the same before tackling Mrs Pengelly.

Brocket's Row, she discovered, sat atop a steep rise in the ground. Behind it, sloping downhill, was an area of rough pasture, plentifully dotted with clumps of weeds and bushes, and surrounded by the crumbling remains of a stone wall. The spinney lay beyond and below it, right at the bottom of the hill, and beyond that, she could see the roofs of warehouses, Dudley Newman's would-be business park. She drove on the short distance downhill until she reached it, then climbed out of the car and stood looking back and upwards towards the houses. The spinney, as a block of trees, would be visible from up there, but it would be too far away for anyone to see what went on in its shady interior. Alan had warned her that, lately, someone had been using the spinney to dump rubbish, but from the road this eyesore couldn't be seen. That was probably why the Council had not been here to put up notices warning against fly-tipping. No one had reported it.

Once she stepped between the trees, Meredith immediately saw what the problem was. Any and every kind of debris was here. Someone had tipped out irregular lumps of concrete. It must have been quite some time ago, because already blackberry bushes had colonised the heap. There was an ancient gas cooker nearby, leaning drunkenly to one side with stinging nettles clustered around its feet. There were several black plastic bin liners. One had split and an unpleasant, rotten smell oozed from it, together with a dark tarry liquid. Meredith skirted these horrors and came upon a worse one, the body of a dead fox with sunken flanks and its jaw open in death as if it was snarling at her. She wondered if it had foraged amongst the plastic bags and eaten something poisonous.

Through the trees, to the rear of the patch of woodland, it was just possible to make out the dark shapes of the warehouses that were all that remained of Dudley Newman's ambitious project. In every sense, literal and metaphorical, the place stank of decay.

She had no wish to linger. It was impossible to tell how the spinney had once looked when local children had played here, and certainly not possible to guess just where Josh and Dilys had found the dead girl. Would Josh be able to pick out the spot after so many years and major changes in the surrounding vegetation? Meredith retreated from the spinney and its horrors, got back into her car, then turned round and drove back up to the top of the hill.

There were eight houses – four sets of semis, standing in a row – cresting the rise and looking out over the town like a raiding party, assessing the target below. Probably there had once been a plan to build a bigger estate of social housing, but that hadn't happened, for whatever reason, and only these eight houses remained. It seemed nothing planned for this outlying area of Bamford prospered – neither Newman's doomed project nor this even earlier one, decided on by some post-war planning committee in a rush of socialist fervour. The houses were a good size but looked their age, and not only in style. The exterior walls had been rendered with pebbledash long ago, a fashion Meredith had never liked. Now some rendering was flaking, and what remained was a dirty khaki in colour – all except one house, the first one, belonging to Mrs Pengelly. The exterior of that house was in good order and painted white. It made Meredith think of one shining clean tooth in a mouth of bad ones. The front garden was tidy, too, with a lawn and a rose bed. But Mrs Pengelly had

Josh to keep all that as it should be. The occupants of the other houses seemed to have lost heart and interest. Renovation of these homes, and installation of modern facilities, would be costly. The best thing would be to knock them down and start again. A modern-day Dudley Newman could do that. But probably, like the spinney, Brocket's Row had been forgotten and left to its fate.

'You want to see me?'

Meredith jumped. So absorbed had she been in studying the front of the house, she hadn't heard the approach of the speaker. She turned now and saw a small, wiry woman wearing jogging pants, a purple fleece jacket zipped up to the chin, and a crocheted beanie hat that could have passed for a tea cosy.

'Mrs Pengelly?' she asked. 'Yes, I was just wondering if you were at home. I'm Meredith Mitchell.'

'Oh, I know who you are!' was the prompt reply. 'You write them books, detective stories. I've read a couple. They're about that man who mends pianos and solves mysteries. I'd have thought he had enough to do with just the pianos.' She pushed open a wooden gate. 'Come on in, then.'

Indoors, the house was far more welcoming than the location. It was warm, and spotlessly clean and tidy. The furniture was old, but looked comfortable. A blue budgerigar in a cage hopped up and down on its perch as they entered, uttering whistles of excitement.

'That,' said Mrs Pengelly, 'is Bobby. I let him out to fly around the room, but not when I've got a visitor. He sometimes perches on your head and if you're not used to it, it feels funny. Would you like a cup of tea?'

Meredith felt that, before she settled in too well, she ought to explain her presence. 'I'm here because of something Josh told my husband. Josh helps us in the garden.'

'I know why you're here,' said her hostess, who seemed pretty well informed about everything. 'Josh told me all about it and I've been expecting one of you to turn up.' She eyed Meredith in an assessing sort of way. 'I thought it might have been your husband. He used to head up the police here, years ago.'

'He thought you might rather talk to me, and I wanted to come and see you. All this must have come as a shock. I thought you might be upset about it all. Also, if they haven't been already, a serving police officer or two might call by.'

Mrs Pengelly nodded and walked out of the room without comment. Meredith could hear the sound of a kettle coming to the boil and a clink of china. Mrs Pengelly returned bearing a tin tray with two mugs on it, a jug and a bowl of sugar.

'I don't take sugar, thanks,' said Meredith, accepting her mug. It had wild flowers painted on it.

'Not many people do, nowadays,' said Mrs Pengelly. 'All kinds of ideas people have now about stuff not being good for you. Burnt toast it is now. Who eats burnt toast, anyway? Besides, you shouldn't go letting it burn in the first place. Do you mind if I switch on the logs?'

While Meredith disentangled this speech in her mind, Mrs P stooped and switched on a fake log fire in the hearth.

'Cheers the place up!' she said. 'Even if you don't have the heat on with it.' She sat down and fixed her visitor with a sharp gaze. 'Mostly people call me Auntie Nina.'

'Please call me Meredith. I realise Josh has told you about the body he and his sister found in the spinney years ago. May I ask, when did he tell you?'

'He didn't tell me twenty years ago, when they found the poor girl,' said Auntie Nina fiercely. 'I'd have reported it.'

Meredith realised that it was best to think of Mrs Pengelly as 'Auntie Nina'. She wondered briefly what had happened to Mr Pengelly. The other woman had divested herself of the purple fleece and was revealed to be wearing a green-and-white striped rugby shirt. It must be in a boy's size. Meredith suddenly realised that her hostess probably shopped for clothes at jumble sales or in charity shops.

'You've got the garden all nicely laid out now, I hear,' Auntie Nina went on. 'It was in a terrible mess before you took on the vicarage. Father Holland, who used to live there, never got round to any gardening. Courgettes, is it, you want to plant next? So Josh says. I never grow anything exotic. Never cooked anything like that, either. Anyhow, one thing led on to another, as it does, and I found myself telling Josh I remembered when your husband was in the police. I was just making a bit of conversation,' observed Auntie Nina, stirring two spoons of sugar into her tea. 'But Josh got really interested. Anyway, later on the next day, when he came home from your place, he said he'd had a word with Mr Markby and told him about something that had happened years back, when he and his little sister were here together. That's Dilys,' she added, in case Meredith wasn't sure.

'He told us about Dilys.'

Auntie Nina shook her head. 'She was a handful, I can tell you! Josh was never any trouble, but Dilys! She was all right with me, but the complaints from other people about her, you wouldn't

58

credit. She'd fight with any of the other kids, knock seven bells out of them. The parents complained, of course. She was disturbed, you see.'

'Sounds like it,' said Meredith. 'And then Josh told you about the bracelet – and the body.'

'That's it. And that was the first I heard of it, believe me. It fair took the wind out of my sails, I can tell you, especially with Dilys taking the bracelet off the corpse . . .' Auntie Nina paused. 'Dilys was always a bit of a magpie, you know. Anything glittery took her eye. She used to hide away bits and pieces she'd taken, but I'd find them and get them back to the owner, if I could. I didn't tell the Social. She was in enough trouble as it was. She didn't need to see more head doctors. She needed time to settle down. But it's still difficult to imagine her taking a bracelet off a dead girl's arm. But she did, so Josh says, and you can believe him. Josh doesn't make things up.'

'I believe Dilys is in prison at the moment,' Meredith said, tentatively.

'Much good that will do her,' said Auntie Nina with a sniff. 'Just make things worse. She feels everyone is against her, you see, and to be frank, mostly people are against her! So she's not wrong. She left here when she was sixteen. She wanted to go her own way, and she did. She went up to London in the end. Got into more trouble there, of course.'

'But Josh stayed here with you.'

Auntie Nina only nodded. The budgie chirruped and pecked at a little bell in his cage. It jangled tinnily.

'Do you know what happened to their mother?'

'Dead. Heroin,' said Auntie Nina briefly.

'Was this before they came to live with you? Or afterwards? That she died, I mean.'

'She died a couple of years after they came here. I was told it was because the heroin had something wrong with it, as if heroin itself wasn't bad enough. Let's see, Josh was just eleven. He took it well, didn't say much. Social Services did try to get them adopted out, but with Dilys being the way she was, no one would take them on. So they stayed here with me.'

'I know twenty years is a long time ago,' Meredith went on, 'but do you recall any time when the children seemed particularly upset? Worried about something, perhaps?'

'The way they were, it would have been hard to tell, wouldn't it?' Auntie Nina pointed out. She paused, and her brow furrowed in thought beneath the tea cosy beanie. She hadn't removed it when she'd divested herself of the fleece, and now Meredith wondered if her hostess ever took the crocheted hat off.

'There were a few days,' said Auntie Nina slowly, 'when they both went very quiet. I do remember that, although I couldn't tell you exactly when it was, not to the day. They'd been here nearly a year, I recall, and it was just at the start of the summer, maybe June. It was during the school term and I did wonder if they'd picked up some bug or other at school. But there was nothing going round at the time that I knew of. Even little Dilys went quiet and was no trouble for about a week. That's why I remember it, because she didn't go quiet often. I kept an eye on them but they were eating all right, even the vegetables. I had terrible trouble getting them to eat vegetables when they first came. They didn't know what they were. After a week, or just a little bit longer, things seemed to go back to normal – or what was normal for them. I didn't know whether to be pleased or not. I had hoped Dilys had begun to calm down. But she hadn't.' A note of sadness entered her voice.

There was a moment's silence during which Mrs Pengelly appeared to be thinking about the past. The past, thought Meredith, is where we need to go now.

'Mrs—Auntie Nina, do you remember any talk in Bamford about a missing student, a local girl, twenty years ago?'

Auntie Nina blinked and returned to the present day. 'What? Oh, yes, the daughter of those people who ran the travel agency. It was in the local paper and in the big daily papers, too. And on the telly news, as well. Lots of people knew the family. I didn't myself, because I never had the time for foreign holidays, or the money, come to that. Besides, I never did fancy aeroplanes – travelling in them, I mean. Up there in the sky with nothing under your feet. I've been abroad, mind. I went to Boulogne on the Channel ferryboat when I was much younger.' She frowned. 'It's a pity neither Josh nor Dilys said they'd found a body, because it might have been her, mightn't it? Even though she'd gone missing over Gloucester way. She'd come back to see her folks; but before she got through her own front door, well, we don't know what happened, do we?'

'No, we don't.'

'It's a terrible world, sometimes. Things you see on the telly, read in the news . . . It's like everyone's gone mad . . .' Auntie Nina paused to meditate for a moment on the state of the world, then she fixed bright eyes on Meredith. 'Your husband's going to look into it, is he? That story Josh told him?'

'Alan's retired. He has reported it. If anyone looks into it now, well, it won't be him, and it all depends on whether they find the remains.'

'Of course,' Nina Pengelly resumed, 'I can understand why the two of them never told anyone. I'm not sure the police will be sympathetic. But the children thought they'd get into trouble again.' Unexpectedly, a look of satisfaction appeared on her face. 'They'll be digging in the spinney, will they? Perhaps they'll take away all that rubbish down there. I've rung the Council twice about it, and they say they'll send someone out. But they haven't. We're not important enough.'

'I don't know whether they'll be digging or not.'

'If they do, I'll know about it, I suppose,' said Auntie Nina. 'Be able to see something of it from my kitchen window, perhaps. I can see the spinney. But I can't see into it, if you know what I mean. But a lot of police cars and diggers and so on, I'd see them all right.'

Meredith drained her mug and returned it to the tray. The fake logs flickered reassuringly. Bobby rang his bell again several times, following that with an impatient squawk.

'If you want to let him out, I don't mind,' said Meredith. 'Even if he lands on me.'

Auntie Nina fixed her with a beady eye that suddenly struck Meredith as very birdlike. Then she stood and went to the cage. There was a flutter of wings and a light draught caressed Meredith's ear. Bobby landed on the back of his owner's chair and perched there, studying the visitor, turning his head so he could assess her.

'Does he talk?' asked Meredith.

'No,' said Auntie Nina, 'but he understands what's going on.'

Pet owners often said that of their animals. Dogs and cats, possibly, thought Meredith. But she wasn't sure about birds. On the other hand, there was something knowing and distinctly unsettling about Bobby's bright gaze.

62

'I looked into the spinney before I drove up here,' she said next. 'I saw it's a bit of a mess.'

'It's disgraceful!' snapped Auntie Nina. 'It never used to be like that.'

'Who lived in Brocket's Row twenty years ago, do you remember?' Meredith made a determined effort to avoid staring back at Bobby, because she felt that in any contest, she'd surely lose.

Nina Pengelly leaned back in her chair and pursed her lips. 'Let's see. Next door to me were the Fletchers, Molly and Keith. He worked on the railway. They're both dead now. The Stokes, at the far end, they were here the longest, moved in before I did. When I say "they", I really mean Maggie Stokes and Fred, her son. Her husband, I never knew him, because he'd left her when their child was about three. That was well before my time here, years ago. When I came to live here, Fred was a grown man.'

Nina paused to consider the past again. 'I don't know if that's why Fred never married – because he felt he had to look after his mother. I think it's a shame, actually, because Maggie was a nice-looking woman and if Fred had found himself a wife, Maggie might've found someone for herself. But as it turned out, Fred never left home, and he's still there.'

Briefly, Meredith wondered whether Mrs Pengelly had ever drawn a parallel between herself and Josh Browning, and the situation with Fred Stokes and his mother.

'When Fred was working, he drove the big lorries, up and down the country and across the Channel, right across Europe. Then he had to give up because of trouble with his back.' Nina allowed herself a grin. 'I sometimes used to wonder what Fred got up to when he drove abroad. He wasn't a bad-looking fellow then. He's getting well on in years now, and he's more disabled. It's made him cantankerous. But I suppose you can't blame him.'

Nina paused to finish her tea. Bobby flew round the room, landed back where he'd started, and resumed staring at Meredith.

'We've got different people living here now. Next door to me here, they're foreign, but they're very good, quiet. Not there all day, out at work. It's not them who go dumping stuff down in the spinney. It's the other houses, between this pair and Fred at the other end. Coming and going all the time, never the same people from one week to the next. The Council puts them in there temporary, until they can find them somewhere better and more permanent. So, of course, they don't bother, do they? Every time they move out, they take their rubbish down to the trees and chuck it. I said the Council hasn't been, but that's not right. They did come once, ages ago, and took away some broken bits of furniture and stuff. But now they need to come back again. The turnover of tenants now is so quick, you blink your eye and there's a new neighbour.'

'Is Mr Stokes on his own there? I mean, he must be getting on.' Meredith hoped this was tactful and her hostess didn't take it as a comment on her own age. It was hard to tell how old Mrs Pengelly was, but Meredith was inclined to agree with Markby's guess.

'Fred is eighty-two,' Auntie Nina told her, which was a lot older than Meredith had thought she'd say. Nearly twenty years older than her hostess.

'His back's got worse over the years, poor man,' Nina was saying. 'It's got so he can't move without pain. Can't bend, can't reach up, can't turn. The last five or six years he's been in a wheelchair. He had a carer who used to come in, morning and evening, but he was so disagreeable she wouldn't come any more, and he didn't want her. I go along there every day to check on him, and I make sure he's got his dinner. That's where I was coming from when you met me, outside the house here . . .' She paused and frowned. 'I don't suppose he's been upstairs in that house since he took to the wheelchair. Well, he couldn't, could he? He gave up trying to get up and down the stairs even before that, and took to sleeping downstairs. I shudder to think what the place is like upstairs now. Must be thick with dust. The Social Services put in a downstairs toilet for him.' The beanie hat bobbed. 'Can't be helped, can it? "What can't be cured must be endured!" Never a truer saying!'

With a rustle of wings, Bobby took flight and made a couple of circuits of the room. Then Meredith felt something land on the top of her head.

'Told you he'd do that,' said Auntie Nina, nodding.

Bobby walked up and down Meredith's scalp a few times. She could feel his claws, not unpleasant, more of a tickling sensation, making her want to scratch the area. Then, suddenly, she felt a painful tug at her hair and, despite herself, she yelped.

'He does that sometimes, too!' said Bobby's owner. 'That's very naughty, Bobby!' she admonished her pet. 'Go on, now!' She clapped her hands and, to Meredith's great relief, Bobby flew off again to perch high on the curtain rail and stare down at her in triumph.

'I'll put him back in his cage,' said Auntie Nina. 'Or he might escape outside when you go.'

Meredith interpreted this as a hint. She realised that talking so much about the distant past had unsettled her hostess. She wanted to stop now. Meredith thanked her and got up.

Nina Pengelly escorted her visitor to her front gate. A wind had sprung up and brought with it the noise of traffic.

'Hear that?' She jerked the beanie hat in the direction of the sound. 'That's the motorway, that is! It's got to be three miles away at least but when the wind's coming from that direction, you'd think it was at the bottom of the hill.'

'This must always have been a quiet spot,' said Meredith, snatching at an errant lock of her hair caught by the culpable wind.

'Very quiet, dear,' said Auntie Nina. 'Never see a soul, like I told you. When we had the other families living here, in the old days, it was a proper little community. Everyone was very respectable, too. And all the time, someone was down there in the spinney burying that girl. It fair gives me the creeps. If people here had known about it at the time, they'd have been that shocked, I don't know what they'd have done. But now, I seldom see anyone.'

As she ceased speaking, and as if in contradiction, they heard the sound of an engine in distress and a battered tradesman's van chugged up the hill. It passed by them and stopped at the far house. A thickset man in a donkey jacket clambered out.

'Fred's got a visitor,' said Auntie Nina. 'That's nice. He doesn't get many. That's Mickey Wallace, that is. He and Fred are old cronies.' She peered towards the new arrival, who appeared to be scrabbling at the letter box of Fred's front door. 'Hang on a minute,' she said to Meredith. 'I'll just see him go in. The key should be there, but if it isn't, I've got one.'

Wallace had apparently found a key, and he opened the door. Meredith was denied a view of Fred Stokes, but from the sound of voices, the thickset man was being welcomed in. The door was shut.

'Nice to meet you, dear,' said Nina Pengelly to Meredith as she turned back to her own front door. 'I'll look for another of your books when I go down to the library!' she called back over her shoulder.

As the door closed behind her, the front door of the end house opened again, as if in some synchronised movement. Meredith, who had been about to get into her car, paused, then slid into the driver's seat and waited, watching through the windscreen. As a precaution, she slid a lipstick out of her bag and turned down the inside mirror, to give herself a reason for lingering.

The first thing she saw was a set of feet and lower limbs, tilted upwards. There was more uneven movement and then a wheelchair appeared, together with its occupant. The wheelchair itself wasn't of the sturdy type she'd expected, but lighter in style and collapsible. She'd already built an image of Fred Stokes in her head, long immobile and probably by now enormous. But the wheelchair's occupant was a withered wisp of a man, bundled up in outdoor clothing that gave him some bulk. But without that, Meredith realised, there would be a near-skeletal figure.

So much, she reproved herself, for trusting to preconceptions. She had known that Stokes had been a lorry driver. Lorry drivers tended to build up their upper-body strength and were generally burly men. Like Mickey Wallace, for example, who now appeared, manhandling the wheelchair fully through the doorway. He paused to pull the door shut behind them and then pushed the chariot and its occupant down the path to his van. There he lifted his friend from the wheelchair with little effort and lowered him into the passenger seat. Wallace folded up the chair with a practised movement, carried it to the rear of the van, opened the doors and stowed the chair inside. He returned to open the driver's door. Only then did he pause, with one hand on the frame of the door, and looked back towards Meredith's car. It was a very direct stare. Meredith lifted the lipstick and busied herself with an inspection of her appearance in the mirror. This seemed to satisfy Wallace. He clambered into his van and the vehicle rattled away. Meredith glanced at her wristwatch. They're going to the pub, she guessed, for a pint and a bacon roll, probably.

Meredith heaved a sigh of relief. Had Wallace decided to approach her car and demand to know why she had been gawking at his invalid friend being helped into the van, it would have been embarrassing. Perhaps she was making another erroneous judgement, but Mickey Wallace looked like an awkward customer.

Markby had received a visitor, too. The knock at the door came about twenty minutes after Meredith left to seek out Mrs Pengelly. He went to answer it and found an elderly man on his doorstep. He was tall, thin and slightly stooped, wearing a raincoat. His hairline was receding and his remaining grey-white hair was thin and wispy, worn a little long. His expression was anxious. Markby thought that he ought to know him, but he couldn't put a name to him. That's how it went when you met so many people in such varying walks of life over the years. Had this man been a witness? A victim of crime?

'My name is Hellington,' said the man on his doorstep. 'Arthur Hellington. I don't know if you remember me? You headed up enquiries locally into the disappearance of my daughter, Rebecca.' Apologetically, he added, 'It was twenty years ago.'

'Yes, of course I remember,' Markby assured him, truthfully, because as soon as the man said his name, his several encounters with Rebecca's near-hysterical parents came flooding back. 'Come on in, won't you?' He held the door open.

Hellington hesitated. 'I don't mean to take up your time.'

'I've got plenty of time!' said Markby. To himself he was thinking that Meredith was right. He did have more time than he had jobs or interests to fill it. 'I was just about to make myself a cup of coffee. Would you like one?'

Hellington, still apologising, accepted his offer and sidled into the hall where he was persuaded to divest himself of his raincoat. Markby showed him into the sitting room and left him while he went to make the coffee. When he returned, he found his visitor standing looking out of the window towards the road, in the same spot where Meredith had stood after he'd told her of his visit to Trevor Barker. Markby set down the coffee mugs and Hellington moved awkwardly away from the view of the road to sit down on the nearest chair, still ill at ease.

Markby decided it was up to him to start the conversation. 'Has Inspector Barker been to see you and your wife? He showed you the bracelet?'

Hellington didn't reply directly except for a bob of the head. Markby took that to mean yes.

'My wife died five years ago.' Hellington's voice was low-pitched and slightly hoarse, as if he had a cold or sore throat. 'She never got over our loss of Rebecca, you see. She was never the same woman again. For a long time we hoped – she hoped – that Becky, as we called her at home, would just walk in the door. She got the idea in her head that Becky had lost her memory . . . and that it might come back, and she'd remember who she was and where she lived.'

'Did you also believe that?' Markby asked gently.

After a moment's hesitation, Hellington shook his head. 'No . . . for a while, of course, but not after the first six months or so. But if believing it helped Brenda, my wife, get through each day, then I went along with it. She kept Becky's – Rebecca's – bedroom just as it was. She wouldn't change anything in the house or the garden, because if it was different when Rebecca came home, she might not recognise it. She might think we'd moved. Eventually, Brenda wouldn't leave the house, because Rebecca might come when the place was empty and go away again. If all this makes it sound as if my wife had gone off her rocker, then I suppose, yes, she had, in a way. But she was all right in everything else. It was just anything to do with Rebecca. For Brenda, time stopped when Becky vanished the way she did.'

'I do understand,' said Markby sympathetically.

'Yesterday evening, when Inspector Barker came to the house and produced that bracelet, to tell you the truth, Markby, I was glad Brenda wasn't there. As soon as I set eyes on it, I knew that Rebecca really is dead.'

'Tell me,' Markby spoke carefully, 'when your daughter first went missing, did you go down to Gloucestershire and discuss things with the investigating team there, even make any enquiries yourself?'

'Oh, yes!' Hellington's voice and manner gained some energy for the first time in their encounter. His voice grew firmer. 'I asked all her friends, and fellow students. I met a young man who was her boyfriend. I spoke at length with the police officers in charge of the search for her. There was an Inspector Parry in overall charge of her case. I must say I got the impression that he wasn't holding out much hope. He didn't actually *say* she was dead, you under-stand. But I think he suspected from the first that they were looking for . . . for a body. The other man I spoke to at length was a Sergeant Carter. I thought he was much more optimistic to start with. Later on, I felt he'd lost hope, too. And they have other cases to deal with, don't they, the police? They can't spend all their time on one enquiry, especially if they draw a blank everywhere.'

'That's true,' Markby admitted wryly. 'But that doesn't mean the case is closed. It stays on file, and if anything new turns up, they'll reopen it.'

He had not added that Inspector Parry and his team had soon realised this would turn out to be a murder case, and that the files on unsolved murders are never closed but remain unfinished business until the killer is named. Even so, he realised as soon as his last words had left his mouth that he should have phrased it differently.

Hellington leaned forward and asked eagerly, 'And now – now Rebecca's bracelet has been found the enquiry will be opened again?'

'Inspector Barker is the person who will keep you up to date on any new developments,' Markby said, feeling that he was chickening out. 'But, you know, we did make every effort to find a trace of her here, at this end, when I was at Bamford. We had absolutely no luck. None of her friends here had seen her or heard from her. We had posters showing her photo around the town, if you remember, and in the local press. Besides, it was on the tele-vision news at the time. If anyone had seen her, or even thought they might have seen her, they'd have come forward. Bamford is – or it was then – a fairly small place. A piece of news like that would be very much discussed in the local pubs and so on.' He knew he was sounding more and more apologetic, even defensive.

'But she *was* here, wasn't she?' said Hellington simply. 'She must have been alive when she came here. Someone *here* killed her and buried her in those woods.'

'Well, not necess—' Markby began.

Hellington leaned forward again. 'All right. Let's say someone killed her miles away, near where she was studying. They'd then have brought her here to bury her. That sounds very far-fetched to me. Doesn't it sound unlikely to you? How would anyone down there know the layout of Bamford? Know about that spot of woodland?' He rubbed his balding skull. 'But the whole thing is unbelievable. I do understand why Brenda couldn't believe it. One reads of things in the newspapers or sees the news on the telly – but it's just as they say, isn't it? That you never believe it will happen to you?'

Hellington settled back in his chair again. 'Inspector Barker told me all about the two children finding the bracelet twenty years ago. If only they'd told someone in authority then. Something might have been done, don't you think? It would have been a lead to follow?' His tone had become a mix of wistful and resentful. 'She was here,' he repeated. 'She was *here*. Brenda was right. Becky had come home.' His eyes filled with tears and he turned his head aside.

Markby also looked away and waited until Hellington had regained his composure. 'The two children were something of a special case themselves,' he explained. 'They were wary of authority and came from a background where the police weren't seen as friends. They were scared, too, of getting into trouble. The boy was just nine years old and the little girl only eight.' *And now that little girl is twenty-eight and in prison*, he thought.

Hellington had set aside his mug, half drunk, and was rising to his feet. 'I should go. Thank you for seeing me, Mr Markby. I realise you're retired now, as I am, and there isn't anything further you can do. I do hope you don't think I'm blaming you for not finding Rebecca twenty years ago. I know how hard everyone tried, both here and in the West Country.'

This, thought Markby, is worse than if the poor chap shouted curses at me and accused me of slack police work. 'I suppose,' he heard himself say, lamely, 'there's no doubt it's Rebecca's bracelet? I know it spells out her name, but . . .'

'Oh, it's hers,' Hellington said. 'We had it made for her as a present when she gained her place at college. We were careful to have it spell out her full name, because she wanted to be called Rebecca now, not Becky. More grown-up. We were very proud of her. I am still very proud of her. I try not to hate the person who took her from us. But I would like to stand in front of him and ask him, why? If he had a reason, you see – whatever it was – it would be preferable to his having no motivation. It wouldn't all be so pointless.'

When his visitor had left, Markby went back to the sitting room and sat contemplating Hellington's abandoned coffee mug. 'Trevor Barker is right,' he murmured aloud. 'I do want another crack at it.'

It was not a purely selfish desire. The sight of Hellington's distress had fuelled the resolve in Markby. The man deserved proper closure after what had happened. It had destroyed his family and his wife's sanity, and had condemned the man himself to live a half-life, filled with shadows.

Chapter 5

If anyone had asked Ian Carter point-blank whether he wanted to make another attempt at solving the mystery of Rebecca Hellington's disappearance, his instinct would have been to reply, 'No, not without some reliable forensic evidence.'

That would have been the first answer, the result of years as a police officer.

He might have continued, if pressed, 'In any case, I've got enough work on my desk at the moment, things happening now, wanting urgent answers. If anything does come of it, it won't involve me. The girl had done what she'd said she was planning to do. She went home and, somehow, died in that part of the world. It was her dad's birthday. Of course, she'd gone home. She never got there, fair enough. But she'd started out. It's not down to me that no one found any trace of her here. It was down to Markby and his team, at Bamford, if they couldn't find her there!'

The realisation that he was sounding more and more defensive would probably have made him stop there. When in a hole, stop digging!

Having neatly lined up the logical sequence, and abandoned the argument, he couldn't stop thinking about it. It was that phone call from Markby. He couldn't put it out of his head. Ian was left with the annoying feeling that perhaps he hadn't done enough, way back then. Besides, since becoming the father of a daughter himself, he better appreciated the agony of Rebecca's family, left in limbo for so long. But, to try and pick up the pieces of a stalled investigation, for crying out loud!

'You're scowling,' Jess told him. 'Don't you like this place?'

The pub was called the Wayfarer's Return and had acquired a good name for food in the short time it had been open. Calling it a pub was a misnomer. It had become a restaurant. Prior to that, the one-time pub had been empty and semi-derelict for years. The considerable amount of money spent to bring it back to commercial life appeared to be paying off. It was early in the evening, but the main area was filling up nicely.

'Sorry,' he said to Jess. 'I didn't mean to look grumpy. It's nothing to do with this place. I've been meaning to come here for weeks. I've heard good things.'

'The menu is extensive,' said Jess, perusing the open card folder. 'I bet they didn't serve Balinese green bean salad in this pub before the makeover!' She then disconcerted him by asking, bluntly, 'Are you out of sorts because Alan Markby phoned this morning?'

'Yes,' said Ian honestly. He briefly summarised that morning's conversation with Markby.

'The children found her – or found a body – and didn't tell a soul?' Jess said doubtfully. 'Didn't tell anyone *for twenty years*? That's hard to believe.'

'Markby believes it. But why did he have to bother me with it? He must know how many cases I've worked on since then. He can't expect me to remember details of them all!'

But I do remember that one, he thought. Markby and I both, we remember. Why? Because we felt cheated, that's it! We felt we should have been able to find the girl, alive or dead, and someone stopped us. That's why he phoned me this morning. He knows exactly how I felt back then – and still feel now.

He sighed and pulled a wry smile. 'I apologise. I really am rotten company. We won't mention the business again. Let's eat.'

So they ate and made conversation about a dozen other things but, inevitably, with the desserts came a long silence. Both seemed absorbed in their own thoughts. In Ian's case he knew it was the Rebecca Hellington case. He didn't know what it was in Jess's case. But she had struck him as being a little absent-minded during the meal. He wondered about that scribbled letter he'd spotted on her table in the canteen, before she whisked it away. She hadn't wanted him to see it and wouldn't welcome any questions about it. Now, as he covertly watched her face, he saw her make an effort to pull herself back from whatever thoughts he wasn't meant to share.

'This is silly,' she said briskly. 'We can't both sit here in silence. Of course you want to talk about Alan Markby. Did you actually meet him, twenty years ago, or was your contact with him only over the phone?'

'I met him twice. He seemed to think I was trying to push an investigation in his direction that had nothing to do with his force. He kept reminding me she'd disappeared in my part of the world. I kept telling him she'd told friends she was going home, so might well have done so. We parted on rather cool terms. Well,' concluded Carter, with a demonic smile of triumph, 'it wasn't on my patch she was found, in the end, was it?'

'She hasn't actually been found now, has she?' Jess pointed out mildly. 'Two kids saw a dead body twenty years ago and one of them nicked a bracelet. The body's vanished and all they've got at Bamford is the bracelet.'

There was silence again. Carter was concentrating on his dessert and Jess let her gaze drift across the room. Though the place was now crowded, one free table remained in a corner, hopeful customers kept at bay by a white card declaring this spot 'reserved'. But a man and woman had arrived and were being led to the table by a waiter who swept the card away in a grand manner. Indeed, his whole general demeanour suggested these were regular and highly valued clients. All this made Jess keen to study the newcomers. In their forties, she judged. The man must have been very attractive when younger and had preserved his looks with care, so that he could still be classed as good-looking. Nevertheless, in Jess's view, there was a certain pretension in his style, hair too carefully styled, casual clothing too expensive. His female companion was about the same age, tall and slender, well dressed and equally high maintenance. She put a hand up to her well-coiffed hair as she sat down, and Jess noted the knuckle-duster of an engagement ring and broad gold wedding band. She made Jess feel like a scruff.

She had betrayed herself, somehow. 'What's up?' asked Carter. 'Something wrong with the food?'

'No, the food is fine. But I'm beginning to feel underdressed. I was watching the new couple, over there, in the corner. They could afford to eat anywhere, by the looks of it. It does say something for the Wayfarer's Return that they've chosen to come here.'

He was following the line of her gaze, and she was surprised by the sudden look of incredulity on his face. 'What is it?' she asked sharply.

He ran the tip of his tongue over dry lips. 'That,' he muttered hoarsely, 'that guy over there with the playboy looks – the one you mean – is Peter Malone, Rebecca Hellington's boyfriend.'

'What?' Jess was so taken aback that she slopped coffee into the saucer. 'Are you sure?'

'Or I'll eat my boots. I interviewed him several times. OK, he was a lot younger then, twenty or so, and now he's forty-something, he's put on weight and has lost the trumpet.'

'Trumpet?' Jess asked, startled.

Ian reddened and said, sheepishly, 'Back then, he looked like one of those angels you see in Italian frescoes. Now he doesn't. But that's definitely Malone.'

'Spooky,' said Jess, after a pause. 'That must be his wife, then. Do you remember her?'

Ian shook his head and dragged his gaze away from the couple at the far table. 'Fate is conspiring against me, Jess. It must be! In twenty years I've not mentioned anyone or anything to do with that damn case. Now, in less than twenty-four hours, Alan Markby is bending my ear about it and Peter Malone walks into this pub. This is going to end up back on my desk, after all these years, and despite the change in location.'

Jess, seeking to reassure him, said, 'Don't panic. It's a freaky coincidence, that's all. If we hadn't been talking about the case, and I hadn't been people-watching, neither of us would have paid that couple any attention. If that *is* Malone—'

'I'm not hallucinating!' he muttered.

'OK, you're not. That's your old interviewee, Malone. His being here is a coincidence. He's done all right for himself, by the looks of it.'

'Yes, he bally has.'

After a moment, Jess asked, 'You must have interviewed other people than Malone? What about the girl's friends?'

'I talked to girls who lived in the hall of residence where she lived, and also to students on her course. She wasn't a girl who had a lot of friends, or that was the impression I got. She was shy, that was the general agreement. She wasn't disliked, but the others found her reserved – hard work, socially. They tried and then gave up on her. The story Malone later told me about how they'd met – that she'd gone to a party and hadn't liked it – seemed more and more to make sense. She wasn't a party person.'

'So, she hadn't talked to any of them about her plans for the weekend she disappeared?'

'A couple of them said she had mentioned going home for the weekend – to Bamford, that would be. But she'd been vague, and they couldn't tell me her precise travel plans, if she had any. She did, apparently, sometimes talk about having plans, without giving any details, and then they'd hear no more. They thought that she either didn't want to tell them her business, or she was going somewhere with Peter Malone. She talked about Malone, sometimes, as a boyfriend. The girls got the impression she was very keen on him. He was known by sight around the hall of residence when he came to pick up Rebecca or bring her home. One or two of the girls thought him fanciable; but Rebecca was on her guard, and she'd whisk him in and out of the place before any of them could get chatting to him!' He sighed. 'I don't think Sophie ever thought that way about me. I sometimes wonder why Sophie married me at all.'

'Now you're getting maudlin – and don't, please, get all gloomy and introverted when you're having dinner with me in a nice place like this!'

He grinned. 'Sorry. It's just . . . having the whole wretched affair suddenly come to life again. Suppose they find a body?'

'Ian,' said Jess, reaching out to pat his hand, resting her arm on the tabletop. 'Take it easy. It's chance, right? Neither you nor Alan Markby could find Rebecca twenty years ago, and no one has found her *now*. They probably won't even search the woodland, beyond a cursory look around. The budget won't stretch to it. It would cost enough to send the bean counters berserk. Don't forget, all there is to go on – any evidence that there was anything there in the first place – is the claim of a couple of children, from twenty years ago.'

'The bracelet,' said Carter. He sounded weary.

'Yes, the little girl, we're told, took it off a body. I would have been too scared when I was eight to do anything like that. Perhaps she found it somewhere else.' Jess leaned in, willing him to listen and knowing his mind was elsewhere, back in time, fixating on the memory of frustration and failure. 'Ian, you're talking about two children who, apparently, were used to the police coming to the door and asking questions – even having the police burst in to search their home.'

'That was when they lived with their mother,' Carter reminded her. 'They were in foster care when they found the body, or so Markby's gardener says.'

'Oh, yes, the gardener, Josh, the little girl's brother. He was still a child who'd been trained from babyhood never to tell the authorities anything – even, if he had to say something, to lie. Now, twenty years later, while his co-conspirator, Dilys, is in prison, he suddenly speaks to Alan Markby. Whatever prompted that, it's still not rock-solid evidence that Rebecca is buried in those woods. We don't know he's telling the truth. The local force will go through the motions and put the file away again.' She glanced briefly across the room. 'So, Malone is dining here tonight with his wife. This place is gaining a good reputation, so why is that strange? There is absolutely nothing to worry about.'

'The Rennies are in the bathroom cabinet,' said Caroline Malone. She was sitting before the dressing-table mirror and applying moisturising lotion to her face. She was a tall, slender woman of the type the Pre-Raphaelite painters had liked. She had a long straight nose, clearly defined lips and a firm jaw. Her blonde hair was usually worn coiled into a knot at the nape of her neck. Before going to bed, she braided it into a single long plait.

Without turning, she could see her husband in the edge of the mirror. He was in pyjamas and dressing gown, and he was scowling as he sifted through the small stack of paperbacks on his bedside cabinet. But it wasn't the reading material on offer that had put him out of sorts, she was sure of that. He'd been like it during the entire drive home.

'You've got indigestion?' he asked, glancing towards her.

'No, I'm fine, but you're not. I'm assuming you ate something that disagreed with you tonight. I thought the food was OK, but I was careful what I ordered. You know that if you eat too much fried stuff, you get a bad stomach.'

Her husband tossed the paperbacks aside. 'I didn't eat too much fried food. I've not got a bad stomach, and I'm not out of sorts.'

'Like hell you're not!' she said crisply. 'You turned all introverted and gloomy halfway through the meal, and you're still brooding. If it's not the food – what, then?' She swivelled on the stool to face him squarely in the mirror.

He hesitated and then sat down on the edge of the bed. 'OK, if you must know, I had a bit of a shock at the pub. I saw someone there I met years ago.'

'Why didn't you go over and speak to him? Or was it a her? Did you have a falling out, whenever it was – years ago?'

He was silent for a moment, then asked, 'Do you remember Rebecca Hellington?'

Whatever she'd expected him to say, she hadn't expected that. Malone felt a spark of unworthy pleasure at seeing her face fall. She even frowned, before she remembered that it would cause lines on her forehead and consciously smoothed her brow. But Caroline was never at a loss for long. She quickly regained her composure.

'Wasn't she that girl who made a fuss at Nick's party and went all weepy? I had to take her over to my parents' place, and hide her in my bedroom. She became a sort of girlfriend of yours later, didn't she? Then she went missing or something. I'm not surprised. I thought her seriously flaky.'

'Yes, she went missing – and they never did find her.' Defensively, he added, 'She was only a sort of girlfriend, nothing serious, and not for very long. But when she disappeared, the police got excited about it. A Sergeant Carter interviewed me several times.'

'I should think he spoke to loads of other people, not just to you!' said Caro carelessly, stretching out her chin and studying her reflection critically for early signs of wrinkles.

She'd not seen any signs of age yet. But if ever she did, her husband thought resentfully, she'd be off to see about getting a chin tuck or face lift, or whatever it was, immediately. He'd often wondered if the underlying reason why she'd never tolerated the possibility of them having children, was the fear of losing her figure. 'We don't need kids,' she'd declared in the early years of their marriage. Later, the objection had been, 'My cousin Nick has enough to go round. I don't want to live in a cross between a playschool and a madhouse, even if you do!' So, that had been that. Caroline always got what she wanted. Or, to turn the expression around, she didn't bother with what she didn't want. No more talk of children of their own. There was something about her vanity and self-absorption that was like a suit of mail. Sometimes, he envied it. Right now, it was really irritating.

'That's who was there tonight, Carter!' he announced, almost in triumph, hurling a metaphorical javelin. He was pleased to see it found a chink in his wife's armour.

'Sure?' she asked sharply, whirling round on the stool to face him directly.

'Absolutely, not likely to forget him.'

'I suppose it was to be expected, that they'd have interviewed you, when it all happened,' she said thoughtfully. 'Could you tell them anything?'

'Of course I couldn't! Rebecca told me she was going home for the weekend, to a place called Bamford, in the Cotswolds somewhere. I thought that was where she'd gone. I told Carter that, more than once. He was an obtuse sort of guy, couldn't seem to get it into his head. In the end, he accepted I wasn't a suspect. Or I think he did, at least. It was hard to tell what he thought.'

Caroline was watching him carefully with that slow, unsettling

83

appraisal she adopted when deciding on whether or not to buy something: a dress, a shade of lipstick, an explanation. She was an interior designer by profession and if something didn't match up, out it went. She was like that with people, too, as he'd discovered over the years. Perhaps she'd picked him because he suited some design she'd hatched for her life. Perhaps, he thought, one day he'd be discarded together with some old curtains and a carpet that was showing signs of wear.

He was being unfair, he decided. He didn't doubt she loved him; and he loved her. He found her exciting, truth to tell. She was watching his face, probably reading his mind.

'So?' she said at last.

'So, tonight, at the pub, he was there. I've just told you! He was having dinner with a woman, a red-haired female.'

'You're *sure?*' she persisted. 'We've all of us changed over the years. You haven't seen him since that time, have you? Perhaps the man in the pub just looked a bit like him.'

'I told you. It was Carter!' The anger crackled in his voice. It convinced her at last.

'Did he see you?' She was always practical.

'Not sure, don't think so.'

'Doesn't matter, then, does it?' Caroline decided.

'Just gave me a shock, that's all. Have you ever been interviewed by the police?' Now he sounded sullen.

'Of course I haven't!' She bridled, then added reluctantly, 'Only by the traffic cops, that time I drove off the road coming home from the races.' She rapped the glass surface of the dressing table irritably. 'They put points on my licence, when it wasn't anything serious. It didn't involve any other car. No one was hurt.'

Malone would have liked to retort that, although no one was hurt, Caroline shouldn't have been behind the wheel. But he didn't say it, because the reason she had been driving was that he had been drinking merrily in the hospitality tent, and so he wasn't fit to drive. Unfortunately, in his own impaired state, he hadn't realised at the time how much over the limit Caroline had also been.

So, he replied now, 'Well, then, try to imagine being grilled by the police because they're convinced you're withholding vital information regarding a possible major crime. They have a way of looking at you as if they suspect you're Jack the Ripper.'

'Don't brood on it!' she advised him, and turned back to the mirror.

It was no use her saying that. He'd think of nothing else for days. Even seeing Carter 'off duty' and dining with a lady friend failed to erase the youthful images of the policeman, etched into his memory. Malone could see him now as clearly as if the fellow sat in this bedroom, in that chair over there, an educated thug, a sort of inquisitorial machine with cold green eyes. He'd been undeniably frightening, and had shown an implacable determination to solve the case. Peter had spent twenty years resolutely forgetting the guy. But you don't forget unpleasantness. You only bury it. Then, when you least expect it, it climbs up out of the grave, and back into your life. He shivered. Was Rebecca going to do that? Climb out of some unmarked grave, if she was dead? They didn't know, did they? Nobody knew.

Solve the case. Malone grimaced. That was whodunnit fiction-speak for you. Bring on literature's finest sleuths. Bring on their hard-drinking, dishevelled television equivalents. Bring on Sherlock

Holmes – or Tintin and Snowy, come to that – or any inspiration thrown up by the talents of the pen. They were all pallid, unimpressive wraiths compared with that guy, Carter, and the horrible reality. But Carter, for all he'd scared Peter witless at the time, hadn't solved the mystery.

Malone was sure Carter hadn't forgotten it, either. But I'm not a scared student now, he told himself. I'm a successful, no, dammit, I'm a *very* successful man. I have nothing to worry about, just like Caroline says.

His wife had finished at her vanity mirror and stood up, slipping off her wrap. Malone decided she looked thoughtful. She was probably wondering whether the old story would find its way back into the local news, and whether he – and, by association, his wife – might be mentioned. She had spent considerable care and many years building up a professional reputation. Hey! So had he! Neither of them wanted their names to appear in the popular press, even if only a passing mention.

He stretched out a hand for the paperback he'd started reading the previous night. It was a whodunnit. On the cover, an artist had depicted a dark shadow looming over a sunlit landscape. Somehow, he didn't fancy it now. He threw it back on the pile and switched out the bedside light.

Chapter 6

Jess was to be proved wrong. A decision was taken to make an exploratory dig in the spinney. The owner of the land, including the area of rough pasture alongside the wooded area, had turned out to be a Canadian descendant of the Brocket family, aged eighty-four, who'd never set eyes on the spot and had no desire to. He lived in Toronto and had to be reminded that he'd inherited this remnant of the family estate. Used to wide expanses of prairie, mountain and forest, he was especially disgusted when told the land in question amounted to no more than a few trees and a scrap of coarse grass and weeds. 'No use to anyone!' he opined. 'If you want to dig it up, go ahead.'

Josh went along with the police team on the first day to point out the spot where he and Dilys had stumbled on the body, as exactly as he could, given the length of time and the changes in the spinney. But Josh, though city born, had become a countryman and he knew about the lie of the land. On the second day one group of searchers gave a shout. Others hastened to the spot and gazed down at the disturbed earth and the long slender leg bones and partially uncovered ribcage, startling white against the black soil and leaf mould. Someone stooped and brushed away more earth where the head ought to be, and the empty eye sockets and open jaw stared back at them.

Trevor Barker, called by the officer in charge of the diggers, in turn called upon Markby. The two men stood, side by side, and stared down at the now fully exposed skeleton. The body was laid out completely straight, as if by professional morticians, except that the head was slightly turned to one side and no one had closed the mouth at the time of death, so that the jaw hung open. A few clumps of what now looked like cotton threads clung to the skull: long, fair hair.

This, then, thought Markby, was what he had been looking for twenty years earlier, without knowing it. He'd been seeking a missing girl. The likelihood that the hunt would end in the discovery of a body had always been at the back of his mind. That was all too often how it did end.

Markby imagined that the dropped jaw was calling up a grotesque greeting to him. 'Hello, where have you been? What took you so long?'

Mentally, he replied, 'I'm sorry. I would have liked to find you before this. I will now do all in my power to help those who must track down the person who put you there.'

Barker expressed himself aloud quite mildly. 'Well, I'll be damned. It's here!'

He was, he explained to his wife later, flabbergasted.

Markby went home, told Meredith about finding the body, and they discussed it briefly. Then he went to bed, as anyone in any other line of work might do. But, of course, he wasn't a police officer any longer, and he'd lost the knack of putting aside the day's discoveries. Sleep was slow to come.

In the early hours of the morning, he slipped out of bed and made a cautious descent of the staircase, because it was inclined to creak. He poured himself a modest whisky and took it into the kitchen, as that was the warmest room. In the cooling night air, the fabric of the house and the wood of the furniture around him settled, as if their joints were stiff, uttering a groan from time to time. There were other odd sounds: a slight rustling, a single sudden crack. Sometimes, it did seem as if voices whispered to him. What caused this illusion he had no idea – other than the fact that he sat at the scrubbed pine table in a house that was over a hundred and fifty years old, and it talked to him. In the company of those long gone, he thought about murder.

When he'd been a younger man, setting out on his career, he had always known that dealing with unnatural deaths would be part and parcel of his work. Each and every death had come as a shock and had been distressing. He had learned to cope with that, as police officers do, but he had never allowed himself to become hardened to the many grisly and pitiful sights, because once that happened, you lost an essential part of your own humanity. You had always to feel pity. You had always to feel anger. What you did not allow yourself was to be swayed in your judgement by these emotions. So, he had never indulged in the 'black humour' that helped some officers deal with horror. Nor had he allowed any officer on his team to indulge in it within his hearing. If you can do nothing else for the dead, you can at least respect them.

And hadn't he met Meredith because of a murder? That young man, the one who kept the Siamese cats. He recalled other cases, too, after he'd met Meredith. The old family grave, opened to receive a new occupant in the very churchyard next door to this house – then still a vicarage – only to reveal a burial far too fresh.

A body sprawled in a wine cellar. And the murders that appeared above all to be so 'wrong': the murders of the young.

He drank the last of his whisky, rinsed the glass and set it, upside down, on the draining board. Then he quitted the kitchen and its ghostly company. At least, he hoped it was only that – and not mice.

He managed to avoid the creaking stair tread, but when he slipped into bed, Meredith stirred alongside him and her voice asked, 'What's wrong?'

'Nothing. I couldn't sleep.'

There was an upheaval in the duvet as she turned towards him and he felt her hand on his shoulder. 'Is it finding the bones of that girl?'

'I suppose so. I'm out of the habit of dealing with murder cases.' He put his hand over hers. 'Don't worry. I'm not going to become obsessed about it. I wish . . . I wish I could have found her twenty years ago.'

'Twenty years ago, you didn't know she was dead, not for sure. It wasn't your case. It was Ian Carter's. He hadn't asked you to look for a body, only to check if anyone had seen her in Bamford recently. No one had.'

'Oh, someone had seen her, more than one person. Josh and young Dilys saw her – and whoever buried her.'

After a moment she said, 'You didn't fail. Carter and – what was his boss's name?

'Parry, elderly fellow. He was grey-haired, getting near retirement, nice enough old boy. He died several years ago.'

'It was Carter's failure, then, and Parry's.' Then she added, 'And her killer's, it was his failure, too.'

Surprised, he asked, 'Oh? Why?'

'Didn't mean her to be found, did he?'

The post-mortem examination quickly established the body to be female and that of a woman of about twenty. Subsequent DNA tests confirmed it as that of Rebecca Hellington.

But Markby had known, from the first sight of the remains, that they would be Rebecca's. They all knew it.

Unfortunately, the examination of the bones would not make it immediately possible to pinpoint the cause of death.

Chapter 7

'It's very good of you to agree to join us, Alan,' the Assistant Chief Constable said. 'And to come early. I'd like a quick private chat before the others get here.' This speech was accompanied by a hearty shake of the hand.

'I'm listening,' Markby said courteously, disengaging his mangled fingers.

The ACC drummed his fingers on his desk. He was a pink-faced, plump man with small eyes and a snub nose. He was usually smiling, so that he often resembled a kindly pig. He wasn't smiling now.

'You and Superintendent Carter are old acquaintances, aren't you? I am assuming you met him at the time, when you were handling the case at this end of things, and he was hunting around the girl's college, interviewing her friends, her boyfriend, trying to learn anything that might explain where she'd got to. Twenty years ago, of course, now.' He sighed. 'This is going to be a tricky one, Alan. But you don't need me to tell you that.'

'I met both Ian Carter – he was a sergeant at the time – and his boss, Inspector Parry, who was in overall charge. They came to Bamford to talk to her parents. Later, Carter came back again to inform me they were putting the case to rest, until such time, if ever, as they had something new to go on . . .' Markby paused.

'My impression was that Parry believed she was dead, right from the start. He was an experienced officer and he read the runes. Sadly, he's no longer with us; Inspector Parry died several years ago.'

'Quite, quite,' said the ACC, nodding and looking suitably sober, as one did when speaking of a deceased colleague. Then he got back to present business. 'So, Carter believed he might find her alive? Was that also your impression?'

Markby replied, carefully, 'I believe he had high hopes at first; he was reluctant to believe she was dead. He kept insisting she'd come home to Bamford – or at least, that she'd set off home but never arrived. He thought I should be able to track her movements at this end. But all I could establish was that she hadn't arrived at her parents' house. No one came forward, in response to our well-publicised appeal, so we had to conclude no one had seen her. I had officers at the train station, interviewing passengers, and down at the bus depot interviewing staff. She normally travelled by the long distance buses. I sought out her local friends from a list made by her parents. I didn't find a thing . . .' He paused. 'Believe me, when Josh Browning showed me that bracelet it was a real bolt from the blue. But I still believe we did all we could at this end, at the time.'

'But your memory of the case could still be of great help, Alan.'

Markby sighed. 'I honestly don't see how.'

The ACC leaned forward confidentially. 'I'll be honest, I don't see how, either – not now, not at this precise moment. But we don't know what this new investigation might turn up. And that's where your memory might prove very valuable indeed.'

'I'm happy to do anything I can, of course . . .' Markby hesitated, before continuing. 'The girl's father came to see me after

Barker had shown him the bracelet. His wife's mind was affected by her daughter's disappearance, and she has since died. Hellington himself is a walking shadow of what he once must have been – a successful local businessman.'

'Ah, yes, the travel agency,' the ACC murmured. 'Well, then, I take it I can tell the others, when they get here, that you're happy to come on board. Thank you.'

Markby opened his mouth to say he wasn't exactly 'happy', and he hadn't actually been given the chance to decline to come aboard anything. But before he could speak, there was a sharp rap on the door and a young constable, with 'keen boy' written all over him, appeared in the doorway. 'All the others have arrived now, sir.'

'Thank you, Jenkins, show them in.'

The die was cast, thought Markby. Can't back out now. All aboard the *Skylark*! I'm now a deckhand.

So, that's how the case conference had begun. In theory, when the gathering had originally been suggested, it hadn't technically been a formal review. But, inevitably, that was what it was always going to become. When he'd been approached and asked whether he'd like to come and see the ACC, and then stay on to meet the others, he'd known what he was in for.

'You don't actually have to go,' Meredith had said earlier, before he set out, and while he was still expressing reservations.

'Yes, I do,' he'd replied. 'It's an obligation. In old-fashioned terms, you'd say it was a matter of honour.'

'OK, Sydney Carton,' she said. 'Mind the steps up to the scaffold.'

So, now he shook Ian Carter's hand and agreed that 'it had been a long time'. Carter had gone grey – looked so much older,

Markby thought – but of course he did! Twenty years! Carter probably thought Markby looked like the Ancient Mariner.

Neither of them chose to mention Markby's phone call to Carter in which he'd sprung the news on him of Josh's revelations. There was no need to mention it. It was why they were all here. It was why *he* was here. He had no one but himself to blame.

Five of them were gathered in the room and each of them had been provided with a rapidly cooling cup of coffee. It had been brought in by the alert Jenkins, all agog at even this brief admittance to the inner circle. He'll talk about it for days, Alan thought. None of the visitors seemed inclined to drink the coffee, although a cautious sip had revealed to him that it was quite good. It hadn't come from some machine, such as the one he remembered from his working days at Bamford. That had dispensed a dreadful concoction that had managed to be both boiling hot and tasteless. Today's coffee had been brewed in some percolator reserved for the ACC and his visitors.

That's what I am, Markby reminded himself. I'm a visitor! I'm here to give them my memories of a failure, a case neither solved nor closed, but lurking in some limbo. 'Rebecca Hellington. Student. Aged eighteen.' That's what the file will tell us. A girl destined always to be eighteen years old, never to become nineteen. When you die, the clock stops and the calendar freezes. You cannot go forward; you cannot go back and undo the sequence of events leading to your death. You stay as you are, or were, at that moment. That is how Arthur Hellington remembers his daughter.

When Rebecca dressed on the morning of her death, she pulled on jeans she would never take off again. Forensics had established she'd worn jeans because, although the fabric had rotted away, a metal button and studs had survived. In the same way, her bra had rotted, but not the hooks and eyes that had fastened it, nor the two half-hoops of underwiring in the cups. Forensics believed that whatever top she'd worn had been made of cotton, because no trace remained. But she'd worn a jacket with an imperishable zip and buttons at the cuffs. Her trainers had survived as well. Thanks to the acquisitive instincts of eight-year-old Dilys Browning, sister of Josh, they now knew Rebecca had worn the bracelet spelling out her name. If they'd known earlier that Dilys had slipped it from the dead girl's wrist, it would have helped. It might even have been of use to Forensics. But Dilys had kept her secret and polished her treasure until the hallmark had nearly been rubbed out. Nothing now could be gleaned from the bracelet and, in every way, they were picking up the trail twenty years late.

Perhaps that explained the blank, official expression on Ian Carter's face, letting them know he had come here with an 'open mind' and had set himself to be scrupulously polite to all concerned. Markby didn't doubt Carter would be polite. He couldn't judge how open-minded he would prove. That inexpressive mask was one Markby recognised well; all officers learned to assume it when necessary. He had donned the same mask himself, in the past, numerous times. It could mean that Carter's brain was totally empty of any new ideas.

The other two occupants of the room showed more animation. One was a young woman of athletic build. Her long dark hair was brushed back and secured with a grip. But, disconcertingly, the fringe of hair over her forehead had been bleached. She looked as alert as a gun dog. The remaining member of the gathering was Bamford's Inspector Trevor Barker, in a well-brushed uniform.

Markby recalled Meredith's quip about Sydney Carton and thought that, if anyone here looked like he was headed for the scaffold, it was Trevor Barker. He noticed that Barker looked critically at Ian Carter. Poor old Trevor must be feeling as if his territory had been invaded.

The woman with the piebald hairstyle was there to put the case for the Major Crime Review Unit. She wasted no time before doing just that. She was confident, fluent and determined; she didn't wait to be invited to speak.

The MCRU was regretfully unable to assign any personnel to the case at the moment. They were currently snowed under with other unsolved cases. They had received an unprecedented flurry of new information on old crimes, much of which held out hope of real progress. They were, of course, understaffed, as everyone knew. They'd repeatedly requested, and been denied, a bigger budget and both more officers and more clerical staff. They were aware that, locally, there was a lot of interest in this case. The national press had also run stories on the discovery of the bones. There was public pressure for some result and MCRU were, of course, willing to help where they could, but—

At this point, the ACC managed to regain control and interrupted her, to say crisply, 'You can't put any more boots on the ground, you mean.'

She flushed and said, 'Yes, sir, if you'd like to put it like that.'

Markby had tuned out the last bit of her speech. It had been clear from the opening words where it was going. Carter had his eyes closed and Barker was chewing furiously at his lower lip. They all understood. They were on their own, she was saying, unless they wanted to wait an unspecified length of time before the unit got round to them. She was not to be denied the final word, however.

'After all,' she said, unable to disguise a note of triumph, 'let's be honest. This is no longer what used to be called "a cold case", is it? Not with the discovery of an *actual* body.'

Markby suppressed the urge to ask what kind of body wouldn't change the situation. A *virtual* body?

'Rebecca's death,' she concluded, 'must be considered the subject of a current investigation by the regular CID.'

She might have added, 'So there, you guys!' Instead, she sat back and turned a defiant stare on the apoplectic Trevor Barker.

'Nor have I got officers and civilian staff sitting round doing nothing!' he yelped.

The ACC knew when the better tactic was to cede the terrain and hope to return to the fray later with more success. He murmured, 'Now then, Trevor . . .' He cleared his throat, placed his clasped hands on his desk and went on, 'With the discovery of remains, this is – as our visitor quite correctly stated –' giving a nod towards the MCRU's representative, 'no longer an old, unsolved case. It's a new one – and geographically it does fall within your remit, Trevor.'

'Yes, sir,' muttered Barker.

The young woman did her best not to look triumphant, but she couldn't quite manage it.

Markby and Carter exchanged looks of resigned understanding. Then they both looked at Barker whose expression now suggested he'd just had news of a disaster in his family. Which he had, in a way, because his team of investigating officers and support staff formed a kinship and all would be affected by any decision taken here today.

'So,' the ACC went on, having now adopted a Buddha-like calm, 'it will be your case, Inspector Barker. We are fortunate in that former Superintendent Markby and Superintendent Carter, who has so kindly driven over from Gloucestershire this morning . . .' he managed to make Gloucestershire sound like the remote heart of the Amazon rain forest, 'will both offer all possible assistance. Together they worked on the original investigation, and have indicated they are willing to put their experience of the case at your disposal, and to help out in any way they can. In your case, Alan, we are keenly aware that we are proposing to drag you out of retirement.'

At this, all the others looked at Markby with something like envy mixed with resentment. He was the man with the bolt-hole into which he could scuttle if things got difficult. He nodded and mumbled something appropriate.

'What about the press?' asked Carter. 'There will be considerable interest, both locally and nationally.'

'A statement will be released to the press tonight, following this meeting, confirming the identity of the remains found in recent excavations in Brocket's Spinney. There has already been considerable speculation, of course.'

'It will be worse when the press get hold of the identity of the remains,' said Barker gloomily. 'Would-be informants will be coming out of the woodwork, and it's a racing certainty that ninety-nine per cent of them will be time-wasters.'

There followed a moment of introspective silence on the part of all present.

Then the ACC said, encouragingly, 'You may be lucky, Inspector Barker. You may get a good lead fairly soon.' He waited a moment for Barker's reply and, when none was forthcoming, asked, 'Now, then, is there anything else at this moment in time?'

It appeared no one had anything further to add.

'Good!' exclaimed the ACC. He didn't actually rub his hands, but he did clap them together. 'Now, then, I believe they've reserved a table for us in the canteen. To lunch!'

At this, all his visitors looked depressed, and they trailed out in a huddle.

'Be sure to insist,' muttered Barker in Markby's ear, as they descended the stairs, 'they pay you a whacking great consultancy fee! I bet they can find the money for that!'

Carter had overheard and muttered back, 'Don't count on it. They couldn't run to a modest restaurant lunch. We'll be lucky to get something better than beans on toast!'

Despite their worst fears, the canteen, no doubt under pressure not to let the ACC down, produced a decent lasagne and a dessert of jelly with fruit in it that brought back childhood memories for Markby.

After lunch, once they were outside the building, they waved goodbye to the champion of the MCRU. Before she drove away she smiled for the first time, turning on them a beaming grin of victory. The three men retired by common consent to the nearest pub and conferred, as Britons like to do, over a pint at a rickety corner table decked with stained beermats and a small clay flower-pot stuffed with little paper tubes of salt, pepper and sugar.

'Dropped in it!' declared Barker. 'That's what. We've been dropped in it.' He had been covertly studying Carter's hair. Though greying, it was thick and strong. Perhaps it was something in the other man's diet?

'I certainly have been,' agreed Carter. 'And I suppose you have, Alan. But you're retired and have every right to refuse to cooperate. I am still a serving officer, so it's my duty to look gracious and offer up such resources as I can contribute to the cause.' He turned to Barker. 'Actually, this is your pigeon, Trevor. The girl's remains have been discovered here. It's your patch. It's likely she died hereabouts. The ACC, back there, is quite correct.'

He could not prevent himself casting a meaningful glance at Markby, and one with a tinge of triumph in it. He didn't say, 'I told you so, twenty years ago.' But the look said it all.

Markby murmured, 'We found no evidence of that, at the time. We know she *intended* to come home, but no one came forward who saw her here. She didn't contact anyone – family or friends.'

'But now we've got a body!' Carter rebutted this mild disclaimer briskly. 'Or you have, Trevor.'

'We may have the remains of a body,' said Barker through gritted teeth, 'but I have not got the manpower. I thought I'd made that quite clear earlier – neither the manpower nor the resources. I do respect the fact, Superintendent, that you've got your own caseload, down there in Gloucestershire. That quite properly has first call on your attention and resources, rather than the body unearthed in Brocket's Spinney. Plus, I don't suppose you want to spend hours trailing round interviewing witnesses who will probably be geriatric by now. I'm not accusing you of being geriatric, Alan!' he added hastily. 'But fair enough, you've retired and we can't expect you to give up a lot of your time.'

'Not all the witnesses are geriatric, either,' said Carter unexpectedly. 'Rebecca's boyfriend, Peter Malone, is still only in his mid-forties and lives locally – I mean, in Gloucestershire. I saw him recently, dining with, I suppose, his wife. I'm willing to track him down and have a talk with him.'

Barker brightened. 'Great!' He turned to Markby.

'I would like – but only if you agree, of course, Trevor – to talk to Dilys Browning,' offered Markby. 'I understand she's in prison and nearing her release date. But I'd like to talk to her before that. Once she's out, the press will get to her; there is plenty of human-interest material there. But someone needs to find out if there's anything she can add to what we already know. We do know she went back on her own to retrieve the bracelet from where Josh persuaded her to throw it away; and she might have seen some activity in the lane leading down to the spinney. I understand you may wish to interview her yourself, Trevor. But my information is that she's difficult and mistrustful. She does know, however, that her brother trusts me. That may just help.'

'Be my guest!' said Barker. 'But she was only eight. It's a bit much to expect her now to remember details.'

'Well, possibly, but there's always a chance.'

The tone of cooperation had been set.

Carter said, thoughtfully, 'I rather like to meet your gardener, Alan.'

'Josh? You can do that today, before you set off home. I left him working at my place. I suppose he's still here. I'll call Meredith and ask. She can stop him leaving before we get there.'

'Good! I know his story is now a matter of record, but I'd still like to hear it from him in person!'

Trevor Barker was looking marginally more cheerful. 'I'll talk to Rebecca's father again. And I'll go and see that old girl, Pengelly. She's had time to shake up her memory, and she might have recalled seeing something going on around that spinney. I understand she can see the damn place from her kitchen window.'

'Ah,' said Markby, 'Auntie Nina! Not allergic to feathers, I hope, Trevor?'

Barker looked startled.

Markby continued, 'Meredith, my wife, called on Nina Pengelly and learned there is another long-time resident of Brocket's Row still living there. A Fred Stokes.'

'Why did your wife call on Nina Pengelly?' demanded Barker, squinting suspiciously at Markby.

'She thought the old lady might be worried. Meredith worked in the consular service, years ago. She dealt with quite a few distressed Brits, among other things . . .' Markby paused, and added, 'We quite look on Josh as part of the household.'

'Well, you're not the local squire,' said Barker firmly. 'My officers and I can handle interviews with Mrs Pengelly – and with this Fred Stokes.'

Carter sat listening to this exchange without comment. His face still wore that bland expression, but Markby suspected he was highly amused.

'Nice place you've got here, Alan,' said Carter later, surveying the late Victorian frontage of the one-time vicarage.

'Well, we were lucky,' returned Markby modestly. 'The Church was selling it off and we wanted – well, I wanted – a decent-sized garden. We're still trying to get it straight, of course, and we're beginning to feel we never will. It was very dilapidated when we bought it and needed everything from rewiring to a new kitchen, new bathroom, new pretty well everything; and no one had taken a paintbrush to it since who knows when. But we've grown very attached to it,' he added hastily. 'Have you managed to find the right home for yourself in Gloucestershire?'

'No,' said Carter frankly. 'I was living in a cramped flat with odds and ends of furniture left over from my divorce settlement. I've moved into a slighter larger place, but I haven't bought any more goods and chattels. Oh, I bought a single bed for my daughter when she comes to stay.'

'Sorry,' apologised Markby. 'I've been down that road myself. I was lucky. Meredith rescued me.'

'No need to apologise. If I haven't moved myself into a better place, and fixed it up properly, it's no one's fault but my own.'

They found Meredith sitting with Josh in the kitchen, where they had obviously been drinking tea and eating chocolate biscuits from a tin with a picture of Victorian children playing in the snow on the lid. Markby thought he remembered the tin from Christmas, when Meredith had won it in a raffle. It had sat in the cupboard ever since, waiting for its moment.

'We can all go into the sitting room now,' suggested Meredith. 'It's a little cramped for more than two people out here.'

Josh had risen to his feet on their arrival, and Markby thought with regret that, faced with a stranger, a police officer and the prospect of questioning, Josh had assumed his most vacant expression. If he carried on looking like that, Carter would dismiss anything Josh said.

At the suggestion they leave the kitchen for a more formal setting, however, Josh's blank expression turned to one of alarm. 'I like it here,' he muttered.

'Fair enough!' said Meredith briskly. 'I'll make you all a fresh pot of tea and leave you to it. Josh and I haven't quite eaten all the biscuits.'

Josh's expression now became guilty, as if he were to be charged with polishing off the contents of the tin.

'It's all right, Josh,' said Markby gently. 'Sit down, for goodness' sake. It's only a chat. Mr Carter is interested to hear about how you and Dilys found the girl in the spinney.'

Josh sat reluctantly and placed his forearms on the table with his hands clasped. It somehow gave the impression he was in handcuffs. He had garden soil under his fingernails and he wore a stretched and baggy hand-knitted sweater, probably the work of Auntie Nina. Without warning, he broke into speech, all the words he hadn't spoken before now pouring out of him in an unstoppable stream.

'I never spoke before, because when I went back to the spinney, she'd gone, that girl had gone. So we thought it best to keep quiet. No one would have believed us, anyway. I told Dilys not to say anything. It's not her fault. I didn't know about the bracelet, that she still had it . . .' Josh paused, 'I knew she had it in her hand on the way home, on the day we found the body, and I made her throw it away. I didn't know she'd gone back and found it again. I only knew that when she gave me the box, a few weeks back, to keep while she's inside.' Josh looked up and, showing animation for the first time, fixed his gaze on Carter. 'She's not a thief, Dilys! She's never been that. But it was pretty, see, and she fancied it.'

'We understand that,' said Carter calmly. 'What I'd like to know, Josh, is how soon you went back to the spinney again, after the two of you had stumbled on the body.'

'It rained for two whole days, so I didn't go back until the second day,' said Josh firmly. 'And then I went on my own. I wouldn't let

Dilys come with me; because if the girl had been lying there since then, the rats might have got to her, and I didn't want Dilys to see that. I'd been waiting for someone else to find her. But after two days, and no one saying anything, I decided to go back and check it out. The rain had stopped. I slipped out of the house while Auntie Nina and Dilys were watching the telly after tea, and I went down there, to the spinney, and she'd gone, the body, I mean.'

'What did you think might have happened to her? To the body?' Carter asked him. 'Do you remember?'

'Of course I remember!' said Josh, sounding cross. It was the first time Markby could ever remember him sounding anything other than phlegmatic or, occasionally, cheerful. 'I'm not daft, you know. I wasn't then and I'm not now!'

They calmed him down with more tea and chocolate biscuits, and he resumed his tale.

'I thought, when I saw she'd gone, that I'd been wrong and she hadn't been dead, after all. That when Dilys and I saw her, she'd been asleep. Probably drunk, like Dilys said, first of all. It was Dilys who later said, on the way home, that the girl was *dead*. But she said it because she'd taken the bracelet and I'd found out. She might have been making an excuse. So, I thought perhaps the girl had woken up and gone off home.'

'But,' Carter suggested quietly, 'you waited for someone else to find her, so you must have thought she wouldn't have moved.'

Josh gestured with one massive begrimed paw. 'I had to check it out, didn't I? I had to go back and see if she was still there. I didn't *want* her to be lying there. I didn't want to think she was dead—'

He stopped and stared down at the tabletop and the biscuit

crumbs on his plate. 'To tell you the truth, it made me afraid our mum could be dead, too.' His voice had sunk to a whisper. 'We hadn't seen our mum in a long time, but no one had told us whether she was dead or not. I thought she might be, because she hadn't tried to see us. But I didn't want to think it. That girl – I thought perhaps our mum was like that, lying dead somewhere. She had long hair, like our mum.'

There were a few minutes of silence after that, because neither of the other two men knew how to break it.

It was Josh who took up the tale again. 'But when no one else found her, and I couldn't see her when I went back to the spinney, I began to think that, really, she couldn't have been dead. She'd woken up and left. But that meant Dilys had taken the bracelet off a live person, and was a thief, and I wasn't going to tell anyone that. On the other hand, it had poured for most of those two days, so perhaps no one else had gone to the spinney and that was why no one had seen her. *I didn't know!* You're asking me to remember now all the things I was thinking back then, when I was nine! It was all a muddle in my mind then and still is. All I know is, I went back, two days later when the rain had stopped, and she wasn't there.'

Josh thumped his hand on the tabletop. His face had grown alarmingly red, his scarlet cheeks clashing with his hair, and for a moment Markby feared he might break down and, like a child, burst into tears.

'It's OK, Josh, take it easy, we understand,' he said. 'We know you must have been in shock, back then. Of course, you didn't know what to think. It was brave of you to go back on your own and check.'

Josh heaved a sigh and relaxed his shoulders. 'Well, then, a bit after that, I saw the girl's photo in the local paper. Auntie Nina always read the local paper, and she still does. I was sure it was her photo, the girl we found, because I'd seen her really close up, in the spinney. The story in the paper said that this girl came from Bamford and she'd left to be a student somewhere. She had been supposed to come home and see her mum and dad; but she'd never turned up. Everyone was looking for her, because no one knew where she was. I knew, because Dilys and I had seen her in the spinney. That's to say, I knew where she'd been on *that* day, when we found her. But I didn't know what had happened to her after that, so I told Dilys we must say nothing, because we'd be in trouble for not telling anyone at the time. Do you understand?'

Josh raised worried eyes, looking first at Carter, for under-standing, and then at Markby, for support.

Together they assured him they understood.

'I puzzled over it, all those years,' said Josh now. 'If she was dead, how could she move? Not unless someone else moved her – and who would do that? So, why didn't someone else find her, like Dilys and I did? Or, if she'd been asleep and got up and walked off somewhere, where had she gone? No one ever did find her. I decided it wouldn't help if I did speak out, because wherever she was, she wasn't in the spinney.'

He drew a deep breath. 'But I should have said something, I know that now. Because now I know she was still in the spinney; only someone had buried her in the two days before I went back there . . .' Josh paused and added, with a kind of regretful recog-nition of a task well done, 'They made a decent job of it, burying her. I give 'em that, because I didn't spot any disturbed earth, back then. But it had been raining, like I said, and that would flatten out any sign of digging. They must have covered her grave over pretty good, with leaves and that.'

He raised his eyes to look at them defiantly. 'I didn't speak out all those years, because I didn't think it would do any good,' he said. 'But then I didn't know Dilys still had the bracelet. When I found it in that box she gave me to keep for her, I knew I'd been wrong and I should have spoken up.' He turned his eyes towards Carter, and there was despair in them. 'We messed up your search for her, didn't we?' he said. 'Because the bracelet spelled out her name. I could have told someone that, and they would have known *who* it was we saw, even if her body had gone.'

Carter leaned forward and said, encouragingly, 'Yes, that's true, but you must have been a very scared little boy. We understand that. If it helps, look at it this way. Because Dilys kept the bracelet, we have that evidence *now*.'

Markby knew he would be forever in Carter's debt for those words, because a cloud seemed to pass from Josh's countenance. 'Yes,' he said. 'That's right, isn't it? It was evidence, and Dilys kept it safe.'

Alan met Carter's gaze and he knew that Carter was thinking, as he himself had thought during the conference meeting, that the bracelet had survived safely but, in forensic terms, it was now useless.

When Josh had left them, Meredith came back and suggested Carter stay for dinner.

Ian thanked her; however, he ought to start the drive back home. 'But there is one thing I think might be helpful.'

They both looked at him enquiringly.

'I'd like to see the place where the remains were found, if you can spare the time to take me there, Alan.'

'We'd better go now, then,' Markby said. 'Before it gets too dark.'

The spinney didn't look any better in the twilight. There was a chill breeze playing around their heads. It rustled the foliage on the remaining trees and made the strands of police tape, some of which had broken loose, flutter like ribbons in a rhythmic gymnastics display. There were rustlings in the undergrowth, and an unseen bird flew through the branches overhead with a rattling sound.

'Pigeon probably,' observed Markby. 'Clumsy blighters.'

Carter said, 'My daughter would call this spooky.'

Markby grinned briefly. 'It *is* spooky. I understand that it was a pretty spot, twenty years ago.'

'Hard to imagine it.' Carter pointed away to the right. 'Where is the grave?'

'Over here. I've got a torch. Mind how you go.'

They trod a wary route through the undergrowth, stumbling and both nearly losing their footing on more than one occasion.

'Here we are,' Markby said, and he shone the torch beam down into the excavated mud. 'You can't see much now. But this is where she was.'

'And where did the children originally find her?'

'You'd need Josh here to tell you that. It wasn't exactly this spot. But it wasn't that far away from where we're standing now.'

Carter grunted and said, 'Thanks for showing me.'

They picked a cautious path back to the road. Carter paused there and said, 'I can hear traffic. Quite a way off. Over there.' He pointed in the direction of the muffled hum.

'That's the motorway. But it hadn't been built twenty years ago, when Josh and Dilys found the body.'

They moved away from the spot and Carter stopped again, this time to point uphill, across a patch of open land. 'What are those houses, up there, right on top of the rise?'

'Brocket's Row. There are only eight of them, four sets of semis.'

'There are still some people living up there now who were residents twenty years ago, as I understood you to say. Who are they, exactly?' Ian sounded thoughtful.

'Josh's foster mother, Nina Pengelly, the elderly woman Meredith went to see the other day. Trevor Barker says he will be talking to her. As you know, I told Barker there is another old-time resident – an elderly man, now in a wheelchair.' Markby added quietly, 'I think I know what's in your mind.'

Carter looked towards him but the light was so poor now, all he could see of the other man's face was a pale glimmer, an almost featureless oval.

'Local knowledge,' said Alan Markby's voice.

'Has to be,' agreed Carter. 'Someone had to know this spinney was here, and they decided to bury the girl in it.'

'Yes,' agreed Markby. 'And then they sat back and watched while the police floundered about looking for her. Even laughed, maybe.'

Carter didn't miss the bitterness in his voice. 'You and me both,' he said. 'They were laughing at us all.'

Chapter 8

Carter made the long drive home without incident or delay, but darkness had fully overtaken him before he reached Cheltenham and the block of flats where he lived. When he'd first taken up his present post, he'd rented a flat in Gloucester, but had soon decided he preferred to look for a home in Cheltenham. It would be a much nicer place for his daughter to come to on her visits. He'd had vague ideas of evening strolls along the streets of fine Georgian and early Victorian architecture, pointing out the details to Millie, and of visits to the theatre there, also with Millie. So far, he hadn't had the chance to take evening strolls – and he hadn't got to the theatre, either. Millie had dragged him to the cinema to see a long, animated film featuring a lot of prehistoric animals speaking modern colloquial English and forming unlikely alliances. To his shame, he'd fallen asleep in the middle of it. Millie had found it hilarious. She'd talked about it all the way home and for the next two days.

The architect of this block of flats had paid the past a token tribute with a mock-Regency facade. The planning committee that had passed the plans would have liked that. Carter wasn't sure he did. He liked things to be honest, what they were, and not pretend to be something they weren't. Perhaps that had been his objection to the prehistoric heroes of the film. Perhaps he had a policeman's literal mind and his imagination had atrophied. Perhaps he needed to spend more time with his child. If only.

The street lighting cast an inadequate orange glow on pavements, and curtains were drawn at all the windows, except for two on the first floor that were dark: his flat. The veiled light behind some of the other curtains shimmered and occasionally grew brighter and then duller. The residents of those flats were watching television. As he climbed the stairs, he heard the muted tones of voices and bursts of music. Once, he heard the sound of gunfire and shouts. Action movies, he thought. He imagined the viewers as couch potatoes, sitting in front of scenes of frenetic adventure. Perhaps they'd all had busy days and were entitled to lounge about.

He opened his door and walked in, experiencing the usual lack of enthusiasm. 'Going home' at the end of the working day was generally a positive thing. 'I'm off home!' he'd hear other officers say, pulling on their coats, hunting for their car keys, their worried or bored faces brightening at the thought of warm rooms with televisions flickering, children running around and – for the lucky ones – dinner appearing on the table. But Millie was back at boarding school; during the upcoming half-term break she would be flying out to France to spend the time with her mother and step-father, not to mention her new baby brother.

The temperature in his flat was lower than outside in the street. During the winter, he'd kept the central heating going, but as soon as March came around he switched it off, because it seemed a needless expense when he was away all day. A weekly cleaner came and dusted and vacuumed, so the flat wasn't dirty. It was just depressing. He wondered now why he'd bothered to make the move from Gloucester. It made no difference where he chose to sleep. Wherever it was, he'd be there alone.

He threw down his coat and briefcase and paused to pick up his post and riffle through it. Nothing of much interest. He tossed it aside and picked up a framed photo of his daughter instead. She was perched on a stile, wearing jeans and a T-shirt with the image of a cat printed on it. She was grinning at the camera and waving. There was open countryside behind her. He remembered that day out as a family, before his wife had left and taken Millie with her.

He went into the kitchen, and it was more discouraging than the living room. Worse, now he couldn't help comparing it with Markby's Victorian kitchen. His mind's eye threw up the memory of the period iron range kept as a 'feature', and the modern cooker. There had been a Welsh dresser with cups and antique plates on it. He was sensitive to odours and he recalled the lingering back-ground aroma of bacon, coffee, fresh flowers. His kitchen here smelled of bleach, because the cleaner was a believer in pouring it down the sink. The units were flat pack. It wasn't that he couldn't have found the money to improve the look of the place a bit. But there seemed no point in it. It was unlikely he'd ever be the owner of a comfortable 'period residence', as estate agents liked to call old houses. Well, not unless someone came along wanting to share it with him. That did not seem likely to happen soon.

Just for an instant the image of Jess Campbell entered his mind, but he thrust it away. No chance.

All the same, Carter went back to the living room and picked up the phone.

'I wondered if you were back,' said Jess's voice in his ear. 'I was going to give you a call soon and ask how you got on.'

114

'If you're not settled in for the evening, you could come over here and I'll tell you all about it.' Carter glanced around the room. It looked depressing, and it was cold. 'I should warn you, it's chilly here.'

'Then why don't you come over here? Have you eaten?'

'Lasagne at lunchtime. How about you?'

'I've had a pizza. I can make you a sandwich, if you want one. Only it would have to be either cheese or tuna, because that's what I've got in.'

'I don't need feeding, but I would really appreciate a listener.' Dear Lord, I sound pathetic! he thought.

'Fair enough,' she told him.

Carter found a bottle of wine in the cupboard, retrieved his coat and car keys and set out again.

Jess's small flat was blessedly warm and, unlike his, managed to be a home and not just a place to sleep and keep belongings. His feelings of guilt redoubled, Carter sank back into a comfortable chair. 'You really don't mind my turning up like this and ruining your evening with work?'

'No, of course not.' Jess grinned. 'You don't have to go on a guilt trip.'

'Is it that obvious?'

'Just tell me what happened. Actually, I really want to know. Did you see Alan Markby?'

'I saw him, and he took me out to the spot where the remains were found. It was pretty desolate. You know what it's like when an area has been searched.'

Jess nodded. 'Is it a remote area?'

'Not really. There are houses nearby. They're old enough to have been there when Rebecca Hellington was buried. But nothing immediately next to the small wooded area where she was found . . .' He paused. 'It's not the first time I've found myself at a scene like that, and I ought to be used to it by now. But it's always depressing.'

She listened in silence while he recounted the highs and lows of his day. More lows than highs, to be honest. She sat on a sofa with her legs tucked under her, her glass of wine in her hand, and her intelligent face – elfin, with its pointed chin and wide-spaced grey eyes – fixed on his. Her red hair reminded him of Josh, although the gardener's was carroty, while Jess's was darker. Auburn, they called that, Carter thought. She wore it cut short. At work she was a human dynamo. Now she looked relaxed, the day's problems set aside. He envied her ability to put the working day behind her and have a private life. But did she? She used to go around with Palmer, the pathologist, although she'd always insisted it was purely friendship. But he'd heard that Palmer had someone else now, a regular girlfriend. Palmer must be out of his skull. As casually as he could, he asked, 'Speaking of wooded areas, is Tom Palmer still seeing that girl who paints trees?'

'Yes, they're planning to move in together. They're house-hunting.'

'What happened to the other one he hung around with for a while – the one who spent her time with Petri dishes and bugs? She went to Australia, but I heard she was coming back here. Did I hear wrong?'

'No, you heard right.' Jess sounded as if she didn't care one way or the other. But it could be a front.

116

'So, he's definitely not getting back together with her, then?'

'No, he was very upset when she accepted a year's research grant and buzzed off without a backward glance.'

'It is upsetting,' said Ian grimly, recalling the departure from the family home of his ex-wife. Jess hadn't said anything. Never mind Tom Palmer not thinking straight, Ian thought angrily, I'm the one who can't summon up the courage to move my relationship with Jess on from where we are now. But would she want that? Would it be a good thing, after all? There were plenty of couples who managed to juggle personal partnerships with professional ones . . . and an awful lot who didn't. Workplace romances were notoriously dodgy. He and Jess formed a good partnership professionally, and they were friends, or he wouldn't be sitting here. But he'd be a fool, he told himself, to try and bring romance into it.

It struck him that she was looking thoughtful, as she had been during their meal at the Wayfarer's Return. Was she thinking the same thing as he was? Or was she thinking about something – or even someone – else altogether?

Just when the silence between them was threatening to become awkward and he was wondering if he ought not to have come here, she spoke.

'So, we're reopening the investigation at this end,' she said.

That's that, then, thought Ian. I'm indulging in pipe dreams and she's thinking about work! Thank goodness he hadn't made a fool of himself.

'We are indeed,' he replied briskly. 'Although it does now look as though the girl carried out her intention to go to Bamford for her father's birthday. Your old chum Markby has done all right,' he added. 'He and his wife are living in a big old rambling place, a former vicarage. She's writing detective stories, all about a piano tuner.'

'Under what name?' asked Jess, ever practical.

'I think her own maiden name, Mitchell.'

'I'll seek some of them out. At least she can consult him for details of police procedure.'

'She could, but he says she doesn't. She makes it up. They're all set in the nineteen-twenties, anyway.'

'I see. What about the witness, the gardener?'

'Big, strong, silent type. Takes off his boots and leaves them outside the kitchen door, but slapdash when it comes to washing his hands.' Carter grinned briefly. 'Imagine the woodcutter in *Little Red Riding Hood*. But we did get him talking.'

'Good witness?'

'Actually,' said Ian, tilting his wine glass and watching the red liquid swirl round inside it, 'a surprisingly good witness, considering he was recalling events that took place when he was nine years old.'

'And the sister is doing time for a violent assault? Wonder what sort of witness she'll be.'

'Markby will find out. He's going to see her. This is to be a joint operation, as I was explaining, although technically it's Inspector Barker's case. He's in charge at Bamford now. He is not a happy man.'

'Don't suppose he is. What should we do?'

Carter appreciated the 'we'. 'I'm going to track down, if I can, Peter Malone. In theory, there ought not to be any difficulty in finding him. I saw him the other evening, so we know he's living somewhere locally. Unless, of course, he drove miles to the Wayfarer's Return for that meal out. I think it more likely he's not far away. I hope so, anyway.'

'He may be in the phone book, although he could be ex-directory. Dave Nugent will track him down on the computer. If Malone is any kind of professional, he'll have a web page of some sort.' Nugent was their technical wizard. 'He'll be surprised to see you – Malone, I mean.' Jess frowned. 'Unless he did see you in the pub, the other night. He didn't give any sign of it.'

'I saw him and I kept my head down,' Carter pointed out. 'He may have done the same.' He refilled his glass and Jess's. 'There is one piece of the jigsaw that doesn't belong. I don't mean it doesn't quite fit. It seems to be out of another jigsaw altogether.'

She raised her glass in a mock salute and grinned. 'Only one?'

'OK, none of it fits together yet – and it won't, until we get going on this new enquiry. How do you remember Markby? As thorough?'

'Extremely thorough. Definitely not one to leave stones unturned.'

'Of course, when you knew him he had made superintendent, and when I knew him he was an inspector. But thoroughness isn't something you learn and then forget. Nor is it something that comes with age and rank. You're thorough, or you're not . . .'

He paused and Jess asked, 'Where is this going?'

'He couldn't find any trace of Rebecca,' Carter said. 'Back in the day, when we were all scouring the country for her, especially between here and her hometown. Neither our investigation nor his turned up a train or bus ticket purchase, or a fellow passenger who'd noticed her. Her family was well known in her hometown, ran a local business. She went to school locally. Not a soul came forward to say they'd seen her, even across the street, exchanged a wave, that sort of thing. She disappeared from *here* and her bones have turned up *there* – and in between, there is a blank.'

He hesitated before adding, 'I'm beginning to work on a theory – and it is only that, as yet. What if she didn't travel to Bamford; or didn't travel when she was alive? She may have had the intention of going home, but she stayed here and she died here. Don't ask me how her body got to Brocket's Spinney – that's the name of the patch of woodland. Desolate spot it must be, too, even when you're not floundering around by torchlight, looking for a grave. Yet someone chose to bury her there.'

Jess raised an objection. 'If someone *here* killed her, how would he know about the spinney at Bamford, and that it'd make a good place to bury the corpse? And it would have taken time to transport her body there. Or did someone at Bamford travel all the way down here to kill her and then ferry her body all the way back again? That hardly makes sense. It would be a pointer to the murderer's identity.'

'It's like I said,' Carter replied. 'We're missing a bit of the puzzle, and I can't even imagine what it looks like.'

Chapter 9

The following day, Markby set about planning his visit to Dilys, researching the task ahead as an actor might prepare for a role. It's difficult for a man of certain years to stand in the shoes of an eight-year-old disturbed little girl. No less difficult to understand the workings of the mind of a twenty-eight-year old with a history of violence and failed bouts of therapy. But he had to make an attempt to get into Dilys's memory. Josh had repeated his version of finding the body several times now, but Markby was particularly keen to hear Dilys's account. After they had stumbled on the grisly sight, Josh had left the scene almost at once. Dilys had lingered to take the bracelet. That had taken some nerve, thought Markby. Dilys had to crouch down right by the corpse, looking into Rebecca's face, wary lest, after all, the eyes might open and the 'dead' woman sit up and demand to know what Dilys was doing. Dilys might well have seen something, some small detail, which her brother had not.

But the trip in semi-darkness to the spinney with Carter the evening before had been both unsettling and unsatisfactory. Had Markby been able to overhear Carter's conversation with Jess Campbell, he'd have agreed a hundred per cent with Carter. As an experienced police officer (even retired), he ought to have got used to such scenes. But he never had, when he'd been a serving

121

officer, and it was no better now. Unpleasant though it was, Markby knew he needed to go back there again for a third time. More and more, his instinct told him the answers were there – or should be there.

The day was dull and a fresh wind had picked up. He pulled on an aged quilted body-warmer over his sweater and set off. It meant driving along a B road lined with stone walls. Last night, coming here with Carter, he'd driven right to the spinney. Today he was going to walk part of the way.

Walk the scene. That's what he'd learned to do, all those years ago, as a young constable. An elderly sergeant had taught him that. 'Surprising what you spot when you're on your own two feet, lad,' he'd said. 'Little things you drive right by in a car. Get out and walk.'

He had to keep a sharp eye out for a spot to pull off the road. Luckily, just before he reached the spinney, he came upon a passing point and a gritted area big enough to let him pull in, park up and set out on foot.

It was a short walk and, in other circumstances, would have been enjoyable, with the fresh breeze in his face. But he didn't find any significant clues. If there ever had been, he was too late. Possibly Barker's search team had been along here already. But if they had – and if they'd found anything – Barker hadn't let him know.

Now he had reached the spinney itself. On his very first visit here, before going to Barker with Josh's story, he'd found the place in the lamentable state later seen by Meredith. Later, he'd been here to gaze upon the bones of Rebecca Hellington amid the havoc caused by the search. The whole area had been churned over and swarmed with the searchers. Last night's brief foray into the undergrowth by torch, with Carter stumbling alongside him, it had been eerily quiet and deserted.

Seeing the place again in daylight, he was put in mind of a huge carcass that had been stripped. The activity, the noise of the search, those had gone, and most of the original rubbish had been removed: the rusting cooker and decomposing material in bin bags, and the concrete rubble. Nina Pengelly would be pleased about that. But there was fresh debris in the plastic blue-and-white police tape that had flapped and danced in the breeze the evening before. It could now be seen to have wound itself, like a tangle of unravelled knitting, around the bushes and trees. It was as though some huge demented spider had been at work. The excavations were everywhere as trenches and holes, making negotiating a path hazardous. He wondered how he and Carter had managed to navigate a way to the grave last night by torchlight without either of them breaking an ankle. Vegetation had been uprooted and tree branches snapped. In addition, following the departure of the police searchers, the sightseers had moved in. The earth was trampled into a sea of mud and scored by tyre tracks. It had rained overnight and the ruts and holes were part filled with water. Takeaway food cartons and soft drink cans littered the area. It was impossible to imagine it had ever been a place where children had played.

Markby picked his way through the debris back to the spot where the bones had been unearthed. He was looking down into the empty grave when his ear caught the crack of a twig and a rustle of leaves. At the same time, he experienced that familiar and unpleasant prickle running up his spine, and knew he was being watched. He looked up and saw, staring at him intently from a short distance away, a young woman.

When recounting this to Meredith later, he admitted to having received quite a shock. Not only because she'd been able to get so close to him unobserved, indicating he wasn't as alert as he might once have been, but because when she saw he'd spotted her, a look of undisguised delight crossed her face. That was more alarming than seeing her there, and she had a further unpleasant surprise for him.

'It's Superintendent Markby!' she exclaimed.

'No, it's not, it's plain Mr Markby!' he retorted at once. 'I'm retired.' (Was he doomed to repeat the last words *ad infinitum*?) He hadn't a clue who she was; being addressed by name completed the discomfiture he already felt.

'But you were the investigating officer here at the time Rebecca went missing?' she persisted. 'I've checked the old newspaper reports. Your photo is in them. Have you come out of retirement to assist in the present enquiry?'

Markby was beginning to be seriously alarmed. 'Look,' he said brusquely, 'you clearly know who I am, and you've been doing a lot of homework. Perhaps you'd tell me who you are and what you're doing here!'

'Sure!' she said brightly and walked towards him, holding out a small card.

'Damn,' said Markby gloomily, taking the card and reading it. 'Press.'

'My name is Tania Morris. I'm a stringer for three national dailies.'

He took another look at her. She was in her mid-twenties,

sturdily built, her fair hair trimmed into a bob that made her look somewhat old-fashioned. A bit, he thought, like an illustration in one of those adventure books for schoolgirls that had belonged to his mother. They'd still had their place in a bookcase on the landing in the family home during his boyhood. His mother had been sentimental about keepsakes. Alan and Laura, his sister, had read the yarns with howls of laughter. Sensibly, this up-to-date example had tucked her jeans into wellington boots. They were fancy ones, green and patterned with daisies, the sort of thing garden centres sold. Meredith owned a pair, not patterned with daisies but with autumn leaves.

'Where are you based?' he asked truculently. 'How did you get here?'

'I drove here from Stratford on Avon. But I'm by way of a Bamford local, too, in a sense. My family lived here for a couple of years when I was young. One year, they booked a family holiday from Hellington's Travel, when I was seven. We all went to the Algarve. It was the year before Rebecca went missing. I don't think they kept the travel company going for much longer after that. I'm not sure. We – my parents and I – we moved on. But, you see, I feel I have a link.' She tilted her head to one side, studying him. 'I'd really appreciate an interview. You remember Rebecca's disappearance. You must have been in charge of the search for her.'

'She didn't disappear from Bamford,' Markby heard himself say, mulishly. 'She disappeared from where she was a student at a teacher training college, over an hour's drive away. I wasn't in charge of the hunt for her. Gloucestershire police force was.'

'But *you* looked for her *here*.'

'Yes, because it was thought she might have come home to visit her family. But we found no trace of her here. No one saw her. That was the extent of my involvement, so there is nothing further I can tell you.'

Ms Morris had her inquisitor's stare fixed firmly on him. 'But she was here, wasn't she?' She pointed at the excavated grave.

Markby was suddenly very angry.

'She was *buried* here. That's all we know! And we didn't know it then!'

He saw her face light up again, as it had when she'd recognised him, and he knew he'd given her an angle for her article. 'You think she died elsewhere and was brought here by her killer to hide the body?' she asked eagerly.

'I'm not giving any interviews,' he said firmly, 'and contrary to what you might think, I am not a party to any line the investigating officers might be following.'

He wasn't fibbing, he told himself. As far as he knew, Trevor Barker didn't have any theories or lines of enquiry. Probably, he would not have told Markby, even if he had. He didn't blame Barker for guarding his turf. In his shoes, Markby would no doubt have done the same.

Ms Morris didn't buy it, however. 'But you're here,' she pointed out, not unreasonably, 'at the scene. Why come here, if you don't have anything to do with the investigation now?'

'Call it idle curiosity.'

'Don't think so!' she retorted, grinning. 'You're on to something. You've got a theory!'

'You, on the other hand,' he snapped, 'apparently have a crystal ball! I have no fresh thoughts on the matter at all!' Now he was fibbing and, what was worse, he suspected she knew. She had a smug grin on her face.

'Good day to you!' he said. He turned and strode back towards his car as confidently as he could while trying to stay upright and praying he didn't plunge ignominiously, face first, into a puddle. Ms Morris would love that.

When he got home, he rang Trevor Barker and warned him a reporter with some local knowledge was in the area and keen for a story.

'She says she's a stringer for three national dailies.'

'Great!' came Barker's voice, gloomily, in his ear. 'Now she'll tell the world and its wife! Did she get any pictures?'

Oh hell! thought Markby. She probably did take a couple of snaps of me on her smartphone before I spotted her.

'I don't know,' he told Barker. 'It's possible. She'll have taken some of the grave, at least.' But he wasn't worried about that. 'I'm not wasting any more time,' he said to Barker. 'I'm calling ahead to the prison to let them know I'm on my way. I understand the ACC is getting me clearance.'

Troubles come in threes, they say, and sometimes, memories arrive in groups. Firstly, the encounter with Tania Morris had sparked recall of those old books of his mother's. Now, hard on its heels, came another image from childhood. When Markby had been five years of age, he had innocently been the cause of a permanent rift in relations between his maternal grandmother and a paternal aunt. In a nutshell, his grandmother had declared that the infant Alan took entirely after her side of the family. He bore a remarkable resemblance to her brother Wilfred at the same age. She had produced a snapshot of said Wilfred, aged five, sitting on a bench with a belligerent-looking terrier for company.

This had been at a Christmas gathering when assorted members of both sides of the family had been gathered. His father's sister, Emerald by name, had taken one look at the snapshot and declared robustly that it was nonsense. Wilfred looked nothing like Alan – and Alan, therefore, did not resemble Wilfred. On the contrary, the young Alan looked exactly like *her* brother, his father, at five years of age. Both women had taken offence, and never spoke again. They were given few opportunities to do so, because his mother had so arranged things that they were rarely invited again at the same time.

So much, thought Markby, for genes. Over the centuries, and in many families, inherited facial traits or other peculiarities (or absence of them) had caused no end of trouble. So there was no reason why he should have supposed that because Josh was tall, red-headed and somewhat shambling in build and manner, his sister Dilys should be made in similar style. Moreover, although they had unquestionably shared a mother, it was quite possible that they had had different fathers. At any rate, Dilys proved to be small, compact and muscular in build, with hair trimmed so short it was difficult to be sure what colour it might be if allowed to grow. The stubble was dark. She had a heart-shaped face, small nose, glittering brown eyes, shaved lines in her eyebrows, studs in her ear lobes and tattoos on both arms. Without the tattoos, studs and belligerent expression, thought Markby sadly, Dilys would have been pretty. As it was, he recalled to mind the squabble between his grandmother and Aunt Emerald, all those years ago – perhaps because Dilys reminded him of the terrier seated by young Wilfred on that bench.

Before being permitted to meet her, he'd had an in-depth chat with the governor.

'We have not had any trouble with Dilys here,' said the governor, a brisk, middle-aged blonde in a business suit. 'It is an open prison, and she has stuck to all the rules. She knows, of course, that if she didn't, she'd be sent straight back to her former prison and her release might be delayed.' The governor smiled cheerfully at him. 'I'm afraid, though, we feel a member of the staff here should be present when you talk to Dilys. The thing is, you mean to talk to her about something very personal, as I understand it. That might set her off. That wouldn't be good for you, and it certainly would be a black mark against her. We don't want that, do we?'

'She might take a swing at me, you mean?'

'Quite possibly.' The governor added quickly, 'We hope not. But your visit is a rather unusual one. And we have a responsibility towards Dilys, too.'

'Has she had any counselling? Anger management? Dealing with unresolved issues dating from her childhood?' he asked.

'We're a prison, not a psychiatric ward!' said the governor. 'But yes, she was offered anger management classes at the previous place. She knew that if she accepted them, it would bring forward her release date, so she agreed. She went to a course of six meetings with the therapist.' The governor shook her neatly coiffed head. 'Sadly, she felt she'd failed.'

'Dilys felt she was a failure?'

'No, the *therapist* thought she'd failed. It seems Dilys sat through all six sessions without saying a word, and hardly moving a muscle. But she did stare – never took her eyes from the therapist's face

– and her eyes held such a look of scorn. It unsettled the therapist considerably. She got rather discouraged. However, on the other hand, Dilys didn't fly into a rage at any time when the therapist was with her, so it was marked down as progress, of a sort.'

Thus when, shortly after that conversation, Markby found himself in an interview room, and the door opened to admit Dilys Browning and a prison officer, he half expected to be given the same silent, unmoving treatment that Dilys had used to demolish the anger management therapist.

He could not have been more wrong. She bounced in, fizzing with energy, with the officer scuttling along behind. He had been thinking of the terrier in the photo and now this whole initial scene almost made him laugh. Dilys and the officer were like a dog owner with an excitable and untrained pet, and this terrier was longing for a scrap.

'Oy!' snapped Dilys, as soon as she set eyes on him. 'What have you done with my bracelet? I want it back. Josh had no right giving it to you. It's mine!'

Her direct question was in tune with the manner of her entry. Markby felt he was the one summoned and she was the interviewer.

'The bracelet is an important piece of evidence and it's in the hands of the police at Bamford. I'm afraid that has nothing to do with me,' he said apologetically. It was a stuffy, official sort of reply and he didn't expect it to go down well with Dilys. It was also not how he'd wanted to start the conversation.

Dilys sniffed and glowered at him. 'I found it!' she said stubbornly.

'Well, I'm not here to argue about that.'

'So what are you here for, then?'

'Just an informal chat,' said Markby firmly. 'Why don't you tell me about the day you and Josh went to the spinney and the bracelet came into your possession.'

Dilys studied him carefully. 'Josh and I went to the spinney,' she said simply. 'And there was a dead woman there. But you know that, don't you? Josh told you, the daft sod.'

'How did you know she was dead? Josh says he wasn't sure.'

'Josh was scared of her!' retorted Dilys. 'He couldn't get away fast enough. I stopped to get a better look at her.'

'Why?'

This simple question successfully threw Dilys into a moment's confusion. She lowered her head and glowered at him. 'I dunno, do I? I was eight years old, wasn't I? You don't think about things when you're eight, you just do 'em.'

'You weren't scared?'

'I don't scare easy!' She fixed him with a challenging eye. '*You* don't scare me, neither. You're not a copper, you're an old guy, and I don't know why they bothered sending you!'

'True, I'm not a policeman any longer, but I was for a long time,' Markby returned mildly. 'I was in charge of looking for that girl in the Bamford area, twenty years ago when she went missing. I really did look hard for her, Dilys, and I found no sign of her.'

'Not hard enough, then,' she retorted. 'Or you'd have found her.'

'Not if someone buried her.'

Dilys bounced on her chair in indignation. 'Oy! Josh and me didn't bury her, did we? Is that what you're saying?'

'No, of course not. It would have been difficult for two young children to do that. But someone did. Whoever it was had to move her a short distance to find the right spot. Then he, or they, dug a good deep hole and put her in it. Then the gravediggers covered the disturbed soil with leaves, bits and pieces of twigs and so on – anything they could find, I guess. They must have disguised it well. When Josh returned two days later, and found the body gone, he didn't immediately think she might have been buried there. Or even that the earth had been disturbed. It was an unexplained mystery to him. Naturally, he thought, well, perhaps she had only been sleeping.'

Dilys sniffed again, possibly to suggest that was stupidity on her brother's part. Otherwise she only pressed her lips together and fixed him with a look that suggested she thought he wasn't too bright, either.

Markby refused to be discouraged. 'What I'd really like to know, Dilys, is whether *you* noticed anyone else in the spinney, or any sign at all of any other presence.'

'What's it like now?' asked Dilys unexpectedly, ignoring his request.

'What is what like?'

She drew a deep breath and asked, impatiently, 'The spinney, of course! What's it like now?'

'In a bit of a mess. Because of the digging.'

'I used to like it there,' said Dilys. 'When we were kids.'

'I know you did, Dilys.'

'How do you know?' Dilys asked suspiciously.

'Josh told me. You used to make camps in the bushes.'

'Seems to me,' muttered Dilys, 'that Josh has been gabbing away about everything.'

Markby persevered. 'Josh believes you and he were there alone when you found the dead girl. But I think perhaps someone else was nearby. I suspect that person saw you and your brother and hid, waiting for you both to leave. But you hung back to take the bracelet . . .'

Dilys glowered at him.

'So, what I'm wondering is, whether you noticed anything else, something Josh might have missed, because he was anxious to get out of there, as you said.'

Dilys made no reply, but she fixed him with such a steady and scornful look that he wondered if he was now about to receive the silent treatment Dilys had apparently perfected for demoralising well-meaning professionals.

'Because I think you were a very observant little girl,' he added artfully.

Mollified, Dilys nodded and some of the scorn faded from her gaze. To his relief, she spoke. But it didn't help. 'I didn't see anyone,' she said.

Markby sighed. It had only been an outside chance.

'But I smelled him,' added Dilys, unexpectedly. She frowned. 'It might have been more than one person but I think, if there were two of them, I might have heard them. Anyway, I smelled at least one of 'em. He'd been smoking – fags, the ordinary sort. You know, not pot. It wasn't that sort of smell. It was just ordinary cigarettes, and he was still there – or he might have only just gone – but the smell of the ciggies was still really strong . . .' She paused. 'That was because of all the trees around, I expect. Smoke got trapped in the air under the trees, you know, like it does in a room.'

Markby leaned forward. 'Thank you, Dilys. Now then, when you went back later—'

'I didn't!' interrupted Dilys. 'Josh wouldn't let me go near the spinney for ages after that.'

'I know you didn't go back to the actual spinney for a few days afterwards. But you did go back to the spot where you threw away the bracelet, when Josh insisted. You went back secretly that same night and found it again.'

'Oh, yeah,' said Dilys with a shrug. 'I went and got it back. It was mine. Josh had no right to make me throw it away. And she *was* dead. I don't care what Josh says. When I took it off her wrist, her skin was really cold and felt odd. And her fingers – I had to pull it over her fingers, because the clasp was awkward. I didn't have time to fiddle with it or Josh would have spotted me. I had to just pull it off as quick as I could. It still caught in her fingers, because they were bent.'

Dilys held up her right hand and made it into a claw shape. 'A bit like that. They were difficult to move, just like they were made out of wood. You go stiff when you die. You don't stay like it. After a while you go all floppy again. Well, I knew that, didn't I? So she was going stiff. She hadn't gone really rigid. If she had, I might not have got the bracelet off at all without breaking it . . .' She paused again. 'I didn't want to break it,' she explained, 'because it was beautiful.'

He must have looked surprised, because Dilys flushed a deep red at having been caught in a moment of weakness, and the belligerent look returned. 'Well, I'd never had nothing like that, had I?'

'You knew about rigor mortis?' Markby couldn't disguise his astonishment. 'At the tender age of eight?'

Dilys nodded and even gave a brief grin. 'Old guy died in the house next door to my mum's. This was before the Social took us away and Josh and I still lived with her. Anyway, the old man's name was Mr Milton and he died sitting in his chair. He'd been watching telly. No one would have known he was a goner; but his daughter came over to see him and she couldn't get in, so she called the police. They came and broke down the door. He'd gone stiff as a board and they couldn't lie him out flat. They had to carry him out like he was still in his chair. They'd thrown a blanket over him but they couldn't straighten him out. It looked funny. I was watching from my bedroom window upstairs, with Jezza. He was my mum's boyfriend at the time and he'd run upstairs when the cops turned up to break in, next door, because he didn't want them to see him, I suppose. Generally, our mum's boyfriends kept away from the police. Anyhow, Jezza told me why it was, how the body had gone stiff and that's what happens when you die.'

Now Dilys gave him a smug look, because she knew she'd successfully thrown him off his planned line of enquiry about their activities in the spinney.

Markby managed to gather his thoughts. He who hesitates is lost; and he'd be lost if he didn't take control of the conversation fast.

'So,' he began briskly, 'when you went back to the lane later, to retrieve the bracelet from where you'd thrown it, was anyone around – in the lane, perhaps?'

Dilys thought for a moment. 'Only Mr Stokes. He lived in the end house with his mum. He saw me and he asked me, "What are you doing there, Dilys?" So, I said I was picking the pink flowers for Auntie Nina. Because I'd thrown the bracelet into a patch of ragged robin. Auntie Nina called 'em that. Fred Stokes said, "That's nice, Dilys." Then he walked on with his hands in his pockets, whistling. He was going to the pub, most likely. He went every evening.' Dilys smiled. 'Sometimes, when he came back late, we'd hear him singing; if we looked out, we'd see him staggering about all over the road. Anyway, after he'd walked off, I found the bracelet. I took it back and hid it.'

'Thank you, Dilys,' Markby told her. 'I appreciate you telling me all this.'

'Don't know why,' said Dilys. 'You won't forget my bracelet, will you? You tell whoever has it now, *I want it back!*'

As Markby drove home, the image of childhood birthday parties, evoked during the ACC's lunch, came back to mind. He recalled the jelly in little bowls, with pieces of fruit in it, and the birthday cake with its candles. He remembered it being sunny, and running around the garden playing tag, or if they were indoors, it would be hunt the thimble or pin the tail on the donkey. He remembered the brightly coloured balloons and the party favours. And then he thought of little Dilys Browning, leaning from her bedroom window in the company of a petty criminal who was her mother's current boyfriend, to watch the stiffened body of the next-door neighbour being carried out, frozen in sitting position, with a blanket over it. It made him feel very sad.

He called at the police station on his way home, and was ushered straight into Trevor Barker's office. He wasn't surprised to find the inspector still at his desk.

'We've learned something,' he reported, taking a seat opposite Barker. 'Allowing for ambient temperature, we can assume that

Rebecca had been dead six to eight hours when the children found her. They came across the body in the late afternoon and she was stiffening – so we can work on the probability she died earlier that day or just possibly in the early hours of that morning. But by the time whoever buried her returned, possibly rigor was wearing off, or had worn off. She had been laid out very neatly, with her body straight.'

He paused and Barker said, 'Easier to dig a trench than a big pit to take a curled-up body. We're not talking some prehistoric burial site, foetal position and all that.'

Markby nodded and added, 'Well, this may just be my fancy, but it's as if someone took trouble over her burial and wanted to do it right. Josh said they'd done a good job.'

'They didn't want anyone to see a fresh grave.'

'True, but I'm wondering if they weren't also showing the dead girl a kind of respect.'

'Another tricky thing, fixing time of death,' said Barker gloomily. Brushing his hair that morning, he'd found the hairbrush clogged with loose hairs. 'It can mislead you, the state of rigor. All sorts of conditions influence the speed it comes on at, or how quickly it wears off.'

'Yes, yes,' agreed Markby, impatiently, 'I know. When was the victim last seen alive, and when was the body found? Death occurred between the two. That's the general rule, and the only one you can be sure of. But let's postulate that she died early in the day and was taken, by some means, to the spinney during the day. Dilys is convinced there was a man in the spinney – she told me he reeked of cigarettes. Let's assume he intended to bury the body while it was still light enough to see what he was doing.'

'But those perishing kids turned up,' said Barker gloomily.

'Yes, the children disturbed him and the would-be gravedigger hadn't time. If he'd waited until he was sure enough of himself to go back that evening, it would have been very dark and he couldn't have moved, except with great difficulty, among the trees and bushes. Carter and I were there last night with torches and nearly came to grief. The gravedigger couldn't use artificial light, because it might be noticed from the houses in Brocket's Row. So, hearing the children coming, he scraped some leaf litter over the body and decided to return the next morning . . .' Markby paused. 'It rained the next day, according to Josh, so that Josh himself didn't go back to the spinney. If he had, he might have stumbled on the act of burial – and who knows what would have happened? As it was, whoever buried her in the pouring rain must have had the dickens of a job.'

Barker leaned back in his chair and tapped his fingers together. 'OK, then, I'll go along with your theory. She lay in the spinney overnight. But we still don't know who left her there. Or who returned to bury her. I imagine, whoever it was, he didn't mind the rain. It kept others away.'

'Fred Stokes was a lorry driver and lived in Brocket's Row,' said Markby.

'Well, I was going to see him today, anyway,' said Barker. He stood up and held out his hand. 'Thanks for your help. You can leave it with me now.'

'Willingly!' Markby assured him. But it wasn't true.

PART TWO

Chapter 10

Nick Ellsworth pulled into the parking area of the fast-food diner. It was situated alongside a filling station forecourt, and was approximately halfway between his home, in Weston St Ambrose, and the offices of the firm of architects in Cheltenham, in which he was a partner. He took pride in being an 'early bird'. It kept the office staff on their toes, so he liked to think, and made a good impression all round. In any case, he enjoyed driving his two-seater sports model through the countryside, still damp with morning dew. It was like setting out on an adventure.

His house was called the Old Forge because once, long ago, it been the village blacksmith's cottage. The forge had been alongside it, spitting red sparks and echoing to the clang of hammer on metal. In its present incarnation it was the sort of property estate agents love to have on their books. Previous owners had converted the whole thing, forge and cottage, into a rambling but spacious family home. He and Cassie, as newly-weds, had begged and borrowed from family to raise the deposit. He'd be paying off the mortgage for years. But they had no regrets. Admittedly, it was a bit isolated for convenience, but wild horses wouldn't drag Cassie out of it.

The early drive meant he missed the worst of the traffic. It meant he also missed the family breakfast, and there was a definite benefit in that. He had three children under school age. The two older ones, twin boys, squabbled; their disputes were marked by flying lumps of banana, squashed egg soldiers and spilled liquids.

Their sister, Libby, was only six months old. Gordana, the nanny, seemed indifferent to the running war between his sons. 'They are little men,' she would say, if their squabbles threatened to turn into brawls. She concentrated on the baby, whom she force-fed like one of those unhappy geese. In Nick's opinion his daughter was becoming visibly doughnut-shaped.

He had mentioned this to Cassie but it had not been well received. ('Don't criticise Gordana or she'll leave!') Gordana frequently dropped hints about leaving, anyway. She didn't like living in such a quiet spot with nowhere to go in her free time. She came from a village somewhere in the Balkans and she hadn't left that, she complained, just to find herself stuck out in the country in England. She stayed because they paid her over the going rate.

Cassie herself sat gloomily drinking coffee and complaining of headaches. This coming autumn the boys would start school; someone would have to ferry them to and fro, because Weston St Ambrose had long ago lost its primary school. The plan was that Cassie and Gordana (if she was still around) would share the school run, until Cassie returned to work full time. She was a web designer.

'So, she's got to stay, Nick!' Cassie insisted. 'To get someone else who will be responsible for three children won't be easy, especially stuck out here at Weston St Ambrose. Gordana grumbles but she'll stay, I'm pretty sure, if we don't upset her. She doesn't mind the boys being boisterous, and she loves Libby.'

Moreover, Gordana was a competent driver who grasped the

wheel with grim determination and stared through the windscreen with unwavering intensity. In her time off, she drove Cassie's ageing Mini; at other times she took charge of the larger family vehicle, with room for the children. Cassie had asked her where she'd learned to drive and she had replied casually that the army taught her.

'No wonder,' Nick had muttered, when Cassie relayed this piece of news to him, 'that she handles the car as though it's a truck!' To which he'd added, 'What was she doing in the army?'

Cassie had replied, crossly, how should she know? 'I didn't like to ask,' she'd added.

Nick had given up worrying about anything at home. He had barred anyone but himself from driving his two-seater. That rule fixed, it was easier to let Cassie and the 'General', as he now referred to Gordana – out of her hearing – sort things out between them. Cassie said he shouldn't call the nanny by any nickname, because one day she'd overhear. Nick was already of the opinion that Gordana spoke, or at least understood, far more English than she let on. What's more, she listened in to any conversation, including telephone calls, and it wasn't simply to improve her English. She just liked to know everything. Cassie informed him he was being paranoid.

No wonder, then, he'd given up on breakfast *en famille* and chose, instead, to drop into the diner for his latte and the fry-up. That was another thing about breakfast at home. No one was prepared to cook him bacon and eggs. Cassie declared fried breakfast to be death on a plate. She didn't eat breakfast, anyway, other than a slice of brown toast and a small tub of organic yoghurt. Gordana, curiously, ate pungent salami and a lot of very heavy bread sprinkled with salt. All in all, it was easier just to get out of the way. He hadn't let Cassie know about the all-day breakfast, of course.

Another reason for stopping at the diner was that a rack on the wall held a selection of daily newspapers. He seldom bought a newspaper but he liked the traditional feel of sitting there, reading one, as he breakfasted. It was what his own father had done, so he looked on it as carrying on a tradition. This morning, even earlier commuters than himself had snaffled both *The Times* and the *Telegraph*, and he had to make do with a tabloid. He took it, together with his coffee and a stick with a numbered plastic flag on it, to a table by the window and, while waiting for his fry-up to appear, opened up the paper.

The café suddenly seemed to have gone quiet. Or he'd gone deaf. All around him people were eating and apparently talking – he could see their mouths moving – but he couldn't hear a word they said, or the chink of cutlery on plates, or the hiss of the machine that produced the coffee. It was like being in a silent movie. This curious silence began the moment his eyes focused on the page facing him, and the image of Rebecca Hellington.

Shock was followed by disbelief and then horror. His first conscious reaction, once he'd managed to get any control of his thoughts and emotions, was that it was a mistake. It wasn't, couldn't be, that wretched girl. This was a pretty standard portrait photo of some other long-haired eighteen-year-old who looked a bit like her. *Come on!* he told himself. *You can't really remember what she did look like.* It was twenty years ago. But a scan of the article under the photo confirmed the identity. Someone had found her body. Strictly speaking, they'd unearthed her bones. Somehow, a skeleton was more shocking than an entire body. Digging up someone's bones, it hardly seemed decent.

The diner burst out of its silent world with a hubbub of noise that made his head reel. He battled to get a grip. How could anyone just 'find' a body – or what remained of it – after twenty years? No one had found her when the entire police force of the county was out looking for her. Rebecca had vanished off the face of the earth for good.

He scanned the accompanying article and learned very little. The police spoke vaguely of 'information received' that had led to the discovery. But it was the 'where' rather than the 'how' that really threw Nick into complete confusion. 'In woodland on the outskirts of Bamford,' the article told him.

He was crumpling the paper in his hands. He knew it and yet couldn't stop himself. The world had begun to spin again. This diner was as chaotic as a hall of mirrors at a funfair. How on earth had the body ended up in some woodland miles away? When he could focus again, he saw the article had been written under the byline of Tania Morris. Ms Morris didn't enlighten her readers beyond reciting the basic facts. That suggested to Nick that she didn't know much else. So she padded it out. She wrote enthusiastically of some plod called Markby. This officer was now long retired but had handled the original investigation at the Bamford end of things, Bamford being the girl's hometown, which she'd been intending to visit when she disappeared. Markby, though now retired, was assisting the new enquiry, said Ms Morris. There was a very small, very smudgy photo of a tall, thin, older guy in a gilet and pullover, rather distinguished-looking. He was standing in some scrubby woodland and staring down at the ground like a country gent coming upon signs of poachers on his land.

The noise was switched off again, as if someone had twiddled the knobs on an old-fashioned radio. The silent movie was running again. Nick sat at the table as if isolated in a thick fog. Twenty years, and everyone had forgotten the fuss and bother surrounding the girl's disappearance. This would knock Pete completely for six. The police had put him through the mill at the time. Pete had described a sergeant, a real eager beaver, whose name had been . . . Nick screwed up his forehead. Carter, that was it.

'You're number four, aren't you? The breakfast?' A middle-aged woman was standing over him with his fry-up. She was speaking very loudly into his ear, so she must have already asked him at least once. He muttered his thanks and she plonked it down, grabbed the plastic flag and made off with it back towards the kitchens. He looked down at the pink bacon, yellow egg yolk, red tomatoes, greasy fried bread triangle and charred sausage and, for the first time, understood Cassie's point of view. He pushed the plate away. He felt sick and knew it wasn't just the food; it was panic.

He thought of Caro – his cousin Caroline who was now married to Pete Malone – did she know about this yet? He'd have to warn her, if she hadn't already found out. If all the fuss started up again, Pete would inevitably be dragged into it, and Caroline with him. Hell's bells, they'd all be dragged into it, including himself. There would be newspapermen hanging round the gate. His partners in the firm would be furious. Cassie would hit the roof. Gordana would leave.

Then there was Pete himself. What would he do when he heard about this? Perhaps he hadn't seen a paper yet – or switched on the news on the radio or television, or checked online. Perhaps, despite all the sources of information that batter us twenty-four hours round the clock, he was still blissfully unaware. Automatically, Nick reached for his mobile phone. Then he realised that he was sitting in a crowded area and this wasn't the place. He needed to get back to the privacy of his car. Surreptitiously, he smoothed out the creased paper and tore down the fold to remove the page with the photo on it. This he stuffed into his pocket. Then he abandoned his breakfast, his half-drunk coffee and the mutilated newspaper, and headed for the exit.

By the time he reached his car, panic had turned to angry resentment. It was so damn unfair. That girl, Rebecca, had never been anything but trouble from the moment Pete had found her snivelling among the plants in the conservatory at Nick's home. It was that time when his parents were away on a cruise and Nick, master of all he surveyed until they got back, had thrown a really good party. Everyone had had a great time except that girl. And Pete, stupid, kind hearted, a little bit drunk, had blundered up to Nick demanding help. Nick had appealed to his cousin and persuaded Caroline to ferry the girl over to her house, a quarter of a mile away, and stash her there for the rest of the night. And that had been the start of it.

It was not surprising, thought Nick bitterly, that the girl had got it into her head that Pete was her knight in shining armour and had fallen for him. She started trailing after him like a puppy. She'd been an absolute pain then and – wouldn't you know it? – twenty years later, she'd popped up as a pile of bones and was managing to be a nuisance now.

In the car park he rang Pete's home number. There was a fair chance Pete wouldn't have left home yet. It was Caroline who answered in her lazy drawl. She worked from home, except when out visiting clients' properties or suppliers of expensive interior furnishings.

'He left five minutes ago. Was it urgent?'

'Listen, Caro, have you seen the news at all this morning?' His voice sounded shaky to his own ears.

'No,' her voice told him, 'it's always doom and gloom. I can't face news until at least coffee break time. What's happened? Someone died?'

'Yes, but not recently. Caro, they've found Rebecca.'

There was a silence. Then Caroline's voice, edgy, 'Do you mean that dippy girlfriend Pete had years ago?'

'That's the one! For pity's sake, you can't have forgotten! They've found her body – well, a skeleton.'

'If it's a pile of bones, how do they know it's her?' Caroline sounded impatient and dismissive. She didn't like bad news. She never had. Just as, when they were children, she'd hated losing when playing board games.

'I don't know. The article doesn't say; but the police have said it is Rebecca, so they must be sure. DNA? That's what usually seems to do it these days, isn't it?'

He heard her give a long-drawn-out hiss. That meant she was cross. But when she spoke, the question really floored him. 'Is that why that blasted detective is hanging around?'

'Detective?' Nick's voice was sounding increasingly croaky to his ears. He felt cold. He had a pain in his chest. Perhaps he was going to have a heart attack. 'Someone has been to see you?'

'No. We went out for a meal, to the Wayfarer's Return, you know it?'

'Yes, yes . . .' he urged her. 'Get to the point, Caro!'

'Don't snap at me or I'll hang up on you. Pete swears he saw that detective sergeant, what was his name, Carter? Pete says he was there, in the restaurant, dining with a girlfriend, or wife, or something. I told Pete that, even if it was Carter, he couldn't have been there on account of Pete. He wouldn't know we'd be there, would he?'

'Did Carter recognise Pete?'

'Don't think so. But if they've found remains, well, perhaps Carter being in the Return wasn't such a coincidence. On the other hand, he might not be a policeman any more. Or, if he is, he must be pretty senior by now. Where did they find this skeleton?'

'That's just it,' said Nick. 'They dug it up in some woods near her hometown, Bamford. Miles away.'

'Well, then,' said his cousin, serenely, 'that's all right.'

'How can it be all right?' Nick yelped. 'Don't be bloody naive, Caro! Not you, of all people!'

There was silence at the other end of the phone for so long that he asked sharply, 'Are you still there?'

'Of course I am! Give me time to think!' Nick waited impatiently and was about to ask her to hurry up, because he was on his way to work and couldn't hang about indefinitely, when she declared in a very cool, confident way, 'This has nothing to do with any of us. So don't panic. They found her on her home turf. That's where all the enquiries will be made.'

For a moment he was almost reassured. Caro, under fire, had

the coolest head of anyone he knew. But there was still that nagging doubt.

'Even so, don't tell me they won't track down Pete again!'

'So what if they do?' asked Caroline wearily. 'What can they expect anyone to be able to tell them after twenty years? He couldn't have told them anything then, and he still can't. *Don't call Pete.* I'll do that. Leave it with me, all right? And stop panicking! OK, they might just contact Pete. But there's no reason for any of them to come near *you.*'

'It'll be Carter again,' muttered Nick. 'He nearly drove Pete to a nervous breakdown last time.'

She gave a sort of exasperated yowl. 'Listen, if, by any remote chance, they do want to talk to you, don't start babbling like you're doing now. Yes, the bones turning up are a bloody nuisance and inconvenient. But it's not a disaster. I'll take care of Pete, and you pull yourself together, Nick! You're flapping like some old hen. What on earth for? *There isn't anything to worry about, OK?*'

She cut the call. Nick switched off his phone and sat staring at it as if Caroline's face was staring back at him with a commanding expression. She was right, he supposed. Fair enough, he'd leave it with her. She wouldn't let the police badger Pete. She certainly wouldn't put up with any harassment they might try towards her. She wouldn't involve him.

He climbed into the driving seat and, as he did so, the crumpled sheet of newspaper in his pocket crackled. It sounded as if Rebecca's photo was chuckling.

Inspector Trevor Barker stood with Sergeant Emma Johnson in Brocket's Row and studied the row of houses.

'They're in a great location,' said Emma, turning and indicating the view behind them. 'You'd think some developer would have got hold of the land and put expensive property up here.'

'Land belongs to the Council,' said Barker. 'They don't put money into social housing any more, do they? Besides, this is an odd position. I know it's got a view, but it's not on any of the main roads hereabout. You can hear the motorway traffic, but these houses aren't connected with it in any way. There's that old warehouse park behind them. No one is going to pay top whack for a luxury house with a load of old storage places behind it.'

'They build anywhere, these days,' said Emma.

Barker drew a deep breath. 'Never mind the state of the housing market. Mrs Pengelly, generally known as Auntie Nina, lives in that one on the left. You take her. I'll go along and have a chat with the old fellow, Fred Stokes, who lives in the house at the other end of the row.'

'Righty-ho,' said Emma, and she set off at a brisk pace.

Barker made his way to the house occupied by Mr Stokes. He stood for a moment, sizing it up. There was a grass patch by way of a front garden and someone had cut the grass. He wondered if Josh had done it. Apart from the sort-of lawn, no one had attempted to create a garden. There were no bushes or flower beds, but no rubbish, either. The house next to it, for example, had an old, rusted Volkswagen standing on piles of bricks instead of wheels. Weeds grew tall around the makeshift blocks. It had been there some time and had the look of permanency about it. At least, thought Barker, with grim humour, no one had towed it down to the spinney and dumped it there with the old cooker and the rest of the stuff.

He walked up to Stokes's front door and rang the bell. He

knew the occupant was disabled, so he didn't expect the door to be opened at once. He waited patiently, and eventually his ear caught the sound of minor collisions and squeaks. The old boy was in his wheelchair. How would he reach up and open the latch? wondered Barker.

'Who is it?' demanded a voice through the door.

'Police . . . Inspector Barker, sir. We're investigating the remains found in the spinney. You've heard about that?'

It was true the old man lived very near the spinney; but if he was housebound, there was no telling how much he knew about what went on around him.

'Of course I bloody know about it!' came back the indignant reply, confounding Barker's doubts. 'There's been no end of noise and comings and goings. You police has no consideration for the elderly. They fixed up some lighting and it was on all night long, and a generator of some sort throbbing away. I couldn't get no sleep.'

'I'm sorry to hear that, Mr Stokes. Can I come in and have a word with you?'

'You has to show me your identity,' retorted the voice.

'Oh, well, if I hold it up by your letter box, will you be able to see it?'

'I might,' conceded the voice grudgingly.

Barker took out his warrant card, raised the flap of the letter box and pressed the card against it.

'Yus, all right,' grumbled the voice. 'I suppose you can come in.'

'Are you able to open the door for me, Mr Stokes?'

'Open it yourself!' was the spirited reply. 'Key is on a string.'

When he'd taken away his warrant card, Barker could see a

string hanging vertically from the opening. He put in his fingers, hoping there was no dog, and fished out the string with the key tied to the end of it.

'Go on, then!' ordered the unseen occupant. 'Just gimme a minute to get out of the way.'

Barker duly waited while Mr Stokes bumped and squeaked his way back from the door, and then unlocked it and pushed it open. A waft of stale air, heavily laden with the smell of nicotine, enveloped him. He was tempted to leave the front door open wide. But he closed it and hoped there was enough oxygen for both of them. An old man in a lightweight, canvas seated wheelchair sat staring balefully at him from the other end of the hall. He looked very small but that, Barker realised, was because he was very thin and huddled into himself.

'You know, Mr Stokes, that isn't very good security, leaving the key accessible from outside.' Barker was sincerely concerned.

'If anyone wanted to get in,' said Stokes, 'they would, key or no key. But why would they? I'm not going to get burglars, am I? I'm a pensioner. I got nothing. Anyhow, no one comes up here, excepting the people who live here. And none of them comes near me, except for Nina Pengelly. She comes every day and gets me my dinner.'

'No one has suggested you have a carer?' Barker asked.

Stokes sniffed. 'I had one for a few weeks. Much caring she did! Fifteen minutes in the morning and fifteen minutes in the evening, and all the time moaning about my smoking. I told her to clear off and not come back. Nina looks after me all right, enough for what I need. I see no one else. *You* found your way here, though, didn't you?'

Barker was seeking some way to answer this when Stokes moved, manoeuvring the chair with surprising dexterity and leading the way through an opening, where formerly a door had hung, into an open-plan area running the entire length from the front to the back of the house.

'Friend of mine did all that,' said Stokes, indicating the place where a dividing wall would once have sectioned off the kitchen area, and presumably referring to the building work. 'So as I could get my chair back and forth. Social Services came along and put in a downstairs toilet. I haven't been upstairs for years. Woman from the Social talked about having one of them stair lifts installed. But I don't trust 'em. What would happen if I got stuck halfway up, eh? I'd be left there like a fly on the wall until someone found me.'

'Your friend is a builder?' Barker wondered whether planning permission had been sought and granted for the conversion; and whether any weight-bearing wall had been removed.

'Turn his hand to anything,' said Stokes.

This wasn't quite an answer to Barker's question but it was as good as he was going to get. He looked around the extended living area. It was exactly that, a combination of sitting room and bedroom, leading into the kitchen area. Barker had been in many people's homes and it wasn't the first room he'd seen like this; but it depressed him, even so. All unnecessary furniture had been removed to allow the wheelchair free movement. There was a single bed placed against one wall, and a chest of drawers that probably held Stokes's clothes. The obligatory large television set – not new but not that old, either – dominated the area, and directly before it stood a battered armchair. Beside the chair was a little table on which stood a tea-stained mug and an ashtray full of stubs. There was one other chair, presumably for the use of any visitor. It was a practical wooden one, with curved back and arms, in the manner of a traditional Welsh chair, but this one had a home-made look about it. The fireplace held an electric fire; the narrow mantelshelf above it was bare but for what looked like a utility bill propped up for later attention. Nicotine was impregnated into everything. The walls and paintwork were tinged an orangey-brown. The stale tobacco odour wrapped itself around Barker like a cloak. There was another odour, too, that of sickness and age. He wondered how soon he could get out of there.

Stokes had placed his wheelchair beside the battered armchair and now heaved himself with difficulty from one to the other. Barker had moved forward to help but was repelled by a growl from Stokes who, once he had collapsed into the depths of the armchair, demanded, 'What do you want, then?'

'I understand you were living here twenty years ago, Mr Stokes. Is that right?'

'Lived here all my life!'

A lifetime spent here. It didn't bear thinking about.

Unexpectedly, Stokes gave a wheezy chuckle. 'And I'm a sight older than twenty now! I'm over eighty. I'm the oldest inhabitant, that's what they call it, right? I've been here longer than Nina Pengelly. She's a spring chicken compared to me!'

He then began coughing and jerking back and forth in the chair. Barker, who had just seated himself on the wooden chair, leapt up and prepared to render first aid. But Stokes flapped gnarled tobacco-stained fingers at him, indicating he wasn't in distress. He was, Barker realised, laughing at his own wit.

'I wonder,' Barker went on, sinking down on to the unwelcoming hard seat of the wooden chair, 'if I could ask you to take your mind back to the disappearance of a local girl, Rebecca Hellington? It happened twenty years ago. Do you remember it? It was in the local papers.'

Stokes nodded. 'I remember that. I didn't know the family personal, like. But I knew of them, because they had a little business in the town, selling foreign holidays. I used to drive the lorries over to the Continent in those days, so I didn't need no foreign holiday.' He began to hunt in his pockets and drew out a small tin and a box of matches. He opened the tin to reveal half a dozen hand-rolled cigarettes. Politely he offered the tin to Barker, who thanked him and refused.

'I'm not supposed to smoke,' said Stokes, putting one of the roll-ups in his mouth and lighting it. 'Doctor said so.'

'Well, it doesn't do anyone any good,' Barker agreed. 'It isn't just the health issues, you know. You could have an accident with a dropped match or lighted cigarette. Looks to me like you've already had a few of them!' He indicated burn marks on the arms of Stokes's chair. In some spots the cloth was burned right through; dark, shiny hairs poking out indicated the stuffing was horsehair. It must be a pretty old piece of furniture, thought Barker. Perhaps the old boy's parents owned it?

'Smoking never did me any harm,' said Stokes obstinately. He was then overtaken by another burst of coughing. 'Too late, now, anyway,' he conceded when the paroxysm was over. 'That girl,' he jabbed his index and middle finger, with the cigarette held between them, at Barker, 'she'd gone off to be a student, hadn't she? Like the young 'uns do. That's where she was when she disappeared, as I recall. Wherever she was doing her studying.'

'You're quite right,' said Barker.

Stokes nodded, gratified. 'I got a good memory,' he said.

'However,' Barker continued, 'wherever she died, she was buried in Bamford, in that spinney down the hill from here.'

The pleased expression was wiped from the old man's face. 'I heard they dug her up. That's what all that business was, with the lights rigged up and the racket and people coming and going.'

'Yes, her remains were found. They might never have been, of course, unless there had been some reason for the spinney to be uprooted and developed. But we were acting on information received.'

Stokes sniffed. 'Them kids had something to do with it, didn't they? I mean, they're not kids now. Nina Pengelly said Josh put you on to it. He still lives with Nina, but the little girl – big girl now – she went off somewhere.' Stokes shook his head. 'She was a real little scrapper, that Dilys. Always in trouble at the school for fighting with the other children. You wouldn't have thought it, looking at her. Just a little thing, she was. But fierce, oh my! Nina had no end of trouble with her.'

'As Mrs Pengelly may have told you, Mr Stokes,' Barker pressed on, 'the two children, as they were twenty years ago, saw Rebecca's dead body in the spinney but they were scared and ran away. They didn't tell anyone at the time. So that's why I'm wondering if you can remember anything odd happening around that time. Any strangers hanging about, for example?'

Stokes frowned and stared hard at his smouldering cigarette. 'You gotta remember I was off driving the lorries a lot of the time. I might not have been here.'

'Actually, you were here, Mr Stokes, because Dilys Browning remembers seeing you in the lane here, on the evening of the day she and her brother found the body. She – she was picking wild flowers on a bank just at the bottom of the lane when you came along and spoke to her.'

'And she can remember that?' Stokes glared. 'She was only a little kid.'

Barker waited without replying. A silence of some minutes lasted while Stokes finished his cigarette and stubbed out the remains in the tin. 'Matter of fact,' he said at last, 'twenty years ago would be about the time I gave up driving the lorries. So, I stand corrected, as you might say. I might well have been here.'

'So, Dilys is right when she claims to have seen you?'

'It's possible,' Stokes said pedantically. 'But I don't recall it. I know I told you I've got a good memory, and so I have, for the big things. But a little thing like seeing one of them kids in the lane, well, they were always in the lane. I must have seen them heaps of times. So you can't expect me, can you, to pick out just the one time? I also saw my other neighbours around the place, on most days, but I don't recall actually seeing any one of them on a *particular* day and maybe just exchanging a word or two.'

This was fair enough. Barker tried another tack. 'So, you retired twenty years ago?' It made sense, if Stokes was over eighty now.

'Didn't want to,' said Stokes sulkily. 'But the back trouble had got worse. A couple of years before that, I was in an accident on the motorway – just south of Birmingham, it was. Not my fault, mind! Some stupid kid, who shouldn't have been behind the wheel of a car, caused it. A real pile up, it was. It made the evening news. Pictures of my lorry stuck across three lanes. The M6 was closed northbound for hours. The driver what caused it, he killed himself, of course, so we had the emergency vehicles – ambulance, police, fire services, motorway maintenance, you name it.' Stokes fell silent for a moment at the memory. Then he added, briskly, 'It was after that the back trouble started. So I might have been here, like I said, but I don't recall anything *unusual*.'

'Perhaps not in the lane. Perhaps in that field between the lane and the spinney?' Barker prompted.

'No, not to my mind, like I said.' Stokes pursed his mouth. 'There were sometimes travellers camped in that field. They used to turn their ponies out there to graze. They don't come no more, not since they built them big warehouses on most of the land.'

Barker had been a policeman long enough to recognise an attempt to muddy the water. His questions had made Stokes uncomfortable. Fair enough, it was a lot to expect the old chap to remember seeing a local child on an unspecified day twenty years before, but Stokes had grown uneasy.

Before Barker could build on this he heard a rattling at the front door. Someone else was pulling out the string and key. Feet stamped in the hallway and a man's voice called out, 'Fred?'

A look of relief flooded Stokes's withered features. 'That's Mickey, come to see me. He takes me down the pub.'

A burly shape filled the door opening and a man, middle-aged but younger than Stokes by some years, entered the room. He stood, staring down at Barker and breathing heavily. He had a square face and thick, unkempt hair; his shoulders were broad, his long arms hanging by his sides. He stood with his feet slightly apart and head lowered. In fact, there was something altogether bovine about him with his solid build and impassive features. Barker couldn't help but think of a bull, snorting over the gate of a field at someone threatening to trespass on his territory.

'He's a copper,' said Stokes, waving a hand at Barker by way of introduction. 'And this is my mate, Mickey Wallace.'

'I know he's a copper,' said Wallace. 'There's another of them down the road, a girl, been talking to Nina Pengelly.'

'He's come asking about those bones,' said Stokes. 'What they dug up the other day over in the spinney.'

'Oh, has he?' said Wallace.

'Yes, I have!' snapped Barker, annoyed. 'I'm Inspector Barker, and I'm just having a talk with Mr Stokes, so perhaps if you could wait outside, Mr Wallace? We won't be much longer.'

'We're done now!' said Stokes firmly. 'I got nothing to tell you that's of any interest to you.' He looked towards Wallace. 'That Dilys, young Josh's sister, she reckons she saw me twenty years ago in the lane. Well, like I was telling the inspector here, I saw them kids in the lane practically every bally day, back then. And they saw me. So, what of it?'

'He's a sick man,' said Wallace heavily to Barker. 'And he's over eighty. You ought not to come bothering him.'

Barker gathered his professional dignity around him like a cape and rose to his feet. 'Perhaps we can talk at some other time, Mr Stokes.'

The two men watched him leave.

Barker found Emma standing by the car. 'How did you get on, sir? I got a cup of tea and had to drink it with a budgie sitting on my head.'

'I got the runaround,' said Barker bitterly. 'Bet my pension on it.' To himself, he thought: *no wonder I'm losing my hair.*

Chapter 11

It was market day in Bamford. Meredith didn't really need to go to the market every week but she enjoyed it there. She liked the jumble of stalls, the heaps of vegetables and fruit, the racks of clothes, the stalls selling the gleanings of house clearances claiming to be collectibles, and the air of general organised chaos. So, she abandoned the piano tuner to his latest sleuthing and set off, shopping bag in hand.

Living in a former vicarage meant living next to the churchyard. Neither Meredith nor Alan bothered about this. It was like an extension of their own large garden. There was even a little door in the dividing wall that allowed her to walk straight out from the garden into the churchyard without having to go round by the road. She stepped through it now and on to the damp grass. There were trees dotted about between the graves, and a thriving resident population of grey squirrels. One ran up a tree trunk at her approach and perched on a branch, staring down at her inquisitively, perhaps hoping she'd brought some food. But he was out of luck today. 'On my way back from the market!' Meredith called up to him. 'Not on my way there!' His bright eyes fixed her for a moment longer and then he scurried away.

A little further on, a small white cat with tortoiseshell patches was prowling amid the headstones, looking for mice. Birds flapped from one tree to another and the jackdaws circled the church tower, uttering their discordant cries. But of other human life there was only one example. Meredith's attention was called to it by the sound of running water and the clang of a metal watering can. An elderly man was stooped over one of the taps dotted around the churchyard for the use of people putting flowers on graves. He stood up as she looked. Can in hand, he turned and set off towards a headstone nearby. He was tall, with wispy grey hair, and wore an old-fashioned raincoat. Meredith walked casually nearer so that she could read the legend on the headstone.

Brenda, beloved wife of Arthur Hellington

There followed the dates of her birth and death, but Meredith did not need to know those. The man was on one knee, carefully arranging the flowers he'd brought in an urn.

She waited until he had finished his task and stood up. Then she cleared her throat tactfully to let him know she was there, and asked, 'Mr Hellington?'

He turned and looked at her vaguely, then in puzzlement.

She hastened to explain. 'I'm Meredith Markby, Alan's wife. You came to see my husband recently, about your daughter.'

His expression cleared and he came towards her. 'Oh, Mrs Markby, yes, of course. Your husband was involved in the search for Rebecca at the beginning, when she disappeared. And now, of course, they've found . . . they've found her.'

He sounded so lost that Meredith said, impulsively, 'There's a bench over there. Would you like to sit down for a moment?'

'Yes,' he said gratefully, 'yes, I think I should.'

When they were seated, side by side, he said, 'I hope your husband didn't mind my troubling him?'

'Of course not. He – he is just so sorry that Rebecca couldn't have been found earlier. Twenty years is a long time not to have any information.'

'Yes, a very long time,' he agreed. He indicated the headstone of the grave he'd been tending. 'My wife, Brenda. She couldn't accept it, you know. She always thought Rebecca would come back; or that we'd hear from her. She thought of so many possible explanations why she hadn't contacted us. Her mind ran on nothing else, and eventually, well, she rather lost her grip on day-to-day reality.'

'When the present investigation is over,' Meredith told him, 'you should be able to bury Rebecca, at least. Even if, well, even if they can't find out what happened. They'll release the . . . body to you.'

'Yes.' He pointed at the headstone again. 'It's a double plot,' he said. 'I intended that I should be buried there with my wife. But now I'll bury Rebecca there, with her mother. Brenda would have liked that.'

There was a silence during which he sat, with his hands loosely clasped, looking towards the grave. Meredith was about to take a tactful leave of him, when he spoke again.

'Some of Brenda's explanations, as she called them, of why Rebecca hadn't phoned or written were rather fantastic. The more so, the longer it went on. Any reports she read in the tabloid press about a disappearance, or kidnapping, she'd seize on. She imagined Rebecca locked in a lonely barn somewhere, or taken to some big city and coerced into prostitution. But first of all, she thought Rebecca might have been injured in an accident, and be lying in a coma somewhere. I understand that's commonly what people fear. Or that Becky had lost her memory. One explanation Brenda returned to constantly was that Becky had had a severe asthma attack.'

'She was *asthmatic*?' Meredith exclaimed, rather more loudly than she would have liked.

'Oh yes,' he said, 'from childhood.'

'Did you – did anyone mention this to the police, twenty years ago, when she disappeared?'

'Oh, yes,' he said again. 'We stressed our concern to the inspector who came up from Gloucestershire to see us, Inspector Parry. He had a young sergeant with him, Carter.'

'So she would have carried an inhaler on her?'

'All the time,' Hellington said.

'Asthmatic?' Markby exclaimed. 'I don't remember that!'

Meredith had abandoned her trip to the market and returned home immediately, after parting from Arthur Hellington, to tell Alan what she'd learned.

'She carried an inhaler on her at all times,' Meredith insisted. 'That would survive being buried, wouldn't it? It would be made of plastic or similar.'

'They found buttons and a couple of zips in the grave,' Alan said. 'There was no mention of anything that remotely resembled the remains of an inhaler. I'll get on to Trevor Barker at once. They'll have to go back and dig again. It could have been in a pocket, and we know the body was moved between Josh and Dilys finding it in the spinney and it being buried. The inhaler could have fallen out then – or earlier, of course.'

'I've looked all through the file here,' Barker assured him. 'There is no mention of the girl being asthmatic.'

'But it must be there!' Markby insisted. 'The parents told Inspector Parry when he came up from Gloucestershire.'

'Well, then,' pursued Barker, 'possibly Parry failed to pass that detail on to us. Or he told someone on your team, and whoever it was failed to make a note of it in the file.'

'Not on my watch!' Markby said firmly.

Barker hurried on. 'Look! Let's assume Parry didn't even mention it to you or anyone else on your team. After all, it was *his* investigation, wasn't it? Not *yours*. It was a liaison job, as far as Bamford was concerned. All Parry wanted you to do was tell him if she turned up alive here. She'd disappeared on Parry's patch and he was looking for her there. He was just closing a loophole when he asked you to look here. No one back then was suggesting she might turn up here *dead*!'

Markby made no reply, he sat opposite the Inspector, still simmering.

Barker plunged on. 'You were asked to check out whether she came home, and you did check – and, as far as could be ascertained then, she hadn't.'

There was a saying: 'When you're in a hole, stop digging!' Barker thought it was time for him to stop, so he did.

Markby raised his head. 'You'll have to go back and search that spinney again, Trevor. Every inch. Dig some more around the grave. Look under all the bushes.'

'The costs of this investigation are spiralling,' said Barker bitterly. 'We'll have to get equipment back, and a search team . . . but you're right, of course. We have to go back and try and find that wretched inhaler.'

'Good morning!' the smart young woman at the desk greeted Ian Carter. 'Can I help?'

'I'd like to have a word with Mr Malone, if he's in today,' Carter told her, adding his name.

'Do you have an appointment?' A note of doubt entered her voice and she began rattling keys on her computer.

'I don't, but if he's here—'

'Yes, he is in the office this morning,' she admitted. 'But he's got an important meeting in half an hour's time. Could you come back tomorrow?'

'I have important things to do, too,' Carter told her amiably. 'I do think Mr Malone would like to know I'm here.'

'Well, what's it about?' she challenged.

'Personal,' said Carter. He smiled at her but remained standing in front of her, immovable.

He saw doubt flicker across her features. Then she reached for the intercom. 'Peter? I know you're waiting on this morning's meeting, but there's a gentleman here by the name of Carter who'd like a word.'

There was no immediate reply.

She frowned, perplexed. 'Peter?'

His voice crackled suddenly from the machine. 'Yes, yes! Send him in, Beth!'

Beth stared resentfully at Carter. 'You can go in,' she said stiffly.

'But you should have made an appointment. He's got other people coming in half an hour.'

'Oh, it won't take me that long!' said Carter cheerfully.

The Gloucester office into which Beth ushered him was large, airy and had a picture window overlooking the Sharpness Canal. There was a glass-and-steel desk and similar modern pieces of furniture dotted around the room, together with the obligatory potted yucca. Malone was standing with his back to the window. Carter wondered if that was deliberate, so that the light didn't fall on his face.

He then, quite irrelevantly, remembered being told by his ex-wife, Sophie, on a visit to Versailles that Marie Antoinette had bad skin. Ladies, in her presence, were warned beforehand to stand with their backs to the light, so that attention shouldn't be drawn to their, perhaps finer, complexions. Why did he think about that? he asked himself. Was it because, even now, his mind threw up the image of that angel on the fresco, in its flowing robes? Malone had made him feel uneasy, all those years ago, by a certain theatricality, an awareness of how others saw him. Even now, when Carter walked in unexpectedly, Malone was striking a pose.

Beth closed the door with a sharp click, and Malone spoke. 'It is you, then. I can't say I'm surprised.'

'You have heard the news, I take it? That Rebecca's remains have been found?' Carter replied with equal brusqueness.

'Couldn't not hear about it!' snapped Malone. 'It's in the press, on the telly, my wife heard about it and called—'

He broke off abruptly, and Carter guessed he had not meant to say that his wife had called him. Those few words and Malone's attitude had already revealed that, although Malone had grown older, and progressed career-wise, he had remained in many ways the truculent youngster Carter had interviewed twenty years earlier.

Now Malone asked, suspiciously, 'You didn't tell my receptionist that you were a police officer, so is this an official call? Or are you just dropping in for old times' sake?' After the barest hesitation, he added, 'I suppose you are still a copper?'

'Oh, yes,' Carter told him. 'I can show you my identification.' He took the plastic folder from his inside pocket and held it out.

Malone took it, glanced at it, and handed it back. 'Superintendent now, eh? Congratulations.'

'You've done well, too,' Carter returned politely, indicating the smart, modern office.

Malone's mouth twisted into a brief, sardonic grin. 'You still didn't tell Beth you were here officially. Why not? Is that standard police procedure now, blag your way in and then spring a nasty surprise on the person visited?'

'Believe it or not,' Carter told him, 'I was being tactful. No need to feed the office gossip mill.'

Malone stared at him for a moment and then said, 'OK, OK. I suppose I should be grateful for that. ' He indicated a chair with a gracious sweep of his hand. 'Please sit down, Superintendent Carter. I'm afraid I am waiting for an important client and can't give you much time. But it will be enough, perhaps. I can't tell you anything now I didn't tell you twenty years ago.'

There was a definite change in his manner. Suddenly, he'd returned to being the suave financial expert, and Carter might have been a client. It was a measure, thought Carter, of how shaken Malone had been to see him walk in.

Carter seated himself. 'It must have come as quite a shock to hear remains had been found and identified.'

'Yes, of course it did!' Malone sat down opposite him. 'Rebecca *had* gone home, hadn't she, after all? Just as she was saying she would; and just as I kept telling you, all those years ago. You didn't believe me, did you? Well, you should have done. If you had, you might have started looking earlier in the right place, instead of wasting everyone's time here, your own included. She'd gone to Bamford to visit her folks. No wonder you didn't find any trace of her here.'

Carter accepted that Malone might have some grounds for feeling aggrieved; but the man now had enough experience of life to understand that Carter's questioning of him, years before, had been necessary. But he didn't want to anger Malone further. He needed his cooperation. 'Any investigation has to start at the beginning, and that was here. Unfortunately, that does mean people get upset,' he said, placatingly. 'Her college was where she was first missed. We don't know how she came to be buried where the bones were discovered. There's a gap, but we hope to fill in the missing pieces.'

The word 'bones' seemed to touch a nerve in Malone, and he twitched. 'Poor kid,' he said, and looked down at the floor.

'You knew she was asthmatic?'

Carter had received an irate call from Trevor Barker shortly before setting out today, demanding to know why no one at Bamford had been informed of this important fact.

'Didn't DI Parry say anything?' Carter had asked blandly.

Apparently not, was the answer. Ex-Superintendent Markby, said Barker, was astonished to hear it. 'And so was I! What were you all playing at, back then?'

Carter imagined Alan Markby jumping up and down in frustration and giving Barker a hard time. The image gave him a moment of unworthy delight. But Barker and Markby both had some justification for being disgruntled. Why didn't we mention it to the Bamford team? Carter asked himself. I suppose I didn't because I thought Inspector Parry would have done so. I was just a junior member of the team, a dogsbody, and he did all the talking. Perhaps Parry thought I had said something. Or perhaps Parry simply forgot. He hadn't been far off retirement. Mentally he'd got a little lazy.

'We all knew!' Malone said now, irritably. 'She carried this little gadget, an inhaler.' He held up his hand with his forefinger and thumb crooked and spaced to show the size of the inhaler.

'Did she use it often?'

Malone stared at him. 'I can't remember! Yes, I remember she had an inhaler and I suppose I must have seen her use it. But not often, no, not to my recollection. She didn't wheeze. Why do you want to know about that?'

'Only because no inhaler was discovered in her grave. If she had one on her, it should, in theory, have been buried with her. Other traces of her clothing were found.'

'Look,' Malone said, a sudden note of entreaty in his voice, 'I have these really important clients and they'll walk in here at any moment. I need to have my head together. If you're going to fill my mind with gruesome images, I'm not going to be able to concentrate! Surely you can understand this?'

'Of course,' Carter told him politely. 'But I would like to run through things again, everything you can remember.'

'I can't do that now! Anyway, haven't you got any records?' Now Malone was really twitchy.

'Indeed, we do. But sometimes, over the years and with the benefit of distance, and hindsight, odd little bits of memory surface. Or things start to look different. Perhaps I could call on you at home?'

'Caroline – my wife – won't like that,' said Malone gloomily. 'But, yes, it would be best if you came to the house, and Caroline heard what you've got to say. I told her I saw you the other evening at the Wayfarer's Return. Did you see me?' He paused and raised his eyebrows. His voice held a note of forlorn hope.

'Yes, I did,' said Carter. 'I was surprised. It had been a long time.'

Malone would clearly have liked to reply that it hadn't been nearly long enough. But if so, he forced these words back. 'I thought you would have done. Sod's law, isn't it? I'll get away from here as early as I can.' He went to the desk and scribbled on a notepad, tearing off the page and handing it to Carter. 'That's where I live. The house is set back from the road but if you see a pub called the Feathers, watch out for a drive opening on the other side of the road. It's got security gates, but I'll make sure they're open to let you in. Can you come about six? Give me a contact number so that I can call you if I'm going to be held up here.'

Carter took the address and put it in his pocket. 'Did you enjoy your meal at the Wayfarer's Return?'

'Not much,' admitted Malone. 'Not after I saw you there!'

A little before six, Carter and Jess were driving along a quiet, tree-lined road on the edge of the city. From time to time they passed driveways barred by security gates or twisting little side-turns that probably led to such properties, set further back from the road.

'Wealthy area,' said Jess. 'Quite a millionaires' row, this!'

'I get the impression Malone has done well, but I'm just wondering,' Carter said, but didn't volunteer what he was wondering.

Jess prompted him. 'What?'

'These aren't recently built properties. Malone and Rebecca first met at a party, out of town, in a large house. When Rebecca was taken by another partygoer, a girl, to her parents' house as a sort of refuge, where Rebecca could stay until morning, it was nearby. That, to me, suggests just the sort of community this is. So, I'm wondering . . . ah, there's the pub and that, over there, must be the entrance to Malone's place. The gates are open. I don't for a minute think that makes us welcome! But here it is. It must be this one.'

Carter turned through opened wrought-iron gates in a tall, thick laurel hedge, and followed a curving gravelled drive to pull up in front of the house. First glance suggested it might have been built in the thirties. It had a definite art deco look. It was rendered white and presented a mix of straight and curved shapes, the windows projecting in rounded bays while the main entrance door – in fact, a double door – stood within a square recess. There was a first-floor balcony above it and, above that, below the roof was a decorative pointed design in several sections. The gardens were laid to lawn and shrubs.

He drew up and Jess, peering through the windscreen, said, 'I had a doll's house like this when I was little. My dad made it. He liked messing around with wood and glue and paint. He made model aeroplanes for my brother; and I got the doll's house. The whole facade was hinged and opened up. But it only had four rooms, two up and two down.'

Carter said despondently, 'I don't think I ever made anything like that for Millie. I never seemed to have the time.' Briskly, he added, 'Let's face it, I don't have the talent for that sort of thing, either.'

They both got out, and as Carter shut the car door, the door of the house opened and Malone appeared.

'Thanks for being prompt,' he greeted them. 'Caroline has invited people over later. I didn't know that when I suggested you come. But come in.'

'We won't take up too much of your time,' Carter assured him and introduced Jess.

'Nice to meet you, Inspector Campbell,' said Malone courteously, bestowing on Jess a charming smile. 'Please, come in.'

The fellow is like a chameleon, thought Carter. This morning he was annoyed at my intrusion and more than a little alarmed. Now he's the gracious host. Carter didn't know whether to be irritated or amused. They followed Malone into a sitting room at the rear of the house, where French windows opened on to a vista of another lawn and more shrubs.

'No flower beds,' muttered Jess. 'What's the betting the grounds are kept tidy by a garden company?'

But Malone was offering them a drink. They both refused politely.

'Caroline will be here in a jiff,' said their host.

On cue, the door opened and Caroline Malone entered, or rather, thought Jess, made an entrance. She was tall, slender and elegant in an outfit of royal-blue palazzo pants and a silk tunic.

It looked very expensive. She wore her long hair coiled into a twist at the nape of her neck.

'I've been curious to meet you, Superintendent Carter,' she said. 'Ever since Peter said he thought he recognised you at the Wayfarer's Return.'

'Inspector Campbell was with you there, I think?' said Malone with just the very slightest hint of malice.

'Winding down,' said Jess cheerfully, 'after a busy day.'

'We've only recently discovered that pub,' said Caroline. 'I thought it very good. But crowded, of course. As soon as anywhere gets a good reputation, people flock to it. Are you both quite sure I can't offer you something? If not alcohol, I can rustle up tea or coffee.'

They assured her, jointly, that they were not in need of anything. Caroline sank on to a white leather sofa and smiled again. Then there was a silence. The visitors were expected to begin.

'This is a very interesting house,' said Jess. She and Carter had agreed beforehand that she should open the interview, simply because the Malones would not be expecting that.

'Thank you!' said Caroline with a twitch of an eyebrow.

'It's my wife's family home,' Malone told them. 'My parents-in-law are sadly no longer with us.'

'It's good that a lovely house like this stays in the family,' Jess responded to this piece of information.

From the corner of her eye, she could see Caroline showing signs of restlessness. Mrs Malone wanted this whole visit over and done with. And it's not, thought Jess, just because she's invited guests over later.

'I was wondering on the way here,' said Carter, turning to

Malone, 'whether it was at a party in this area that you first met Rebecca Hellington?'

Jess, the observer on this trip, saw Caroline's face freeze in disapproval and Malone flush red. 'Yes!' he said briefly and glanced at his wife.

Caroline effortlessly caught the ball lobbed at her. 'As a matter of fact we both met Rebecca for the first time that night. The party was held at the home of my uncle and aunt. They were away, and my cousin Nick threw the party.'

Now it was the visitors' turn to be disconcerted. Carter was startled to hear his theory confirmed so promptly. Besides which, Caroline's role here was more than as a support for Peter Malone. She'd been at the party. She'd known Rebecca. I slipped up! he thought furiously. I slipped up twenty years ago when I was talking to anyone I could find who knew the missing girl. I spoke to her boyfriend. I spoke to fellow students. I spoke to girls in her hall of residence. But I didn't speak to anyone who'd been at that party. Malone told me, told me quite openly, how he'd met Rebecca, and how he'd arranged for her to be given refuge elsewhere. But because that had happened weeks before she went missing, and before they started actually dating, it didn't appear to have any bearing on her disappearance later.

When he spoke, he feared his voice sounded quite hoarse. 'Is this the house to which Rebecca was brought to escape the party? Were you, Mrs Malone, the fellow guest who kindly offered her a bed for the night?'

'Of course,' said Caroline with a gracious smile. 'Didn't Peter tell you?'

She's turning the knife, thought Carter, almost feeling the pain.

She's letting me know I should have been talking to her twenty years ago.

'Of course, Peter and I weren't married, we weren't even engaged then,' Caroline continued smoothly. 'But he was Nick's friend and when he asked me to look after a girl who was feeling unwell and wanted to leave, naturally, I agreed.'

'I told him all that at the time!' snapped Malone to his wife. He turned to Carter.

'Well, not exactly, Mr Malone,' said Carter mildly. 'Yes, you told me how you arranged for one of the girls at the party to take Rebecca under her wing and take her to her home nearby. But you didn't tell me your now wife's name.'

'There was no point!' Malone was clearly exasperated. 'It has no bearing on Rebecca's later disappearance. Before, when I told you about the party, it was because you wanted to know how she and I met.'

'Nor did you mention to me this morning at your office, when you suggested we talk to you at home, that you had subsequently married that partygoer.'

Malone stared at him in apparently genuine bewilderment. 'Why should I? How has what any of us has done, during the twenty years since Rebecca did her vanishing trick, any bearing on what happened to her later? Anyhow, there was no time earlier to explain anything to you, Superintendent! I was expecting a client. My PA had already told you that!'

Carter turned to his wife. 'What do you remember of Rebecca, Mrs Malone?'

Caroline smoothed the silk of her sleeve where it covered her slim gold wristwatch.

She's controlling, thought Jess. It's not much of a hint but it's a hint, all the same, that our time here is limited.

'I really only know what I learned at the party, and it wasn't much. My cousin came to where I was with some other girls. He told us another guest, Peter, had come across a girl, in the conservatory, who wasn't feeling well. She wanted to go home, but the people she'd come with didn't want to leave. Peter couldn't take her himself. He'd been drinking – and anyway, he hadn't come in his own car. So, I suggested I ferry her over to my home, this house. My parents were out for the evening. I said I'd take Rebecca, as I later learned her name, away from the hurly-burly and bring her here. She could crash in my room. My parents wouldn't check on me. They knew I'd gone over to Nick's. He's my cousin, so they wouldn't be worrying where I was. They'd just go to bed when they got in. And that's what happened. I got back from the party in the early hours and Rebecca was asleep on my bed. So, I went into a guest bedroom and slept there for a few hours. Then I woke Rebecca and drove her to the bus stop in time to catch the first service of the day into Gloucester. I left her there and came back here to bed.'

'Rebecca caught the bus all right,' Malone said. 'I went over to her hall of residence the following evening and checked.'

'Yes, you did,' said Caroline.

Jess didn't miss the disapproval in her voice, or the glance she cast her husband. *This is all your fault*, the glance said. *You're responsible for the police sitting here, when we're expecting other visitors.* I wonder, thought Jess, if they really are expecting anyone?

'Can I have your cousin's surname, Mrs Malone? The host at the party. Is he still living in the area?' Carter asked Caroline.

She stared at him in a way that ought to have turned him to stone, but Carter, thought Jess in amusement, was proof against that!

'I can't think why you want to know!' Caroline Malone said. 'My cousin is Nicolas Ellsworth and he's a partner in a firm of architects in Cheltenham. Yes, he was the host of that party, but that doesn't mean he knew Rebecca. People turned up in groups. Friends brought friends, you know how it is. I suppose he might have said hello to her when she arrived. She was hiding in the conservatory when Peter found her. Right, Pete?'

'Stuck in a corner crying,' confirmed her husband. 'Caroline and I smuggled her out through the door into the garden and round the side of the house to where Caro had parked. We didn't want others to see her – see someone in distress.'

'I'd like your cousin's address or a contact number,' Carter said. 'I could, of course, call at his office—'

'Just drop in, as you did on me!' said Malone, resentfully.

His wife cast him a warning look. She turned to Carter and said, 'Nick lives in Weston St Ambrose. His house is called the Old Forge.' She was now definitely cross. 'Are you going to bother him? Because he and his wife have three little kids, all under five. And he won't be able to tell you anything. I don't suppose he even remembers her at the party.'

'I take the point,' said Carter. 'I will be tactful and may not have to trouble him for long. I know Weston St Ambrose. Have you a home phone number for him?'

She rose silently and went to a little Victorian bureau in the corner. When she returned she handed him a slip of paper, in silence.

Carter thanked her and pocketed the paper. On impulse, he asked, 'Does this house also have a conservatory?'

She stared at him. 'This one? Yes, as it happens.'

'Could we see it?'

'Whatever for?' Now Caroline couldn't hide her exasperation, but she was ready to do anything to get them out of the house. 'Show them, Peter, would you? I have to go and check on the canapés.' She rose in a rustle of silk. Their audience with her was over.

'This way,' said her husband.

To reach the conservatory they had to pass through a dining room. At one end of the long, well-polished table a small stack of plates, napkins and cutlery awaited the expected guests. There was to be some sort of finger buffet, he guessed.

The conservatory was a large one, of a date with the house. It contained comfortable soft furnishings but not a lot of plants. As if he read Carter's mind, Malone said, 'In my mother-in-law's day, this place was full of potted plants and vines of all sorts. It was like Kew Gardens. She had what they call green fingers.'

Jess murmured, 'No one could hide away in here!'

Malone stared at her as if he'd forgotten she was there. 'What? Oh, no, well, I'm no gardener and neither is my wife.'

'But you have an attractive garden outside.' Carter indicated the view through the conservatory's glass walls.

'Some garden maintenance firm looks after it!' snapped Malone, confirming Jess's guess. 'Always did, I guess. My late mother-in-law didn't trouble herself with outdoor planting, the muddy sort of gardening. She liked to garden in comfort, in here.' He waved a hand carelessly around him.

'And the house where the party was held? The house belonging to Mr Ellsworth's parents? The conservatory there would be very like this one?'

'Originally the houses were exactly the same,' Malone told them. 'My wife's grandfather and his brother were builders; they built both houses as family homes, one for each of them. The houses were identical.'

'And did your wife's cousin inherit the family home, as your wife did?' Carter asked.

Malone drew a deep breath. 'I can't imagine where you're going with all these questions. They have nothing to do with – with Rebecca's disappearance. If you must know, Nick's parents, Caroline's uncle and aunt, sold up and retired to a cottage near the coast. So, Nick didn't get the chance. He might not have wanted to keep it, anyway. He and Cassie, his wife, like living in Weston St Ambrose.'

'When I first saw Weston St Ambrose,' Carter said, reminiscing, 'the place had virtually closed down. Now it seems to be expanding again.'

'Well,' Malone conceded, 'you know how it is. Places get fashionable. Weston St Ambrose is on the up, or so Nick tells me. It still wouldn't suit me.'

Caroline Malone had not reappeared. The canapés obviously needed a lot of attention.

'Well, thank you for showing us,' Carter said. 'We'll be on our way. Please say goodbye to your wife from us.'

Malone couldn't hide his relief.

'Well?' asked Carter when he and Jess were driving back. 'What do you think? Are there really guests, or were those knives and forks just decoration?'

'There probably are guests, last-minute ones!' Jess gave her opinion. 'We might have lingered, and if no one turned up, they'd look foolish. I reckon Caroline rang round a few friends hastily, when her husband called her to let her know we'd be dropping by at six.'

'That's what I thought,' he agreed. 'It wasn't arranged a long while ago.'

'Absolutely not!' Jess grinned. 'Or Malone wouldn't have invited you to come this evening. Plus, it's inconceivable that his wife had arranged something and hadn't told him about it, despite his claim when we arrived. The minute you were out of his office this morning, he was on the phone to warn her and give her time to set up something, so that we wouldn't hang about.'

'He doesn't want me back in his life,' said Carter after another couple of minutes.

'No disrespect, but people do feel that way about us, the police . . .' She paused. 'Are you going to talk to this cousin?'

'Certainly am! He probably won't have anything to tell us, but I want to rattle Malone's cage a bit more!' After a few moments of silence, he added, 'Tell me, Jess, why do I now think that party was so important in all this? I didn't think so at the time of Rebecca's disappearance. Now I just feel as if those two houses, belonging to related families, located close together and built to the same design . . . I feel as if they hold the key.'

'It's called instinct,' Jess told him.

'Coppers don't act on instinct, they act on evidence,' he retorted.

'Then call it experience,' she said.

They drove on in silence for a little while and then Carter asked, 'What happened to the doll's house your father made for you?'

'It got put up in the attic when I was too big to play with it any more. I dare say it's still there.' Jess smiled. 'My mother never throws anything away.'

'And your parents still live in the same house?'

'My mother does. My dad died.'

'Of course, sorry, you did tell me that before. So, it's a family home, and one day either you, or your brother, may live in it?'

'Probably not,' said Jess, staring out of the window. 'It's a family house. It needs a family.'

'No sign of any children in Malone's house,' Carter commented. 'Not even a photograph. But that was built as a family house and has stayed in the family, Caroline's family.'

'You know,' Jess returned after another pause, 'somehow I don't see Caroline in the role of mother. In a way . . .' She paused.

'Go on,' he prompted.

'Well, in a way, Peter Malone isn't just her husband. He's sort of her child, too. I mean, she'd defend him to the last. And she's possessive, yes!' Jess's voice suddenly held a note of satisfaction. 'Yes, that's the word that came into my head when I first saw her! She's kept her family's house and she's got her grip firmly on her husband. I bet,' Jess added thoughtfully, 'that when they were younger, she didn't like Rebecca hanging around.'

'I'm beginning to think nobody did,' Carter replied. 'Even when I first interviewed Malone, twenty years back, he was keen to underline that his relationship with Rebecca wasn't serious.'

'That could just be because he wanted to distance himself from the investigation into her disappearance,' Jess pointed out. 'Having a detective turn up and quiz him must have made him jittery. He was very young.'

'Now he's not so young but still as jittery!' Carter returned grimly. 'It makes me very curious to meet Nick Ellsworth, the party-giving cousin.'

When his unwelcome visitors had departed, Peter Malone returned indoors to find his wife in the kitchen, making up a cup of the herbal tea she drank. She believed it helped her to control her weight.

From the worktop, over her shoulder, she asked, 'Gone?'

'Gone.'

'Let's hope they don't come back.' Chink, chink went the spoon against the china mug.

'That stuff,' her husband said, 'looks like something you'd mix up to feed pot plants.'

'You ought to try it.'

'I did – once. By the way, I don't think they were fooled by those plates you set out in the dining room. They knew it was a last-minute thing.'

She turned, nursing the mug in her hands. 'Did they say so?'

'Didn't need to. I thought the redhead might laugh out loud.'

'Let her do what she likes. They've gone, and that's all that matters.'

Malone eyed his wife. 'So, am I expecting any mystery guests? Who?'

'No one.' She smiled. 'They sent a last-minute cancellation.'

He gave an exclamation of anger. 'Dammit, Caro, you can't treat people like this! As if they were fools!' After a moment, he added, 'Me included!'

Now she put down the herbal tea and came over to him, slipping her arm around his waist. 'Come on, darling,' she coaxed. 'Don't make such a fuss about it. It doesn't matter a scrap what they thought. They're professionals. They don't expect to be made to feel welcome and they know people find it tacky, having them in the house.'

'*Tacky?*' He stared at her in amazement. 'Good Lord, Caro!' He shook off her encircling arm and went to the window where he stood, staring out at the garden. 'Don't make an enemy of Carter. He's like a terrier. He doesn't let go.'

'Pete,' she said, 'he *has* to let go if he has nothing to hold on to.' She smiled. 'And he has nothing. You couldn't tell him anything. He has no reason to come back.'

He turned to look at her. 'You're confident of that, are you? Sure I've got nothing hidden, nothing further I could tell Sherlock Holmes there? No murky secrets in my past?'

'I'm absolutely sure!' she exclaimed. 'Why on earth should you? I know you. You're my husband. For goodness' sake, don't let that man Carter get to you.'

He continued to stare moodily at her. 'Well, someone, somewhere, has, haven't they? A murky secret? And don't underestimate Carter, either!' Malone nodded towards the mug of herbal tea. 'You carry on drinking that witch's brew.' He set off towards the kitchen door. 'I need a whisky.'

The sun was setting in Bamford that evening and there was a scent of rain in the air. They'd seen it fall tonight – and that wouldn't help the searchers, thought Markby. He and Trevor Barker stood, side by side, in the road by the spinney, watching the crouched figures move methodically through the tangle of undergrowth. From time to time, a yelp of displeasure indicated someone

184

had plunged his leg into a puddle of cold water, deep enough for it to lap over the top of a wellington boot and settle around the unfortunate's foot.

A figure scrambling its way towards them revealed itself as Sergeant Emma Johnson. 'The search leader says he thinks there's no point in going on tonight. The natural light is too bad, and artificial lights aren't helping much with all the bushes and so on around, casting shadows.'

'Call them all off, Sergeant,' said Barker resignedly. 'We'll call it a day.' To Markby he said, 'We'll have another go tomorrow morning but, frankly, I don't think there's a snowball's chance of finding anything. It's not there, Alan. It's a tiny object; it could have been lost anywhere between where she died and here, where her bones were found. That could well be a sizeable stretch of country, and we can't search it all. I can't even justify spending more money on looking in this spot . . .' He paused. 'And even if we did find it, would it tell us anything? After all this time, it will have degraded and it would be unlikely we could prove it was hers. A lot of people carry those inhalers.'

'Fair enough,' Markby agreed with a sigh.

They turned away and saw that a small crowd of onlookers had drifted in from somewhere and now stood watching. It was wonderful, thought Markby, how a crowd could materialise as if from nowhere at the first sign of any official activity. These onlookers probably lived in Brocket's Row and, seeing the lights and movement down the hill from their kitchen windows, decided to follow each other to the spot where 'something was going on'. They formed a huddled dark mass against the sinking sun, and among them Markby's eye was caught by a movement. A red pinpoint was moving regularly up and down, as a smoker took the cigarette from his mouth and replaced it, between drags. But the height was odd. The smoker was either extremely short or seated. Beside him, Trevor Barker had noticed the same thing, and Markby heard him give an exclamation.

'Well, I'm damned, that's Fred Stokes.' Barker set off determinedly towards the red glow and Markby followed. He saw then that the answer to the puzzle was that the smoker was seated in a wheelchair.

Stokes had a companion with him, a burly man, who stood alongside the wheelchair with a hand resting on the back of it in proprietorial fashion.

'Well now, Mr Stokes,' Barker hailed the occupant of the chair. 'How did you get here?'

The burly minder spoke in reply. 'In my van!' he said.

'Ah, yes, Mr Wallace!' Barker acknowledged the burly man before returning his attention to Fred Stokes. 'Not a pleasant evening for you to be sitting about in the damp air. You'll be taking a chill, if you don't watch out.'

The smoker coughed and wheezed. 'You again, is it?' he said hoarsely. He waved the cigarette in the general direction of the scene. 'Thought you'd finished. What's brought you back, then?'

'Oh, we're very thorough,' said Barker.

Stokes was squinting up at Markby in the poor light. 'I know you, too, don't I?'

'This is former Superintendent Markby,' Barker told him.

'Oh, aye,' said Stokes. 'Now I remember. You used to run the police here, didn't you? Some time back? Not a copper any longer, then?'

'No, Mr Stokes,' said Markby with resignation, 'I'm retired.'

'Fancied you might be,' returned Stokes. 'You'd be a bit long in the tooth to be still a copper now.'

'Very true,' agreed Markby. 'Have we met in the past, Mr Stokes?'

Stokes gave a disagreeable grimace. 'You never nicked me, if that's what you mean. Nor did anyone else. I've always been a law-abiding man, me.'

'Pleased to hear it,' said Markby affably.

Stokes gave him a suspicious look before turning his attention back to Trevor Barker. 'When are you going to take them lights away?' he grumbled. 'I can see them from my window. They keep me awake. That's why I asked Mickey to bring me down here.'

'We won't be much longer,' Barker assured him.

'Oh well,' said Stokes. 'Better than the telly, I dare say.'

The burly man, Wallace, stamped his feet like a restless horse and gripped the handles of the wheelchair. 'We were on our way to the pub, when we saw you were busy again here. Best be getting along, Fred!' He manhandled chair and occupant away towards a white van, parked a little way off.

'Cigarette smoke,' said Markby quietly to Barker. 'Dilys smelled it in the spinney when she and Josh found the dead girl.'

'Old blighter,' said Barker uncharitably. 'I'll have to talk to him again. But although he may be a physical wreck, there's nothing wrong with his brain. He's as artful as a cartload of monkeys.'

'I'm considering having a badge made!' Markby said suddenly, and Barker looked at him in surprise. 'No, nothing to do with the police, Trevor. Just a label reading: "Retired. Do not approach."'

Chapter 12

'It's certainly a pretty house,' said Jess.

They had taken the precaution of parking at the edge of Weston St Ambrose and walking to the Old Forge.

'Don't give them the chance to see us coming,' Carter had said grimly, adding, 'I still can't get over how this place is changing so fast. When I first visited here, Weston was like that village in folklore, the one that appears only once in a hundred years – and you have to watch out not to be caught there at nightfall, or something like that, or you're stuck for the next hundred. Now look at it! It's got a supermarket, for goodness' sake!'

'Not much of one,' said Jess. 'And that was here the last time we had a murder to investigate locally. The one involving the Writers' Club. Anyway, your ex-wife's aunt lives here.'

'Yes, Monica, and I'd quite like to call on her while we're here. Not just a social call, you understand. She might have some gossip about the people who live here.' He nodded towards the Old Forge.

Jess grinned and they walked towards the front door. They were not as unobserved as Carter had hoped. Someone was watching out. The door flew open as they got there and they were confronted by a splendid figure. She was a strongly built young woman with long black hair and the sort of dramatic features seen in Victorian paintings of historical scenes; but she was dressed in fashionable jeans, boots and a baggy orange sweater with the sleeves pushed up above her elbows.

'You are police,' she announced in a strong accent. It was not a question but a simple statement.

'Yes,' replied Carter. He showed his identification.

She dismissed it with a glance

'You're Mrs Ellsworth?' he asked doubtfully.

Her large dark eyes glittered as if this were some kind of insult. 'No! I am Gordana. I am nanny.'

Beside him, Carter heard Jess mutter, 'Yipes!'

'You will come in,' ordered Gordana.

She pulled the door open wide and, obediently, they stepped into the hall, which had the form of a large, low-ceilinged square room with a stone paved floor. Carter guessed it must have formed part of the original forge. In the distance a baby was wailing. Before they had time to look round properly, there was an interruption. Two small boys erupted into the space, yelling at the tops of their voices. They were each armed with plastic weapons, playing at space adventurers, and were clashing them with as much violence as they could muster. Carter wondered if he ought to interfere, because if either combatant landed a blow on the other, some damage might be done; the howls of pain that the wounded warrior would set up promised to be even worse than the battle cries. However, seeing there were visitors, the pair skidded to a halt. They lowered their weapons and stood, side by side, staring up at the newcomers critically.

In their wake panted a woman in her early thirties, with short fair hair, freckles and a strained expression. She clasped a red-faced baby to her chest.

'Boys, boys!' she wailed. 'Oh, Gordana, can't you take them out?'

'Mrs Ellsworth?' asked Carter again, sure this time he had the right woman.

'Yes, yes, I'm Cassie Ellsworth,' she gasped.

'They are the police,' Gordana told her in dire accents.

'I know, Gordana! It's OK! Superintendent Carter? And, um, Inspector—?'

'Campbell,' Jess supplied helpfully.

'We've been expecting you. I'm sorry about this.' She gestured towards her sons.

The baby, perhaps by way of making its own presence felt, started to wail again. Cassie began to pat its back and make soothing noises. Gordana took up a position hovering protectively over the two boys. Jess had been studying them. One was dark-haired and one was fair. The dark one was slightly taller, but only marginally, than the fair one. Their features were otherwise identical, with small noses and widely spaced bright eyes. They also sported the same hairstyle, a chopped-off bob with a fringe.

'They're twins!' Jess exclaimed in delight.

Cassie Ellsworth turned her attention to Jess. 'Yes! People don't always realise . . . that's Dominic.' She pointed at the fairer one. 'And this is Oliver.'

Dominic said, 'Hello, are you really a policeman?' He scowled at Carter. 'You're wearing the wrong clothes.' He transferred his critical gaze to assess Jess, top to toe. 'So are you. You're just pretending.'

'We are real police officers, even in the wrong clothes,' Jess told him. 'Hello, Dominic. Hello, Oliver.'

Being directly addressed, Oliver reluctantly muttered, 'Hello!'

'They haven't got the right clothes. They're not police. I think they're aliens,' declared Dominic.

'Don't be silly, dear,' said their mother.

'I'm one of twins,' Jess told Cassie with a smile.

Cassie's expression brightened. 'Oh, are you? Perhaps we could talk about that sometime?' The baby squawked and wriggled. 'I mean, obviously not now because you've come to talk to my husband about something else. But I'd be glad to hear of your experience of being a twin. Did you get along well when you were children?'

'Pretty well,' Jess told her.

Cassie looked despondent. 'Dominic and Oliver squabble a lot.'

'They should be strong, they are little men,' opined Gordana, flinging back her mane of dark hair and looking even more like the mother in a Greek tragedy.

'We're brother and sister,' explained Jess. 'Perhaps that helped when we were little. Two boys or two girls might fight more.' She looked at the two boys, standing side by side. 'I think you'll find,' she added, 'that even if they quarrel a bit between themselves, they'll stick together against a third person.'

'Yes,' agreed Cassie dismally, 'usually me.'

Carter, fearing he'd been forgotten in this discussion of child-rearing, cleared his throat noisily and said, 'I'm sorry we're bothering you, Mrs Ellsworth!'

'Oh, it's all right,' said Cassie. 'Gordana, please take Libby and – take them all out somewhere.'

Gordana plucked the baby from Cassie's grasp, which made it

squawk again, and disappeared with the twins in tow. Dominic's voice floated back to them, maintaining, 'I still think they're aliens!'

'She's very good with them,' Cassie confided. 'We couldn't manage without her. I live in dread that she'll leave. Please, come and meet Nick.'

She led them into a cluttered, untidy sitting room looking out on to a patio area, where the children's father, who had wisely not joined the welcoming party, was waiting for them. He advanced towards them, a stockily built, sandy-haired man with a broad face and a small nose. The twins take after him, Jess thought.

'Hi!' Ellsworth greeted them, stretching out his hand. 'Superintendent Carter?' They shook hands.

'This is Inspector Campbell.' Carter introduced Jess.

'Sorry about the racket in the hall,' Ellsworth apologised. 'This is a rather noisy house, I'm afraid. I could have met you in my office, but that's a bit cramped and – well, not very private.'

Carter thought to himself that there wasn't much privacy to be had in the Old Forge, but at least they didn't share the space with Ellsworth's business partners and office staff. 'Keep it in the family,' he said aloud, and smiled to show he meant no sarcasm.

'Oh, yes, absolutely,' Ellsworth agreed. 'Please, do sit down.'

His wife reappeared. 'Coffee, everyone?'

They told her they'd love to have coffee.

'Where are they?' asked her husband nervously – referring, presumably, to his brood and not the coffee mugs.

'Gordana's taken them out. They've gone over to the churchyard to look for squirrels.' Cassie disappeared towards the kitchen.

'Gordana manages them very well,' the children's father told his visitors. 'Cassie worries that she might leave. It's a bit quiet here in Weston St Ambrose. Nothing for her to do in her time off.'

Carter thought, but didn't say aloud, that it wasn't very quiet in the Old Forge.

'Where is Gordana from?' asked Jess.

'Oh, don't ask me,' returned Ellsworth. He frowned and hesitated. 'Eastern Europe, somewhere. Cassie knows more about her than I do. Cassie hired her. She used to be in the army, apparently. Not my wife – Gordana was in the army.'

'I see. Well, Mr Ellsworth, you will already know we are looking again at the disappearance of Rebecca Hellington. You remember her?'

Ellsworth looked despondent. 'Oh, yes, I remember her. I remember all the fuss when she disappeared. Poor Pete Malone – he's married now to my cousin, Caroline – had a terrible time. That was down to you, mostly.' He stared morosely at Carter.

'My job was to find the missing girl,' returned Carter. 'I didn't.'

Jess asked a question. 'How did you learn that the case had been reopened, Mr Ellsworth? Did Malone tell you? Or your cousin, perhaps?'

Ellsworth blinked nervously. 'What? Oh, no, I told her. I told Caroline. Well, not that the case was reopened, but that remains had been found and identified as – as Rebecca. It was in one of the tabloid papers. I don't eat breakfast at home. Usually, I stop off at a diner attached to a filling station. They have the dailies there for any customer to read. It was in either the *Express* or the *Mail*, I think.' He frowned. 'I wanted the *Telegraph*, but someone else got to it first.'

'And you saw a report of the discovery of a skeleton near Bamford, identified as that of Rebecca?'

'Yes. It was a nasty shock.' Ellsworth reddened. 'It was very sad, of course. But well, you know, upsetting. I phoned Caro, my cousin, right away.' He leaned forward, hands clasped, and said earnestly, 'It's nothing to do with any of us. She didn't—well, the body was buried at Bamford. So poor old Pete was proved right. He'd said all along that she'd gone home for the weekend. She'd told him she meant to do that. It was her father's birthday, or her mother's, I don't remember which—'

'Father's,' said Carter expressionlessly.

'Well, then . . .' Ellsworth made a gesture with both hands, spreading them wide. 'That's what she did, then, poor kid. And someone there bumped her off, I suppose, and buried her.'

A rattle of crockery heralded the return of his wife, and relief crossed Ellsworth's face. 'Ah, coffee!' he exclaimed.

There was a pause while coffee was handed round. Cassie hesitated and sat down. 'I'll go away again in a minute,' she promised.

'Did you ever meet Rebecca Hellington, Cassie?' Jess asked her pleasantly.

'Oh, no,' said Cassie. 'It was before Nick and I met.'

Ellsworth said, rather loudly, 'My wife is ten years younger than I am.'

'Yes,' chirped Cassie, 'I must have been still at school when it all happened.' She cast a fond look at her husband and he flushed an even darker shade of red. 'Anyway,' Cassie went on, 'I didn't know anything about her until Nick came home and said he'd seen in a newspaper that human remains had been dug up in a wood. They belonged to some girl Pete dated, years ago. I mean, talk about dramatic!'

'No one had ever told you?' Jess sounded surprised. 'About the disappearance of Peter Malone's girlfriend—'

'Why should we?' Ellsworth interrupted, suddenly truculent. 'Cassie never knew her! And it's not something we talked about, Pete, Caro and I. It wasn't a pleasant memory. Peter nearly had a nervous breakdown, Superintendent, after you finished with him!'

'I was only a sergeant, then,' Carter offered.

'You scared him witless!' Ellsworth declared.

'Can't think why,' returned Carter. 'He had expected, surely, to be interviewed?'

'He hadn't been prepared for the third degree.'

'I hardly think it was that!' snapped Carter, angered enough to let it show. He caught Jess's eye and continued more calmly. 'It may have seemed that way to Mr Malone, at the time. I'm sure, if you talk to him about it now, he wouldn't describe it like that.'

'He has described the experience to me, Superintendent, as it seemed to him at the time. He felt then he was treated unfairly. He still feels that. So, I hope it's not going to happen again? You – and Inspector Campbell here – you were at their place yesterday, putting Pete through the mill. Can't you realise that this . . . episode . . . has scarred his whole life? Yes, I know you have to talk to people who knew the girl, but can't you see? Pete couldn't help you twenty years ago, and he sure as hell can't help now! Why aren't you all at this place, Bamford, where she was found? Instead of messing about here, you should be looking there!'

'Oh, someone is, believe me,' Carter assured him. 'We are

liaising closely with Bamford. I've been to the scene of the discovery. It's in woodland, as reported in the news. But it's not a big area of trees, just a small spinney.'

'It seems incredible to me,' muttered Ellsworth, 'that no one found her twenty years ago, when the . . . the burial was fresh!'

'Oh, but someone did find her.'

Ellsworth looked startled. 'But we understood—'

Carter continued, 'That is to say, they came upon her before she was buried. Two children stumbled over her body, but they were scared and didn't tell anyone.'

'Poor little souls,' said Cassie.

'Yes, it's altogether a very sad story.'

'It sounds extraordinary to me,' muttered her husband.

Cassie began to collect empty cups, rattling them together. 'I'll take these back to the kitchen, if it's OK with you. I wasn't around at that time. Can't help, sorry.' She fled with her tray.

'Tell us about the party,' Carter invited Ellsworth.

Ellsworth's moment of aggression had evaporated. 'Oh, that. You mean the one I threw at my parents' house, I suppose. Look, it was just a party. My people went on a holiday cruise. Anyhow, I had the house to myself and I threw a party.'

'And you invited Peter Malone?'

'Yes, I invited Pete. I knew him, but we weren't close friends at the time. We used to play a bit of tennis together, belonged to the same club. Pete was usually happy to make up a doubles foursome. Later, of course, he married my cousin and became a family member. I didn't, before you ask, invite Rebecca to the party, not directly. I didn't know the girl.'

'So, who invited her?'

Ellsworth threw his hands in the air. 'I don't know! Not now, not then! I'd never met her before that night, I told you! Someone brought her along. You must have been to parties when you were young, Superintendent! You know how it is.'

'Oh, yes,' Carter said vaguely. 'So, you really have no idea who brought Rebecca?'

'No!' Ellsworth made a visible effort to regain control. He had begun to sweat. 'I barely spoke to her. Just said "hi" when she was introduced, told her to help herself to a drink . . .'

'Where did the drink come from? Was it your parents' private supply?'

'No!' Ellsworth snapped. 'Bloody hell, I wouldn't hand out my dad's good whisky and prized bottles of wine!' He drew a deep breath. 'It was one of those "bring a bottle" affairs. And people did – bring a bottle or two, mostly plonk or cans of beer.'

'And when did you see or speak to Rebecca again, at the party?' Jess interposed.

Ellsworth's head snapped round and he stared at her as if he'd forgotten she was there. 'I didn't – or if I did, I don't remember. It was noisy and crowded, with people moving between rooms, some dancing, some going out into the garden and some—' He broke off.

'And some of them going upstairs?' asked Jess when he fell silent.

Ellsworth turned a deep red. 'Not if I saw them and could stop them. I'd told them upstairs was off limits. They sneaked out into the garden into the shrubbery if they wanted to— Well, I suppose that's what they did, if they needed privacy.'

'How about into the conservatory?' Carter asked sharply.

'The conservatory?' Ellsworth blinked at him, momentarily confused. 'I don't know – why do you ask?'

'Malone found Rebecca crying in the conservatory. So he says, anyway. He claims that's how they met and got talking.'

There was a silence. Ellsworth leaned back in his chair and eyed his visitors. When he spoke, his voice was under control and his eyes sharp. 'Look here, are you saying that someone tried it on with Rebecca in the conservatory and that's why she was in tears?'

'I don't know,' said Carter simply.

'Well, I certainly bloody don't!'

'And then your cousin, Caroline, took Rebecca to her house for the rest of the night?'

'Yes, left her there and came back to the party. Pete had been asking for someone to help – he said one of the girls was feeling iffy. It turned out to be Rebecca. That's all I know.' Ellsworth drew another deep breath. 'It was the first time any of us had ever met her. I wish it had been the last!'

Carter raised his eyebrows. 'Because?'

'Because she . . . because of the way it all turned out. What do you think?' Ellsworth almost snarled.

Carter glanced at Jess and got to his feet. Ellsworth couldn't hide his relief. He stood up too, and so did Jess.

'We understood, from Peter Malone, that you didn't get to keep the family home, as your cousin did,' Jess said blandly. 'Are you sorry? I understand the houses were identical, built by your grandparents.'

'What?' Ellsworth appeared genuinely startled. 'Why on earth were you talking about that, my old family home? That's got nothing to do with this.'

'They are very attractive houses, with a family connection,' Jess explained, maintaining her bland expression. 'I expect you regret letting yours go.'

Ellsworth looked partly convinced by this explanation but still ruffled. 'Yes, they were identical, but I didn't "let it go", as you put it . . .' He paused and added, 'My parents sold up and moved to the coast, bought a nice little cottage near St Ives. I'm not sorry. We like it here, Cassie and I. I do still own the St Ives cottage, as it happens. They left that to me. Cassie and I use it for family holidays. She and the kids spend most of the summer there, with Gordana.'

'Nice,' said Jess.

'Yes,' he told her stiffly. 'It is. The old house – the one you were asking about – is still there, but it's rather different now, unfortunately. The people who bought it turned it into a B&B, extended it to the rear and destroyed much of the gardens.'

'Oh, dear,' said Jess pleasantly. 'Does that mean the conservatory isn't there now?'

'No, they knocked it down for the extension.' There was a brief mocking gleam in Ellsworth's eyes. Just for the fraction of a moment, but Jess saw it. No use us poking around there! he's thinking.

Cassie Ellsworth reappeared to say goodbye to the visitors. She was holding a length of broken plastic in her hands.

'Dominic has broken his light sabre,' she told them all. 'It must have happened just before Gordana took them out.'

'Thank God,' muttered her husband.

'You'll have to get him a new one when you're in Cheltenham, Nick, or they'll squabble over the one that's left.'

'No chance. Take Oliver's away, too.'

'Nick! That would be unfair!'

'The racket they make is unfair to me!'

The visitors, realising that they'd been forgotten in this moment of domestic disharmony, quietly slipped away.

'Well, what do you make of all that?' Jess asked Carter as they walked away from the Old Forge.

'That Mr Ellsworth is a very nervous man. Perhaps that just comes from living with those kids.' Carter gave an unexpected chuckle. 'A lot of people see us as alien, so Dominic isn't alone in his opinion. Let's go and see Monica. This way.'

Monica Farrell's cottage stood diagonally across the street from the church and churchyard. As Carter and Campbell approached, their ears were assaulted by ear-splitting shrieks and whoops, marking the progress of the twins as they raced between the tombstones. They were even afforded a brief glimpse of Gordana, striding out, her orange sweater a vibrant patch of colour among the greens and greys, her dark hair fluttering, and the baby, Libby, strapped to her back in some sort of frame, like a rucksack.

'Goodness, Ian!' exclaimed Monica, 'and Jess, too! This is an unexpected pleasure.'

She ushered them into her cosy sitting room. It was in its usual comfortable muddle, with cushions and crocheted blankets, books and two cats lazing in a splash of sunlight falling through the small window. One cat got up and stalked out the moment it spied strangers. The other one came to sit down by the new arrivals and fix them with a basilisk stare.

'We had some business in the village,' Carter explained to her.

'So, I thought we'd call by. I'm sorry I haven't been over to see you for a while.'

'You're a very busy man, I understand that,' Monica replied. 'Where was your business in Weston? Or am I not allowed to ask?'

'At the Old Forge – do you know it?'

'Ah!' said Monica, smiling. 'Dominic and Oliver.'

'You know them, do you? They're over the road in the church-yard now, with the nanny, Gordana,' Jess told her.

'I thought I heard them. Nice, sensible young woman, that.' Monica gave a nod of approval. 'Intelligent, too.'

Carter looked surprised. 'Oh, you're acquainted with Gordana? Do you know where she comes from? It seems to be a mystery.'

'Of course it's not a mystery!' Monica retorted. 'She comes from Montenegro. She's spending time in England to brush up her language skills. When she has free time she sometimes calls here and we have long chats. She has a degree in molecular chem-istry. She studied in Germany.'

'I wonder if her employers know all that!' murmured Carter. 'They seem to think she was in the army.'

'Oh, Cassie and Nick,' said Monica. 'I've had little to do with *him*. I understand he's very successful. They don't seem to lack money. They run three cars. They have to, I suppose. Cassie and Gordana both drive Cassie's Mini, unless either of them has the children with her. Then they drive a monster like a little bus. Nick has a sporty number he probably fancies himself in. He shoots off each morning like a racing driver.' Monica paused in consideration. 'Cassie seems a pleasant young woman, a bit harassed, I fancy!' She gave a sudden hoot of laughter. 'I don't know that Gordana herself was in the army, but her father is, or was. I understand Montenegro has quite a small army nowadays. Now then, I dare say you have time for a cup of tea?'

'Well, we've just had coffee at the Old Forge . . .' Jess said hesitantly.

'I bet you didn't get cake!' said Monica. 'I made a fruit cake yesterday – and if I say so myself, it turned out rather well!'

'I wonder,' said Jess, when they'd been supplied with a generous slice of cake apiece, 'if you've ever met Nick Ellsworth's cousin, Caroline Malone. Her husband's name is Peter. We called on them yesterday for a brief chat, to do with a case that Ian's investigating.'

'That girl, I suppose? The one who went missing twenty years ago?' Monica replied placidly.

'Well, yes,' Jess sounded her surprise. 'You know about that?'

'Well, I read my newspaper and there was a piece in that about a body – or rather, a skeleton – being found somewhere, not here. I do remember the original case, when the girl disappeared. Very sad.'

'I worked on the original case,' Carter told her. 'I was a sergeant then, just made, and keen, you know. I didn't get very far. That is to say, I didn't find the missing girl.'

'Well, if she wasn't here, you couldn't, could you?' Monica retorted in a brisk but kindly way. 'She'd gone home to see her parents, I understand.'

'Oh, everyone is very keen that we should believe that,' Carter muttered. 'Well, perhaps she did, at that!' he added. 'But her parents saw nothing of her, and nor did anyone else in her hometown.'

'And that's what you came here today to talk to the Ellsworths about – the missing girl?'

'Indirectly,' Carter said 'Trying to fill in the gaps, you know . . .' He paused. 'It's a bit like a jigsaw. The outer frame is complete, and pieces of the picture here and there filled in, but there are gaps, and I have a horrible feeling that some of the pieces are missing. I had hoped that Nick Ellsworth might supply a missing piece or two, but he didn't.'

Monica said in a quiet, absent-minded sort of way, 'Sometimes the pieces aren't missing. They've just fallen on the floor. They always seem to land upside down.' More firmly, she added, 'I'm afraid I don't know the Malones. I may have seen them, if they've called at the Old Forge, but I wouldn't have known who they were.'

The impromptu tea party over, Jess collected up the plates and cups and carried them out into the kitchen. Monica followed.

'Ian's reading my newspaper,' she said. 'So we have five minutes for a chat about you. How are you getting on? Millie always asks about you when she writes to me from school.'

'Give Millie my love,' Jess said, turning on the tap over the sink. Displacement activity, she thought to herself as she did so. I know what's coming next and I want to avoid it! Better to meet it head-on! 'Millie isn't still planning a future for me and her father, is she?'

'Oh, in every letter,' returned Monica calmly. 'She's at that age.'

'Can't you discourage her?'

'No,' said Monica, 'not in any way that wouldn't make matters worse. She'll sort it out in her own mind, eventually. She's a bright kid.'

'Yes, she is. She's a determined one, too.'

'She's very like her mother,' Monica informed Jess. 'But I don't think you've met Sophie?'

'No. I've . . . I've heard a little about her. But, honestly, Ian doesn't talk much about his ex. He does talk about Millie . . .' Jess paused. 'Actually, I've got someone else lurking at the back of my mind at the moment. Not romantically! I've just heard from my brother.' She went on to explain about the possible arrival on her doorstep of Mike Foley.

'Been very ill?' mused Monica. 'Poor chap. Could be anything in those camps, I suppose, from measles to cholera.'

'I don't know what's been the problem. Simon is vague, and it's slightly worrying.'

'You've met the young man before, have you?'

'Oh, yes, in the dim and distant past, when both he and Simon were medical students. I just have this rather fuzzy image of an athlete running round a track. Not much to go on.'

'No photos anywhere? You know, taken at some athletics event to record your brother's presence, but with other people in the background?'

'I hadn't thought of that!' Jess exclaimed. 'I'll look out my old photo collection. You ought to be the detective, Monica!'

As they were leaving the cottage, half an hour later, Carter dropped back to allow Jess to precede him so that he, in his turn, could have a quick private word with Monica.

'Have you heard from Sophie lately?' he asked, diffidently. 'All OK, with the new baby and everything?'

'I've had a couple of emails,' Monica told him. 'Photos of the new arrival attached. At the moment he looks like a blob.'

'I'd heard the new arrival is a boy. Millie is quite pleased.'

'They're calling him Tristan,' Monica said.

Carter couldn't help looking startled. 'Why?'

'Don't ask me. I suppose Sophie has her reasons.'

'Yes,' Carter returned. 'Yes, she usually does. Pass her – and Rodney – my good wishes when you next communicate.'

Carter and Jess's walk back to their car through the village and passing the front of the Old Forge was not unobserved.

'Where have they been?' Nick demanded of his wife. 'They left here nearly an hour ago!' He scowled. 'Is Gordana back with the children?'

'She came in twenty minutes ago,' Cassie told him. 'Didn't you hear them?'

'She took them to the churchyard, you said. To find squirrels or something? That's the direction those two detectives came from. Do you think they've been talking to Gordana?'

Cassie folded her arms and surveyed her husband thoughtfully.

'Honestly, Nick, you really are getting paranoid about Gordana. Why should the police want to talk to her? What about, for goodness' sake?'

'Us!' said her husband fiercely. 'I told you, that girl snoops!'

'Of course she doesn't!' Cassie set off back towards the sound of wailing from Libby that had just broken out to the rear of the house. 'What have we got to hide? I haven't got any secrets. Have you?'

'No,' he said sullenly. 'Of course I haven't.'

Later that evening, just as they were all going to bed, the phone rang shrilly in the Old Forge.

Cassie answered. 'It's Peter!' she called out to her husband in surprise.

'What's up?' Nick asked into the receiver.

'Sorry to disturb you, Nick,' came Malone's voice. 'Hope I didn't wake you. I just wanted to ask – did Carter come today?'

'Yes, he . . . he brought a colleague with him, a red-haired woman. It's all OK, Pete. I think they got what they wanted.'

'What was that?' Malone's voice sounded suddenly sharp.

'Well, nothing, really. I think it was just background stuff.'

'I just wondered . . .'

There was a rustling sound in the background that Nick couldn't identify. 'Where are you?' he asked Malone.

'In the garden. I didn't want Caroline to know I was calling you. She worries. Nick, listen, is there *anything* you were able to tell the police – anything at all – that I . . . I might have forgotten?'

'Well, I don't know what you told them, do I?'

'Nothing new. I've said it so often now that it comes out like a record. It's beginning to sound unconvincing even to me. Nick, is there anything – can *you* think of anything I should know? I keep thinking there must be. It's difficult to explain, but I feel as though Carter believes I do know something I haven't told him. He may even know exactly what it is. But he wants to hear me say it. He thinks I must know it, too, you see. But I can't say it, because I don't know what it is – or I think I don't know what it is . . .' Malone's voice tailed off miserably.

'Are you OK, Pete?' Nick asked. He was starting to get seriously concerned. 'You haven't been drinking, have you, old son?'

A brittle laugh echoed from the phone. 'Two small whiskies, and a glass and a half of Beaujolais with dinner. Caroline keeps an eye on that sort of thing! Listen, Nick, don't tell her I rang, OK?'

'I won't say anything. I might ring her myself tomorrow, is that OK? She'll be expecting me to give her an update. Perhaps I should have rung this evening, but there was a bit of a rumpus at home when I confiscated a plastic toy weapon of Oliver's. It was a bit unfair of me, because Dominic had broken his and I was just evening things up. Not Ollie's fault, though, I'll have to buy them both new ones.'

'Yes, ring her tomorrow. She will be expecting to hear from you. Just as long as you don't mention this call . . .' A pause and then Malone added, 'Carter does suspect me, you know. I can't blame him, I suppose. It would all make sense, wouldn't it?'

'No, of course it wouldn't! No one could seriously imagine you had anything to do with Rebecca's disappearance. Get a grip, Pete!' Nick said sharply. 'Carter's floundering and he keeps coming back to you because he doesn't know where else to go, except to me—' Nick broke off. 'And I can't help him, can I?' he continued. 'We none of us can. Listen, are you still there?' It struck Nick that the silence at the other end of the phone had an absent feel to it. Pete was there, he was pretty sure of that. At least, he hadn't cut the phone link, because Nick could still distinguish those garden-at-night sounds. There was a distant sharp bark. A fox? It was followed by the faint hoot of an owl. Trees rustling. But Nick felt Malone had tuned out the sound of Nick's voice. 'Pete?' he repeated more loudly.

'Yes, I'm still here, still listening.' Pete sounded desperately tired, like a man who had made a long and arduous journey.

'Get some sleep. You've had a difficult day.' It sounded trite, obvious advice, but what else could he say?

* * *

'Poor old Pete,' said Nick, climbing into bed beside Cassie. 'He's creeping out into the garden to make his phone calls in secret now.'

'I know she's your cousin,' mumbled his wife from the pillow, 'but she can be jolly scary!'

'I think Pete might be cracking up.'

'Why?'

'Obvious, isn't it? The police hanging around their place and ours, that wretched fellow, Carter, with his suspicious stares and the way he has of doubting everything you say.'

'Did he doubt what you told him today?'

'No! I'm not talking about me. I'm talking about Pete. You can't blame the poor chap for feeling persecuted. Damn waste of everyone's time.'

'If Pete can't tell them anything new, the police will soon realise that and stay away.'

He didn't answer. No point in arguing with Cassie, as well as everything else.

Jess spent the evening looking for old family snaps. She did have some, but they dated from her early childhood. If there were other, later ones – of the sort Monica had suggested might exist – she didn't have them here in her flat.

They must be at her mother's house. As she'd told Ian, her mother kept everything.

Chapter 13

Visitors, whether expected or unexpected, appeared to be the order of the day, and not only in Gloucestershire. At the Bamford end of the investigations, the day started well. Markby, on seeing from the window that it was a nice, bright, promising morning – just the day to be out in his garden – announced to Meredith that he would be devoting his time to catching up on chores in the neglected vegetable plot. He really felt he had 'done his bit' in the Rebecca Hellington enquiry. 'And I can't be giving all my time to that. I've got other things to do!' he pointed out cheerfully to Meredith over his toast and marmalade.

'I expect you have,' said Meredith.

'Let's face it, there's nothing much else I *can* do,' he continued. 'I've interviewed Dilys, shown Ian Carter where the skeleton was discovered, and I've done my best to support Trevor Barker.'

'Yes,' returned Meredith and, seeing that Alan seemed to expect a more detailed answer, repeated, 'Yes, you have.'

'Trevor's a good man, reliable. Ian Carter will do a good job at his end of things, and Jess won't leave any stones unturned.'

'No, she won't.'

'All right,' exclaimed her husband, putting down his cup of coffee. 'What is it?'

'Nothing. I just didn't think you'd get bored with the investigation so soon. You were so keen!'

He stared at her, appalled. '*Bored?* I am not bored! I wish you'd make up your mind. First you asked if I was bored because I didn't have any detecting to do. Now that I've been doing my best to help out the ACC, you reproach me for not running round like a demented sniffer dog. I'm very keen that it all turns out as it should; I trust Ian and Trevor to see that it does.'

'If I didn't know you better,' said Meredith calmly, 'I would suspect you of *pique*.' Seeing that this accusation left him bereft of speech for the moment, she went on, 'I might suspect that you'd love to be running the whole thing and, because you can't, you're adopting a grand attitude and pretending you don't care any more. Rot! Of course you care dreadfully, and you don't fool me, ex-Superintendent Markby!'

'I am retired!' said her husband firmly. 'So, get thee to thy piano tuner and let him sort out everyone's problems. I am going into the garden. Josh is supposed to be coming today to give me a hand putting up the frame for the beans.'

Josh was waiting for him. He hadn't called at the house first, but this was normal. Markby guessed he'd walked through the churchyard and entered the garden through the Victorian door in the wall. He'd already gathered together the poles of the bean frame and the plastic netting that would be thrown over it. It struck Markby that Josh looked cheerful. He wouldn't ask why. If Josh wanted to tell him, he would, in his own good time. And so he did.

'You went to see our Dilys,' said Josh, hammering poles into the ground.

'Yes, I was very pleased to meet her.'

'She liked you, too,' said Josh happily. He looked up as he spoke, his face crimson with effort, its colour clashing with that of his mop of red hair.

You could have fooled me, Markby almost replied. I got the impression Dilys thought I was a dead loss.

'Good,' he said aloud.

'She doesn't like a lot of people,' Josh reminded him.

'So I understand.' Obviously, he needed to show how much he appreciated Dilys's approval. 'I'm glad she . . . we got on all right.'

There was a pause in the conversation; but now it had begun, Markby decided to take the opportunity to ask a question or two. That would show Meredith he hadn't lost interest. Pique, indeed!

'Dilys told me something interesting,' he began. 'She said she remembered, when the two of you found the body in the spinney, the smell of cigarette smoke trapped under the trees. Do you remember that?'

'Not really,' said Josh. 'But if Dilys said she smelled smoke, she did. Dilys doesn't make things up.'

'It makes me think,' said Markby, 'that someone was in the spinney and watching you and your sister. After you left, that person buried the girl. That's why, when you went back, you didn't see a body.'

'Bit of a job that,' observed Josh, 'burying a body all on your own. He'd have needed to dig down quite deep, because otherwise foxes would've dug her up again, or even any dogs sniffing round there. Even if they hadn't dug her right up, there would've been scrape marks. I didn't see any.' After a few minutes, during which Josh concentrated on the bean frame, he added, 'He did a good job, like I said, whoever he was.'

Markby had more he wanted to say, but he decided to let the matter rest for the moment. So, they discussed the layout of the rest of the garden. The conversation didn't return to the body in the spinney until it was time for their coffee break. Because the sunshine was so pleasant, they hadn't retreated to the shed, but sat outside it on an old wooden bench.

Meredith had appeared with the two mugs of coffee, and asked after Mrs Pengelly. 'How is she today?'

'Auntie Nina? Oh, she's fine, Mrs Markby.'

Meredith disappeared back to her piano tuner while Markby reflected that she had done an excellent job of introducing the subject he wanted to discuss with Josh, without raising any suspicions.

'It must be a bit lonely up there in Brocket's Row, for Mrs Pengelly, I mean. She's lucky to have you around some of the time. But there's—well,' Markby gave an apologetic smile, 'I was going to say there's not a lot going on up there. But there's been an awful lot going on! Normally, I meant, it must be very quiet.'

'She doesn't mind,' said Josh.

'I did meet one of your neighbours, Fred Stokes, when the police were searching up there the other evening. He recognised me from years back, when I was still professionally active. He assures me I never arrested him! He is rather annoyed about all the activity around the spinney, I understand, especially the artificial light at night.'

'Oh, you don't need to take any notice of Fred,' said Josh. 'He likes to grumble.'

'I understand Mrs Pengelly, Auntie Nina, takes him his midday meal every day. That's very good of her.'

'She likes looking after people,' explained Josh. 'And Fred eats

212

pretty well the same thing every day, so she doesn't have to think about it. He likes sausage and mash or cottage pie. Auntie Nina makes a good cottage pie. She makes a good steamed pudding, as well – syrup or dried fruit. But Fred doesn't eat that. He hardly eats anything at all, Auntie Nina reckons. He keeps going on cigarettes.'

'Yes, I heard he's a heavy smoker.'

'Always has been,' said Josh. 'That's what he does all day, smoke and watch the telly, until Mickey Wallace comes over to collect him and take him out to the pub for an hour. Auntie Nina says Fred ought to be dead, not eating, just smoking, never going out much or getting any fresh air. But he's tough, you see. He doesn't look it but he is.'

'He must have been a much bigger man once, years ago, when he drove the lorries,' Markby remarked.

Josh thought about this and nodded. 'When we were kids he was a big bloke, carried a lot of weight. He looked like a giant to Dilys and me. But he was always friendly to us. He used to walk off down into Bamford to the pubs every evening and back, never needed anyone to take him. It's a shame he lives like he does now, but it's how he wants it.'

The bench on which they were seated was opposite the door into the churchyard and now both of them were attracted by a rattle from that direction and stared across. The latch was moving up and down.

'Someone's trying to get in!' said Josh indignantly, rising to his feet.

At that moment, the door creaked open and a female form stepped through it into the garden.

'Tania Morris,' said Markby with a sigh. 'She's a reporter, Josh.'

'Well, she's got no right coming in like that, uninvited!' said Josh truculently. 'What does she report on?'

'Local news mainly, I suspect. In this case, that means the body in the spinney. Brace yourself, Josh.'

'She's not talking to me!' growled Josh.

But Ms Morris had spotted them and was marching confidently towards them with a beaming smile on her face. No wellington boots with daisy pattern today, noticed Markby. Today she wore knee-high suede boots with little tassels and a short jacket embroidered with some sort of braid. She looked, he thought, a bit like a hussar. He rose reluctantly to his feet to greet her.

'Just the person!' she hailed him cheerfully, as if they'd bumped into one another in the street and not in his vegetable garden.

'I don't know what's brought you, Ms Morris,' he returned. 'But I don't think I can be of any assistance to you.'

'Not you, Mr Markby! Although any chance of a chat is welcome. But this is the person I was hoping to see!' She pointed at Josh, who backed away with an expression of alarm. 'It is Josh Browning, isn't it?'

'I got nothing to say to you,' muttered Josh. 'What do you want me for, anyway?'

She had reached them now and seated herself uninvited on the bench. Josh shuffled a bit further away from her.

'Oh, come on, Josh. You must realise yours is a true human interest story! I've been checking on you. Readers will love it.' She smiled up at him encouragingly.

Markby could have told her she was wasting her time. 'I don't think he wants to talk to you, Tania,' he said. 'Kindly leave. If not, you'll be trespassing.'

'Only a civil offence, Alan,' she returned chummily. 'As I'm sure you know.' She turned her attention back to Josh. 'I called at your home,' she said, 'in Brocket's Row. Your landlady, Mrs Pengelly, said you were working in this garden today. I understand she used to be your foster mother? I'd really love to talk to you about your childhood – and your sister's. How the two of you found the body I mean,' she flowed on, disregarding Josh's manifest panic and Markby's rising ire, 'such a disadvantaged background makes wonderful copy. And then, finding a dead body! How old were you?'

'Nine,' muttered Josh, turning an appealing look on Markby.

'Gosh!' exclaimed Tania, producing a small recorder. 'Tell me how it happened.'

'Switch that off!' thundered Markby.

She was so surprised at his fury that she obeyed and sat looking at him, momentarily discountenanced.

'You are attempting to talk to an important witness. It's completely out of order. It's interfering in the investigation of a serious crime.'

She rallied. 'I don't think so. Anyhow, I'm after the background story, and that's not interfering with any enquiries that might be ongoing. Speaking of which,' she hurried on, changing tack and switching her attention to him. 'Why have the police been searching in the spinney again? What are they looking for?'

'If you want to talk about that, you'll have to talk to Inspector Barker,' he told her. 'Although I wouldn't advise it. And by the way, I don't want to see any more photos of myself in the daily press.'

'Oh, I don't need another photo of you,' she retorted. 'But I'd love one of you, Josh!'

Josh reacted as if he'd been stung. He dashed into the shed and shut the door. 'I'm not coming out!' they heard his muffled voice from within. 'I'm not coming out until she's gone!'

'My goodness,' said Tania, not a bit discouraged. 'He is shy, isn't he?'

'You heard him,' said Markby. 'He means it. So, off you go!'

'Oh, well,' she replied, still undeterred, 'I'll catch him somewhere else. It might be worth talking to Mrs Pengelly again.'

Through the shed door came a roar of anger. But it didn't bother Tania. She strode off across the garden, the tassels on her boots jiggling, and went through the door into the churchyard. She didn't close it. Markby got up with an exclamation of annoyance, and went to shut it. He caught a glimpse of her disappearing between the headstones. He returned to the shed and tapped on the door.

'You can come out, Josh. She's gone.'

Josh emerged, cautiously. 'I won't put up with her bothering Auntie Nina!'

'She wants a story, Josh, and she's determined. You'll have to watch out.'

'She hasn't met our Dilys,' muttered Josh. His forehead creased in a worried frown. 'Dilys is due out soon. If that reporter woman goes asking my sister for pictures and stories, Dilys will knock her flat. And if she does that, it will violate her probation and she'll go back inside!' He turned to Markby. 'So don't let her. Can't you stop her?'

Markby sighed. 'I'll have a word with Inspector Barker but I can't promise anything. However, she's not going to get her story here. If I drive over to the DIY superstore and buy a good, strong bolt, can you fix it on that door today? Just so we don't get any more surprises.'

'Sure,' said Josh. He scowled. 'She's got a bloody cheek, she has.'

Markby, who had never heard Josh use any kind of strong language, stared at him in surprise.

'Where are you calling from?' Caroline Malone asked.

'From the car park at the filling station. Has Pete left for work yet?'

'He drove off five minutes ago. What's all this about, Nick?' She was already beginning to sound exasperated.

'That Carter fellow came to see us yesterday,' Nick Ellsworth explained. 'He brought a red-haired woman with him, small, sharp-eyed, by the name of Campbell.'

'That's the woman he was dining with at the Wayfarer's Return,' Caroline said, thoughtfully. She regained her brusque tone. 'So? You knew they'd turn up. Did you let the twins loose on them?'

'What do you mean?' he replied, nettled. 'They're not Rottweilers!'

'As good as. I should think Dominic and Oliver would disrupt any police visit pretty efficiently!'

'Look here!' Nick rose to the defence of his offspring. 'They aren't that bad!'

'Yes, they are! Otherwise, you wouldn't leave home early and eat fry-ups for breakfast in the café at that filling station where you are now! I don't blame you for preferring to breakfast in peace. I'm not getting at you. At times like this, the twins must be very useful.'

'As it happened,' said Nick with dignity, 'the woman, Inspector Campbell, is herself a twin, and she was delighted to meet my sons.'

'Merry hell!' returned his cousin. 'Well, then, what did the intrepid sleuths have to say for themselves?'

'After Gordana took all the kids out to the churchyard . . .'

'The *churchyard*! What on earth for?'

'To see the squirrels! Listen, stop rabbiting on about my sons. I'm trying to tell you something.'

There was a pause. 'Go ahead,' Caroline invited. 'I'm not stopping you.'

'Well, Cassie made them coffee and they sat there and chatted. Caro, they seemed obsessed with the houses.'

'Which houses?'

'Your house and my parents' old house, the ones our grand-fathers built. They kept talking about the conservatory and the gardens.'

'So? Let them! Perhaps they are an item and they're house-hunting. What did you tell them?' Her voice sharpened.

'Nothing! Anyhow, they left *on foot.*'

'They must have had a car. Wasn't it parked out front at your place?'

'No! They'd obviously parked it somewhere else. They left on foot and were going in the direction of the church – and the churchyard. They were gone for ages, at least an hour. Then I saw them coming back, still on foot. What were they roaming around Weston for? Where had they been? I think they went to find Gordana and chat to her. Cassie says I'm paranoid.'

'I'm with Cassie on this one, Nick. Anyway, chat to Gordana about *what*?'

Nick drew in a long breath. 'Well, I don't know, do I? But Gordana snoops. Cassie says she doesn't, but I know she does. She was in the army, you know, back home, wherever home is.'

Caroline gave a hiss of exasperation. 'You really are the limit, Nick! I'm sure that nanny of yours wasn't ever in any army. That's your imagination going into free fall. Why are you so hysterical about all this? *What did you tell the police?*'

'Nothing! I just wish they'd stop hanging around – and that I knew what they're thinking!'

'Thinking, Nick, is your trouble!' she retorted unkindly. 'You never stop, and your imagination is totally uncontrolled, like I said. Pull yourself together! I mean it. If you carry on like this, the guys in the white coats will come for you. Go and have another coffee and a doughnut at that eatery where you are.'

'Got to get to work,' he replied gloomily.

'So, go to work. And listen, don't bother Pete! He's a bit fragile about all this.'

'Yes, I realise that, Caro. Pete . . . well, never mind. Speak to you later.'

When he'd cut the call, Caroline sat staring at her phone for some minutes.

But Peter Malone was not at work. He had been there briefly earlier, walking in through the door as usual, first thing, and greeting anyone he encountered, including Beth.

She handed him a sheet of paper as he walked past her. 'This is the seating plan for the eleven o'clock meeting in the boardroom. I've put name cards by each place and I'm organising coffee and sandwiches.'

'Great, Beth, thanks,' he mumbled, taking the diagram and entering his office without glancing at it. Moments later, he came out again. 'Beth? Who smokes?'

She stared at him in astonishment. 'In this building? No one. It's not allowed!' She sniffed. 'I can't smell any cigarette smoke!'

He waved a hand. 'No, I didn't mean that! I meant, do you know if anyone working here is a smoker when not here at work? Does anyone slip out now and again for a quick fix of tobacco?'

'I have no idea!' retorted Beth stiffly. 'The company encourages employees to take personal fitness very seriously.'

'Right, then,' he replied, 'I'll just step out and buy a pack somewhere – and go for a stroll alongside the canal for fifteen minutes. I need the fresh air.'

She was looking at him as if he'd suggested something so highly improper as to be criminal. 'You don't smoke,' she said firmly. 'I know you don't.'

'Well, I want a cigarette now, thanks!' he returned sharply. Seeing her face redden, he added, 'I'm under a bit of stress, Beth. If I'm to chair that eleven o'clock meeting, I need . . . I need to go for a walk and think things through.'

'Oh, all right,' she conceded, reluctantly. 'What do I tell anyone who asks where you are?'

'That I'll be back in half an hour. I've got my phone if it's an emergency.'

The call had come through to uniformed branch at three thirty, by which time not only had Malone missed the important eleven o'clock meeting, coffee and sandwiches provided, but he hadn't contacted his office and was not answering his phone. The constable who originally took the call inclined to the view that the missing man would return soon of his own accord.

'Got held up somewhere, I dare say,' he informed Beth. 'It's only a couple of hours, isn't it? Or perhaps he just forgot this meeting?'

'Mr Malone does not forget meetings entered in his diary. If there were the slightest possibility of his doing so, I am there to remind him!' snapped Beth.

'Lucky fellow. Well, he doesn't qualify as a missing person in our diaries until a couple of days have gone by. So, cheer up! He'll turn up.' The constable unadvisedly gave a chuckle he might have thought was reassuring.

He was talking to the wrong person. 'Nonsense!' stormed Beth. 'Mr Malone is a very responsible person! He wouldn't miss an important meeting without sending a message, at the very least. His car is still in the car park, so he can't have gone far. And he has his phone with him. But it's switched off. That's not normal!' Beth played her trump card. 'This isn't just an ordinary missing person, you know. Your Superintendent Carter came to see him the other day. I think it was something to do with an investigation. You ought to tell Superintendent Carter. I'm sure he would want to know.'

The constable assured her he would pass the report on to CID immediately.

'Well, be sure and make it straight away!' ordered Beth. 'Like now!'

Realising he'd been handed a hot potato, the constable did as bid. The news reached Jess, who phoned Malone's office immediately. 'No sign of him yet?'

'Not a thing! It's nearly five. I'm sure something's wrong.' Beth drew in a deep breath, lowered her voice and went on, dramatically, 'He asked me if I knew anyone who would have *cigarettes*. He doesn't smoke. The building is a smoke-free zone. No one here smokes.' In a whisper Jess had to strain to hear, Beth added, 'First of all, they were all shirty here because I rang the police. Well, it was a very important meeting and it had to go ahead without him, so they were all in a bad mood. It was really inconvenient. Then, when he didn't turn up, they sort of forgot me and got cross with him in his absence. Now, well, they're all getting a bit fidgety about it, muttering in corners.'

'OK, Beth. Leave it with me. Just to check, you've been trying his phone, I suppose?'

'It's still switched off,' said Beth gloomily. 'It shouldn't be. He doesn't switch it off when he's away from the office. I need to be able to get in touch with him, especially on an important day like today.'

'Has he perhaps gone home?' Jess asked. 'There could have been an emergency.'

'He would have let us know!' insisted Beth.

'Has anyone checked to see if his car is still in the car park?'

'Yes! Of course I checked! And it is!' Beth declared indignantly.

'Have you rung his house?'

At this Beth became suddenly less assertive. 'Well, you know, I wouldn't want to get him into any trouble – or upset his wife, or anything.'

Jess was beginning to get the feeling all was definitely not well. A nervous breakdown, perhaps? Everyone who knew Malone seemed to be worried that, with the discovery of the remains at Bamford, his former experience as a possible suspect in the disappearance of his girlfriend would be playing on his nerves. Nick Ellsworth had been very keen to stress that. She reassured Beth that they would start immediate enquiries, and then went to find Carter.

'Honestly,' she said, repeating Beth's account to him, 'I think

Beth was almost more worried that he might be a secret tobacco addict than that he'd just disappeared. But it sounds dodgy. He is acting out of character. Perhaps we should be concerned.'

Carter had received the news with evident displeasure. 'Blasted man. What's he playing at? You've told that PA, Beth, to let us know immediately if he turns up at the office?'

'Yes, but I don't think he will. It's got a bad feeling to it, Ian. This eleven o'clock meeting was an important one. If, for any reason, he couldn't make it, Beth insists he would let her know. I believe her. She called us on her own initiative. Not everyone in the firm is happy that she did.'

'She's got more sense than they have. Has anyone telephoned his house? Got in contact with his wife?'

'Frankly,' said Jess, 'I got the impression they are all a bit scared of his wife. Anyway, no one on his staff, or among his work colleagues, wants to spread panic.'

'No,' said Carter with a sigh. '*They* don't want to spread panic. They leave it to the police to do that.' He stood up. 'All right, come on, let's go and find Caroline Malone. If we're lucky, he's been crying into his beer in a pub somewhere and will show up at home, maudlin but intact. Or, if not, he may still have been in touch with his wife.'

Chapter 14

'What on earth do you want?' snapped Caroline Malone, opening the door to find Carter and Jess on her doorstep.

She was wearing another of those palazzo pants and silky top outfits, noted Jess. This one was in black and white, very striking but intimidating. Caroline's eyes sparkled with anger as she placed herself in the centre of the door opening, barring the way.

'You were here the day before yesterday, for pity's sake! Now what's brought you?'

'We are sorry to trouble you again, Mrs Malone,' Carter said courteously. 'But I wonder if we could have a word?'

'Pete – my husband – isn't here. He's at work. He does have to work, you know! If it's urgent, I'll ask him to call you when he gets home.'

'In fact, Mrs Malone, your husband isn't at work. He hasn't been in the office since a little after nine this morning. His PA contacted the local police, because he missed an important meeting and she had thought his manner strange. We're hoping you can help us locate him. I'm sorry if this is a shock.'

The colour had been draining from Caroline's face as he spoke and her usual confidence was evaporating. To Jess's eyes, she appeared to be dwindling physically. Just for a moment she looked like an image of a Pierrot in a black-and-white baggy costume, a marionette version, hanging limply and disjointed from the puppet-eer's strings.

She said very quietly, 'Nonsense!'

'Perhaps we could come in?' Jess prompted gently.

Caroline looked at her as if she'd never seen her before. Then she stood aside and gestured to them to enter.

As they followed her to the large room in which they'd talked on their previous visit, they heard a rattling noise from somewhere in the house, on the ground floor.

Caroline saw they'd heard it and her face flushed. 'That's not Pete, if you're thinking I've got him stashed somewhere where you can't get at him. It's Lenka, my weekly cleaner. This is her day.' This domestic detail served to help her regain some poise. 'She'll make us all tea. I'll go and tell her.'

She walked out quickly towards the sound of a vacuum cleaner that had just started up. The noise of the vacuum was abruptly switched off.

'Tea is a good idea,' Jess murmured. 'She may need it.'

Caroline was back in a few minutes, coming in with a brisk step, and apparently restored to her usual self. She held a mobile phone in her hand. 'Lenka will be here in a jiff. I'm sorry, I didn't ask you if you have a preference when it comes to tea.' She raised her eyebrows.

'However it comes,' Carter assured her.

She nodded. 'I drink herbal teas myself.' She gestured vaguely around her at the seating. 'Please, anywhere . . .'

They sat. There was a further rattling, this time heralding Lenka, who turned out to be a young woman with pink hair. She marched in briskly with the tray and plonked it down on a low glass-topped table. 'There you go!' she said. She eyed Carter and then Jess but added nothing more. They knew they'd been rumbled as police. Caroline had not needed to tell Lenka that. Lenka knew.

When this house was built, thought Jess with wry amusement, tea would have been brought in by a parlour maid in a black dress and white apron. Probably, that maid would have been just as quick to identify plain-clothes police officers.

Lenka had retreated to her vacuum cleaner. They could hear it buzzing in a muffled way through closed doors, like a very large bumblebee trapped against a windowpane. Caroline indicated her visitors should serve themselves. She put her phone down beside her and sat back on her white leather sofa, her bone china mug of herbal tea resting in her cupped hands. 'Now, then,' she said calmly. 'What's all this?'

'Perhaps,' Jess suggested, 'you might like to telephone your husband's office and check whether he's back.'

'I just have. He's not.' Caroline's tone was bleak.

'We understand from his PA, as Superintendent Carter explained earlier, that the meeting was scheduled for eleven o'clock.'

'Yes, yes,' Caroline said impatiently. 'Pete spoke about it this morning before he left. Beth says his car is still in the car park. He can't have gone very far. It's not like him to miss an important meeting, but there has to be an explanation. Have you tried the hospitals?'

Carter nodded. 'Not personally, but someone else has rung round. Yes, the car's still there. I've seen it there myself. Beth also tells us he asked her for cigarettes.'

Now Caroline couldn't control a start of surprise. 'Cigarettes?

What on earth for? He doesn't smoke – and it isn't allowed, anyway, in the building.'

She leaned forward, set down her tea and grabbed the phone beside her. 'Nick?' she asked them, as she scrolled down the stored numbers. 'Have you asked Nick Ellsworth?'

Carter was shaking his head as she was connected. 'Nick? Just a quick call to ask if you were in touch with Pete this morning. OK, what? Yes, if he rings you, call me – and ask him to call me. I don't know. The police are here. They say Pete walked out of his office and hasn't come back. His PA phoned them. She told them he was acting strangely. He wanted cigarettes. OK, thanks.'

She cut the call and sat back again. 'He hasn't been in touch with Nick.'

Jess said, 'As to the cigarettes, that could have been just an excuse to go out. When he discovered there were none to be had, he told Beth he would go out to buy some and walk by the canal for a few minutes, presumably to smoke a couple. It suggests he was stressed about something. Has he been worried?'

'Of all the stupid questions! Of course he's stressed!' Caroline burst out, eyes blazing. She turned her attention to Carter. 'You're hounding him again! Just as you hounded him twenty years ago! It's that wretched girl! Ever since she's turned up again—'

She broke off and Carter said mildly, 'Rebecca hasn't turned up again in person. Her remains have been found.'

'Dead or alive, she—' Caroline stopped, set down her mug of herbal brew and leaned forward. 'Listen to me, both of you! Pete is a kind man. He's always been a kind person. He rescued, if that's the word, Rebecca from Nick's party and persuaded me to bring her here, because he was sorry for her. Damsel in distress was a role she played very well. After that, she started clinging to him, her rescuer, her hero! He couldn't get rid of her and he was too kind to tell her outright he wasn't interested in her, not in the way she wanted.' Caroline heaved a sigh. 'Then she told him she was going to see her parents for the weekend, and none of us ever saw her again. But you lot were there immediately, weren't you?' She glared at Carter. 'Making out that Pete knew something he wasn't telling you! Suggesting—'

Carter broke in to defend himself. 'No investigating officer at the time suggested anything to Mr Malone.'

'Don't try and wriggle out of it!' she snapped. 'OK, you insinuated that he knew more than he was telling. He didn't! He'd told you all he could and you just wouldn't let go! He nearly cracked up over it. Ask Nick. He'll tell you.'

She leaned back against the sofa cushions, a study in black and white on a creamy white background. Like a still from a nineteen-forties film, thought Jess.

Quietly, Caroline went on, 'And all the time Rebecca had done what she'd told Pete she was going to do. She went home to that place, Bamford. And someone there killed her – or she had an accident – who knows? But someone buried her there and you've got her bones to prove it. But you still don't give up, do you? No, you're back here straight away asking your questions! And now – and now . . .' Her voice trailed away.

'We have to ask you,' Jess told her gently. 'Did he appear even *more* distressed this morning than he has been of late?'

'Of late?' She raised her head and stared at Jess. 'You mean, since the girl was found? He's been going downhill since that day . . .' She paused. 'But this morning, if you must know, he seemed more preoccupied with the meeting at eleven. I was quite pleased, actually, that he was only worrying about that – that he had something else on his mind. Anything to take his thoughts away from you and your precious investigation!'

The phone beside her on the sofa emitted a tuneful ringtone. She grabbed it, 'Oh, Cassie, hi. Yes, that's right. I thought he might have spoken to Nick. OK, right, well, if you should hear from him. Yes, they're still here.' The last words were accompanied by a glance towards the visitors. She cut the call.

'Cassie Ellsworth,' Caroline told them. 'Nick rang her in case . . . well, just on an off chance. Nick and Cassie, they've got a place at St Ives, Nick's parents' cottage. They go there for breaks and we've used it, too. But he hasn't been in touch with Cassie about it, and there's no landline link to the place.'

'We'll ask the Devon and Cornwall police to check it out. Have you got the address?'

Caroline stood up in silence and went out of the room. A few minutes later, she came back with a slip of paper. She handed it to Jess.

'Would you happen to have a key to this place?' Jess asked.

'No, it doesn't belong to us. But I know a neighbour down there has a key for emergencies. I don't know her name. Cassie will tell you, or she can give you a key.'

Jess went out of the room. In her absence, there was another awkward silence.

'What's she doing?' Caroline asked aggressively.

'Arranging the check on the cottage.'

Jess was back. 'They're checking now. Someone is asking Cassie Ellsworth for details of the neighbour with the key.' She leaned towards Caroline and added, sympathetically, 'We're doing our best to find him, and we will. Sometimes – if a person has a breakdown – he, or she, just goes away somewhere, to be alone. Quite often, the missing person comes back after a couple of days. Sometimes they book into a hotel room. Or they go to a holiday property, like the place in St Ives. In normal circumstances, we don't consider an adult to be a missing person unless they've been gone at least forty-eight hours.'

'Not Pete!' Caroline told them firmly. 'He doesn't do this, doesn't just take off and not let anyone know where he's going. His office needs to be able to find him. The business is international; financial information comes in at all hours from around the world. He always lets me know if he's going to be even half an hour late. Now I don't know where he is.'

If she was aware this contradicted her previous insistence that there must be a simple explanation for Malone's disappearance, she didn't seem aware of it. The energy had seeped out of her again. Caroline's head was bent. She didn't look up but asked, through a mane of fair hair that had slipped loose from the hairpins, 'The canal. He told Beth he was going for a walk. Are you looking . . . are you looking along the bank?'

'Even as we sit here,' Carter assured her.

'Find him!' she said bleakly.

On their return, Carter and Jess found Sergeant Phil Morton waiting for them. He looked like the bearer of bad news. This wasn't necessarily the case, as Morton's normal expression wasn't cheery. But at the moment, he looked gloomier than usual.

'A Mr Nicolas Ellsworth rang to speak to you, sir. He's very upset. He says, can you call him back straight away? He's at work but I've got the number for his direct line.'

'OK, I'll call him now.' To Jess, Carter added, 'What's the betting he hasn't anything useful to tell us but he's keen to remind us that, whatever is going on, it's all our fault. Correction, all *my* fault!'

Carter braced himself as he waited for the connection.

'What's all this about Pete being missing?' Ellsworth's voice, in his ear, jangled with emotion. 'How the hell can he be missing? Caroline – his wife, my cousin – she's going out of her mind!'

'He walked out of his office early today. It's not been possible to contact him.'

At the other end of the phone, Ellsworth's breathing was so laboured that Carter began to fear the man might be having some kind of attack. 'Listen!' Ellsworth croaked.

'I'm listening, Mr Ellsworth.'

'Pete rang me late last night. We were going to bed. I've not told Caroline about this, because Pete asked me not to. He was calling from his garden, all very secretive and odd. He didn't make a lot of sense. When Caroline called me earlier – while you were at her house – I still didn't mention it to her, because I don't know what's going on and I don't want to make a problem for Peter. Frankly, Carter, I think the poor bloke is going out of his mind. *I warned you*, Superintendent, when you were at my house. I warned you Pete was taking all this very badly. He's like a lot of these intellectually very clever guys. He finds day-to-day problems a bit difficult to handle.'

Carter, heroically, forbore to remind the speaker that Peter Malone wasn't the one who fled his home every morning to eat breakfast at a filling station diner. But his expression, when he put down the phone, rivalled Morton's for pessimism.

He looked at Jess and said, 'The signs aren't good. Apparently, Malone was hiding in his own garden late last night, making an incoherent phone call to Ellsworth and swearing him to secrecy. Ellsworth's opinion, for what it's worth, is that Malone is going quietly crackers . . .' He paused. 'We're going to have to hope he's not.'

'He'll turn up,' said Jess encouragingly.

'When Rebecca went missing, twenty years passed before she reappeared. Let's hope it doesn't take Malone that long!'

It didn't take twenty years. A canoeist found Malone's body in the canal that evening as the light was failing. The area had been cordoned off when Carter arrived; sightseers were being chivvied away by a couple of uniformed officers.

'Member of the public who found the body is over there, sir,' Carter was told.

He ducked under the tape and made his way to the spot.

'I wasn't sure that was what it was!' declared the unlucky canoeist. A very young man and probably unused to sudden or unnatural death, he was seated on the bank, wrapped in a thermal blanket. Someone had given him a plastic cup of tea. His pale face peered up at Carter, the emergency lighting that had been set up lending his features an eerie sheen. 'I was on my way back, it was getting too dark – and suddenly there was this hump in the water. I thought it was a sack of rubbish. I was pretty angry, because a thing like that could sink a canoe. I gave it a push with my paddle and it bobbed up and down and I saw – I saw a head.'

His features twitched and he fought to control them. Carter guessed he wasn't far off bursting into tears. 'I mean, the . . . the shape, the hump, it was bobbing up and down and suddenly rolled sideways and . . . I saw a face . . . his eyes were open. He was looking at me as though I could help him! But I couldn't . . .' His body shook and the undrunk tea slopped out of the cup.

Carter made his way to the canvas tent erected over the body, which had been laid out on the ground. Huddled in the tent he found the doctor, an older man, hunched over the sad sight, and another constable.

'Looks like a straightforward suicide,' said the doctor, glancing up, as the newcomer squeezed in. 'He even filled his pockets with stones, in the old-fashioned way of people who want to drown themselves. Don't see that so much, these days.'

He flashed a torch on to the dead face. Carter looked down on Malone in sick recognition. Death has a way of smoothing out stress and the signs of ageing. He was looking down at that angel again, the one on the fresco, trumpeting a message upward into the heavens; the young man he'd met twenty years earlier.

'Put the stones in an evidence bag,' he ordered.

The constable moved to obey. Then he asked, 'This, too, sir?' and he held out his hand. On the palm lay a sodden packet of cigarettes.

'Did he smoke any?' asked Carter dully.

The constable eased open the top of the box. 'Looks like he only smoked one, sir.'

'Steadying his nerves,' said the doctor in a matter-of-fact way. 'Poor devil,' he added, with more compassion.

'Not devil,' Carter muttered, 'angel . . .'

But the doctor and the constable didn't understand and looked at him in puzzlement.

'I should have seen it coming!' Carter muttered. 'Ellsworth warned me. He told me how distressed Malone was about being questioned again. I should have realised.'

He was slumped on Jess's sofa. She wished she'd had something stronger to give him than a glass of cheap white wine. But her drinks cabinet didn't run to brandy or whisky. There was barely enough wine left in the bottle to top up his glass. But she could do her best to stop him sinking into melancholy.

'Nonsense!' she said briskly. 'How? He was a grown man, not a teenager full of angst. OK, when you interviewed him twenty years ago he might have been vulnerable. But not now! He worked in the financial world. For that you need good nerves, or so I've always understood.'

'Tell that to his wife! She – and that cousin of hers – are threatening to make an official complaint. I'll be taken off the case.'

'How can they make out you harassed him? You interviewed him once, very briefly, at his office, and we called on him together, once, at his house. And when we were at his house, his wife was with him. He wasn't on his own. It wasn't like one of those old cops and robbers movies, where the police gang up on a suspect in a bare room, lit by a single unshaded bulb, threatening to rough him up!'

'All right,' mumbled Carter into his wine glass. 'You know that. I know that. But the widow and the old friend are breathing vengeance. They want blood – mine!'

'Of course,' Jess went on mildly, 'there is another possible explanation why Malone jumped into the canal. Some people might say it's an obvious reason. Let's suppose he killed Rebecca, twenty years ago. He drove the body to Bamford in an attempt to make it look, if she were ever found, as if she had gone home. He was lucky, or thought himself lucky, because the body wasn't found. Don't forget, Malone was the person who kept insisting, from the very first, that she'd gone home to visit her parents that weekend. No one else has come forward to corroborate that. Alan Markby found no trace of her – and I know, from my experience working with him, how thorough he was! Now the body *has* been found, and the police are back on the case. Malone had thought he was safe. Now he knew he wasn't. Is it any wonder that he cracked up?'

Carter leaned back, cradling the empty wine glass in his hands, 'So, how are we going to prove that now? If it is the reason.'

'Do you think he killed her?' Jess asked him quietly. 'Or did you suspect it, twenty years ago?'

He smiled tiredly. 'I didn't know twenty years ago, and I'm beginning to fear that now I'll never know.' There was a silence, then he added, 'Oh, well, if I'm suspended on sick leave pending enquiries, it will at least give me time to go and visit my daughter.'

'No one is going to charge you with breaking any kind of rule regarding interviewees, not while I've got anything to do with it!' said Jess fiercely.

He looked at her in surprise.

Chapter 15

Nina Pengelly studied the plate with the meat pie, gravy, mash and carrots, and wondered whether, if she added a couple of sprigs of broccoli, Fred would eat them. Fred was difficult about greens. Really, she thought crossly, it was worse than trying to feed a child. That reminded her of when Josh and Dilys were small and first came to live with her. They wouldn't eat anything green, either. Josh was all right now, easy to feed. Nina did wonder how they'd get on if Dilys came back, when they let her out of prison.

'Still,' she said aloud, addressing Bobby who was perched nearby, 'after prison food, I dare say she won't be picky.'

She placed a tea cloth over the tray and turned her attention back to the bird. 'You've got to go back into your cage, so be a good boy,' she told him. 'I'm going to be opening the front door and we can't risk you flying out, can we? The other birds would kill you. Come along.'

She walked into the sitting room and Bobby flew after her. She stood by his cage and indicated the open door. 'Come on, now.'

He hopped from chair back to chair back and then, obligingly, flew into the cage and on to his swing.

'I won't be long,' Nina told him, shutting the door carefully.

She went back to the kitchen to retrieve the tray and set off down Brocket's Row towards Fred Stokes's home. It was a nice day, she thought, not too hot and a pleasant light wind. Up here, at the top of the hill, it could get pretty gusty and when it rained, my, you really knew it. But today . . .' She paused and sniffed. There was a funny smell in the air. It didn't come from the dinner on the tray, that was for sure!

Nina stood, looking around her, scenting the breeze like an animal. She walked on a few steps. The smell – a horrible, acrid smell – was getting stronger. It was getting more pungent the nearer she got to Fred's house.

Nina began to run and then, because it was difficult to do that and not drop the tray, she stopped to place the tray on the ground and hurried on without it. There was no one at home in any of the houses between hers and Fred's, she knew that. They all went out to work. Whatever it was, it had to be caused by something at Fred's!

She had reached the house. She ran up to the front window and peered in, hoping to see him sitting in his armchair in front of the telly, waiting for her to bring in his dinner as she always did. But she couldn't see anything. Had he closed the curtains? No, the obstacle to seeing into the room didn't come from curtains. Had she suddenly gone blind? No, she could see all around her quite clearly. But the window was totally opaque. Behind the glass was a swirling black mass.

Nina ran to the front and scrabbled at the letter box for the key on a string behind it. She should have brought her own key. She'd had Fred's key for years but she'd got into the habit of using the key that hung behind the door. Her fingers touched the string and she hauled out the key, fitting it to the lock with fingers made clumsy by panic. In her mind she was delivering a tirade of accusation and blame targeted at her neighbour. Silly old fool! How many times had she told him about smoking so much and being so careless when putting the lit cigarettes down? It was nothing short of a miracle that he hadn't caused a fire before now!

The door opened and a great mass of black smoke billowed out and enveloped her. She started coughing and spluttering as it entered her chest and stung her eyes, making them water. She rubbed at them, determined to keep them open, and managed to call his name. 'Fred? *Fred!*'

But that was a waste of time. Nina ran back to where she'd abandoned the tray and snatched the cloth from it. Folding it into a triangle, she tied it over her face and ran back. She still couldn't see inside the house through the smoke. As fast as it billowed out through the open front door, fresh clouds of dark grey poured into the hall from the living room. Drawing breath was well-nigh impossible, but the poor visibility didn't trouble her, because she knew her way. She ran her hand along the wall and advanced down the hallway until she found the opening into the room where Fred must be. She was trying to hold her breath and knew she couldn't hold it much longer.

The open front door meant the hall now acted like a flue. The smoke was drawn out along it and rolled in great clouds into the open air. For a moment or two it thinned indoors and allowed her to make out the shape of the chair and the form huddled in it. She grasped his jacket and hauled him on to the floor. He fell like a rag doll, unconscious. Kneeling beside him, she leaned across his inert form to grab his wrists and her fingers knocked against a bottle lying on the floor. It was square and flat – a whisky bottle, she thought. Who bought him that? Then she began to scramble backwards, dragging the inert Fred Stokes with her. There was no weight to him. But, even down here at floor level, it was so difficult to catch any breath that she doubted they'd make it into the hall.

When she did manage it, she found dragging her load was even more difficult because the hall was narrow and Fred had to be manoeuvred through the doorway and turned at an angle to face the front door. Afterwards, she could never work out quite how she did it. All she did remember was that, as she continued hauling Fred along with her, there was a crackling sound from the room they'd left and a sudden bright red-and-yellow flame leapt up and flickered through the doorway and into the hall. Her ears were filled with a roaring noise and the crash of something exploding, probably the television set. Nina knew she couldn't pull Fred along much further. She realised he might be dead. But it wasn't in her nature to abandon him, even though the fire was gaining strength in the room they'd left. She'd die here with him, in the hallway.

And then salvation came in the form of someone else. Another person was there, incredibly. Someone had pushed through the smoke and had grabbed Nina and was tugging at her. Nina thought that the would-be rescuer probably didn't realise that she, in turn, was gripping Fred – and she couldn't tell them. But the rescuer was strong and determined. Nina, still linked to Fred, was hauled along the hall, through the door, a painful exit over the step, and out into the front garden. Here it was still smoky but there was enough air to take a painful breath. Nina began to cough. Her chest hurt, her throat felt as though someone had sandpapered it, but she was breathing. Someone else was shouting, a woman's voice. She thought she heard the voice shout 'fire' and 'ambulance' but, still holding Fred's wrists, Nina drifted into unconsciousness.

Then they all came at once, or it seemed as if they all came at once: the fire engine and an ambulance and a police car and another car carrying Mr and Mrs Markby and Josh. The noise they all made brought her back to consciousness, and there were people all over the place in all different sorts of uniforms. There were paramedics kneeling beside her, and she tried to tell them not to bother about her, to go and see to Fred. She was all right. But her voice wouldn't come out properly and she couldn't make them understand.

One of the paramedics pointed to a young woman, and told her that she was her rescuer. Apparently, after calling the emergency services, the same girl managed to get a message to Mr Markby to tell Josh what had happened – because, somehow, the girl knew Josh was working at the Markbys' house. So Markby told his wife as well, and they all turned up.

Josh was kneeling beside her and shouting, *'Auntie Nina!'*

She wanted to tell him she was all right, but she couldn't. In any case, she had no time to worry or puzzle over it further because, just after that, she passed out again and didn't come to until she was in the hospital.

'That was some tight hold you had on old Fred,' said Josh. 'We couldn't get you to let go of his wrists.'

Nina was propped up in a hospital bed with an oxygen mask over her face. She raised a hand to scrabble at the mask and managed to lift it enough to ask, 'Fred?' Her voice sounded, to her own ears, like the low growl of an angry tomcat. That would never do. She must speak better than that!

'He didn't make it, Auntie Nina,' Josh told her. 'I'm really sorry.'

Nina made a gesture of resignation, then scrabbled at the mask again. 'Girl?' she croaked. The sound was better than the growl, but not much.

'Who got you out?' Josh was good at guessing what she meant. 'Her name is Tania Morris and she's a newspaper reporter. She was on her way to interview you. I'd already told her she was to leave you alone. But it's just as well she didn't take any notice of me!' Josh gave a wry grin. 'She saw the smoke coming out of Fred's door and ran over to see what it was. She could just make out the shape of your body lying in the hallway, so she pulled you out – and Fred, too. She's a big, strong girl,' added Josh, approvingly.

'Fire?' whispered Nina. The whisper sounded more human than either of the sounds she'd produced before.

'You mustn't try and talk, Nina,' said a nurse, appearing by the bed.

'I'll talk to her,' said Josh firmly. 'She doesn't need to talk to me. I know what she wants to ask.' He turned his attention back to Nina. 'Fred, the silly beggar, must have dozed off sitting in that old chair while he was smoking, and the cigarette came into contact with the horsehair stuffing. The fire people told us that horsehair stuffing in very old furniture is one of the worst things for making that kind of smoke. He was probably asleep when the fire started. Perhaps he didn't even know. Just inhaled the smoke and . . . went.'

241

Nina made a square shape with her hands. 'Bottle.'

Josh frowned. 'What bottle?'

'Whisky!' croaked Nina.

'You want me to bring you in some whisky?' Josh was genuinely shocked. 'I've never seen you drink anything but a glass of sherry at Christmas! Anyway, they wouldn't allow it here!'

At this Nina looked so furious that she didn't need to try and speak. Josh got the message.

'You don't mean for you. OK, sorry! Who for, then?'

Nina stretched out a hand for the glass of water by her bed. Josh handed it to her and she sipped it carefully, before handing it back to him. Josh replaced it and waited.

'Fred,' wheezed Nina. 'Fred had a bottle of whisky.'

'Someone must have given it to him,' said Josh. He frowned. 'Mickey, perhaps? I don't know why he'd do that. Fred was a beer drinker. Always empty beer cans lying around the place. I collect . . . I used to go over there and collect them up when the recycling bins were due to be put out, and put them in the right one. I never saw a bottle of whisky. Well, if he had one and drank it all, no wonder he went to sleep so soundly. A blessing, I suppose, if he never knew anything about it.'

Nina steepled her hands like a roof.

'Oh, his house is burnt out pretty much altogether,' Josh told her. 'Downstairs everything's gone and upstairs isn't safe. The house next door got a bit of damage. All the other houses are all right. But the Council's sent people up to look at them all. We'll have to keep an eye on that. But don't you worry about that now.'

Nina flapped her hands to either side of her.

'Oh, you don't have to worry about Bobby!' exclaimed Josh.

'He's all right. I'm looking after him.' He leaned forward. 'Police and firemen said you were very brave, Auntie Nina. They said you were a heroine . . .' Josh paused. 'But I knew you were a heroine, anyway, before that, because you took on Dilys and me when we were kids.' Josh reached out and took her hand in his massive paw. 'I was really scared I'd lost you, Auntie Nina. It gave me the fright of my life when I saw you lying on the ground and the paramedics all round you.'

Nina patted his arm with her free hand and then drew a 'D' in the air with her forefinger.

'Yes, well,' Josh went on, a little awkwardly. 'I thought it best not to send a message to Dilys. Not just yet. She might, you know, freak out like she does.' He drew a deep breath. 'Dilys'll be out soon and she needs an address – or else they'll put her in one of their hostels, and she doesn't want that. So, would it be all right if she came back to Brocket's Row for a bit?'

At that Nina dragged down the oxygen mask and croaked indignantly, 'Of course it is! It's her home!'

By the time Meredith came to the hospital to visit her the following day, Nina Pengelly was dressed and sitting in a chair beside her bed. Meredith was glad to see she was managing without the oxygen mask Josh had described and her voice, though very hoarse, sounded human, at least.

'Awful squawks I was making yesterday!' she informed Meredith huskily. She leaned forward. 'I wanted to go home today but they want me to stay until tomorrow.'

'It's probably a good idea,' Meredith told her. 'They've got to be sure your lungs aren't damaged.'

'They're a bit sore, when I breathe,' said Nina, 'but you'd expect that, wouldn't you? I'm not going to get better any quicker sitting here than I would at home. Hospitals are very unhealthy places.' She frowned and took a few wheezy breaths. 'That girl what pulled Fred and me out – they didn't keep her in. They checked her over and let her go home. Said she should come back if she felt bad. Why couldn't they do the same for me?' She reached for a glass of water on the bedside cabinet and took a long drink.

'I'm sure,' said Meredith firmly, 'that Josh would be happier knowing you're under medical supervision for the next few hours. It won't be long, and you'll soon be back in Brocket's Row.'

'Josh says the Council's looking at all the houses. There's nothing wrong with mine!' Nina's voice grew louder with agitation and she was overtaken by a burst of coughing.

'You see?' said Meredith, when Nina was silent again, panting and taking swigs of water in between breaths. 'It's best you stay another night here. Take the opportunity for a good rest. I'm sure you need one after all your exertions yesterday. I'm very sorry about poor old Fred. Especially after you tried so hard to save him.'

Nina leaned forward and gripped Meredith's arm. 'Listen, Mrs Markby, there was an empty whisky bottle by his chair. I felt it with my fingers when I was on the floor, trying to grab hold of Fred. One of those flat half-bottles with a square shape, you know?'

'Yes, I know. Not surprising, then, that he fell asleep so soundly.'

'No, no!' Nina insisted in gravelly tones. 'You don't understand. He never had whisky. Josh took out the empties to the bins, and any other rubbish. Josh never saw a whisky bottle. Fred was always a beer drinker. He had the supermarket deliver it to the door. I told him it was downright embarrassing, having booze brought to the house. But he'd just say, well, he couldn't carry it. He used to grumble about the charge, mind you. He never had anything else delivered. I bought enough food for him as well, when I shopped for me and Josh. Fred paid me a little bit weekly to cover his share. He only had a pension. He had no money to buy something that cost as much as whisky!' She had released Meredith's arm. 'Someone must've bought it for him.' Nina drew a very long, wheezy breath. 'Can't talk any more, dear. Thanks for coming to see me.' She waved a hand towards the door and added, 'Tell your husband about the whisky bottle. It's not right.'

'I will,' promised Meredith.

'I suppose,' Markby said, 'that his pal Mickey Wallace could have bought it for him. Nobody else would. Nina Pengelly wouldn't.'

'She's very worried about it.'

Alan shrugged. 'Well, I'll mention it to Trevor Barker. But if someone was kind enough to buy the poor old devil a present . . .'

'A present that killed him!' said Meredith fiercely.

'If he'd drunk enough beer, he'd have gone to sleep very soundly,' Alan pointed out.

'Perhaps,' said his wife, unconvinced. 'But Nina says to check with Josh. Josh used to carry out Fred's household rubbish and recyclables to the bins every week. Josh never saw a whisky bottle, ever.'

'Well, Nina didn't *see* one, either, did she? Not in all that smoke. Her fingers touched the shape on the carpet and she judged it to be an empty whisky bottle . . .' He paused. 'Anyway, there will be a post mortem. They'll carry out tests.'

'If there was a whisky bottle,' Meredith insisted, 'it should still be there in the ashes and rubble from the fire. Trevor should ask the fire service investigators. The coroner likes to know all that sort of thing, doesn't he?'

Chapter 16

'I've come to see you, Trevor,' Markby told him, apologetically, 'because my wife isn't going to let it go. I admit that it does seem a bit odd to me, too. You don't happen to know the result of the fire service investigation, do you? Of course, I understand that you really can't tell me details ahead of the inquest. But if they found something suspicious, something they'd request police help with . . .'

'Well, as it happens, I can tell you,' Barker told him, 'because the fire investigator has been in touch – and also the hospital path lab. Anyway, you are involved in the reinvestigation of the Hellington case and it may well impinge on that. Yes, there was a glass whisky bottle and it was recovered from the scene of the fire. Because it was a flat bottle – some people call it a flask – the side in contact with the floor was protected from the smoke, and also from water and anything used in extinguishing the fire. Fingerprints, or partial prints, have been recovered. Some are Fred's. Some belong to a person unknown. Of course, they could belong to a till operator in the supermarket where the whisky was most likely purchased. But there are also a couple of good prints on it, and some partials, that do match prints on record.'

'Let me guess,' said Markby. 'Mickey Wallace? Why are his prints on record?'

'Yes, Wallace's prints. They only show he handled the flask and was most probably the person who gave it to Fred. The reason his prints are on record is that Mr Wallace is one of those people – I can never understand them – who have a liking for exotic pets, reptiles mostly. He and Mrs Wallace took a cruise in the Caribbean. It stopped, among other places, at Dominica. There Mr Wallace illegally acquired an iguana. To be exact, a species called the Lesser Antillean iguana. It's very rare, threatened, and doesn't breed well in captivity. How he managed to hide the creature while he was on the ship, goodness only knows. But he was caught trying to smuggle it back into Britain. It wasn't the first time he'd been nabbed. A couple of years before that, he drove back from Spain with three small tortoises hidden in a suitcase. He'd reckoned to sell them for a couple of hundred pounds apiece. We suspect he'd done it before and got away with it. So, we have Mr Wallace on record as a small-time but regular smuggler in that line of trade.'

'So, he most probably bought and gave the whisky to Fred.'

'There is something else . . .' Barker paused. 'You'll have to keep this to yourself for a bit. The post-mortem tests have shown that Fred had drunk a lot of alcohol, yes. But he'd also ingested a lot of a common medication prescribed for sleeplessness. The old combination of booze and sleeping pills.'

'Sleeping pills? Had he been prescribed them by a doctor?'

'No, but there are a lot of them out there and if someone really wants to get hold of some, well, it wouldn't be impossible. The main thing is . . .' Barker hesitated, 'tests are still continuing on the empty flask, not just the exterior, but also the interior. It does begin to look as if the pills were crushed up and added to the whisky in the bottle.'

There was a silence. Then Markby broke it, asking, 'Are we talking suicide?'

'Possibly, but at my own meeting with Stokes, I found him a tough old fellow, cantankerous and bloody-minded I wouldn't have judged him suicidal . . .' Barker paused. 'His life was limited by his health and mobility problems, but I don't think he was the sort to brood on that. Mrs Pengelly brought him a hot meal every day. His mate, Mickey Wallace, took him out to the pub two or three times a week. Otherwise, he didn't like people very much. He refused to have a carer. His lifestyle suited him fine. The only thing that was upsetting him of late was the excavation carried out in the spinney and the discovery of the remains.'

'I see . . .' Markby said softly. 'So, are we talking here about Stokes being at least one of the people who buried Rebecca? For twenty years he'd got away with it, and then . . .'

'And then we dug her up,' said Barker.

'It would answer one big question,' Markby mused. 'What happened to the body Josh and Dilys found? How come, when Josh returned a couple of days later, it had disappeared? Answer, Fred and possibly someone else had buried it. Dilys remembers smelling cigarette smoke in the spinney the day they found Rebecca. Fred, as we know, had always been a heavy smoker with the sad but probably inevitable results!'

'Oh, but the old boy didn't start the fire,' Barker said immediately. 'The horsehair-stuffed chair had starting burning, but the fire was started at the back of the house – in the area you might like to call a kitchen, although he never made more than a cup of tea there.'

Markby stared at him. 'Is that certain?'

'Oh, yes. I dare say,' Barker went on, 'we were supposed to think that Fred's smoking habit was the cause. But the fire service investigator is quite clear on this point. At the back of the house, the window into the kitchen area had recently been forced and something like a Molotov cocktail had been thrown in. You know the sort of thing, petrol in a bottle with a lighted rag stuffed into the top? It burned away for some time in the kitchen area, on the floor where it landed. The kitchen floor was covered with ceramic tiles. They're not flammable, but some flames did reach a wooden storage cabinet. That would have burned slowly for some time before bursting into flame. Because the furnishings in the downstairs area had been stripped to the minimum, and there wasn't any carpeting down – to facilitate Fred's wheelchair moving around – the fire could well have been contained in the kitchen area. It did spread, but relatively slowly, along skirting boards, other paintwork and various items of rubbish, like empty boxes, lying around. It only really got going late in the day, after it had reached the front of the house where Fred had a little more furniture and his television.

'Had he been alive, there would have been plenty of time for him to raise the alarm. But he was already dead, we now know. The investigator's opinion is that the petrol bomb was tossed in around two hours before Nina Pengelly came to the front of the house with the old chap's dinner.'

Markby considered this for some minutes while Barker waited, watching him closely.

Markby said at last, softly, 'The booze and pills should have killed him – did kill him – so why bother to set a fire? And set it so incompetently?'

'If you ask me,' said Barker, 'whoever gave him the spiked whisky then panicked and decided to try and cover the real cause of death, hoping that the body would be burned.'

'It's got to have to do with the burial of Rebecca Hellington and the discovery of her skeleton!' Markby said firmly. 'There is no other reason why anyone would want to go to such lengths to kill someone like Fred Stokes. He was disagreeable but harmless! However you look at it, Trevor, the fact is that Stokes and Wallace are the prime candidates for burying the body. They thought they'd got away with it. But now Rebecca's been found and they started to panic. Wallace is the younger man, and the way he'd see it is, he has more to lose, half a lifetime. I don't know whether either of them killed her, but I am pretty sure they both buried her. Stokes was over eighty. You'd been to interview him at his house once already. Wallace couldn't rely on him not to crack. If he confessed to the burial, then perhaps they would also be charged with abduction or even murder. Wallace couldn't be sure. Fred had to be taken out of the equation.'

Barker decided to act as devil's advocate. 'All right, in theory, the more you think about it, the more obvious it seems that Wallace and Stokes are the most likely pair to have buried the girl. Stokes drove a lorry. Perhaps he picked her up. Her father says she didn't hitch-hike, but perhaps on that one occasion she did. On the other hand, Stokes told me that, around the time she disappeared, he'd given up driving due to an injury. We couldn't reasonably expect him to produce a twenty-year-old work schedule, showing where he was on a particular day . . .'

He paused, before continuing. 'There's quite an age difference between Wallace and Stokes,' he added. 'Were they friends, back then? Would Stokes involve Wallace in this sort of caper? Oh, and by the way, Dilys now claims to remember smelling cigarette smoke in the spinney, but the twenty-year-old memory of someone who was then eight years old isn't going to carry much weight in court!'

'We – you – won't get any further,' Markby pointed out, 'until you go and see Wallace and hear what he's got to say.'

'All right,' agreed Barker. 'I'll pay a social call on the man. As of this moment, he hasn't done anything criminal that we can prove – at least, not in this matter. It's a big jump from smuggling tropical pets to arson. Do you want to come along?'

Wallace, they discovered, lived in a street lined either side with Edwardian brick terraced houses of the sort that had started out as homes for upwardly mobile tradespeople and clerical workers. The street had gone down socially but was still clinging, here and there, to its former respectability. In some places efforts were being made to reverse the decline. Some houses, perhaps the first homes of younger couples, had fashionable blinds. On the other hand, some, perhaps rented or even squats, had lace curtains varying between dingy and torn. Some woodwork hadn't been painted in years. Some was painted in alarming colours – fire station red or a bilious lilac.

Wallace's door and window frames were egg-yolk yellow. Almost every house had a vehicle parked outside it. Outside Wallace's home stood his white van.

'Well, at least he's in!' said Barker, adding mistrustfully, 'What's the betting he's got a pit bull terrier?'

'He's not going to set it on the police, Trevor,' said Markby.

'You hope!'

Wallace was, indeed, at home – and he wasn't alone. The door was opened to reveal not a snarling pit bull terrier but an equally fierce-looking woman with improbably orange hair, wearing a tight black sweater and purple leggings.

'Who are you?' she demanded, suspiciously, looking from one to the other. She had large gold-coloured earrings hanging from her ears and the loops bounced around as she moved her head.

'Police,' said Barker briskly, producing his ID.

'What do you want?' was her next question.

'We'd like a word with Mr Wallace. Is he at home?'

This question was answered by a shout from the rear of the house. 'Who is it, Samantha?'

'Coppers,' shouted back Samantha. She eyed them again, concentrating on Markby whom she subjected to detailed scrutiny. 'And one of them is getting on a bit.'

'What do they want?'

'To speak to you!' yelled Samantha over her shoulder, earrings swinging madly. She turned back to the visitors. 'They're all legal.'

'What are?' asked Barker.

'His pets. I know he was daft enough, two or three years ago, to try and bring in that lizard thing. It was only because a bloke had it in a sack and come up to us in the street to ask if we were interested. I told Mickey at the time, don't touch it. He couldn't resist it, of course. But everything he's got now is legal.'

'Bring them inside, then, don't stand telling the entire street our business!' came a roar.

Samantha stood aside to allow the two visitors to enter and slammed the door behind them.

'He's in the back. Go through!' she snapped. She stamped up the stairs on platform soles and left them to find their way.

They found Wallace sitting in a crowded room full of glass tanks. The room seemed overheated, and the tanks supplied the reason.

'Snakes!' exclaimed Barker in undisguised horror. 'I should have expected it!'

'It's my hobby!' said Wallace. 'And you know it, don't you? All that fuss they made over the iguana I brought back from my holidays, and them little tortoises before that. Anyhow, all this lot is legal, like my wife was telling you – and telling the whole street.'

He was slumped in a chair, clad in a turquoise-and-yellow shell suit, and clasping an opened can of lager. He didn't rise to greet them. His small dark eyes surveyed them beadily, moving from one visitor to the other.

'Do you ever let them out?' asked Barker, giving each tank a quick check to make sure it held its occupant.

'Not often. Some of them move pretty quick,' said Wallace. 'Sit down, if you want. What's it about, then?'

'You've heard, I expect, about the fire at Fred Stokes's home?' Barker asked, taking a chair furthest from a tank. 'You know Mr Stokes has died.'

'Of course I know!' Wallace sipped from the can. 'He was an old mate of mine. I'll miss him.'

'He'd apparently drunk a whole half-bottle of whisky and fallen asleep in his armchair.'

'Daft old bugger,' said Wallace.

'Did you buy the whisky for him, by any chance, Mickey?'

'Why should I?'

'Your fingerprints are on the bottle.'

254

The room had gone quiet. Even the reptiles appeared to be paying close attention. Snakes can't hear in the way mammals do, Markby seemed to recall from school biology lessons. They don't have ears. They go by vibrations in the bones in their heads, or something of that sort. And they may have poor eyesight but they have an excellent sense of smell.

Policemen also learn to substitute one sense for another, he thought wryly. When words aren't spoken, they pick up other signals. He was picking them up now. Wallace was deeply shocked. His broad, stolid face didn't show it. The dark eyes were still. The hand holding the beer can didn't quiver. The turquoise shell suit was still slumped in an ungainly way, like a collapsed bell tent. He hadn't moved. But he'd begun to sweat. Markby could smell it. Wallace was reeling. He hadn't been expecting to see the police in his home so soon after the death of Stokes. The man shifted his considerable bulk in the chair. Markby thought that the shell suit did him no favours.

'So what if I did? I was doing him a good turn. He was old and he never went out, except when I took him for a couple of pints of an evening. He sat there watching telly all day, and he didn't understand half of that.' Wallace was gaining confidence. 'And he'd been sent round the bend by all those lights and digging down in the spinney. It's down to your lot, that is.'

'It was very good of you to take Mr Stokes out for a drink,' said Markby. 'He's very fortunate to have you as a friend.'

Wallace transferred his attention to Markby. 'Thought you'd retired,' he said.

'Oh, I have!'

'What you doin' here, then?'

'I'm here as an observer only. You and Mr Stokes had been friends for some time, I'd be right in saying?'

'You would.'

'How did you first meet him?'

Wallace considered the question for some time. 'We were in the same line of business, you might say. Transport.' He put down the can on a nearby occasional table. 'You want tea or anything? I'll give Samantha a yell.'

'Please don't trouble her!' Barker said hastily. 'We're fine.'

Markby glanced at him. Barker drew a deep breath and gave him a slight nod.

'It's like this, Mickey,' Markby picked up the questioning. 'As you know, I've been helping out with the investigation into the death of Rebecca Hellington. You and Mr Stokes were in the crowd watching the police work in the spinney.'

'We were,' agreed Wallace. 'But you'd already found the body, hadn't you? What had you gone back for?'

'Just making sure we hadn't missed anything!' said Barker. 'We're very thorough!'

'So are the ruddy Customs and Excise! How they found that iguana . . . I had it tucked away in the suitcase, really snug. It wouldn't have come to any harm, you know. I'd have looked after it properly. And if the bloke who sold it hadn't sold it to me, he'd have flogged it to someone else!'

'Mr Wallace!' Markby drew the conversation determinedly back to the body in the spinney. 'We are not here about an iguana. Rebecca's father is still alive and desperate to know what happened to his daughter.'

'Dare say he is,' said Wallace.

'At the moment we don't know, and neither do the Gloucestershire force, *how* she died. But we do know she was buried in the spinney. We also know *when*, because two children saw her body prior to the act. So that's the first thing we have to clear up: how she came to be buried there.' He drew a deep breath and glanced at Barker again. 'No one at the present time is suggesting that either you or Stokes killed her.'

The shell suit heaved. '*What?*' yelled Wallace. 'I should bloody think not!'

'Mickey,' Trevor Barker asked, quietly, 'did you help Fred Stokes bury her body? If you did – and you could have had reasons for doing that which have nothing to do with her death – you might well be able to give us important information that could lead to finding out how and when she died and, indeed, if her death was the result of a deliberate act, or came about because of an accident of some kind.'

Wallace was silent for a moment. 'Can't you tell nothing from the body, about how she died?'

'Unfortunately not,' said Barker. 'We only have the bones. Although they are intact, examination of them has told us nothing.'

'You know, Mickey,' Markby told him, 'when I was investigating at this end, twenty years ago, my chief purpose was to find out whether Rebecca had come home that weekend. We tried everything we could think of, spoke to everyone, but no one had seen or heard from her here. So I told my colleagues in Gloucester that she hadn't come home, or there was no evidence that she had. Yet now we know – I know – that she was here. I'd dearly love to know how she got to the spinney. I do think you could tell us. So, I'd like you to consider it very carefully.'

Wallace shifted in his chair and the material of his shell suit rustled. 'There ain't nothing to consider. I'm sorry for the family, course I am. But I can't help you.' His expression hardened. 'You dress it up very nice, but however I look at it, it seems to me you're saying we killed her, Fred and me!' Wallace narrowed his eyes and gave Markby a resentful stare. 'And we didn't.'

'But if you *didn't* kill her, then helping us find out who did can only help you – and Fred's memory.'

There was a long silence, broken by a rustling from one of the tanks as its occupant moved across the sandy floor. Barker glanced apprehensively at it and then leaned forward. 'Just tell us what happened, Mickey.'

The shell suit heaved again like an eruption on the sea floor, a mass of turquoise and yellow on the move, as the wearer hauled himself to his feet.

'All I did,' he said firmly, 'is buy old Fred a bottle of whisky. Not my fault if he drank it all at once and passed out . . . and then the place caught fire. He was always leaving lighted fags around. Now then, if you two have said all you've got to say, I know *I* don't have anything more to add.'

As they walked out of the room into the hallway, sounds of rattling and scrabbling could be heard from upstairs, to the background of Samantha demanding, presumably to an empty room, 'Where the hell are they? Mickey!'

Wallace opened the front door and stood aside to allow the visitors to leave. As soon as they stepped outside, he began to shut the door, but not quickly enough to cut off the sound of his wife's voice.

'Mickey!' The sound was louder and echoed around the hallway, suggesting that Samantha was leaning over the upper banister. 'Mickey! Have you moved my sleeping pills? I can't find them!'

Wallace slammed the front door. On the pavement his visitors looked at one another and then Barker reached up to ring the bell. The door remained shut but, through it, Wallace could be heard shouting and Samantha giving as good as she got.

Barker rang again, then stooped and lifted the flap of the letter box. 'Mr Wallace! Open the door, please!'

There came the sound of confused mutterings. Then the door opened halfway and Wallace's unlovely countenance scowled at them through the gap. 'If you want to come in again, get a warrant! I've said all I've got to say!'

'Oh, we don't want to talk to you just now, Mickey,' said Barker genially. 'We'd like a word with Mrs Wallace.'

'What about?' demanded Mickey.

There was a clunk of platform soles on the staircase. A form could be seen dimly behind Wallace.

'Mrs Wallace? Samantha?' Barker called out. 'Do I understand you've mislaid some sleeping pills?'

'What's it got to do with you?' demanded Samantha.

'Want us to tell her, Mickey?' asked Barker.

Chapter 17

Carter put down the phone. 'You're not going to believe this,' he said to Jess Campbell. 'But Trevor Barker believes he knows who buried Rebecca. The culprits are the old man, Fred Stokes, who lived near the spinney, and a friend, Mickey Wallace. Unfortunately, Stokes is dead, after drinking whisky laced with sleeping pills. Wallace bought the whisky and his prints are on the bottle. He doesn't deny that. But Wallace's wife is missing some prescription sleeping tablets, issued only days ago by her doctor. A fire was later started in Stokes's house, but failed to destroy the evidence. The bottle, with traces of alcohol and the drugs inside it, survived the fire. Barker thinks Wallace will cough to burying the body. They are confident he will eventually also admit to lacing the whisky with crushed pills and starting the fire.'

'What are you going to do?' Jess asked him, after a moment's thought.

Carter got up from his chair and walked up and down his office a couple of times before going to his favourite place to think, by the window, gazing down on the car park. 'Barker's asked me if I want to drive up to Bamford and sit in on the interview with Wallace. I'm banned from going anywhere near Mrs Malone. In fact, at the moment I can't see where I can go except to Bamford. I've hit a solid wall here. What's more, if it helps find out the truth about Rebecca, I have to go.'

'Do we know how Caroline Malone is? Obviously very distressed, but is she being treated by a doctor?' Jess asked.

Carter grimaced. 'Mrs Malone can handle things without medication. She's consulting her lawyer.'

'You didn't harass him to the point where he threw himself into the canal!' Jess protested hotly.

'Try telling her that.' Carter turned to face her. 'Well, in the absence of any communication yet from her legal representatives, or from the police complaints service, I'm left in limbo. I can't deal with Mrs Malone directly now. However, Jess, you can. So, you take over here while I drive up to Bamford.'

'You want me to go and see the widow?' Jess asked, unable to disguise her dismay.

'No, no! Not right away. Just check over everything we've done so far. Something might strike you.'

'I would ask Caroline to come here and stay with us,' said Cassie. 'But she might find the children a bit of a strain.'

'Yes,' said her husband, simply. 'She can't stand . . . children.'

'It's such a pity,' Cassie sighed. 'If she had any of her own, she'd feel differently.'

'Possibly,' said her husband. 'I wouldn't count on it.'

'But just sitting in that house and thinking about Pete . . . she must be very shocked and depressed. She ought to get away somewhere. Perhaps she'd like to go down to St Ives and stay at the cottage for a bit?' Cassie frowned. 'But it would be a little lonely for her there on her own.'

'Look, leave it to me,' her husband told her. 'I'll take care of it. I've booked a few days' compassionate leave. I'm the executor of Pete's will, apart from anything else. Plus, Caro is hell bent on involving the police complaints system. I'm trying to talk her out of it. I want a word with the solicitor about that. I'm hoping he'll advise her there isn't a case. Depends how he feels about the police, I dare say.'

'I suppose she feels she wants to blame someone,' Cassie pointed out. 'It's quite natural . . .' She paused. 'Nick, when Pete phoned you that evening, you know, when he phoned you very late, from his garden?'

'I didn't think you'd remember that!' he returned in surprise. 'You were half asleep when I told you.'

'Not that much asleep – and not deaf, either! Are you sure Pete didn't say anything that might suggest he was thinking of . . . of suicide?'

'Suicide? *No*. I realised he had a lot on his mind and he was finding it very difficult to cope with it all. I mean, for twenty years he'd been able to put Rebecca's disappearance out of his mind. Then, up pops a skeleton and all cards are on the table again. Of course he was struggling to cope with it. But that's not the same as being suicidal . . .'

Nick paused. 'We've all been struggling to cope with it – Caro, me . . . You know, Cass, when I think back to that party, the one I threw while my people were away, I remember how I thought it had all gone swimmingly, a really good bash.' He rubbed a hand over his skull. 'I suppose his mind must have been drifting towards suicide. I should have realised it.'

'It's not your fault!' said Cassie, shocked.

'The fact is, in a way it is all my fault—'

'You can't blame the fact that you gave a party, darling!' insisted Cassie. 'And you couldn't stop him walking into the canal, if he'd decided to do that.'

'That doesn't mean there aren't other things I could have done, should have done! But the years went by; the Rebecca business seemed over and forgotten. Pete and I never talked about it. I should have done more to talk to Pete.'

'Therapy!' said Cassie firmly. 'He needed professional therapy. You couldn't have supplied that, Nick.'

'No, I couldn't. Well, Caroline isn't likely to go seeking professional therapy. It is down to me to talk her through this. She is my cousin. I'll pop into Gloucester first, see the solicitor and have a word about probate for Pete's will. There might be a delay, you know, because of the way he died. Inquest and so on. After that, I'll drive over to see Caroline . . .' He hesitated. 'Cassie,' he said, in a different voice, 'you and the kids mean an awful lot to me, you know. Since they found Rebecca I know I've been a bit difficult to live with. I'm sorry about that and . . . and everything.'

'Thank you, darling, and I do know. You have been a bit nervy lately. But you've been worried about Pete, so I understand. But you shouldn't have taken Oliver's light sabre away, just because Dominic broke his.'

'Oh, all right, I'll buy Dominic a new one and return Oliver's. But I do wish they could learn to play quietly.'

He walked out of the room and Cassie heard him exclaim, 'Oh, Gordana! I didn't realise you were in the hall. What is it?'

'Boys are in the sandpit in garden,' came Gordana's voice. 'I come in to find plastic little buckets. But I can't find little buckets.'

'They're outside in the greenhouse!' Cassie called.

Gordana's footsteps beat a retreat and Nick put his head round the door. 'I told you! She snoops!' he hissed.

Cassie watched him drive away, thoughtfully. Then she sighed and walked into the garden to find the twins building an elaborate castle in the sandpit, with determination written all over their faces.

'I found the buckets,' said Gordana, pointing.

'Yes, I see. Have you checked on Libby?'

'Baby is sleeping and boys are playing very well, no fighting.'

Cassie brightened. 'Perhaps they're getting along better.'

'So, can I have rest of day off?' asked Gordana. 'I need to go shopping, maybe go to Gloucestershire Quays?'

'Oh, yes, I suppose so. Yes, go by all means.'

A few minutes later, she heard the Mini being driven away, and almost at once, as if the sound of Gordana's departure had been a signal, a wail from the house announced that Libby had awoken from her nap. Cassie set off back indoors.

'I'm not surprised to see you,' Trevor Barker told his visitor. 'I've got Wallace in custody and, now you're here, we can interview him properly.'

'Including about the fire in Stokes's house?'

'Certainly! It nearly claimed a second victim in Nina Pengelly.' Barker scowled. 'But it didn't bring about Fred's death – the whisky and pills did that. Of course, if he hadn't already been unconscious when the fire reached him, then it would have resulted in his death from inhaling the smoke, especially from the burning horsehair.'

'A murderer who believes in belt and braces,' said Carter.

Trevor Barker grunted and they both sat in silence for a moment or two.

Then Carter asked, 'What about this Wallace?'

'Stokes's only close pal and drinking companion. He's quite a bit younger than Stokes. At the time the body was buried, I'd guess Wallace was in his late twenties.' Bitterly, Barker added, 'Now he keeps snakes.'

'Why present his old chum with a bottle of whisky laced with crushed tablets? I mean, why *now*?'

'My guess,' Barker told him, 'is that Fred's nerves were showing signs of strain. Wallace must have started worrying. In addition, I'd paid a call on Stokes to question him. Perhaps that brought Wallace to his decision? If so, I'll have to live with that. Or perhaps it was the second search we made in the spinney? The first time Wallace, and Fred, knew what we were looking for. The second time, they didn't, and that could've rattled them. Anyhow, it seems that Wallace decided to silence his old mate. He did it in the most merciful way he could think of. Give the old chap a bottle of whisky as a treat, having tampered with it first, and then leave it to human nature, knowing Fred wouldn't limit himself to just one tot.'

Carter sighed. 'OK. You say Stokes used to be a truck driver?'

'That's right, but he claims to have just retired around the time of Rebecca's disappearance. I get where you're going, Ian. Perhaps, against usual practice, she did hitch a lift? If both Stokes and Rebecca lived in Bamford, she may even have recognised him and not hesitated to get into his lorry? But it would mean that Stokes had driven his lorry down to the Gloucester area on some job, wouldn't it?' Barker drew a deep breath. 'We have checked him out. He did retire about that time. He applied for a disability pension. Back trouble. And how did Wallace become involved? Did Fred knock on his door and ask Wallace to help him bury a dead girl? It's hardly likely.'

Wallace sat in the interview room with folded arms and a sullen expression on his face. He turned a bloodshot gaze on Ian Carter. 'And who's that? When you come to see me at my house, you had that Markby with you. I thought you were having to trawl round the old folks' homes to find enough p'licemen. I've read about the cutbacks. But I didn't realise things had got that bad! This one's got grey hair, as well.'

Wallace shifted his gaze from Carter's greying but thick mop to glance at the top of Barker's head; but if he had been going to mention the inspector's thinning hair, he wisely decided not to.

'This is Superintendent Carter from the Gloucestershire force. He was involved in the original investigation into the disappearance of Rebecca Hellington,' Barker almost snarled.

'And you got nowhere, I suppose?' Wallace said, disagreeably, to Carter.

'At the time, no – I didn't get anywhere,' Carter confessed.

'So, that's it, is it?' Wallace leaned forward. 'Now you think you're going to pin it on me and poor old Fred, are you? Improve the clear-up rate? Rub out the black mark on your record?'

'You gave "poor old Fred", as you call him, a bottle of booze full of crushed sleeping tablets!' snapped the irritated Trevor Barker.

Carter said, 'I'm not trying to pin anything on you – or on the late Mr Stokes, or anyone else! But Inspector Barker has to investigate the discovery of a body locally; and I have an unsolved disappearance in my part of the world. We both think you can help us.'

'You think wrong, then!' snapped Wallace.

Barker had his anger under control now. But there remained a gleam of malign satisfaction in Wallace's eyes. He knew he had very successfully managed to rile both of the police officers facing him.

Quietly, Carter continued, 'No, I don't. I think I'm right. Even if it was *all* you did, I believe you and Stokes buried the girl. We know where. We don't know why.'

Wallace's eyes opened wide in shock. 'Why? *Why?* Wouldn't you, if you found a dead body in your truck?'

There was a peculiarly tense silence. Trevor Barker asked, blandly, 'Would you like a solicitor, Mr Wallace?'

Wallace leaned back and the chair creaked under his weight. 'Bloody old fool, Fred! His nerve was going. It was you lot fooling around in that spinney got him jumpy. He was getting ready to spill the beans, I could tell. I didn't want to . . . to do what I did. But I had no choice, and you can't say he didn't go happy!'

'What about Nina Pengelly? She nearly died trying to rescue him.'

'She should have minded her own business,' was the disagreeable retort. 'All right, then, I want a solicitor. But I don't want one who looks about twelve years old.' He glared at them. 'And I'm not confessing to murdering that girl! Not now, not ever! Not with a solicitor present or without one! *Because Fred and I didn't kill her!*'

Chapter 18

'I'm a self-employed man,' began Wallace. 'I have been, these last twenty or more years.'

The solicitor had arrived and sat beside him, a middle-aged man with baggy eyes and an air of disenchantment. Every line of his attitude announced he'd heard it all over the years.

'I had a coupla jobs when I left school – warehouseman,' Wallace went on. 'But it was dead boring, shut indoors all day moving stuff from one end of the shed to the other, stacking it on one shelf, taking it off another. Pay wasn't much. So, I thought to meself, I can do better than this on my own! Move things about outdoors, on the road. Fetch and deliver. I borrowed a few quid from my old man, and I bought a used pickup truck, a Toyota, a red one.' Wallace stopped for a moment and looked reflective. 'It was a good buy, that pickup. It was a 1995 model and, at the time I bought it, that made it only a couple of years old and it didn't have a lot of mileage on it. I kept it a long time. Then I needed something a bit bigger and contained, you understand. Moving things in the open pickup, they tended to get wet when it rained. I had a tarpaulin, mind, to put over cargo.'

Barker looked as if he couldn't stand much more of this, but he managed to control his impatience. Carter kept quiet, understanding that Wallace was still moving things, only now they were his memories. He was being methodical, stacking them in order.

'Now, Fred Stokes,' said Wallace, and Barker sat up and looked more alert. 'He was a real trucker, once. Drove them big rigs all over the place – abroad, too. You wouldn't believe it, looking at him now. I knew him from the pub, not well, but I knew he'd had to retire because of his back, after he was involved in a big pile-up on a motorway. The whole pub knew that. He groused about it non-stop. He was short of cash, too, only had the disability pension. Well, I got an enquiry about a job. It was moving antiques. Someone had bought an old bed at auction. A Victorian thing it was, with a walnut headboard all carved with cherubs and grapes and things. And the weight of it! The chap wanted it taken down to a house near Gloucester. So, I got the job. It was all dismantled, in pieces, but I needed someone else to give me a hand. Fred's bad back had stopped him driving the trucks, but he was still pretty handy. He was a lot bigger chap in those days, really beefy. So I offered him a few quid to come with me, and help me out with this bed. We got it on my pickup and tied the tarpaulin over it and off we went. We went early in the morning to beat the worst of the traffic. It wasn't a bad run.'

'Can you tell us the address to which you took it?' asked Barker.

Wallace shook his head. 'I keep all the records for seven years, like you got to, self-employed like I am. But we're talking twenty years ago! My records and my memory for details don't go back that far!' Unexpectedly, he chuckled. 'I do remember we had a hell of a job getting it through the door of the house we took it to! Anyhow, we did it. Fred refused to manhandle the pieces up the stairs, on account of his back, and the house-owner had to

help me with that. Then we set off home. It was about, oh, midday
. . .' He paused and looked up, enquiringly. 'Any chance of a cup
of tea?'

'When you've finished,' said Barker.

Wallace shrugged his heavy shoulders. 'Well, we were pretty
thirsty that day, twenty years ago, after lugging that bed around.
Getting hungry, too. So, we decided, before we drove home we'd
stop at a pub somewhere, for a pie and a pint. We'd already
decided to drive back along the minor roads, country route,
because by then the motorways and main roads had got busy.
Anyway, we were in no hurry and it was a nice sunny morning,
a Saturday, early June. You can get all sorts of weather in June,
but this was really summery. Anyhow, we were driving along,
keeping an eye open for a nice pub. You don't get a pub unless
there's a few houses around; and there were some nice houses
along the road we were taking. You couldn't see too much of
them, because they were in big grounds, had high hedges and big
gravel drives. Really wealthy lot, they were, who lived round there.
You could just see the roofs and top floors poking up above the
hedges and bushes. They weren't that old, I reckon, built sometime
in the nineteen-thirties, I'd guess.'

Carter raised his head and stared at Wallace as if he was about
to ask him something, but he kept silent so as not to disturb the
flow of the story.

'Then we saw this pub and it looked a nice place. The car park
was only small, and there were a couple of cars already parked in
it, so we didn't try and turn in there. We just pulled off the road
and parked up on the verge. There was nothing of any value in
the back of the pickup, only some ropes and the tarpaulin lying

in a heap. Anyone could see there was nothing worth pinching. And it was quiet along there.'

Wallace stopped speaking and frowned. They waited impatiently. Then Wallace's brow cleared. 'We had ham and chicken pie. They'd got it at the counter under a glass dome. Sort of looked home made. It was pretty good, I remember. They put a bit of salad with it. Not that I'm keen on salad, as a rule. But a pub like that always gives you salad. Not the sort of place that gives you pickles. They gave us a bit of that French bread, too. It was a swanky sort of place, like I said. So we took our time and had a nice little meal. We must have been in there about an hour or just under.

'Then we decided we'd better get going. We didn't check the pickup; we didn't see the need to. It was where we'd left it. We drove off back to Bamford and it didn't take long, maybe another hour and a half. When we got here I dropped Fred off first. I didn't drive up the hill to Brocket's Row. I stopped at the bottom just past the spinney. Fred said not to bother to drive up to the top, he'd walk. So he got out and started back alongside the pickup, to the beginning of the road up the hill. I was going to drive on but I heard him shout and then he slapped the side of the pickup to attract my attention. He came back and opened the passenger door of the cab and stuck his head in. "Someone's been messing around in the back," he said. That's his words. I remember. I asked what he meant. He told me the tarpaulin and ropes were still there but they'd been moved. The tarpaulin had been folded over when we put it in there after unloading that bed. Now it was stretched out flat. Only it wasn't really flat, there was a bump in it as if something was underneath it. The ropes were all pushed together up one end. So I got out and went back with him to investigate. We got up into the back and pulled off the tarpaulin . . .' Wallace paused. 'And there she was.'

He fell silent and, at last, when he showed no sign of speaking again, Barker urged, 'Who was?'

Wallace looked at him in surprise. 'Who do you think? That girl all the fuss is about. Of course, we didn't know at the time who she was! Hadn't a clue. Nor how she'd got there. Except, of course, it must have happened while we were in the pub having our pie and pint.' Wallace drew himself up and said, fiercely, 'Someone dumped her in my pickup. Bloody cheek!'

Carter asked tersely, 'Any sign of rigor?'

Wallace moved his head to look at him, his expression suggesting he was glad someone had asked a sensible question. 'It was just starting – and she was cold. I reckon she hadn't been dead long, though. But she was dead, no mistake.'

'Signs of injury?'

He shook his head. 'No, not that we could see. Her eyes were open, and her mouth. She looked . . .' Wallace paused, and when he spoke again his tone had softened. 'She looked scared, poor kid. She was only young, I'd say eighteen or nineteen. Of course, I'm not saying she had been scared when she died, because we didn't know that! But I suppose she probably was. Anyway, she looked scared. It upset me, upset Fred too, to be honest. Apart from the fact that she was in my pickup and we'd got a dead body on our hands! What were we supposed to do with her?'

'Contact the police!' said Barker crisply.

Wallace rolled his eyes. 'Do me a favour,' he said. 'What would the p'lice have said? Think they would have believed us? Not a chance. And don't forget, I'd just started out in business on my own account. I couldn't let the police impound my vehicle while they crawled all over it looking for clues. Besides, no one would believe us. I wouldn't have believed it meself if someone had told me they'd parked a pickup in a quiet back road, while they went to the pub, and when they got back, someone had left a dead body in it! I mean, people do take advantage if anyone is clearing out a house and hires a big skip. It's left sitting outside all night long unattended. House-owner gets up in the morning and finds people have chucked all sorts of stuff in there. But not in a pickup truck, and not a dead body!'

Wallace shook his head. 'Fair makes you wonder!' he observed in a philosophical comment on the ways of the world.

'So, what did you do, Mickey?' asked Carter.

Wallace looked at him. 'Got rid of her, that's what. What anyone in my predicament would do.'

'How?' snapped Barker.

'Decided to bury her in Brocket's Spinney. We were parked right by the place, after all. Couldn't be more convenient. We argued about it for a while, because Fred was worried she'd be found. It wasn't as if no one ever went in the spinney. Local kids played there. Eventually, he agreed. So we lifted her out of the back of the pickup, carried her into the trees, and put her down. She had stiffened up a bit more by then and that worried us a bit. She'd be more difficult to bury when rigor had really got her. We covered her over with leaves and branches while Fred stayed there on guard, like. We didn't cover her to hide her from anyone else, but because Fred didn't like looking at her. I drove home to get a couple of tools to do the job – spade and a shovel.'

'Fred lived nearer, just up the hill,' Barker pointed out. 'Why didn't *you* stay on guard? Let Fred go up the hill to his house and get some garden tools? He must have had some.'

'Sure he did,' growled Wallace, 'and he'd got an old mother as well, what he lived with. If she'd seen him setting off down the road with a couple of digging tools, she'd have asked him where he was going and what for.' Wallace drew a deep breath. 'She'd have been a witness! That's what she'd have been. You lot know all about witnesses. Now me, I lived on my own at the time, I wasn't married then.' For a moment Wallace sounded wistful. 'So I went home and got what was needed and went back to the spinney. It must have been just about three-quarters of an hour later.

'I couldn't see Fred when I got there and I thought, at first, he'd been nervous and cleared off. But I could still smell cigarette smoke, pretty strong, so I reckoned he was nearby. I called out, quiet, and he heard me. He came out of the trees, pale as a ghost and shaking. Some kids had come to the spinney and they'd found the body. That gave me a shock, because I thought for sure the kids would have run off to tell someone. But Fred said, perhaps not. He knew those children, brother and sister. They lived up in Brocket's Row. The Social had put them with Nina Pengelly. They – well, the girl mostly – had caused a lot of trouble in the school, fighting. Fred reckoned there was a good chance they wouldn't tell anyone about the body – or, if they did, no one would believe them.

'So, we decided to get on with it and bury her. It had started to drizzle with rain by then, too. That would discourage visitors. We made a decent job of it, put the poor lass in the ground neatly.

Luckily, we'd laid her out straight when we took her off my pickup, or we'd have had a job laying her out, because rigor had really got to her now. As it was, when we picked her up, it was like lifting a board. I tried to close her mouth and eyes, but it was too late for that, and we couldn't. We buried her as deep as we could, then put a lot of leaves and branches and stuff on the top, together with a bag of rubbish someone had dumped down there and we emptied out. Then we made off. The next day it rained heavy, I remember. We were a bit worried the earth might be washed away and she'd be seen, or foxes might go digging. But neither of those things happened. The kids either hadn't said anything or no one had believed them, because no one went down to the spinney looking about. We reckoned we'd got away with it.'

He frowned. 'Funny thing, Fred said he saw one of the kids, the girl, later on that evening, after we'd buried her. She was picking flowers up by the houses. It reassured him, because she was acting like nothing had happened. Yet now we know it had, because she'd nicked the bracelet.'

Wallace looked at the two police officers and said conversationally, 'You wouldn't believe a little girl like that would go robbing a body, would you? But she'd taken a bracelet off the corpse, it said in the paper. Honestly, kids!'

Carter leaned forward and asked, 'Mickey, think hard. Could you take us – take me – back to the road with the big houses in it? Where you stopped for your pint and lunch?'

Wallace looked unhappy. 'I couldn't, to tell you the truth. Not to be sure. I'd just as likely take you to the wrong place! You gotta understand. It wasn't our neck of the woods. It was all strange territory to us. We'd been just driving around looking for a place to eat . . .' He paused. 'I can tell you the name of the pub, though. I've a good memory for a decent pub. It was called the Feathers.'

Carter leaned back and let out a sigh. 'Yes,' he said softly, with real satisfaction. 'Yes!'

All the others in the room looked at him then, even the solicitor, a spark of interest showing in his weary eyes.

Carter turned to Trevor Barker. 'I'd like to leave this interview. I need to contact my base. You don't need me any more, I think.'

'Superintendent Carter leaves the room. Interview is suspended,' said Barker, glancing up at the clock on the wall. He added the time.

'We'll resume without you,' Barker said, in the corridor outside the interview room. 'I'll continue, with Sergeant Johnson sitting in. This has to do with something Wallace said, doesn't it? Was it the name of the pub?'

'Yes,' Carter said. 'Now I know where Rebecca died.'

Chapter 19

Nick Ellsworth had left Gloucester a little later than he'd expected. He'd spent longer with the solicitor than planned. Then, perhaps because he wasn't looking forward to visiting his cousin, he'd stopped for a black coffee, and to mull over what he should report to her. The solicitor had been very doubtful about involving the police complaints department. If Mrs Malone was set on it, it would be wise to consult further before taking things to the next step. He, the solicitor, felt there wasn't enough to make a case. He hadn't handled anything like it before. He'd like to take more experienced advice.

That made a lot of sense to Nick. But it wasn't what Caroline wanted to hear. Hear it she would have to, and from him.

'I'll be writing to Mrs Malone, of course,' the solicitor had continued. 'But perhaps it might be a good thing if you had a word with her first. She's in a highly nervous state, isn't she? That's how it seemed to me when we spoke. You're a family member. It would be better coming from you.'

Oh, great! Good thing for whom? Not for me! Nick had wanted to say to the man. *You're the legal eagle. You're getting paid for advice, not to pass the buck!* As it was, he'd mumbled and promised to have a word with Caroline.

By the time he'd reached the road where she lived, he was

sweating as if he'd run a mile. He wanted a drink. A whisky would help. There was the pub, the Feathers, but he couldn't go in there. He was breathing with difficulty and wondered if he was going to have a heart attack. He almost wouldn't mind being taken ill – not seriously, of course – if it would mean he'd get out of this visit.

The opening into the drive of the Malone home was coming up and the security gates stood open. That puzzled him briefly. But he had too much on his mind to worry about that. The dreaded moment was at hand and couldn't be avoided. He had no idea what state he'd find Caroline in. She was a strong personality. But Pete's death – particularly the manner of it, and the suddenness – had inevitably taken a dreadful toll.

He wondered if Cassie's suggestion that Caroline take some time to go down to Cornwall to the cottage might not have been a good one. He'd dismissed it when Cassie spoke of it, but after all, for Caroline to stay alone in her own house for the next week or two would place a definite strain on her already shattered morale. Yes, he'd suggest the cottage at St Ives. Fresh air, sea breezes, the beach, the Tate St Ives gallery, the Barbara Hepworth museum . . . Caroline had studied art. She'd like to visit the Tate St Ives gallery now it had been refurbished. He began to feel more optimistic as he drew up before the house. He mopped his brow, sat for a moment to settle his mind, and got out of the car.

The house looked deserted. Was she in town somewhere? He should have phoned first. He hadn't, because that would have meant telling her over the phone what the solicitor had said. He would still have had to face her later. Better get it over and done with. But if she was out, the visit could decently be put off. Yes, he could only try, and if she wasn't here . . . let the ruddy solicitor phone up or write one of his expensive letters and give her the discouraging news.

After a moment's hesitation he walked round to the back of the building. There was no one in the garden, and for a moment he stood looking at the lawns and bushes. This garden had memories for him and they weren't good ones. The earlier nausea was creeping over him again. Then, as his gaze roamed around, it caught a movement behind the kitchen window. Nick went to the kitchen door, knocked and called out.

'Caro? It's Nick! Can I come in?'

He didn't hear a reply but she must have heard him call out. Tentatively, he tried the door handle. It turned beneath his touch and the door swung open, revealing the large, well-planned kitchen with its flagged floor and expensive fitted units. Caroline was there, leaning back against a worktop, sipping from a bone china mug of what he guessed must be one of her herbal brews. She looked up as he came in, but didn't speak. Her long hair wasn't twisted into a knot as usual, but hung long and loose like a damsel in a Pre-Raphaelite illustration for some courtly romance. She was dressed head to toe in mourning black, and that slightly shocked him. People didn't go into such deep mourning these days, did they? There was no reason why she shouldn't, of course. But somehow, with her long dark-blonde hair, pale complexion and slender build, the unrelieved sombre attire seemed more consciously dramatic than sorrowful. Her face was a mask, expressing nothing.

'Caro?' he asked. He knew his voice sounded nervous. 'Caro? How are you?'

She moved the mug away from her lips, turned her head slightly to set the tea down on the worktop and then turned back to face him. She gripped her upper left arm with her right hand, as if to steady it or prevent some involuntary movement.

'The gates were open,' he said. He had to say something. If only she'd speak!

But she only nodded and made a slight gesture in his direction.

'You expected me?' he interpreted. 'You've been expecting me to come and tell you how I got on with the solicitor? Say something, Caro. I understand how you must be feeling. But, please, say something.'

She made a single, slow downward movement of her head. Another nod? Then she spoke at last.

'Tell me, Nick,' she invited, and her voice was low and husky, as if she had a sore throat. 'Tell me how I ought to feel. You, you of all people, ought to have some idea. Tell me how it feels when someone dies.'

He'd known this visit was going to be difficult but it had started even worse than he'd feared. Had Caroline gone a bit loopy, too? Like poor Pete? Aloud he said, as soothingly as he could, 'Cassie and I are really very sorry about Pete. Cassie is very worried – we both are – about you being here, in the house, all alone. You know the cottage at St Ives is at your disposal, if you feel a need to get away.'

Caroline didn't reply to this. Nick, feeling he was sinking into mud, floundered on. 'You can come and stay over at Weston with us, but the children are a bit noisy. We want you to know that we're here to support you in any way you think we can. Don't blame yourself, you couldn't know . . .' There was a dangerous spark in his cousin's eyes. Desperately, Nick concluded, 'You

shouldn't feel – I mean, none of us could have guessed that he'd
. . . he'd do what he did.'

'*You* don't know why he did it? Walked into the canal?' Caroline's
voice was dangerously calm, and it worried Nick a lot. He
wondered if she'd been taking something, some sort of medication.
She was keen on those weird herbal brews, but normally she didn't
take pills. Now wasn't a normal time, however.

'You don't know why he wanted to drown himself? Yes, you
do, Nick. You know very well why he did it.' She sounded gently
reproachful. 'Don't lie to me, Nick.'

'You can't blame the police, Caro!' Nick began again, unhappily.
'I've, er, just come from the solicitor. He thinks, if you want to
go through the police complaints procedure, we should take further
advice first.'

'What do I complain about?' asked Caroline in that husky,
almost dreamy voice that frightened Nick far more than shouting
or crying would have done. 'That my husband was driven to kill
himself? Or that he did it because my *own cousin*, and *Pete's old
friend*, couldn't keep his mouth shut?'

Nick felt the blood drain from his face. He desperately wanted
to sit down but he was mesmerised by that slender black-clad
figure, now swaying slightly to and fro. It was like being faced
with a cobra, head raised, ready to strike, and deadly. Bloody hell!
he thought. She's flipped! She's lost her marbles. And she thinks
I spilled the beans!

'Caro,' he said gently, 'you're under a lot of stress. Why don't
you go into the lounge and sit down and I'll call a doctor.'

She raised her eyebrows. 'Oh, call a doctor? You wanted to do
that once before, didn't you? When that wretched girl collapsed

out there.' Caroline made a slight gesture of her head towards the garden behind them. 'But you didn't, Nick, did you?'

A wave of anger suddenly surged through Ellsworth. 'No, I didn't, and you didn't, and we should have done, Caro! You know we should have done!'

'She was dead,' Caroline said, simply. 'No point, was there?'

Nick felt a bead of sweat trickle down his forehead and knew that she could see it. He wanted to put up his hand and wipe it away, but he couldn't. He stammered, 'It-it was your fault, Caro, you—'

'My fault!' After speaking so quietly, her voice suddenly split the air in a cross between a squeal and a shout. 'And was it *my* fault that my husband went into the canal? No, Nick, *yours*! You just couldn't keep quiet, could you? The moment you saw in some tabloid rag that her body had been found, you went to pieces! You had to tell Pete! And Pete couldn't cope—' She broke off, choking on further words.

Nick stared at her in horror. '*I didn't tell Pete!* I swear it, Caro! I never said a word to him about what happened that day!'

'Don't lie to me! Why else would he take his own life! *You told him!*'

Suddenly, Nick felt a strange calm, some defence mechanism of the mind kicking in, he supposed. 'No, Caroline,' he said. 'I didn't tell him. I didn't need to tell him. He worked it out for himself. Perhaps he didn't know exactly what you did, but he knew that *you* killed Rebecca!'

'He didn't know!' she screeched. Turning, she snatched up the tea mug from the worktop and flung it at him.

Nick managed to swerve so that the mug missed him and

shattered on the floor, but the tea sprayed his face and neck. Taking advantage of his momentary confusion, Caroline grabbed a kitchen knife from a wooden rack. She flew across the floor and, under the force of her body colliding with his, he staggered and slipped on the wet flags, crashing down full length, momentarily winded. A nearby stool fell as well, just missing his head and adding to the racket. Then she was on him. Her face was only an inch from his, white, wild-eyed, her mouth working and a stream of obscenities and accusations pouring forth. She stabbed down at him with the knife. Her strength was doubled by her fury but he managed to grasp her wrist and push her arm to the side. He saw the blade flash past his face, only just missing him, and heard it scrape on the flagged floor.

Then she raised it again.

He found himself thinking, *She really is going to kill me. I'm going to die.*

Jess Campbell put down the phone, sat for a few minutes in thought, and then went in search of Sergeant Phil Morton.

'Phil? The superintendent's been on the line from Bamford. There's been a development.' Briefly, she summarised the information Carter had given her: the outline of Wallace's confession, including the body that he and Stokes claimed must have been put in the back of his pickup while parked in the road near the Feathers pub.

Morton listened, gave a low whistle, and asked, 'What does he want us to do?'

'I'm not sure. But I think perhaps we should drive out to the Malone house and get the widow talking.'

283

Morton looked unhappy. 'That's a bit tricky, isn't it? She – Mrs Malone, I mean – is already kicking up the devil of a fuss about police harassment and her husband being driven to suicide. Sit and talk is the last thing she'll want to do.'

'The more fuss a witness makes, generally the more likely it is he or she has something to hide!' retorted Jess. 'You know that, Phil.'

'Oh, sure, once witnesses start squawking about their rights and wanting their high-flying lawyers, there's a chance they know they'll need them. But in this case, Malone has only just died. It's a bit insensitive, isn't it?'

'If she's got nothing to hide, Phil, I agree. It's hellishly insensitive. But the superintendent thinks she has got a lot she can tell us. I've only met her twice and I judge her to be pretty tough beneath the willowy, fashion-plate appearance. Frankly, I think this might be the very time to tackle her. She may be more talkative now, when her guard is down, than she was the first time the superintendent and I went to see them both. Then she left the talking to her husband and she'd planned the meeting all out, complete with the suggestion of guests about to arrive. This is the ideal time.'

Morton raised an eyebrow but made no reply.

'Well, anyway,' Jess conceded, 'I agree we'll have to be very tactful when mentioning Peter Malone. But Mr Carter has left this in my hands, so I say we go straight out there, OK, Phil?'

'If you say so,' said Morton, unhappily.

'Then off we go!'

'Upmarket sort of area, this,' commented Morton, who hadn't visited the locality before. He slowed down, peering through the windscreen at the neighbourhood around them. 'Nice houses. Worth a bob or two.'

'There's the pub!' Jess exclaimed. The Feathers pub was coming up on the left-hand side. 'Slow down, Phil. If that man Wallace is telling the truth, he parked his pickup around here, on the verge. And that opening in the hedge over there . . .' She pointed across the road. 'That's the entry to Malone's house.'

'Looks like Mrs M may already have a visitor. There's a Mini parked up there under the hedge.'

'That might not be someone calling on her. A visitor would be more likely to turn into the drive. We'll go in, Phil.'

Morton obligingly turned into the drive and pulled up before the front door where a black Mercedes two-seater was already parked.

'Now that's definitely a visitor,' said Jess. 'What's more, I know who it is. I've seen the car before. It belongs to Nick Ellsworth, Mrs Malone's cousin. It was parked outside his house in Weston St Ambrose when we called on him. Come on, let's join the party.'

They climbed out and, as Morton closed the driver's door, they suddenly heard an extraordinary noise – a high, piercing screech – followed by a crash as of falling furniture, and then more screaming.

'Round the back!' exclaimed Jess. 'Come on, Phil!'

Nick felt oddly resigned. Perhaps this was how Pete felt when he walked into the canal. Death was inevitable. It had to come at some time and he was meeting it now. If anything, his strongest emotion was one of sadness. He wouldn't see Cassie and the children again. He was so sure of his fate he had even closed his eyes, shutting out the crazed face glaring down at him. He opened them again when Caroline gave an unexpected gurgle. Through the haze of sweat and panic, he saw that a strange arm had come out from somewhere and snaked itself around his cousin's neck. As he stared up disbelievingly, Caroline's pressure on his chest was lessened. She raised her free hand to claw at the intruding arm, and then jerked backwards, dropping the knife. Suddenly, there were two bodies wrestling on the floor. One was Caroline and one was—

'Oh, my God!' croaked Nick, propping himself up on one elbow. 'Gordana!'

'Get the knife!' yelled Gordana, grabbing a handful of Caroline's hair to hold her opponent steady, and causing a yell of pain and fury from Caroline.

The knife, yes, the knife, where was it? He saw it lying a couple of feet away and scrabbled for it. 'Got it!' he gasped. He rolled over, sat up and saw that Caroline was now prone on the kitchen floor, with a triumphant Gordana sitting on top of her.

'Call police!' ordered Gordana, breathlessly.

'No need, we're here!' came a sharp, authoritative voice from behind them.

To his astonishment, Nick saw the red-haired woman inspector, Campbell, and another officer he didn't know.

'All right, we'll take it from here. Phil! Arrest Mrs Malone, would you?'

Morton hastened forward. Gordana reluctantly released her prey and got up.

There was another scuffle, during which Caroline managed to

spit at Nick and hit the target. Phil Morton eventually managed to manoeuvre Mrs Malone outside, but with great difficulty. During the process, Caroline continued to pour an amazing choice of insults at him, at Nick, at Gordana and at Inspector Campbell. Some were targeted individually and some a general denunciation of their personal characters and intellectual abilities.

Once she'd been dragged outside the house, the unfortunate sergeant bore the full force of her rage.

'This is my house, you lout! Let me go! How dare you drag me out of my own property? I'm going to sue the boots off every bloody copper in the sodding force!' were just some of the words they could distinguish.

Jess Campbell was apparently unfazed. Nick supposed in her line of work she was used to this kind of scene. Now that Caroline was safely secured and out of the way, he was beginning to feel deeply embarrassed. How on earth was he going to tell Cassie about all this?

Campbell turned her attention back to him and to Gordana. 'Neither of you is injured?'

Both shook their heads. Nick wiped spittle from his cheek. 'What are you doing here, Gordana?' he gasped. 'I mean, thanks and everything. But why are you here?'

'Yes, Gordana,' said Jess. 'I'd like to know that, too.'

'I follow him!' said the still panting Gordana, nodding at Nick. 'Today I follow him first to Gloucester, then here. I know he was coming to see her! I knew it was very dangerous for him.'

'Why?' asked Jess. It seemed an obvious question.

Nick, too, chimed in with, 'How did you know?'

'Ah,' said Gordana, wisely, and addressing Jess. 'I knew, when

I first see them together, that Mr Ellsworth and this woman have a secret.'

'Oy! Hold on!' yelped Nick.

'It is not *love*, no!' Gordana shook her head and frowned, supporting the dismissal of this idea with a scornful wave of her hand. 'People who have been lovers look at one another in a *different* way. The way Nick and Caroline look at one another, when they think no one sees, is the way of people who share some very bad knowledge.'

Nick muttered a protest again, but this time without conviction.

'It makes me very worried, because they are a nice family, Cassie and children and him.' Gordana pointed in the direction of the now invisible Caroline. 'But she is not nice.'

'That bloody woman is certifiable!' They heard a distant yell from Caroline. 'Let me go! Go back and arrest that maniac nanny!'

Gordana nodded towards the sound of Caroline's voice. 'She is the crazy one. Nick and Cassie, they don't see she's crazy. But me,' declared Gordana, with satisfaction, 'I know she is crazy when I first see her; and she looks at him – Mr Ellsworth – in a way that isn't good. So I watch out, and I listen. When her husband drown, I know she blame Nick. She wants revenge.'

From what they could now hear, Caroline – outside, in Morton's grip – was spitting and growling like an angry cat. The sound was cut off by the slam of a car door.

'Well, thank you again, Gordana,' said Nick, gathering up what shreds of dignity he had left. Hell's teeth, he felt a fool. 'I'm sorry I said you snooped.'

'Yes, yes, of course I snoop!' snapped Gordana. 'Someone must keep eyes open.'

Nick belatedly got to his feet and dusted himself down. 'Inspector Campbell,' he said, 'I'd like to make a statement. I should have made it twenty years ago.'

Chapter 20

Back at Bamford, Trevor Barker had resumed the interview with Mickey Wallace.

'So, you admit to burying the body of Rebecca Hellington, with the help of the late Fred Stokes?'

'Yeah, I admit it,' Wallace growled. 'Satisfied?'

'Only up to a point, because now we come to a more recent matter, the death of Stokes. Why on earth did you do that, Mickey, give your old friend a bottle of whisky laced with your wife's sleeping pills?'

'For the same bloody reason as I helped bury the girl!' Wallace yelled, his voice echoing round the small room. 'Because I hadn't any choice!'

There was a prolonged silence.

Emma Johnson broke it, remarking, 'Deciding to murder an old pal, that's some choice.'

Wallace gave her a look of disgust. 'Where did you get her from?' he asked Barker. 'Listen, old Fred was going to spill the beans about burying the girl. He said he wouldn't, but I knew he would. He was old and tired and scared. If it had only been about burying her, perhaps that wouldn't have been so bad, but I was afraid you'd try and pin her death on us as well.'

'So, what did you do?' Barker asked, without commenting on the last words.

'You know what I did. I wanted to be sure of the old man, and that meant he had to go. But I didn't want him to suffer, of course I didn't! He was my old mate. So, I bought the whisky and I pinched the pills from the medicine cabinet at home. My wife's a poor sleeper. She says I snore and keep her awake. Anyhow, she gets these pills from the doctor. I crushed them really fine and put them in the whisky. Then, when I drove Fred home from the pub, the evening before, I took the whisky out of my pocket and gave it to him. He was surprised, but he was pretty pleased, too.'

'He didn't question why you were suddenly so generous?'

'No,' said Wallace. 'I told him I'd had a win on the horses. He knew I like to place a bet now and again. So I left him with the whisky and – well, went home.'

'And the fire?'

Wallace was silent for a while, then sighed. 'Nothing went right,' he said. 'I knew if he was found dead, there would be some kind of post mortem, right? So I thought, if there was a fire, the smoke would do for him. He wouldn't know anything about it, because he'd be unconscious from the whisky and pills. That was my plan, see? Only knock him out with the pills and alcohol, then nip back and start a fire. He wouldn't know a thing about it. I was trying,' Wallace added, wretchedly, 'to be kind!'

Emma looked as if she would say something, but Barker glared at her and she changed her mind.

'Go on, Mickey. What happened?'

'I meant to allow time for the pills to work. Then go back in the early hours of the morning and start the fire. So, I slipped out of bed about two in the morning, grabbed my clothes and went downstairs to dress. But I thought I'd better make sure he was unconscious. So I rang him.'

'What, at two in the morning?' Barker exclaimed.

'He slept right by the phone!' Wallace retaliated. 'I knew he'd pick it up if he woke up. If he didn't wake up, well, I'd know the whisky and pills had done the trick, right?' He drew a deep breath. 'I told you, nothing went right! I rang his number and, I couldn't believe it, he answered! He was still conscious, wide awake!' Wallace dwelt on the unpleasant shock he'd received. 'I nearly dropped my mobile. But I just put it down. Needed a drink myself by then! I sat down and wondered what had gone wrong. That combination of whisky and pills ought to have felled a horse. Well, first of all, I realised he hadn't drunk the whisky, or not enough of it. What had probably happened, I reckoned, was that he'd sat up late, watching the telly, until he fell asleep in the chair. Then, when I phoned, that woke him. He hadn't gone to bed. He must have drunk the rest of the whisky after I called.

'To make things worse, Samantha had woken up. She sleeps light, like I said. And she came marching downstairs wanting to know what I was doing, why I was all dressed ready to go out. We had a bit of an argument. Then we went back to bed and I didn't move until six in the morning, because she'd wake up again, you could put your money on it!

'About six thirty, I got up and called out to Samantha I was going over to my lock-up to see about a load. I approached Brocket's Row from the other direction, not from the spinney. I took the motorway and turned off a mile or so from those houses, parked up in a field, and walked the rest of the way to Fred's house. I'd rung him again on the mobile, on the way, and this time he hadn't answered so I reckoned the whisky and pills had done the job at last.

'But I soon found out I had another problem. When I got to Brocket's Row, it was quite busy. It was so much later than I'd planned, like I said. The other people living up there were getting ready to go to work. I ducked into Fred's garden shed and sat there until it was all quiet. It was just before ten by then. I couldn't go round to the front of the house and push some lighted rags through the letter box. That was also my original idea. But in broad daylight there was a good chance Nina Pengelly would see me. She's in and out of the front of her house all the time. So, while I was waiting in the shed, I made up a petrol bomb, Molotov cocktail, what they call it. There's a big old hedge between Fred's back garden and the one next door. I reckoned Nina wouldn't see me, if she chanced to go out into her back garden. I levered open one of the windows at the rear of Fred's house, lit the rags and tossed the bottle in. Then I scarpered, back over the field to my van, and drove home. The fire didn't catch and spread as fast as I'd thought it would. Well, *nothing* went as I'd thought it would. You've seen Fred's place.'

Wallace looked enquiringly at Barker, who nodded. 'Well, it was pretty bare of furniture and stuff, to leave a free area for his wheelchair. I should've taken more account of that. If I could've pushed the lighted rags through the front door, like I intended first, the fire would have caught on faster. The wooden staircase would've gone up like tinder, for a start. As it was, it seems it didn't get going until later, and then Nina Pengelly turned up, didn't she? Not one single thing went right.'

Wallace sat back in his chair. 'I didn't mean for Nina to get hurt. I thought if she saw the fire, she'd run and call the fire service. I didn't know she'd go in there like ruddy Wonder Woman and try and save him!' His features puckered into an unlovely scowl, a mix of truculence and self-pity. 'I can tell you something for free,' he said to Barker, 'it ain't easy planning a murder. Of course,' he added, 'I don't say some people aren't good at it. But you coppers don't catch *them*, do you?'

'Sooner or later, we usually get our man,' said Barker, wishing he didn't sound so corny. 'If it makes you feel any better,' he added on the spur of the moment.

'Well, it don't!' snarled Wallace.

There followed a few moments of silent introspection on the part of all present. It was broken by Wallace who, when he began to speak again, did so in a voice that held genuine sorrow.

'I didn't want to harm Fred. I made sure he didn't suffer. We were mates for twenty years or more. We were bound together, you might say, by the business of finding that girl in my truck, and burying her. There's nothing like a secret for tying two people together stronger than any rope, or chain. But he was old, and scared, and you and your lot kept hanging round the spinney. I thought he'd break. But I didn't want to do it. I had a dog once, spaniel it was. I really loved that dog. But he got old and started making messes all around the house, and that got Samantha riled. So, in the end, I had to take him to the vet, have him put down. It was a bad day. I still miss the spaniel. I'll really miss old Fred.'

Chapter 21

Early the following morning, Jess also conducted an interview, the interviewee being Nick Ellsworth. Carter had driven back from Bamford the evening before, arriving too late for the drama, but in time to be informed of Caroline's arrest, and Nick's expressed wish to make a statement. He now sat in. A fourth person present was the solicitor called in to protect the interviewee's rights. He wasn't a duty solicitor, but one requested by Nick. As he had previously known both Nick and Cassie socially, and played golf with Nick, the wretched man was looking understandably bewildered.

'I'd like you to do it,' Nick had told him. 'The other guy, the one I saw yesterday morning in Gloucester, is my cousin's solicitor and will probably be representing her.'

'What are you being charged with?' asked his golfing friend.

'At the moment, disposal of a body with the intent of obstructing or preventing a coroner's inquest. Obstructing the police in their enquiries. Oh, and possibly accessory to murder.'

'Good God, man!' gasped the solicitor. 'What on earth have you been doing?'

Now Nick took a deep breath and began, addressing the two detectives. 'As I told you when you came to Weston St Ambrose, everything springs from that party I threw at my parents' home while they were away on a cruise. The Norwegian fjords, I think it was, and they were gone for two whole weeks – so, well, you understand.'

Carter and Jess both nodded.

Nick regarded them glumly. 'At the time I thought the party was a roaring success. Now I know it was an unmitigated disaster! Well, I couldn't know then, could I?' He gazed at them in appeal.

'Go on, Mr Ellsworth,' encouraged Jess. 'Why did it turn out to be a disaster?'

'Not at the time!' protested Nick. 'That's what I'm trying to explain. But it was at that party that Pete met Rebecca; and my cousin Caroline met Pete, and decided he was the man for her. So, it turned out pretty quickly to be the eternal triangle, isn't that what they call it? More like infernal triangle, if you ask me.'

Nick leaned forward and went on, earnestly. 'You've got to understand Caroline. She's my cousin and I know her very well. I've got on with her well, all my life – until she lost it in the kitchen and flew at me with a knife! Only, I'm getting ahead of myself . . .' His voice trailed away.

'Take your time,' invited Jess.

'Caroline was always strong-minded, even as a kid. When we played games, she made the rules. If there was any dispute, she settled it. There could be no argument. I think, looking back, we were all a bit scared of her, and we didn't dare argue. She hated, really hated, losing at games, of any sort. Board games, guessing games, sports, you name it. She could never be second in anything. She had always to be first, you see. On the other hand – the plus side, if you like – she was fiercely loyal in her friendships.'

'Loyal or possessive?' Jess asked quietly.

Nick considered this. 'Both,' he decided. 'You might say, she didn't distinguish between the two, in her mind, anyway. If Caro was your friend, you could always count on her. She expected, still does, to be able to count on you. I believe, for her, it was a matter of honour, you see. That's why she flew at me with that knife. She believed I'd betrayed her. I hadn't, had I? You know that. Will you tell Caroline? I want her to know I didn't betray her.' He looked at them, pleadingly.

'Gordana's right. We did have a secret, and Caro thought it was safe with me. I misjudged Gordana!' Nick added. 'She did understand Caroline. Perhaps, where Gordana comes from, all the loyalty and honour stuff makes a lot of sense. Vengeance, too, for all I know. Anyhow, she picked up the vibes that escaped me altogether!

'When poor Pete did what he did, Caroline thought I'd betrayed her and had told Pete all about what happened. But I didn't ever even consider telling him! I couldn't have done, I was involved and – well, in the end, I didn't have to tell him. He worked it out for himself.

'Pete was never a fool. He couldn't know the details: the when, how and where. But he understood Caroline. So, he sat down and thought about it until he'd got it figured out. Caroline and I – and the police, too, I reckon – we all thought Pete was brooding over it like some half-bonkers romantic poet. Well, you, the police, might have thought he'd done it, killed her. Did you?' Nick asked suddenly, staring at Carter in a very direct way.

Asked so directly, Carter could only reply, 'To be frank, I didn't know. I was prepared to believe he hadn't done it. But I did also believe he knew a lot more than he was saying. Well, we won't know now, will we?'

'I do,' said Nick. 'I've tried to explain Caroline to you. Let me explain Pete, if I can. Above all, you have to remember, Pete was a numbers man. He was a financial wizard. He could sense a flaw in some money project a mile off. If there was one, he'd find it. If his calculations didn't add up, he'd start again from scratch and work at it until things did add up.'

A sudden realisation seemed to pass across Nick Ellsworth's face. 'I think,' he said to Carter, 'that he was a bit like you.'

At this, Jess turned a thoughtful stare on Ian Carter, and Carter was so startled that he couldn't say anything at all. Then, to his dismay, he remembered old Inspector Parry, sending him off to interview Malone, because Parry's theory was that he and Malone would understand one another. Had Parry not been so wrong?

'So,' concluded Nick, 'I didn't have to tell Pete, did I? About Caroline and Rebecca? He worked it out. He solved the puzzle. Trouble was, poor chap, he couldn't live with the result he'd arrived at . . .' Nick paused. 'Bloody shame,' he added, sadly. Then, more sourly, 'Caroline will never agree. She'll always blame me, insist I told him what happened. But I really didn't. I didn't have to, as I said.'

'Nick,' said Jess, 'you've told us the why, more or less, but not the how and when. What exactly is it that Caroline believes you told her husband?'

'What?' Nick roused himself from some reverie into which he'd sunk. 'Oh, right. So, we have to go back twenty years. It was a Saturday morning. Caroline had suggested I drive over for a game of tennis. You've seen the house. It's much the same now as it was back then, when her parents were alive. One thing has changed, though, in the garden. The tennis court has gone. It was a grass court and it was located at the very back of the grounds, in a corner, surrounded by tall laurel hedges. There was a gap, like a gateway, for players to access it. The idea, I think, of the thick laurel bushes was to muffle the noise, so there was less disturbance for any other garden users. The trouble was, if a ball flew out of play, nine times out of ten it would disappear into one of the laurels. You had to burrow into all that greenery to try and find the wretched thing. It played havoc with your whites. When Caroline inherited the house, she dispensed with the court, had the laurels dug up.

'However, there we were, that Saturday morning, having an enjoyable game. Suddenly, Caroline let out a pretty ripe oath and mis-hit the ball. She was staring out of the court towards the opening in the hedges. So I looked in that direction and saw Rebecca. She was standing there, framed by the dark green leaves, staring at us. It gave me a shock, because we'd understood from something Pete had said that Rebecca was going home for the weekend. It was her father's birthday. Seeing her there wasn't just a surprise, it was a bit creepy, too. She looked sort of . . . odd, very tense and determined. Her face was very white. It was as if she'd sprung out of some old Greek legend, a woodland spirit of some sort. The reason she'd popped up there, out of nowhere was, as we quickly found out, that she'd manoeuvred a showdown with Caroline.

'I believe now that Rebecca had deliberately told Pete she was going to Bamford, so that she had a free hand to seek out Caroline. Perhaps she intended to travel on to Bamford later. That's possible, I suppose. I don't think she was particularly pleased to see me, or not at first. She'd imagined she'd find Caroline alone. But then she seemed to accept my presence. I suspect she thought I was insurance. Caroline was a strong character, and facing her all on her own might have seemed OK to Rebecca when she was planning it. But in reality, well, actually facing Caro and seeing the anger already on her face, perhaps Rebecca trusted that Caroline wouldn't overreact with me there. But then,' Nick added wryly, 'she didn't know Caroline well enough!'

'What was the showdown about?' prompted Jess when Nick fell silent again.

'Pete, what else?' He looked up in surprise. 'Rebecca had decided to hang on to Pete. She had also realised that Caroline had her eye on him. She was a funny sort of kid, Rebecca. She was pretty enough in a mousy sort of way; and she seemed harmless. You know, one of those quiet little women with a will of iron? Caroline had certainly underestimated her, and so had I! Anyhow, she marched across the court and made an obviously rehearsed speech, facing Caro over the net. They were like a couple of finalists at the end of a Wimbledon match, only without the sporting congratulations and commiserations. Rebecca was telling Caro that she wasn't ready to concede defeat. It boiled down to Pete being *her* boyfriend, and Caroline should keep her hands off him.'

Nick shook his head ruefully. 'She really ought not to have tackled Caro like that. It was never going to work. As soon as Rebecca paused for breath, Caro let fly with a riposte, I suppose you'd call it. And what a riposte! I don't suppose Rebecca had ever heard anything like it or faced up to someone so furious. I remember, she stepped back as if a gale force had hit her. A gale force described Caroline all right.'

'Did you try and intervene?' asked Jess. Having earlier seen something of Mrs Malone when she lost her temper, she could well imagine the scene.

'Hah!' exclaimed Nick. 'Some chance! I did manage a couple of words, but the pair of them didn't want my opinion! They both brushed me aside. It was bloody awful!' Nick's voice throbbed with remembered embarrassment. 'Talk about a catfight! And that's what it became, because Caroline took a swing at Rebecca with her racquet. I jumped in and managed to deflect that. I even got the racquet off Caroline. But it didn't help. They went from yelling at one another to trading punches.'

'There was no one else at home on the property?' asked Carter curiously.

'Unfortunately not. I was stuck there, trying to be referee and in danger of getting clouted myself by both of them. And then—' Nick broke off. His face and manner changed. He began to look wretched. 'Something neither Caroline nor I had expected happened. Rebecca began to wheeze and cough and gasp for air. Her face became discoloured. She put her hand in her pocket and took out this little plastic gadget, an inhaler. I hadn't known she was asthmatic and I'm sure Caro didn't know, either. It . . . it got worse and Caro was still shouting at her and trying to grab her and shove her out of the tennis court area, but I could see that Rebecca was really in trouble. She sank down on to her knees, puffing the inhaler into her mouth and sounding . . . quite dreadful. I shouted to Caro to stop trying to wrestle with Rebecca, because something was really wrong.'

Nick fell silent for so long this time, head down and staring at the tabletop, that eventually Carter said, 'You have to tell us, you know. We understand it's distressing. But we must know.'

'Yes,' Nick said dully. 'Yes, I know you must. But it's . . . it's worse in memory than when it was real, somehow. At the time it was all action, no time to think. Now it's all "what ifs" and "I should've". Mostly, it's what I didn't do, rather than what I did. You see, Caroline was so quick; and I truly hadn't imagined she'd do what she did.'

'Which was?' asked Jess.

'She snatched the inhaler away from Rebecca and held it up in triumph. Rebecca stretched out her hand. She was pleading for it, but Caroline just stood there, holding it up out of reach. You know, the way bullying schoolchildren do when they've got hold of something belonging to their victims. I yelled at Caroline. What did she think she was doing? Was she crazy? "Give the girl the ruddy inhaler! She really needs it!"

'"I know," said Caroline. She had a dreadful smile on her face. "But I'm not giving it to her." Then she . . . she laughed and . . . and she hurled the inhaler into the laurels.'

Nick fell silent. The solicitor looked aghast.

'You believe your cousin meant to kill Rebecca by withholding her medication?' Jess asked carefully.

'Oh, yes, that's exactly what I mean. I now believe Caroline *was* crazy at that moment. Just as she was in the kitchen when she attacked me. Of course, I ran over to the laurels and tried to get the inhaler back. But it was a little thing, and dull-coloured. It didn't show up like a tennis ball, and it hadn't caught in the leaves. It had fallen to the ground somewhere and I couldn't find it. I was panicking, too, because I knew how important it was. But I couldn't . . . I couldn't lay my hands on the damn thing! When I realised that, I backed out of the hedge and turned to see what the situation was with Rebecca. She . . . she was collapsed on the ground, lying motionless in a huddle. Caroline was standing over her, looking down at her with such an expression . . . I don't know how to describe it.'

'Satisfaction? Hatred?' Jess suggested.

Nick shook his head. 'No, worse. Contempt. That's what it was, contempt. I shouted out something, I couldn't tell you now exactly what the words were. I wanted her to phone for an ambulance. But she just looked up and stared at me, and said, very calmly, "Don't bother, Nick, she's dead!" I rushed over there, because I couldn't believe it. Rebecca's eyes were open but not seeing me. I knelt down and tried to find a pulse, but I'm not a doctor, haven't even got any first-aid training. She did appear to be dead. I told Caroline we still had to call an ambulance or a doctor. We weren't qualified to say she couldn't be resuscitated.'

'"No," said Caroline, simply. "I don't want her resuscitated. I want her dead and out of the bloody way."

'I told her, we still had to call someone. After all, you can't just push a dead body aside and carry on with what you were doing before! At the very least, you've got to report it.' Nick looked down at his clasped hands. 'Caro said, I shouldn't be a fool. How were we going to explain it? I said, why not just say she had an attack of asthma, a really bad one? It was the truth. The circumstances need not come out. But Caroline said she'd have her inhaler on her, wouldn't she? Someone would be bound to ask about that. So, we both – Caro and I – went back to the laurels and hunted for that wretched inhaler.

'Caro wasn't so confident any more. I think she realised the possible consequences of what she'd done. She wasn't sorry for poor Rebecca, lying there. She was still angry with her. But she realised *we* were in a fix. She, Caro, kept muttering about that "blasted girl" and "bloody nuisance from the start". But we couldn't find the inhaler. I was in a flat spin by then, I don't mind admitting, and that didn't help. We kept bumping into one another. We got scratched. We had to give up. Caroline was getting more and more furious, and most of it was directed at me now. "I don't know why you insist on wasting time like this!" she said. "We're not going to find it and I'm getting filthy!"

'I said it was still not too late to call the ambulance, even if we hadn't found the inhaler. But Caroline bit my head off again, and told me I was a fool. How would we explain the delay? I'd had enough, by then, of Caro haranguing me, as if I'd done something shameful, and not her. Worse than shameful, *criminal*. She'd known what would happen if she kept the inhaler from Rebecca and we didn't get help. I asked her, how about she came up with some positive ideas instead of insulting me?

'She thought for a moment, then a big smile crossed her face. "No problem!" she said. Her solution was simple. We should get rid of the body. Of course, I asked how? I thought it was a damn stupid suggestion. But Caro is very level-headed, well, most of the time, except when she has freaked out on a couple of occasions – like the day of Rebecca's death, and yesterday. That Saturday she'd been raging at Rebecca, then she'd had a moment's panic, and finally she turned her guns on me. But after that, once she'd got it all out of her system, she was as cool as a cucumber.

'She took charge, just as she did when we'd played games as kids. We'd put the body in my car, she decided. We'd drive out into the countryside and just tip the poor kid into a ditch. She'd be found by someone, eventually. "Dog walker, probably," Caro said. "It always seems to be people walking their damn dogs."

'She wouldn't be missed for a while, because Pete had told everyone she'd gone to Bamford to visit her family. She'd probably told others, students in her hall of residence, the same thing. It would be Monday before she was missed. So, so stupidly, I went along with it. It was cowardly of me,' Nick admitted, looking shame-faced. 'But Rebecca was dead and I couldn't help her now. I could help protect my cousin. Family, and all that, you know. So, I did. But it didn't work out the way Caro suggested.

'We put Rebecca into the back of my car and drove off. But we'd barely turned on to the road, only gone a few hundred yards, when Caro ordered me to stop. There was a pickup truck parked on the verge, under some trees. No sign of the driver. It was just past a pub called the Feathers. That's still there, by the way. "Look!" Caro said. "We can put her in the back of that! The driver must be in the pub. He won't know. He'll drive off and be miles away, with luck, before he finds he's got a passenger!" I was appalled. I asked what on earth she thought the poor bloke was going to do? "Not our problem!" said Caro, as if it really wasn't.

'So, it's what we did. "Bye, bye, Rebecca!" Caro said as we threw her in and dragged a tarpaulin over her. "You won't get in my way any more!" She was as pleased as punch, really cock-a-hoop! She even wanted to go back and finish the game. I told her, "No, thanks!" and went home. I never played tennis with her or anyone else on that court again.'

There was a silence. 'That's it,' said Ellsworth. 'I've never regretted anything so much in my entire life. I'm very sorry. The worst of it is, if we'd called an ambulance, even too late, we'd have brazened it out somehow. There were no witnesses to what had happened, the fight, and so on. Pete . . . Pete would have been horrified and shocked. But he'd be alive today.' Nick looked up, a picture of misery. 'Wouldn't he?'

'We can't know that,' Jess said, knowing that it didn't help.

'I do. There's . . . there's something else.' Nick was staring past them at the far wall. 'I wasn't going to tell you this bit, but I will. It makes me sound like some sort of ghoul. But I might as well come clean. The whole tawdry business has preyed on my mind for years. After – after Rebecca's death, I felt physically ill for weeks. I couldn't sleep. My work suffered. My parents thought I was having a breakdown, and perhaps I was. Caro didn't appear to worry about it at all. She wouldn't. Eventually, I managed to shove it to one side and get on with life. I met Cassie. We have the kids. I didn't forget, but I managed not to worry so much about being found out, because no one found Rebecca. No pickup driver came forward to say a body had turned up in his vehicle. That seemed inexplicable to me, but it did seem as if we'd got away with it. Caro saw it as proof we'd done the right thing in dumping the body the way we did. She was able to dismiss it.

'She had a clear field to target Pete, and got her man. They were married. Her mother passed away; a couple of years later her father died, too. He left her the house, and she and Pete moved in.

'As I told you earlier, she had the tennis court obliterated. It was almost the first thing she had done when they took over the house. It was because of what had happened there, I'm sure. Perhaps I'm wrong in thinking she'd completely put it out of her mind. Anyhow, I happened to drive over to the house on the day the work was being done. Morbid curiosity made me walk down to the spot and watch the landscapers at work. They were taking out the laurels and the branches were stacked up, all those big green glossy leaves. The ground where they'd been rooted was well churned up. I looked down at it casually, not searching or anything, but there it was. I saw it lying in the earth. So I picked it up and put it in my pocket. I've still got it at home. It's rolled in a piece of tissue paper. I keep it in the little box I stash cufflinks and bits and bobs in. You'll find it there, if you look.'

'Find what?' asked Carter, surprised.

'Rebecca's inhaler. It was so muddy it was hardly recognisable, more like a lump of earth than anything. It was the purest chance I spotted it. I picked it up, because I couldn't really believe it for a moment. I examined it and there could be no doubt. No one else, no one in our family, used one. You know? It was as if the poor kid spoke to me. I couldn't throw it away again. I put it in my pocket. Some things are meant, aren't they?'

'So, the lab's got it,' Carter said later, speaking to Markby on the phone. 'I'll be sending a report to Trevor Barker. Now we have to wait and see. Any DNA on the inhaler will be degraded but the mud and laurel roots protected it over the years. Possibly enough DNA might be retrieved to show that it was handled at least by Rebecca, which puts her at the spot. If our luck is really in, there may even be a trace of Caroline's DNA. That would really clinch the case against her. She's not denying anything, by the way. She doesn't seem to care any more. She still blames her cousin for her husband's suicide. Nick Ellsworth handled the inhaler when he picked it up while the landscapers were at work, so his DNA is going to be on it. However, at least he preserved it as he found it, all carefully wrapped in tissue and put away. He never unwrapped it, he says. He didn't want to look at it again. He kept it, because he couldn't bring himself just to throw it away. It's still got dried mud on it. He didn't do as your young friend, Dilys Browning, did, and polish the life out of the thing!'

'What's happening about Mrs Caroline Malone?' asked Markby. 'I understand you've arrested her.'

'She's being assessed to establish if she's in a fit state to stand trial. When she attacked Ellsworth, it was only two days after her husband committed suicide. She's as sane as you or me!' Carter added darkly. 'But she's got a bloody good lawyer!'

Chapter 22

Dilys was back, as Nina Pengelly kept reminding everyone, and they were gathered for the celebration tea party. There was a cake, with 'Welcome home, Dilys' iced unevenly across the top. There were paper napkins, because Nina intended everything to be done 'properly'. For that purpose, she had taken her own mother's best tea set from where it usually resided in a display cabinet. The guests were Alan and Meredith together with Tanya Morris, who had been invited as a thank you for rescuing Nina from the flames.

Bobby was bouncing around in his cage, swinging vigorously on his perch and twanging his bell. But he wasn't allowed out to fly round the room. 'Too many of us here,' explained his owner.

'Mrs Pengelly going into the burning house is a great story,' said Tania.

'So is yours, dragging both Nina and Fred out,' Meredith told her.

'You've got to take a few risks if you want a story,' Tania replied calmly. She leaned towards Dilys and lowered her voice to urge, under cover of renewed activity from the cage above their heads, 'But the papers will also pay for a good human interest story like yours, Dilys.'

'Oh, would they?' returned Dilys sourly. 'I'm not a freak show.'

'Of course not! But you're a very interesting person, Dilys!' cajoled Tania. 'And your story's really fascinating.'

'You reckon?' asked Dilys curiously, eyeing Tania up and down.

'Absolutely! It won't just be in the local press. It will go national.'

'Oh, leave her alone!' ordered Josh. 'Auntie Nina didn't ask you to come just so you could keep on about your ruddy newspapers.'

Meredith had been observing this with some amusement. Josh might be against the idea, but she suspected that featuring in newsprint might already be appealing to Dilys. Tania is going to get her story! she thought.

But it was something else that was on Dilys's mind right now. She put down her cup of tea and fixed a stern gaze on Markby. 'You said you'd see about my bracelet. Well, where is it? I told you, I want it back.'

'You really shouldn't have taken it, Dilys, dear,' said Nina reproachfully. 'And off that poor dead girl.'

'Well, she didn't want it any more, did she?' retaliated Dilys, with spirit. She turned to her brother. 'And I was right, wasn't I? She was dead. You said she was asleep!'

'The thought of it gives me the shivers,' said Mrs Pengelly.

'Then don't think about it!' snapped Dilys. 'Listen, it's mine and I want it.'

Markby exchanged glances with his wife. 'Well, now, Dilys,' he said. 'We discussed that with Mr Hellington, the girl's father.'

'Oh, yes?' said Dilys suspiciously. 'What's it got to do with him?'

'It was the very last gift he made his daughter, and it means a great deal to him to have it back again. However!' Markby held up his hand to forestall a furious outburst from Dilys. 'He recognises that, because you took it, it wasn't buried with Rebecca, and that led eventually to her body being recovered.'

'There you go, then!' said Dilys. 'What's he got to complain about?'

'So, after some discussion, he asked us, Meredith and me, if you would like to accept this, in place of the bracelet.'

Markby took a small box from his pocket and handed it to Dilys with some ceremony.

Dilys took it as if it might explode in her hand. 'What is it?'

'Open it, love!' urged Mrs Pengelly.

Dilys opened it and took out a silver chain with small attachments. She held it up, stretched out, and the attachments could be seen to spell 'D-I-L-Y-S' in silver letters.

'We thought,' said Meredith, 'a necklace might be more useful than a bracelet.'

There was a silence while Dilys contemplated the jewellery. Then a rare smile spread across her pugnacious features. 'Yeah,' she said. 'All right, then. I'll keep this one instead of the bracelet. The old man can have that. I like this one better.'

'Well,' said Meredith as she and Alan drove home, 'that's that. I'm glad it all got sorted out . . .' She hesitated. 'I do rather hope this success doesn't mean you will want to look up all your old unsolved cases!'

'What makes you think I had that many unsolved?' he protested. 'But don't worry. I'm very glad to have the mystery of Rebecca answered. But now I really am retired!'

* * *

For Jess it was the end of a long day and the end of a case. She didn't feel tired, or not very tired. But she was experiencing that sort of mental and physical wind-down that comes when the job is done and everything tidied away. It was a pleasant feeling, and she was enjoying it, until she reached home and received a mild surprise.

There was an unknown car parked outside the big old house, now divided into flats, where she lived. She made a note of it, in the way that police officers automatically do. But anyone would have made a note of this vehicle. It was an old Morris Minor. Bit of a museum piece. No, such a description would insult the owner. A classic car, that was the expression! Whoever owned it, it had been beautifully maintained.

As she got out of her own car and shut the door, the door of the Morris opened and a tall gangling figure emerged awkwardly, like a hermit crab from its adopted home. The figure unfolded to its full height, revealing itself as a very thin man with hair bleached almost white by the sun, deeply tanned skin, and eyes so sunken in his wasted features that they appeared almost to belong to a death's head.

The apparition spoke tentatively. 'Is it Jess?' Anxiously, he added, 'You did get Simon's note – about me?'

Jess found her voice. 'Yes – yes, I did. You're Mike.'

Monica's voice echoed in her head. 'Everything from measles to cholera.' It had been something drastic to reduce the very fit young man of distant memory to this scary figure. Simon had been right to warn her. No, she couldn't take this visitor to see her mother, or not until he'd made a much fuller recovery from whatever illness it had been. Her mother, always worrying about Simon's health, would freak out completely.

'It's been a long time. I wasn't sure . . . Simon insisted you wouldn't mind. I didn't intend to call on you unexpectedly,' Mike was saying. His voice was strong. 'I was just conducting a recce, seeing where you lived.' He half turned and indicated the Morris. 'This belongs to my uncle. He's most unhappy at letting me drive it. It's his pride and joy.'

'I can see . . .' Jess pulled herself together. 'It's a great old car. Have you been waiting long?'

'Not long, just a few minutes.'

'Right, well, then, you'd better come inside. The flat's a bit untidy.'

'I expect you've been busy all day,' he apologised. 'I really didn't mean—'

'It's fine, honestly!' Jess broke in. 'We've just wound up a tricky case. It's a good time for you to call, really it is.'

If you loved *An Unfinished Murder*, look out for the other
Campbell and Carter mysteries in the series . . .

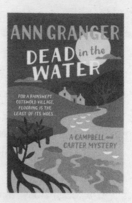

All available to buy in paperback and download in ebook.

For more information visit:
www.anngranger.net
www.headline.co.uk